TEMPEST

'This book blew me away. The non-stop action kept me constantly hungry to read more and to read faster' joyousreads.blogspot.com

'*Tempest* is boldly original and a complete page-turner' nicegirlsreadbooks.com

'I loved this book. It will stick with you even after days of finishing it' smittenwithbooks.blogspot.com

'Beautiful and sad. This book actually touched my heart' thefairytalenerd.com

Books by Julie Cross

Tempest
Vortex

TEMPEST

TIME WILL TEAR THEM APART

MACMILLAN

First published 2012 by Macmillan Children's Books

This edition published 2012 by Macmillan Children's Books
a division of Macmillan Publishers Limited
20 New Wharf Road, London N1 9RR
Basingstoke and Oxford
Associated companies throughout the world
www.panmacmillan.com

ISBN 978-0-330-54380-4

1 3 5 7 9 8 6 4 2

A CIP catalogue record for this book is available from
the British Library.

Typeset by Nigel Hazle
Printed and bound by CPI Group (UK) Ltd, Croydon CR0 4YY

To my editor, Brendan Deneen,
whose vision collided with mine to create this book.

SATURDAY, 11 APRIL 2009

My name is Jackson and I can travel through time. Now, wait, it's not as exciting as you might think. I can't go back in time and kill Hitler. I can't go to the future and tell you who wins the World Series in 2038. So far, the most I've ever jumped is about six hours in the past. Some superhero, right?

Recently I've acquired a sidekick with mad talent for the hard-core science stuff. The one request Adam insists I follow is documentation. A record of nearly every moment from this point on. Actually he wanted the eighteen years prior to today, but I talked him out of it – for now. Maybe if I avoid recording detailed accounts of my many fantasies starring a certain incredibly hot girl, or the dream where I play for the Mets as a last-minute substitute, I could cut my work in half. But who knows, those entries might be crucial to the country's economic stability. Or something equally important.

Even though I'm going along with this journal idea, it

doesn't mean I buy into it. It's not like the world's going to end just because I can jump around in time. Or that I'll serve some greater purpose, like saving the human race from dying. But as Adam says, I must be like this for a reason and it's up to us to find out why.

Cool ending, huh? Actually it's just the beginning.

chapter one

TUESDAY, 4 AUGUST 2009, 12.15 P.M.

'How far back should I go?' I asked Adam.

We kept a good distance between us and the long line of kids corralling around the polar bears.

'Thirty minutes?' he suggested.

'Hey, let that go!' Holly snatched the bag of candy one of the day-camp kids had swiped from a toddler's stroller and threw an exasperated look in my direction. 'It'd be nice if you would actually *watch* your group of kids. It's your summer job too, you know!'

'Sorry, Hol.' I scooped Hunter up before his kleptomaniac habits got any worse. 'Hold up your hands,' I told him.

He grinned a toothless smile and opened his chubby hands in front of my face. 'See? Nothing.'

'Let's keep it that way, all right? You don't need to take other people's stuff.' I set the kid back down and gave him a shove towards the others, who were heading for the large stretch of grass reserved for campers having lunch at the zoo.

'Hey you,' I said, grabbing Holly's hand and twining her fingers in mine.

She spun around to face me. 'You have a soft spot for the klepto kid, don't you?'

I smiled at her and shrugged. 'Maybe.'

Her face relaxed and she tugged on the front of my shirt, pulling me closer before kissing my cheek. 'So . . . what are you doing tonight?'

'Um . . . I've got plans with this really pretty blonde chick.' Except I couldn't remember what we had planned. 'It's a . . . surprise.'

'You're so full of it.' She laughed and shook her head. 'I can't believe you forgot your promise to spend an entire evening with me reciting Shakespeare . . . in French . . . backwards. Then we were supposed to watch *Titanic* and *Notting Hill*.'

'I must have been drunk when I said that.' I glanced over Holly's shoulder before kissing her quickly on the mouth. 'But I'll agree to *Notting Hill*.'

She rolled her eyes. 'We're supposed to go see that band with your friends, remember?'

A little girl from Holly's group tugged on her arm and pointed towards the bathroom. I darted around her before we could discuss my inability to make plans two weeks in advance and actually remember them two weeks later.

'Yo, Jackson, over here,' Adam said, nodding towards a tree.

Time for precise and exact time-travel planning.

'Are you coming with us to see that band tonight?' I asked.

What I really wanted to know was if he remembered it.

'Um . . . let's see. Spend an evening with your high-school friends, who, I've heard, are like a real-life version of *Gossip Girl*. Not to mention blowing an entire pay check on an appetizer and a couple of drinks.' He shook his head and smiled. 'What do you think?'

'I see your point. How about we hang out in your and Holly's neighbourhood tomorrow?'

'Sounds good.'

'All right, on with it. I can't eat while smelling camel ass, so we might as well experiment now.'

Adam tossed my journal on to my lap and threw a pen on top. 'Write down your goal, because time travel without a goal is just . . .'

'Reckless,' I finished for him, trying not to groan.

'The gift shop is right behind us. I've been watching for the last hour and the same girl's at the register.'

'You've been checking her out, haven't you?'

Adam rolled his eyes and pushed his dark hair from his forehead. 'OK, so, you set your stopwatch and then jump back thirty minutes. You go into the gift shop and do whatever it is you do so a girl remembers your name.'

'It's called flirting,' I said quietly so no one else would hear. Then I focused on writing my notes before Holly got back from the bathroom.

Goal: Test theory on someone who has no knowledge of the experiment.

Theory: Events and occurrences, including human interaction, while travelling into the past will NOT affect the present.

Non-geek-speak translation: I jump back thirty minutes in time, flirt with the girl in the shop, jump back to present time, walk back into the store and see if she knows me.

She won't.

But Adam Silverman, winner of the 2009 National Science Fair and a soon-to-be MIT freshman, won't confirm this conclusion until we've tried it from *Every. Single. Angle.* Honestly I don't really mind. Sometimes it's fun, and until a few months ago, nobody except me knew what I could do. Now that the number has doubled I feel a little bit less like a freak.

And a little less lonely.

But I've never been friends with a science geek before. Although Adam's more of the bad-boy-hacking-into-government-websites kinda geek. Which is beyond cool, in my opinion.

'Do you know for sure you can jump back *exactly* thirty minutes?' Adam asked.

I shrugged. 'Yeah, probably.'

'Just make sure you note the time. I'll record the seconds you're sitting here like a vegetable,' Adam said, placing a stopwatch in my hand.

'Is that really what I look like when I jump? How long do you think I'll be like that?' I asked.

'I'm guessing that a twenty-minute excursion, thirty

minutes into the past, will leave you catatonic in the present for about two seconds.'

'Where was I thirty minutes ago, just so I don't run into myself?'

Adam clicked his stopwatch on and off about ten times before answering me. He's so totally OCD. 'You were inside, looking at the penguins.'

'OK, I'll try not to end up over there.'

'We both know you can choose your location if you really concentrate, so don't give me that "I don't know where I'll end up" shit,' Adam said.

Maybe he was right, but it's hard not to think about *anything* but one place. Just one, tiny, half-second thought about any other location than the one I was aiming for, and I'd end up there instead.

'Yeah, yeah. *You* do it then, if you think it's so easy.'

'I wish.'

I get why someone like Adam is so fascinated by what I can do, but for me, I don't exactly consider it a superpower. Just a freak-of-nature occurrence. And kind of a scary one at that.

I glanced at my watch, 12.25 p.m., then closed my eyes and focused on thirty minutes in the past and on this exact spot, though I really, truly have no clue how I do this.

The first time I jumped was about eight months ago, during my first semester of college. I was sitting in the middle of a French poetry class. I nodded off for a few minutes and woke up to a cold breeze and a door slamming me in the face. I was standing in front of my dorm. Before I even had a chance to panic, I was right back in class again.

Then I panicked.

Now it's fun, for the most part. Even though I still have no idea what day or time I travelled to that very first jump. As of today, my known record jump is forty-eight hours in the past. Jumping to the future has yet to work, but I'm not going to stop trying.

The familiar sensation of being pulled into two pieces took over. I held my breath and waited for it to stop. It's never pleasant, but you get used to it.

chapter two

TUESDAY, 4 AUGUST 2009, 11.57 a.m.

When I opened my eyes again Adam was gone, along with the rest of the kids and my co-workers. The horrible splitting sensation stopped, replaced by the light-as-air feeling I always get during a time jump. Like I could run for miles and not feel a bit of ache in my legs.

I looked around. I was lucky – everyone was too busy looking at the animals to notice me materializing out of thin air. So far I hadn't had to explain that one to anyone, thankfully. I hit the start button on the stopwatch and glanced at the giant clock above the zoo entrance.

11.57 a.m.

Pretty close. I strolled over towards the shop and walked inside. The girl at the register looked about my age, maybe a little older. She leaned on the counter, holding her face in her hands, staring at the wall.

Whenever I do these little experiments I have to constantly remind myself of one very important fact:

Hollywood gets everything wrong when it comes to time travel.

Seriously.

OK, here's the weird part. The chick at the counter could punch me in the nose, maybe even break it, and when I jumped back to the present time it would be sore or bruised, but not broken. Why it's not broken is a whole different (unanswered) question, but the point is . . . I'll remember being punched.

If I broke *her* nose, then went back to the present, she'd be totally unhurt and wouldn't remember a thing. Of course, I'm supposed to be testing that theory right now (again). Well . . . except I'm not going to punch her. Either way – same outcome.

'Hey,' I said to her. 'Do you guys sell . . . sunscreen?'

She didn't even make eye contact, just pointed to a wall to the left. I walked over and snatched four different bottles and then dumped them on the counter. 'So . . . are you at NYU or—'

'You know, you can buy these somewhere else for, like, half the price,' she snapped.

'Thanks for the tip, but I need some now.' I leaned on the counter right in front of her.

She straightened up and started ringing up my purchase. 'Four bottles? Seriously?'

OK . . . so much for flirting. 'Fine, I'll just get one. I guess you're not working on commission.'

'You work at a day camp?' she asked disdainfully, eyeing my green staff shirt.

'Yep.'

The girl snorted back laughter and snatched the credit card from my hand. 'You really don't remember me?'

I had to pause for a second to process her words. 'Um . . .'

'Karen . . . I sat behind you in economics all semester. Professor Larson called you unbalanced and said you needed to get a better grasp on realistic finances for college students.' She rolled her eyes at me. 'Is *that* why you have a job?'

'Nope.' Totally true. I don't even get paid. I'm a volunteer, but I wasn't about to tell *her* that. She had obviously already made up her mind about me. 'Well . . . it was nice to see you again, Karen.'

'Whatever,' she grumbled.

I left the store quickly. Jumping back to the present didn't require the same level of focus as going into the past, mostly because I always have to come back to my present before I can jump again. Adam calls the present my 'home base'. He's mastered the art of dumbing it down for me to understand. And baseball analogies are my favourite. Hopefully I wouldn't return to a bunch of strangers staring at my catatonic state.

chapter three

TUESDAY, 4 AUGUST 2009, 12.25 P.M.

When I opened my eyes again Adam was standing over me. 'Jackson?'

'Dude, you need a breath mint,' I mumbled, shoving him to the side.

'You were a zombie for one point eight seconds. I was almost right. Pretty soon I'll have enough data to produce exact calculations. You didn't sustain any injuries this time, did you?'

'Nope.'

I knew exactly why he'd asked. Last week, I jumped a few hours back, lost my concentration and ended up in the middle of traffic instead of inside my apartment. A huge truck ran right over my leg. When I jumped back to home base I felt this sharp pain shooting up my thigh and then it was gone. A light purple bruise appeared, but otherwise my leg was perfect, even though that truck totally should have shattered my bone.

I stood up and dusted off the back of my pants.

'Apparently we had a class together. But I totally pissed her off just now. Well, in the past. You know what I mean. So if the theory is wrong and I *did* change something, she'll be annoyed when she sees me again.'

'Let's find out.' Adam waved to Holly. 'Hey, Hol, we'll be right back.'

I grabbed Hunter, who was inching his way off the grass and towards the pile of abandoned backpacks, looking for some loot to stash in his pockets, no doubt. 'Come shopping with us, little dude.'

The three of us strolled through the door as the girl at the register was dumping a box of key chains into a plastic container. I stopped and stared at her, playing dumb. 'Weren't you . . . in my economics class?'

Her eyes lifted and she actually smiled a little. 'Yeah . . . Professor Larson.'

Ding, ding, two points for Jackson Meyer. She didn't remember my pissing her off. Just like I said. Nothing changed as a result of my jump thirty minutes into the past.

'Karen, right?' I said.

Her eyebrows lifted. 'And you're Jackson, the French-poetry major, right?'

Adam groaned and shoved past me. 'Don't see anything I want in here. Let's go.'

I ignored Adam and lifted Hunter up on to the counter. 'English lit. too. I have a double major.'

Even though my little excursions to the past didn't change anything in my home base, there were *some* advantages, like getting information. So I guess, in theory, time travel to the past *did* change something.

It changed *me*.

Adam, Hunter and I left the store and all of us stopped outside and came face to face with Holly. She had a handful of garbage she was dropping into a bin outside the store. I took her hand and pulled her over to a tree that we could hide behind.

'Adam's got a thing for that chick in the store. I was trying to help them hook up.'

Holly laughed and I nudged her backwards so she was leaning against the tree. 'Did Hunter steal anything?' she mumbled, but my lips were already on hers, preventing her from speaking clearly.

'Not that I know of.' I kissed her again and felt a drop of water land right on my cheek. Both of us pulled apart and looked upward just as the sky opened up and rain came down in huge sheets.

'Damn! I thought it was supposed to be nice all day,' Holly said.

We left our tree and made a run for the grassy area where Adam and the other staff were already lining up the kids.

A few of the little ones screamed as a loud clap of thunder rumbled through the zoo. 'Are we getting on the bus?' I asked Adam.

'Yeah,' he shouted over the sudden storm.

All the kids started running in jagged lines, pulling backpacks over their heads. Holly and Adam ran up to the front of the line and I hung back to push along the stragglers as we jogged to the exit.

Luckily the bus was parked right in front. By that time my clothes and tennis shoes were completely drenched. Just as I lifted the last kid on to the bus steps, I saw a red-haired girl, about ten or eleven, standing outside, alone. Her back was to me and all I could see was the hair and the blue jeans and the long-sleeved shirt. Water dripped off the end of her long braid.

My heart pounded all the way to my ears as theories spun through my head.

It couldn't be her.

But what if it was?

I moved towards the girl and heard Holly shout through the rain, 'Jackson, where are you going?!'

'That girl's not with us,' Adam said. 'Come on. Let's go!'

My steps got longer and faster until I finally reached her. I tapped her shoulder and the girl turned around instantly. Her eyes widened for a second and then her expression smoothed into a smile. If it was somehow her, would she even recognize me?

The rain pounded against the pavement and a bolt of lightning lit up the now-dark sky.

'Jackson!' Holly shouted again.

My heart sank back down. The little girl's eyes were blue. Not green. It was both a relief and an utter disappointment. 'Um . . . sorry. I thought you were someone else.'

I turned around and ran back towards the bus. Dozens of little heads were watching me through the windows. I trudged up the steps and shook the rain from my hair. All the eyes had moved from the windows to me, standing in the aisle. Holly's gaze locked with mine for a second, but I stepped right around her and slid into the seat next to Adam.

I felt a twinge of guilt when Holly took an empty spot, alone, without asking any questions. And I knew she wanted to. The way everyone was staring, it must have been quite a scene.

'What was with the kid you were chasing?' Adam asked.

I had to look away from him. 'Nothing . . . she just looks like someone. False alarm. No big deal.'

Adam leaned his head closer and spoke again after a minute of silence. 'She looks like Courtney, right?'

I sighed but finally conceded by nodding. 'It's stupid. I know.'

'It's not stupid. It happens to people all the time.' He drew in a quick breath before whispering, 'Wait . . . you don't think . . . hmm . . . it's an interesting theory, but way too many logistical problems.'

'Just forget it,' I said before he could drill me with questions. 'Please.'

There was no way around it. My twin sister was dead. Four years later and it still haunted me. *She* still haunted me. Mostly because I missed her so much.

When we were filing off the bus Holly waited for me and stepped in my path. 'You OK?'

I stared at her eyes, full of concern, then shrugged. 'Yeah, why?'

Her face fell and she turned her back on me. 'Nothing . . . never mind.'

OK, so I totally sucked at the personal boyfriend shit. Holly never came right out and said that, but I knew she was thinking it.

I took her soaking wet backpack off her shoulder and threw it over mine. 'So . . . you want to come over later . . . maybe dry off before we go out anywhere?'

She jumped off the last step and on to the pavement before facing me and smiling. 'Sure.'

I wrapped one hand around her blonde ponytail and squeezed water out of the end. 'I think you're going to need a blow dryer.'

She reached up and rested her hands on my face, her light blue eyes turning serious, like Adam had been a few minutes ago. 'Are you sure you're OK? What were you—'

'I'm just a little bit of a freak sometimes, that's all.' I forced a grin and turned her shoulders towards the front doors so we could get out of the rain.

chapter four

THURSDAY, 29 OCTOBER 2009, 6.00 p.m.

Tonight, me and my sidekick are implementing a plan that has been in the works for a while: stealing my medical records from Dr Melvin's office. Adam's convinced we'll find something in there to indicate why I'm such a freak of nature. But seriously, does he think 'Crazy Time-Traveller' will be stamped on the outside of the folder?

I've spent the week observing Dr Melvin's erratic and very inconsistent schedule. Basically he's always working. Except two nights ago. This experiment will involve a two-day time jump into the past (my current record), and some very scientific and devious manoeuvres.

Adam's on his way back from College now and is probably pulling out his hair, trying to come up with all the formulae beforehand. I've done my part, writing down my goal and now I just have to rearrange my plans with Holly. Adam's trips home have been so last minute since school started that I keep cancelling on Holly. But she's totally busy with classes and some kind of dancing team. She'll probably be relieved. Besides, I can still make it to dinner, just not the movie . . . speaking of dinner – shit! I'm already 15 minutes late . . .

More data entry later.

29 OCTOBER 2009, 9.30 p.m.

OK, so, maybe Holly didn't take the change in plans as well as I thought she would.

'Come on, Holly, open the door.'

Two girls zipped past me in bathrobes, giggling.

'She doesn't want to see you,' Lydia sneered. 'This is exactly why I decided against men. I've been telling Holly for nearly a month that she needs to do the same.'

I fought back the urge to shout at Holly's eternally angry roommate. Her arms were spread in front of the door, blocking me. Like I might try to knock it down or something. 'Lydia, don't you have a Sylvia Plath Fan Club meeting to go to?'

Music started playing from the other side of the door.

'You're just darling, Jackson. Now I'm really not giving you my key.'

I banged my head gently against the wall next to the door. 'Please let me in.'

'Don't forgive him. He'll just screw with you. Again and again,' Lydia shouted.

OK, I am seriously going to strangle this chick.

A door flew open behind us and I turned to look at the girl standing with a thick textbook cradled in her arms. 'Jackson, I'm really sorry, but I've got to study. And Lydia, please shut up. No one cares about your angry men-hating rants.'

The music coming from Holly's room cranked up even

louder. I turned to Lydia and shouted over the noise, 'I'll pay you a hundred dollars to hand over your key and disappear for the night.'

I waited for her lecture about violating the dorm rules or some shit about women giving up the metaphorical 'keys' in life.

To my surprise her dark eyebrows lifted and she said, 'Make it two hundred.'

I opened my wallet and pulled out a credit card and thrust it in her hand. 'Just take this.'

She dropped the key on to the floor in front of me and took off down the hall. I sighed with relief.

'Thank you!' the girl behind me said.

I snatched the key from the floor and held it to the doorknob. 'Hol, please talk to me.'

The only answer I got was the chorus of a Pink song. I put the key in the door and opened it slowly, expecting to see Holly standing on the other side, waiting for me. So she could steal the key and shove me out again.

A red shoe flew across the room and slammed into the far wall, above the window. I stepped inside and shut the door before glancing around the room. Holly's feet stuck out from the closet along with the ends of her blue bathrobe.

I wasn't sure if she'd heard me come in but then again, maybe the shoe was meant for me. Wouldn't be the first time a girl had thrown a shoe at me, but for Holly it was a bit out of character.

I had to dodge a brown sandal as I crossed the room to turn off the stereo. As soon as the music stopped, she quit digging through her junk, crawled out of the closet and stood right in front of me.

'I have good news,' I said, attempting to smile but it didn't quite go with the mood. 'Lydia's actually willing to turn off her angry-girl mouth for the right price. She won't be back until tomorrow.'

'Seriously? You paid my roommate to leave?'

There wasn't even the slightest hint of amusement on her face. A knot formed in my stomach.

'Tell me what's wrong. What did I do?' Just by saying this I had admitted that I knew it was more than just cancelling a movie. Very stupid on my part. I reached out my hand, but her arms stayed folded over her chest.

'You're always hiding stuff from me, running around with Adam like a couple of little kids.'

'Are you jealous? I know he was your friend first, but maybe we can work out a schedule.' *Bad. Very Bad. The absolute wrong thing to say.* I cringed, waiting for her to shout or grab another shoe to launch in my direction.

She turned her back on me and walked over to her desk, sifting through a pile of papers. 'Fine. You're right. It's no big deal.'

It would have been impossible to insert even one more drop of sarcasm into her voice. And it hit me like a gust of icy air. I ran my fingers through my hair and tried to come up with something decent to say. Or to decide if I should run. Instead I went for a change in subject. 'Did you . . . lose something? You were digging through the closet?'

'Yes. One of my memory cards.' She slammed a book

against the desk, her back still to me. 'I really need to study, OK?'

I snatched a couple of shoes from the floor and tossed them back into the closet. 'Well . . . maybe I could help—'

'No,' she said quickly before hitting the power button on her computer monitor. She let out a breath and her shoulders relaxed. 'Seriously, Jackson, just go so I can get something done. Please.'

The sarcasm had dropped from her voice, leaving only an exhausted and slightly exasperated tone. She was giving me an easy way out of this argument. But curiosity took over and I opened my mouth again. 'Hol, why are you so pissed?'

She shook her head a little. 'I'm not . . . *mad* at you.'

I let out a frustrated sigh. 'Then what . . . ?'

What do you want from me? I had started to say because I really didn't know. But the words got stuck in my throat when I saw the drop of water fall on to the piece of paper in front of her. I took a couple of steps towards her and she turned around, giving me a one-second glimpse of her tears before she leaned her head against my chest, hiding her face. 'You never tell me anything . . . It's . . . It's like you have this whole other life and I can't be in it.'

Hearing the tears trembling in her voice hit me harder than I expected. I should have run when I had the chance. I wrapped my arms around her and squeezed her shoulders. 'I don't mean to push you away. I'm . . . I'm sorry.'

Holly ducked under my arms and flopped down on the bed, her blonde hair spilling around her. She groaned loudly. 'I hate that I can't stay mad at you.'

I released the breath I didn't even realize I'd been holding and lay down next to her, burying my face in her neck. 'I thought you said you weren't mad.'

She slapped her hands over her eyes and pressed down hard. 'I *was* mad. Past tense.'

'Does this mean we get to have make-up sex?'

She cracked a smile, then her mouth formed a thin line again. 'Only if you promise no more secrets . . . ever.'

Not possible. No way.

I slipped my fingers inside her robe and glided them up and down her back. 'You'll cave either way.'

She raised an eyebrow. 'Try me.'

'OK, I promise.'

'Liar.' She laughed and pulled my shirt off, tossing it over the lamp. 'Lydia's going to be such a bitch tomorrow.'

I loosened the tie on her robe. 'She's at least two hundred dollars richer, so there's nothing to bitch about. And when is she *not* angry?'

'Never. But thank you for one night free of feminist lectures.'

I leaned over and whispered, 'Consider it your make-up gift.'

She wiggled out of her robe. 'Do I get anything else?'

'Like a new car?' I asked.

'No.'

'A pound of that really expensive non-dairy chocolate?'

She kissed the length of my neck. 'You know what I want.'

I groaned loudly. 'Not a chance.'

'Please.'

'You're turning me into a complete freak. Or worse – a chick.' I made the mistake of turning my head. One glimpse of the tears still drying on her cheeks and I caved. 'If you tell anyone, I will kick your little ass. Got it?'

She mimed zipping her lips, then snuggled up to me. 'Do you think you can manage a British accent this time?'

I laughed and kissed her forehead. 'I'll try.' Adam and my medical records could wait.

'OK, on with it.'

I rolled my eyes then took a deep breath. '*It was the best of times, it was the worst of times. It was the age of wisdom. It was the age of foolishness . . .*'

My ninth-grade English teacher always made us recite Dickens while standing in front of the class. I hated it. For Holly I didn't mind too much, but I'd never tell her that.

'Do you think he did the right thing?' Holly asked after I'd recited the first few pages.

'You mean Sydney Carton? Getting his head chopped off so the woman he loves can be with another man?'

Holly laughed and her lips vibrated against my chest. 'Yeah.'

'No, I think he's a complete moron.' I kissed the corner of her mouth and she grinned at me.

'You're lying.'

I pulled her closer and kissed her again, ending the discussion that would inevitably lead to spilling out more secrets than I cared to share.

'You weren't aiming those shoes at anyone earlier, were you?' I asked in between kisses.

She leaned over me, her hair forming a yellow curtain around us. 'I didn't even know you were in here.'

'OK, good, because that red shoe had a really pointy heel. You could take someone's eye out with that.'

She laughed really hard and then kissed me again before whispering in my ear, 'I'll save it for all my other boyfriends.'

I woke up early the next morning to Holly's alarm buzzing loudly in my ear. Blonde hair tickled my nose and a strand fell right in my mouth. She slammed her fist into the snooze button before mumbling, 'I set it so you wouldn't miss your eight o'clock lab.'

'I can skip it today.' I pushed her hair from my face and kissed the back of her neck. 'Go back to sleep.'

She pulled my arm tighter around her, then muttered something nearly incoherent, but it sounded like, 'Tell me a secret.'

This was Holly's favourite game. I usually responded with a random and stupid remark like, 'I used to have a crush on Hilary Duff.' But after last night's argument I owed her a little better than that.

I touched my lips to her ear and whispered, 'I'm crazy about you.'

I could practically hear her smile right before we both drifted back to sleep.

My eyes opened again two hours later. This time to the sound of someone knocking on the door. I reached for my jeans and yanked my T-shirt over my head before shaking Holly. 'I think Lydia's back.'

She groaned and grabbed her robe from the floor, then opened the door. Two men pushed past her and strode into the room.

'What . . . ?' Holly said, grabbing the sides of her robe and tying them tight.

One of the men, the shorter one with red hair, slammed the door shut. 'That's him,' he said to the other man.

'What's going on?' I asked.

The shorter one looked right at me. 'Are you Kevin Meyer's son?'

My heart rate sped. Something had happened . . . When was the last time I'd seen my dad . . . ? *Two days ago*, I remembered. He'd been out of the country since.

'Is he . . . OK?'

Holly drew in a breath and moved closer to me, squeezing my hand. I could guess the theories spinning through her head – *company plane crashes into a mountain somewhere, leaving the CEO's only child without a single living family member.* Sweat trickled down the back of my neck.

The taller of the two men reached into his jacket and flashed a badge, too fast to read it. 'You need to come with us.'

Cops . . . maybe FBI? Investigative reporters? Or maybe my dad's pharmaceutical company was being charged with money laundering or some other scandal. My dad and his clan of business advisers had drilled into me, on many occasions, the lengths reporters will go to get information for a story. And the quick flash of the badge, not letting me really see what it said . . .

I shook my head. 'I'm not going anywhere.'

'Jackson, maybe you should . . .'

I held my hand up to silence Holly before turning my eyes back on the men. 'What paper are you with?'

The two men looked at each other and the taller one shrugged before uncertainly saying, 'Newspaper?'

I raised my arm and pointed at the door behind them. 'Get out. Both of you.'

Holly slowly sidestepped behind me from her place next to the door, without turning her back on the intruders. From the corner of my eye I saw her inching backwards towards her dresser, reaching for something. A cellphone? Pepper spray?

'Are you currently involved with any government agencies?' the short one asked. 'Have they approached you with information?'

These dudes are seriously pissing me off. I quickly scanned the room for a makeshift weapon and slowly reached for a tall floor lamp.

Before I could open my mouth to speak, one of Holly's shoes flew across the room and hit the man on the side of the face. His head snapped in her direction. I could see a heel print burning bright red above his eye. I felt the blood rush to my face as my heart threatened to beat out of my chest. I swung for the fences. The lamp's glass shade connected squarely with Holly's shoe print. He crashed backwards, his body slamming against the door. A shard of glass had opened a good-sized gash above his left eye.

Crouching low, with his arms spread wide, he dived for my legs. Instantly my feet went out from under me and I smashed face down into the tiled floor.

The other man stepped over our tangled bodies as he advanced towards Holly. She inched backwards with her right hand behind her back.

'Just cooperate, and no one will hurt you,' the advancing man said to Holly.

Before he could complete the sentence she revealed her right hand. Her clenched fist erupted in a well-aimed stream of pepper spray. 'Get out of my room!'

'Hell!' he shouted, leaning over and rubbing his eyes.

Holly darted around him and ran towards the door.

The tall man and I both scrambled to our feet. While he was distracted by his partner's screams I followed Holly to the door.

From behind me I heard: 'Freeze! Don't move!'

I turned in time to see the tall man's hand plunge into his half-unzipped jacket. His hand emerged, tightly gripping a semi-automatic pistol. He aimed directly at my head using his one good eye, his vision obscured by the flow of blood.

I sucked in a breath, knowing I was in over my head. Defeated. Holly's hands froze on the knob, her back now pressed against the door.

The short guy held up one hand and kept the other one over his eyes. 'No . . . not yet. Only if he jumps.'

Jumps where? Now my heart was really thudding. They couldn't possibly know about . . . could they?

I took a large step backwards, but tripped on the lamp now lying on the floor, and felt something catch around my ankle. Once again my feet went out from under me.

A booming sound rang in my ears, followed by Holly's scream. Then everything seemed to stop – my heart, my breath . . . time.

Holly fell to the ground and I wanted to shout, to drop down beside her, but the second the seeping red blood started to show through her robe, I jumped. This time, I couldn't seem to control it.

But right before everything turned black, I saw it. Her chest rose and then fell again. She was alive and I just left her there.

chapter five

I spat out a mouthful of something straw-like and realized I was lying face down in the grass. Somewhere. Somewhen. My heart was pounding. It hadn't even felt like a jump.

The sun warmed the back of my neck. I shouldn't have felt the heat so much. I didn't usually in a normal jump. *Something* was different.

It must have been a dream . . . or I hit my head. Maybe I didn't even have a fight with Holly? Maybe none of that happened? Acid churned in my stomach just thinking of the sickening image of her lying in a heap on the floor.

I pulled myself up from the grass and tripped over something, falling flat on my face again. And I felt the painful impact of my body colliding with the ground. Based on how much it hurt, this was definitely home base. My black bag lay at my feet. I must have dragged it with me.

After forcing my eyes to focus, I realized this was Central Park. Right near my building. My legs felt like lead as I stepped closer to the pavement. I pulled my phone from my pocket and tilted it so I could see the time. It was completely blank. After banging it against my thigh a few times I gave up and asked a woman passing me on the pavement. 'Do you know what time it is?'

'Four thirty,' she said as she jogged past.

The aches running through my entire body were so intense I had to stop and sit down on a bench.

'You OK?' an old man asked from beside me.

'Fine, thanks,' I said, leaning my head back. I just needed to rest for a minute. Right before I closed my eyes, the old man's newspaper came into focus and I jolted upright after reading the date.

9 September 2007

What in the freakin' hell is going on?

'Is that . . . um, today's paper?' I asked.

'Yes, sir,' the man said before going back to his casual whistling.

Nope. Can't be right. Just some weirdo reading a paper that's two years old. I stared at it for a few more seconds. A large drop of water fell on to the date at the top of the page. We both looked up at the sky to see the dark clouds moving in. The man folded his paper and stood.

'Didn't say anything in here about rain today,' he said before walking off.

OK, so far all I had was a newspaper that said this exact day was two years in the past. Well . . . the past for *me* anyway.

I ran down the pavement as the raindrops grew more frequent. I spotted a police officer standing under a tree and raced towards him, not caring in the least about getting soaked.

'Excuse me, officer. Do you know today's date?'

'The ninth,' he mumbled, not even looking me in the eye.

'Of September?'

He snorted a laugh. 'Yeah.'

'Of 2009, right?'

He rolled his eyes and pushed past me. 'Damn kids! 2009?'

The panic that followed his words felt like caffeine being injected straight into my veins. I used the bottom of my shirt to wipe the rain from my eyes and searched for a third source.

Henry, one of the doormen at my building, would be perfect, but was there another me here somewhere? Couldn't risk it. I took off in the opposite direction to my building, towards the coffee shop.

The raindrops were cold as ice and my teeth chattered as I opened the door to Starbucks. The chick at the counter straightened up and smiled. 'Haven't seen you for a while.'

I scanned the empty tables for an abandoned copy of *The Times*. 'Um . . . yeah. I've been busy. With . . . you know, school.'

She laughed and I turned to face her. She looked a little familiar, but it could just be the uniform. 'Come on, you've been tramping around Europe all summer.'

I have? 'Well, it was just a week in Germany.'

She started working on an order, though I don't know whose. No one else was standing in line. 'So, what about the rest of the summer?'

'I've been working a lot,' I said over the whirl of the steamed-milk machine.

'Working?' She shook her head and then paused in the middle of stirring. 'Wait, didn't you say you were staying in Spain until December?'

'Uh . . . plans changed and—'

'So why didn't I see you in school last week? They gave your locker to some freshman.' She slid a cup across the counter.

I couldn't move a single muscle. I just stared at the cup on the black marble surface as the pieces snapped together. Lockers, meaning . . . high school. Europe . . . meaning senior year . . . First semester in Spain, senior year.

Senior year . . . meaning 2007.

'What the . . . ?' I muttered under my breath.

I couldn't even manage a three-day jump and now here I was two years in the past? Beads of sweat formed across my forehead. And I *did* remember this girl. She was one of a handful of scholarship students at *Loyola Academy*.

Loyola Academy, meaning . . . my high school. That I graduated from. In 2008.

Which, apparently, hadn't happened yet.

'Jackson? You OK?' the girl asked.

She knew my name. My face. I came here every day – in high school – and paid by credit card. With my name on it. So yeah, that made perfect sense. All the other shit didn't. Or it did, but it shouldn't. My nineteen-year-old self shouldn't be in the era of my seventeen-year-old self.

I had to lean forward to keep from passing out. How the hell did I get here? 'Sorry, I have to go . . . just wanted to say hi.'

I stumbled out the door and leaned against it, catching my breath. Did 2009 even happen? Never, in all my time-travel experiments, had I felt so disoriented. Actually this time jump, this moment, felt as real as the one I had left. Starting with the aches, the cold raindrops, the heaviness of my legs, my heart.

If I just try and go back, maybe I can fix it. The images flashed through my mind – Holly looking so panicked, Holly bleeding and falling to the ground . . . Holly still breathing.

But for how long? And it was my fault. All my fault.

I squeezed my eyes shut and forced back tears. The only thing I could do to keep from panicking was try to get back.

Back to 30 October 2009. Which had officially become the worst day of my life. With my back pressed against the door and rain hitting me in the face, I closed my eyes and forced myself to think of 2009.

Right away I felt the pulling-apart sensation and lost my focus. But it was too late. I was already headed into the unknown.

chapter six

My eyes were still closed when I inhaled the aroma of cherrywood and lemon-scented furniture polish. No rain. No sound of people. Or trucks ready to crush my legs. Finally I looked around and immediately recognized the location.

My dad's office.

Through the clear glass windows surrounding the large corner office I could see the traffic on Fifth Avenue. It was either morning or evening. And a weekday most likely. Adam had always warned me about my lack of direction during a time jump.

'*Who knows where the hell you'll end up?*' he had said.

I shook the thought from my head, reminding myself of my next most important task: to find out the current day and time of this location. So I walked over to the computer and turned on the monitor. It was locked, requiring a fingerprint scan to gain access.

The phone next to the keyboard had numbers on the tiny screen. Just as I leaned closer to look at them, beeping sounds rang from outside the door. Like a code box for a garage or something. I couldn't remember my dad's office ever having a code to get in. The whole building was secure.

Unless this was the future! What if I'd gone beyond 30 October 2009?

I didn't have time to contemplate that last question because it suddenly occurred to me that if this door opened and Dad or someone came in, there was a chance they'd freak upon seeing a version of me that shouldn't be here. On this day. Or this year. Whatever year that was.

I stepped into the coat closet to the left of the desk just as the door opened. Footsteps echoed across the floor and suddenly an arm was thrust right past my face. I pressed my back against the side of the closet, holding my breath, and watched Dad hang his long winter coat.

Clue number one: *It's cold outside.*

I could eliminate a few months. The door swung shut, but not completely. A tiny filter of sunlight streamed through, enough so I could see Dad shuffling around his desk.

A loud buzz sounded through the silent office and I nearly had a heart attack thinking someone must know I was here.

'Yes?' Dad answered.

The phone. Duh.

'Everything went as planned,' a man's voice boomed from the slightly muffled speaker.

'Full report, please, Agent Freeman.'

Agent?

It sounded like whoever was on the other end of the line snorted. Then Dad said, 'Now!'

'All right, all right, sorry. The two subjects, one male, one female, arrived at the scheduled destination unharmed.'

'I don't think you understand the definition of a *full* report, Agent Freeman. Should I dock points from your training exam?' Dad said in a threatening tone.

'Fine. Thunder walked with the usual friends and arrived in time for jazz-band rehearsal at 7.02 a.m. And Lightning arrived at the scheduled location at exactly 7.58 a.m., two minutes before the bell for homeroom. It would have been earlier, but she felt the need to stop for hot chocolate.'

He had to be talking about Courtney and me.

Courtney. Who died 15 April 2005.

But Thunder and Lightning? Code names?

I couldn't write it down. Not here. So I closed my eyes, pressed my back more firmly against the closet wall, and forced myself to repeat the facts over and over. *I'm pre-April 2005. Apparently some kind of agent followed us to school and reported back to Dad.*

Yeah, I'll admit he's a pretty high-profile guy, being the CEO of a major pharmaceutical company. But having us followed by PIs or whatever the dude on the phone was seemed a bit extreme.

'She walked alone?' Dad asked, pulling me from my thoughts.

'Yes, sir.'

I could hear Dad pacing the floor now. 'What about the girl two floors up? Peyton.'

'I heard from a source she has the flu.'

'And you didn't feel the need to give me this information? Had I known, I would have accompanied—'

'I've done six months of life-threatening missions for the CIA, in the middle of the desert. I can handle a couple of twelve-year-olds walking to school.' There was a pinch of annoyance in his voice.

The CIA followed us to school? Or maybe a retired or ex-CIA agent Dad had hired followed us to school?

Dad sighed. 'My apologies. And thank you for the report. This is my first time not tailing them myself. I didn't realize it would be so hard.'

What?!

'Stop worrying. You've got half the CIA on constant watch. Those kids couldn't be more safe if you rolled them around in a bulletproof bubble.'

'Agent Freeman, I wouldn't take any situation lightly. Even walking a couple of kids to school. And you understand my most important policy?'

'Never interfere except when no other option exists,' Agent Freeman recited. 'I watched Thunder and a couple of friends drop eggs from his window on to that Russian man's car the other day. Didn't breathe a word.'

Dad chuckled. 'That was two days ago, right?'

'Yes, sir. January eleventh.'

So it's 13 January. And I'm twelve. Well . . . not me, the other me. The other me is twelve. I did a quick calculation in my head, concluding that it was 2003.

2003? Holy shit!

'I'll take care of it. For the record, that Russian guy is an asshole, but I certainly don't condone dropping objects from windows twenty floors up. Especially considering the fact that it's illegal in New York. That's all I needed. I'll expect an hourly update.'

I didn't even hear Dad's feet move or any kind of sound to indicate he was approaching, but with one swift motion the closet door flew open, a hand clapped over my mouth and he pulled me out by the front of my shirt.

A second later he shoved me against a wall, pinning his forearm against my throat. He leaned his weight forward, leaving me with no escape.

Actually I had a great escape. Time travel. But seeing my dad's face, smooth and confident, seven years younger, it wasn't exactly easy to focus on jumping out of this year.

'You're younger than the others,' he stated flatly. 'How the hell did you get in here?'

What others?

His forearm still pressed against my throat and I couldn't breathe, much less answer him. Right now I was seven years older than the kid he probably had breakfast with this morning. It made sense he wouldn't recognize me.

The calm expression remained plastered on his face, but his eyes flickered with anger. Maybe even hatred. It sent a shiver down my spine to see my dad look at me that way.

'How do you want to do this?' he asked. 'Gun? Poison? Lethal injection?'

I was literally frozen with fear. He eased his forearm off of my throat, only to grip it tightly with his fingers.

'Or I could kill you with my hands,' he added.

I could almost feel the blood vessels bursting in my eyes. On the verge of blackout my vision was narrowing to a small window, just large enough to see his face. I didn't know if he could kill me while in a time jump or not, but the threat alone was a good enough reason to jump out of 2003. So I just left without even saying a word to my dad. A man who apparently possessed the ability to kill someone with his bare hands.

Who. The. Hell. Was. He?

chapter seven

SUNDAY, 9 SEPTEMBER 2007, 5.05 P.M.

Rain hit my face again, landing in my open mouth. I felt dizzy, sick . . . freaked. My father had just tried to kill me.

As in dead. By his own hands.

Obviously he didn't know it was me. And he had the CIA following the younger me around just to prevent my death. The craziness of that alone was too much to grab on to at that moment. Someone knocked lightly behind my head and I jumped, completely startled.

That's when I realized I had been leaning against the door of Starbucks. Again.

In 2007. Exactly where I left from.

The girl from behind the counter, and from my high school, poked her head outside and stuck something in front of my face.

'You left your cellphone on the counter,' she said.

I took it from her hands and stared at her for a long moment. 'It's 2007, right? Senior year?'

The panic in my voice was such a contrast to the

people all around me, strolling the streets of Manhattan on a Sunday afternoon. Didn't they know the world had just flipped upside down? Or that it might end in some catastrophic event preventing me from ever returning to the future?

Of course not. Only *my* world had turned over. Not anyone else's.

'Yep, it's 2007,' the girl said to me with a bewildered smile.

Obviously she thinks I'm nuts.

'And that's a cool phone. Where'd you get it? I've never seen that model and my sister works for—'

'It's a prototype. I've got a few connections. Shouldn't even have it out in the open.' I stuffed the phone in my pocket. 'Um . . . I'll see ya later.'

The rain had slowed to a very light drizzle, so I took off running across the street and towards the park. Nothing could make anything about the last few hours seem normal. The only activity I could do to keep from panicking was to write it all down. Just like I had promised Adam.

Adam. If only I could see him now. Or Holly . . .

I walked a little ways until I found a tree to sit under and pulled out my journal, hoping to calm myself down. But the thought of those two names had sent my heart racing. Especially the last one. I tried not to think about her . . . tried to focus on the details. The scientific facts. But the truth was, since the first day I met Holly, when she ran right into me, dumping her smoothie all over my shoes, I hadn't been able to stop thinking about her. Something I'd never really come right out and admitted.

At first Holly was just the girl I couldn't have. Not only did she have a very devoted boyfriend, but she had a million smart-ass comments about the rich, privileged kids we were in charge of. At least she did until she found out I was one of them. That shut her up for a while.

People always want what they can't or shouldn't have. That alone seemed to pull Holly and me together like a couple of magnets. And I know it wasn't just me gravitating towards her. It went both ways.

I had to get back to 2009. My eyes closed and I forced myself to focus every ounce of energy on where and when I needed to be.

chapter eight

A while later, I was right back in my spot by the tree, writing down everything I could manage. It was a desperate attempt to stay connected, grounded to reality. Plus this way there'd be a written explanation of my recent adventures for Adam or the future Adam, if someone found me lying dead somewhere.

SUNDAY, 9 SEPTEMBER 2007, 6.30 p.m.

In the last forty-eight hours, I've made seventeen attempts to get back (or forward, actually) to 30 October 2009, and they all failed. The second attempt threw me back to February of 2006, outside in the middle of a snow shower. I nearly froze my ass off. Everything is jumbled in my head. Sometimes I feel alive, and other times I'm convinced this is some freakish purgatory. There're too many dates to remember, too many times. Do I even exist anywhere? Am I actually someone if I don't have a real home base?

With every attempt, I ended up in some random past

date. Then I came back here. As if there's nothing in the future. Like 9 September 2007 is THE END OF THE WORLD. Right now I'm so exhausted I can't even think about time travel. Maybe if I just close my eyes for a few minutes . . .

'Hey, kid. Get up.'

Someone shook my shoulders, then jabbed a finger into my chest.

I sprang up from my spot in the grass and nearly ploughed into the two police officers standing in front of me. The sun had completely set while I slept. I glanced at my watch.

8.15

'You can't sleep here,' one of the officers said.

'Sorry.' I snatched my black bag off the grass before shuffling towards the pavement. I wanted to throw the stupid bag in the Hudson. It felt symbolic of my selfishness. My stomach twisted in knots again. This was my punishment for ducking out. For leaving her there to die. I pressed the heel of my hands over my eyes and forced myself to focus. Stay sane. Curling up in a ball of grief two years in the past wouldn't get me a step closer to saving Holly. Or to figuring out what the hell was going on with my dad and that weird trip back to 2003.

I crossed the street and walked into a diner. Every step was agonizing. Something must have happened to drag me this far into a state of complete exhaustion. And pain. Like knives poking me all over. Was it all the jumping? Or the home-base jump?

Food. I needed sustenance of some kind to keep me going, even though eating was the very last thing I wanted to do right now. This was like a bad case of the flu, the feverish, delusional state my mind was in. A mix of physical and emotional, and I didn't know which one dominated.

'Is it just one?' the hostess asked.

I nodded and followed her to a table near the door. I ran through the nightmare again in my mind. Not the craziness that followed leaving 2009, but the event just before. That was my nightmare, and it was still crystal clear.

Who were those men in Holly's room? Why were they asking about my dad? About government people approaching me? Did it have anything to do with Dad's behaviour in 2003?

'*That's him,*' one of them had said. And could they have somehow known what I can do?

'Can I get you something to drink?' the waitress asked.

'Coffee, please. Oh, and where is your restroom?'

She pointed to my left. I stumbled into the bathroom, leaned my back against the wall and closed my eyes.

Please let it work this time.

chapter nine

Exhaust fumes filled my nostrils, horns honking all around. I opened my eyes and stared at the front bumper of a bright yellow cab.

'What the hell!' someone shouted.

I leaped off the road. 'Sorry, I . . . tripped.'

'Idiot! You coulda been killed.'

Only in New York City could someone materialize out of thin air and get no more than the usual angry driver reactions.

I raced to the safety of the crowded pavement, shielding my eyes from the blazing summer sun. Not easy to get your head around when you're exhausted and just came from a cool, dark evening.

I leaned against a lamp post to catch my breath. I could still picture Holly's face as the bullet ripped through her. The image I had just tried so hard to focus on. Obviously it didn't work. Again.

Suck it up and try again, Jackson.

I finally glanced around and recognized the streets

of Manhattan. I knew where I was, just not *when*. The newsstand outside my building had no customers, so I stepped up to make a purchase, keeping my eyes on the revolving front door that my father almost always used.

The doorman, Henry, glanced in my direction, squinting into the sun. I snatched a Mets cap from the rack and threw it on, pulling the front way down, concealing my face.

'I'll take this hat and *The New York Times*.' I handed the man a slightly damp fifty from my wallet.

'Mets fan, huh? Well, I guess I'll forgive you.' He boomed with laughter, and it must have drowned out the footsteps of the person approaching.

'*Wall Street Journal*, please,' a very familiar voice said beside me.

I turned my back to my father as quickly as possible, then shifted my eyes to the newspaper clutched between my fingers.

1 July 2004

Yep, he would recognize me. *Wow, Jackson, I just saw you a few minutes ago. What's with the facial hair and the extra four inches?* That'd go over real well. And how the hell did I get so far back again?

All I could do was keep my back to him and head in the other direction.

'Hey, you forgot your change!'

Luckily he didn't run after me. It was safer to take the long way around Central Park before heading to my usual spot. Time travel was kicking my ass and I had to rest. Even though I felt great now, the second I jumped back to 2007,

I'd feel like hell again. Like I had the plague or swine flu.

A flash of red hair came out from behind a tree. Long skinny legs stuck straight out. My feet moved twice as fast. It was like chasing water in the middle of the desert. Like she would disappear if I didn't get to her quick enough.

'Courtney?' I said, but my voice was constricted.

She kicked off her pink and green tennis shoes and leaned back against the tree, a book resting in her lap.

'Courtney!' I said again, much louder this time.

Her head poked around the tree and she squinted into the sun, probably trying to focus on my face. Then she tossed her book into the grass and stood up slowly. 'Yeah?'

I froze to my spot, staring at her in amazement. She was really here. Alive. But the irony of the situation was gut-wrenching.

My girlfriend, who should be alive, was dead (or dying) in 2009, and my sister, who I'd already lost once, was sitting in the grass here in 2004, sunbathing and catching up on the latest Harry Potter book. She wasn't even sick yet.

As she walked closer, this tiny voice hidden in the back of my head spoke a little louder. Adam's voice, running through the pros and cons of me talking to this younger version of my sister. Was this something that would potentially end the world?

At this point, I had lost the ability to think rationally and all I wanted was to grab on to something real and familiar. So I did, probably the most idiotic thing possible.

With a few long strides I closed the gap between us and pulled her into a tight hug, squeezing her around the arms, making sure she was actual solid matter. I was absorbed in my special moment when her piercing scream went right into my ear. Then she lifted her leg and kneed me in the balls, before wiggling out of my grip and backing up slowly.

'Calm down, Courtney,' I gasped, putting my hands up in the air. I could tell by the way her eyes darted around she was about to run. 'Please . . . don't go. Give me a minute.'

Her green eyes were huge orbs. 'Just leave me alone. My . . . My dad's coming . . . any second.' She pointed behind me. 'Look, there he is!'

Stupid me fell for her trick and I looked over my shoulder. She started to run past me, but I grabbed her around the waist. I needed to tell *someone*. To make them believe me.

'I promise I'm not going to hurt you,' I said, right into her ear. Then I pulled out my wallet and stuck it in front of her face. 'Take this. Look through it. I'll let go of you and sit by the tree. Deal?'

Her whole body stiffened, but she didn't fight me. Then I remembered the man called Agent Freeman following us to school in 2003. Was he watching her now? Maybe he was slacking on the job. 'I know you have every penny of your allowance from the last three years under your mattress despite the fact that I've told you it'll all burn up in a fire and Dad will never let you buy a motorcycle when you're sixteen, even if you pay for it yourself.'

Her breathing hitched for a second, but she didn't say anything. I tried something else, pointing at a nearby tree. 'You watched me fall out of that tree and break my arm eight years ago.'

I released her and walked slowly backwards a few steps before sitting down in the grass by the tree. She spun around to face me. 'Jackson?'

'Yeah,' I said. Then I tossed the wallet over to her and watched as she rifled through it, pulling out picture IDs, credit cards, photos.

Her eyes dropped down to the grass to meet mine again. 'Oh my God, you're . . . big . . . and . . .'

'I can . . . time-travel,' I managed to sputter out, knowing the reaction it would bring.

To my pleasant surprise, her feet stayed planted even as I lifted myself off the ground. I spent the next thirty minutes explaining exactly how I got here, but I left out some details. Like what happened to Holly and that part about Dad and the mysterious CIA agent. Courtney just stood there, wide-eyed and listening, until I finally stopped talking.

'I fell asleep, didn't I?' she asked.

I smiled for the first time in what seemed like forever. 'No, I promise this is real.'

She took a step closer, her nose wrinkling as she scrutinized my face. 'You . . . *look* like my brother. Just . . . older.'

I laughed. 'I thought you would have taken off running by now.'

'I haven't ruled it out,' Courtney muttered.

She touched my cheek and patted it gently. 'Damn, it is you. It has to be.'

'When's the last time you saw me? The younger one.'

'Four days ago. You're supposed to be at baseball camp

in Colorado.' She reached up to touch the top of my hat and pulled off a tag.

'Dad was at the newspaper stand right next to me; I had to hide my face a little.'

'So you can really time-travel?'

I nodded.

We both stared at each other for a minute longer until she finally spoke again. 'Aren't you going to explain a little better, like the science part? This is really freaky, you know.'

'Right, OK, I'll try my best.' Both of us sat down in the grass across from each other. Courtney folded her legs underneath her, looking much calmer than I would have expected. 'So, 2009 is my present year, OK?'

'Yeah,' Courtney said.

'For some reason, I can't get back there. Like the universe shifted two years into the past. I've been bouncing back to 2007 for two days now.'

Her eyes were huge. 'Why? And how did it work before the universe moved or whatever?'

I kept my eyes on the grass and plucked out little pieces. 'I don't know why. But before I would only jump an hour or two, sometimes a couple of days. Then I would just end up back in the same place, like I never left.'

'How do you even know what time is yours?' she asked.

'Basically, I have a home base. And the jumping part is like a boomerang. I'm thrown out somewhere and then I circle back. When I'm in those other years, like this one, I feel like a shadow of myself. And nothing I do during a jump changes anything in my home base.'

'Nothing?'

I shook my head. 'Not so far.'

She glanced sideways at a man riding by on a bike. 'So if you had a gun and murdered that guy, he would still be alive three years in the future?'

'I think so, but I'm not gonna try.'

'Like *Groundhog Day*,' Courtney said, staring over my shoulder.

'Huh?'

'You know, the movie where he keeps repeating the same day over and over. He tries to kill himself by dropping a toaster in the bathtub, then wakes up on the same day again.'

'I hadn't thought about it like that but yeah, that's a good comparison.'

'Can you go from here to another year, like 1991 or something?'

'No, I have to tag up.'

'Tag up?'

'Like when the other team catches a fly ball and you have to tag up before running to the next base. If I tried to go back five years right now, I'd open my eyes and be right back in that diner bathroom in 2007.'

She let out a breath and shook her head. 'So weird.'

'Definitely.' My mind sank deeper into analytical mode. Adam's influence. 'You know what's really weird?'

'What?' Courtney asked.

'When I jumped out of 2009, it felt different. Like I was light as air. Normally it feels like I'm splitting in two. And every attempt to jump forward in time since I got stuck in 2007 has felt like I'm splitting apart.'

'So it was just that one time that it felt different, and that's when your universe shifted.' Her forehead wrinkled and I could guess she was playing with theories. Finally she shook her head and smiled. 'It's just so crazy. Do you have some kind of evidence from the future?'

I rolled my eyes. 'What, like lottery numbers? Do we really need more money? Besides, you already saw my wallet. Everything in there is from the future.'

'Right, I forgot about that.' She picked up my wallet that had been tossed into the grass and started sifting through it again.

I watched every movement she made, studying it, memorizing it. Waiting for her to disappear. 'You're taking this really well.'

'Maybe I'm just in shock,' she said, picking up my licence and pulling it close to her face. 'Wow, so we're, like, nineteen? How do I look? Please say my boobs get a little bigger.'

I swallowed the lump forming in my throat. *Don't tell her.* Better yet, don't think about it. She's here now. *Focus on that.* My hands were shaking, but I kept my face as calm as possible.

She looked up after my long silence. 'What is it? I'm fat, aren't I?'

I forced a tight smile and looked away from her face. 'You look beautiful and not in the least bit fat.'

'You're family – you have to say that.'

'Maybe, but it's still true.'

'Tell me something about the future, something really cool.' Her face was eager, like a gossip columnist digging for dirt.

I knew exactly what she'd want to hear. 'I have a girlfriend.'

As predicted, her face lit up with interest. 'What's her name?'

'Holly,' I said, leaning my head back against the tree. It felt like the wind got knocked out of me, saying her name out loud for the first time since I left her. But I knew it would distract Courtney from asking about herself. I had to play the part, even if it hurt.

'What does she look like?'

'Blonde and gorgeous. Blue eyes.'

'Yeah, I could see you with a blonde model-type. Probably working in Paris, building her career.'

I laughed. 'She's from Jersey and she's a little too short to model and almost never wears make-up.'

Courtney grinned. 'I like her already.'

'Me too.' I put my arms around her and gave her shoulders a squeeze. She didn't protest this time.

'Jackson?'

'Yeah?'

'I have to tell you a secret.' She turned her face so it pressed into my shirt. 'I kissed Stewart Collins at Payton's birthday party last week.'

'I knew it! You guys were gone way too long in the kitchen, and then he had that stupid grin on his face. I could have punched him.'

She giggled. 'Exactly why I didn't tell you.'

My arms tightened around her. 'I miss you so much.'

This was something I never would have said in 2004, but in reality, it had been four years since I talked to my sister. Grief swept over me. I had to get away. This was too hard. Too much. Nothing would change.

I gave her one last squeeze and whispered, 'Goodbye, Courtney.'

Then I jumped out of 2004 and headed back to my own version of purgatory. 9 September 2007. Again.

chapter ten

My eyes flew open and I watched three drops of blood fall into the porcelain sink. A hand reached out and stuck a paper towel right under my nose. The bloody nose was yet another piece of evidence that this exact moment in time was my new present. My new home base.

But something was different. I had been alone in the restroom when I left. If I knew Adam's formula, I'd be able to figure out exactly how long I'd been leaning against the wall in this bathroom, looking like a vegetable.

'Here you go, son. You should pinch the nostrils,' a deep voice spoke right into my ear.

A tall, dark-skinned bald man stood beside me.

'Thank you,' I said, and for a second he looked at me like maybe he recognized me, but everything was jumbling together and he was gone before I could even think twice about it.

My nose only bled for a minute, and after washing my hands I left the restroom.

The waitress set my coffee on the table. The same

waitress who'd greeted me before I went into the restroom. Damn. Same place. Same time.

She smiled as I slid into the booth. 'Ready to order?'

I pointed to the first item on the left side of the menu, not even caring what it was. 'I'll have that.'

'Grilled salmon with seasonal vegetables?'

I shrugged and then nodded. Just as she started to turn away I remembered something.

'Wait! I forgot to ask . . . Do you have a copy of today's paper?' It was pointless, but I had to check.

'Of course, I'll be right back with that.'

I tapped my fingers on the table waiting for the answer I already knew. She dropped the paper in front of me and I groaned as soon as I read the top. 9. September. 2007.

Always the same. Eighteen times now. It was eight thirty at night. A couple of minutes had passed, but that was all. I'd been in the past for the longest stretch yet.

'Is everything OK?' the waitress asked.

'Sorry, I'm just disappointed the final performance of . . .' I glanced down at the headlines, '*Annie* is cancelled. Love that song, "Hard Knock Life".'

The waitress twisted a loose strand of hair around her finger and shifted her weight. 'Yeah . . . uh . . . your dinner should be ready in a few minutes.'

I pulled my journal from my bag because Adam's voice rang through my head again. This used to be fun. Like an adventure. But with each failed attempt to save Holly, Adam's words began to take on a much deeper meaning.

'You have to document everything, down to the minute.'

'Why?'

'First of all, so you know how old you really are. Second, so you know if you changed anything. And third, in case you forget.'

I didn't change anything. Ever. But I still recorded it all, using Adam Silverman's genius format. I laughed out loud the first time he wrote it out, casually, like it was a packing list for summer camp. But the thing is, most of this stuff didn't ever apply to my previous record of a two-day jump. That's why I never took it seriously. Now I did.

TIME-TRAVEL PRIORITY CHECKLIST

STEP 1: IDENTIFY CURRENT DAY/TIME
9 September 2007, 8.30 p.m.

STEP 2: MINUTES PASSED IN PREVIOUS TIME (1 July 2004)
165 minutes

STEP 3: IDENTIFY AGE, IN THIS YEAR, OF SFF
(self, friends and family)
Jackson Meyer (the younger me): 17 years old
Kevin Meyer: 42
Adam Silverman: 16
Holly Flynn: 17
Courtney Meyer: deceased

STEP 4: CREATE COVER OR CURRENT IDENTITY
(change as needed)
My younger self should be in Spain until December. For now I will assume the identity of my 17-year-old self since we don't seem to be bumping into each other. Only if

needed while interacting with someone I know.

STEP 5: RECALL BASICS (current events, technology . . .) Widespread panic may occur upon mentioning John and Kate will split up, thus ending the show 'John and Kate, Plus Eight'. Keep cellphone hidden at all times.

I ran through everything that happened once more to get my facts straight. After I jumped out of 2009, I landed in 9 September 2007 around 4.30 in the afternoon. Now it was getting close to 9.00, but all my attempts to go forward added up to nearly three days. Very little time passes in home base while I'm in a time jump. But the feeling like I'm dying from the flu or something was completely new. And I only felt shitty in this year. Probably because I hated being stuck here. Karma. Or maybe all the time jumps were making me feel like this. Frying my brain or some shit like that.

'Jackson Meyer! Is that really you?' a voice rang through my ears, pulling me out of my hazy depression.

I glanced up to see my favourite high-school Spanish teacher. 'Miss Ramsey, how are you?'

'Great, but I thought you were in Spain for a semester.'

This was the part where I had to remind myself who I was.

CURRENT IDENTITY: *Seventeen-year-old student who should be spending a semester studying in Spain, but is sitting in a Manhattan restaurant, alone, on a Sunday night.*

'I came back early.'

She slid into the booth across from me. 'I can't believe how much older you look after one summer.'

I laughed nervously. 'It's all that San Miguel. Puts hair on your chest.'

She cracked up and her thick glasses slid down her nose. 'I hope you sampled all the great Spanish wine.'

'Of course. I drank a bottle a day.'

She laughed again. 'That can't be true. So . . . will I see you roaming the halls soon?'

I forced back the disgusted look I knew was about to take form on my face. *No way was I going back to high school.*

'Probably not. I'm thinking of taking my GED – just tired of the whole high-school scene.' The waitress dropped off my dinner and I picked up the fork and stabbed a spear of asparagus half-heartedly.

'You look a little glum. Is everything OK?'

I nodded. 'Just jet lag. I got back a few hours ago and it's still two in the morning for me.'

This wasn't far from the truth. In terms of actual time, I hadn't slept much in two days. Of course, only hours had passed in this year.

This stupid freakin' year.

'Sorry to hear that. Well . . . I'd better get back to my date.' She nodded her head in the direction of a man sitting alone at a table using a spoon to examine his teeth. She leaned closer to whisper, 'This is the last time I use an Internet dating website.'

'You can always fake a stomach ache . . . or food poisoning.'

She smiled before turning around. 'Take care, Jackson.'

I grinned until she had her back to me, then dropped my eyes to the journal lying on the table. I plugged away at writing the details of my latest excursion, and was so engrossed in other years that I didn't even notice the waitress standing in front of me, tapping her toe against the floor.

'Sorry, did you say something?'

'Is everything OK with your meal?'

I looked down at the now-cold salmon. The fishy smell was revolting. 'Yeah, it's fine. Could I have my check now?'

She placed it in front of me. 'Do you want me to box that up for you?'

'Um . . . no, thanks.'

The plate disappeared, along with the waitress. The idea of bringing leftovers with me had taken on a new meaning with all the time-travel theories spinning through my head. This was the stupid shit Adam and I would have tossed around while playing Guitar Hero and drinking shots of Crown Royal. I'd start it and Adam would take it twenty steps further than my brain could ever comprehend.

Questions like, if I did get back to 2009, carting my doggie bag, would the salmon be two years old? Or if I went into the past again, would the fish still be in the box? Technically, it wouldn't have been born yet. Can a living thing travel to a time before it's born?

Then, if we could, we'd test it out.

Trying to make plans without Holly or my father catching on was difficult. Holly always knew when I wasn't telling her the whole truth or when I was feeding her a complete load of crap. Right now, I'd give anything to go back. Even if it meant listening to her shout at me again or being locked out of her room for hours.

The waitress was on her way back, so I pulled out my wallet and stuck a credit card on the edge of the table. I flipped through the pages of my journal, looking for something to help me form a plan. Any plan. My fingers froze on the page with '13 January 2003' across the top.

The credit card was removed from the table and the waitress stomped away while I continued to stare at the words I had written:

I THINK MY DAD WORKS FOR THE CIA!

Just thinking about my dad's hands around my throat, the anger hardening his eyes, put life back into my muscles in the form of a major adrenalin rush. He never said he was CIA. But he sure acted like it, in that moment. Not that I knew any more about the Central Intelligence Agency than Hollywood had presented me with. Still, I knew something. A CIA agent (or former agent) would be following me and my sister on the morning of 13 January 2003. I don't know why this was my current point of focus, but the idea that I could see the face to go with the voice coming through the phone seemed like a good reason. Honestly, most of my actions over the last couple of days had been driven by anything but logic, just a lot of fumbling through time (literally), searching for something concrete to grasp on to. Something real. Facts. Answers. I closed my eyes and focused on the date four years in the past.

chapter eleven

MONDAY, 13 JANUARY 2003, 7.35 A.M.

The sun blazed in my eyes again, but this time an icy breeze swept over me, stinging the ends of my ears. I stood outside a coffee shop a few blocks from my building. The door opened and an inviting gust of warm air rushed out. I ducked inside and grabbed the morning paper off an empty table.

I confirmed the date and felt a small amount of satisfaction. It was nice to know *when* I was for a change.

My legs felt so light they were like rubber. I sank into a chair and rested my head on the table. A few deep breaths later I lifted my eyes and looked around.

The only problem was . . . I didn't know what I was looking for. Why would it matter if my father worked for the CIA? Although . . . come to think of it . . . it might explain the angry dudes with guns storming into Holly's dorm room. The idea that my dad had a hand in what happened to Holly made me sick to my stomach. As much as I wished the blame didn't rest on me, I hated the idea of it being my dad's fault. Still, if I put on my logical (sane) hat for a minute, there were only a few scenarios that could explain everything. I forced myself to sit down and go through these in my head before I made any crazy, impulsive moves . . . although it didn't really matter since I wasn't in home base. I shook that thought from my head and set it aside . . . for now. I grabbed a scrap of paper and a pen to jot some theories down, even though I couldn't take something back with me. Not in this kind of jump. But seeing the words on paper right now would help.

1. My dad, the CEO, is secretly well trained in the art of killer self-defence and paranoid about the safety of his children to the point where he hires an injured ex-CIA agent to follow his kids everywhere. But that doesn't explain Dad's ability to follow us without me or Courtney ever noticing!
2. My dad DOES work for the CIA and his day job is a cover, but he's totally the good guy and it's not his fault that a couple of dudes with guns decided to threaten his one living family member because he refused to hand over a secret government password that, if it fell into the wrong hands, would potentially set off nuclear weapons across the world. He just forgot to tell me to watch out for these dudes. Or maybe they got to him first . . . in 2009 . . . I mean, how would I know without going back?
3. My dad does work for the CIA as a spy and found out in 2009 about my being a time-traveller. He decided that I and anyone I'm associated with are a threat to

national (or world) security and must be locked up (or killed) to keep the world from being destroyed.

4. Again, he's an agent for real, and found out that his own son was a freak and had to be studied with brain scans a few times a year and eventually used by the government as a lab rat. Or sold to Russian spies.

OK, so maybe these theories sounded a little too much like summer box-office hits, but seriously . . . some CIA agent (or maybe he's an injured, one-legged ex-CIA agent) was following my twelve-year-old self and the twelve-year-old version of my twin sister. So, yeah, my theories have a *lot* to live up to. And even if options two to four had less than a one per cent chance of being possible, they ruled out the solution of just asking my dad, in 2007, what he really did for a living. Although I kind of ruled out confronting him before this list, right after the strangling incident.

I trudged up to the counter to buy some coffee and come up with a plan to spy on the guy Dad had spying on the younger me and Courtney. 'Large regular coffee.'

The man nodded and took my money, then I slid over to wait. 'Small hot chocolate with skimmed milk and extra whipped cream.'

My head shot up when I heard that voice. The man handed me my coffee and I snatched it and turned quickly away. I knew as soon as I heard her speak that my plans to follow the seemingly invisible Agent Freeman wouldn't happen. Not when I so desperately wanted to talk to my sister again.

How could I do this? Lure her somewhere without Agent

Freeman seeing me? Or what if I could lure her somewhere and he *did* follow? Then I'd get to see him, and since this jump didn't change anything . . . who cared if he saw me? As long as I could get Courtney alone for a little while.

Then it hit me like a sack of potatoes. The stupid password Dad gave us. Courtney and I would roll our eyes any time he mentioned it and we made him give it up in high school. '*Never go anywhere with someone who doesn't know the password*,' he had recited every single day from the time when Courtney and I started kindergarten.

It was like a bad PSA announcement. Over and over. Another example of what up to now I'd just dismissed as Dad's overprotective paranoia. But today it might actually be useful.

I turned back around and looked at the twelve-year-old version of my sister: Bright green stocking hat and matching mittens, white ski jacket, uniform skirt sticking out from under her jacket, cheeks pink from the cold, yet so bright and healthy. As she handed the guy at the register her credit card I breezed past her and muttered, 'Go fish.'

She jumped and dropped her wallet on the counter before looking at my face. We'd been given careful (and annoying) instructions to listen to anyone with this code. But no stranger had ever walked up to us and given us 'the password'. The younger me probably would have thought it was a joke. Courtney was a little more serious. Still too humiliated to tell her friends about it, but more responsible.

I slid next to her, keeping my eyes forward. 'Do I look even a little familiar to you?'

I could feel her eyes burning into the side of my face. Then she whispered, 'You look kinda like my brother.'

I couldn't help smiling. 'Wanna hear a crazy story?'

'OK?' she said slowly.

'I can't believe this,' she muttered for, like, the twentieth time. 'So you talked to me before? How many times?'

'Just once.' After Courtney had skilfully managed to sneak out of school between homeroom and first period, we were in a little store around the corner from the school. I told her the same version I had the first time. She was right. This was like *Groundhog Day*.

And I couldn't stop looking around, waiting to get a glimpse of the sneaky spy, Agent Freeman, but so far he was nowhere to be found.

'If you knew where you were headed, why didn't you think to wear a coat?' she asked.

I rolled my eyes. 'Funny. I didn't have time to pack.'

She rocked back on her heels and then leaned against one of the bookshelves. 'How long has it been since you left the future? The 2009 future.'

'I'm not sure exactly how long, but it feels like forever. You want to go somewhere else with me?' *Somewhere Agent Freeman might follow.*

'Sure, but we should get you a coat first. Short sleeves in ten-degree weather is not a good way to blend in.'

I smiled. 'A twelve-year-old with a credit card. So dangerous.'

She snorted a laugh and then we left the store and headed out into the cold air.

Courtney at twelve was different than I remembered. I always got along well with my sister, but she just seemed so bubbly and adorable to me now. Mature, but still a little girl with an imagination. Exactly why I could feed her my crazy freakin' story and she believed it. Kids are much more accepting than grown-ups. Even so, there was a limit to what a kid will believe, but it was like Courtney could see through me, knew I wasn't lying.

She used her credit card to buy a new coat from a department store before we planned our next adventure.

'How do you do it, the whole time-jumping thing?' she asked.

We were at the Met, blending in with the tourists. 'I don't know how to explain the actual jumping part. How do you explain breathing?'

'Do you think I can do it?'

I turned my eyes from her face. 'Good question. Go ahead and try.'

She smiled and shook her head. 'Why can't you just tell me if the older me has superpowers? I need to mentally prepare myself for something like that.'

I hesitated, feeling the grief sweep over me like it had the last time, but I forced it down and kept my eyes straight ahead before answering. This wouldn't last much longer. Someone would come for her soon. 'Sorry. Can't break the ethical codes of time travel. I'd get booted out of the club.'

I sighed with relief when she didn't seem to notice me balking at that question.

'Damn. This has to be because of Mom, right?' She said this like it was common knowledge. 'Dad's not a time-traveller. Superpowers come from a superparent.'

'Or a vat of toxic waste,' I added.

Courtney giggled and shook her head. 'I doubt it.'

Adam and I *had* gone in the genetics direction just a couple of times with our theories. One being the time when I'd thought I saw a younger version of my sister wandering around the zoo. We never even came close to any concrete theory, let alone a conclusion. We did have a pretty elaborate plan to steal medical records, one that never happened because I ended up in 2007. But it was my records we were trying to steal, not my mother's. Courtney and I never knew our mother. She died from childbirth complications just days after we were born. Dad didn't want to talk about her, and after I turned seven or eight I stopped asking questions. It's hard to want something like a mother when you've never had one. I didn't know any different.

I stopped and Courtney turned to face me. 'You think it was Mom?' I asked.

Even if I wanted to get hold of her records, where would I look? She's been dead for so long. Besides, medical records aren't exactly easy to steal.

Courtney shrugged. 'Could be why Dr Melvin always does those scans of our heads.'

I didn't know if it was Courtney's revelation or just a lack of sleep and food, but I got dizzy all of a sudden, feeling even lighter than I had a couple of hours ago. 'I need to sit down.'

She dragged me by the hand over to a bench. 'You look really pale. Are you OK?'

Beads of sweat formed over the back of my neck and trickled down my shirt. 'I'm just . . . tired.'

I lay all the way across the bench and closed my eyes. Courtney swiped her hand across my forehead, removing the cold sweat. I needed to get out of here before I passed out in the past, or something worse, which might require medical attention. *That* would be interesting. Where the hell was the spy? This whole trip would be pointless if I didn't see him.

I opened my eyes and put a hand on her cheek. 'I don't think I should stay here much longer, OK?'

Her eyes were teary. 'I won't remember this, will I? Like, when you go back to 2007, *that* me won't remember this?'

My throat tightened and I had to force out the words and force back the tears. 'I don't think so.'

She nodded. 'It's kinda like daydreaming, isn't it?'

'Exactly. Something you do when you don't want to face the real world.' I stood again, very slowly, and she put her arms around my waist. 'I love you, Courtney.'

'I love you too, even if I never tell you,' she whispered.

I could feel myself going back, but not by choice. One second she was in my arms and, just like that, cold air replaced the warmth of her body.

Courtney would never have left Holly there dying. She was the brave one. Always did the right thing. And if nobility counted for anything, I would be the one buried under the ground, not my sister. But not only am I still alive, I'm the twin that got handed the time-travelling superpower.

Just as the darkness swept over me a short stocky man about my age came running up behind Courtney, followed by my dad. I tried my best to memorize his face. Focused on it for as long as my body would let me.

'There she is!' I heard the other man shout.

'Don't shoot him!' Courtney screamed. But then they were all gone. Or I was gone. Back to purgatory.

chapter twelve

SUNDAY, 9 SEPTEMBER 2007, 9.20 P.M.

'Hey! Are you all right?' a man's voice shouted into my ear.

'He was gonna run out of here without paying, then I saw him just pass out,' the waitress said.

'How long has he been unconscious?' someone else asked.

'About ten minutes,' the waitress said.

Great. I'd never be able to show my face here again. I stared straight up at the ceiling, willing myself to get off the floor. It was a slow process, but I eventually managed to stand, with the help of the manager.

'Sorry, just a little light-headed . . . um, low blood sugar,' I mumbled.

The manager stepped in front of me. 'Maybe we should call an ambulance, instead of the police?'

Police? Damn!

The waitress was tapping her foot again, holding up my wallet. 'His credit card was declined. I think it's a fake or a copy of some kind.'

Uh-oh. 'Actually I've got another one and some cash.'

'Yeah, two dollars. And I tried the other cards. All declined,' the waitress said.

I glanced around her shoulder, looking for my Spanish teacher, Miss Ramsey. She'd get me out of this mess. But an older couple was now seated at her table. Must have been a short date. 'Just let me call . . . my dad.'

A police officer was already strolling inside with another one following. He snatched the wallet from the waitress's hand and pulled out my licence. 'Issued in 2008? Interesting. And these look like the real deal. Professional.'

That's because they are real. And when did I run out of cash?

The officer holding my wallet glared at me, then looked over at the manager. 'We'll take care of this. Probably drugs.'

'It usually is,' the manager said, shaking his head.

'And with the looks of this wallet full of false documents, I'd guess addict and dealer,' the officer said.

The sneer on his face really pissed me off and I opened my mouth again. 'Yeah, because drug dealers find it helpful to make false documents that only work a year from now.'

'Smart-ass,' he muttered under his breath.

I tried to move away from them, but the cop not holding my wallet blocked my way while the other grabbed my arms and put handcuffs around my wrists. Anger bubbled up in me and I started to wiggle away.

Don't make this worse, I told myself. *And don't bother with jumping*. I'd just end up right back here and my vegetable state would probably make me look even more like a drug addict.

Every single patron in the place stared as I was led out of the restaurant and into the back of a squad car. *Seriously, could my life get any worse right now?*

Yes, it could. Now I'd have to call my dad to bail me out of jail. My dad who almost killed me in 2003. *This should be a freakin' blast.*

'Hey, Meyer, someone's here to see you,' the police officer said.

I rubbed the blurriness out of my eyes and sat up from the bench I had passed out on in the cell. My jail cell. Because I'm a bad-ass criminal. Or a really irresponsible time-traveller who fails to collect proper and authentic documentation.

The footsteps echoed down the hall, growing louder. My stomach flipped over and over. I didn't know how I'd react to seeing my dad again. Even without the CIA thing and the trying-to-kill-me part, I'd have been nervous to have Kevin Meyer, the CEO, come bail me out of jail. Especially when I wasn't the right me. Would he know the difference?

'If it's all right, I'd like to have a word with the kid before you let him go,' a female voice rang out from down the hall.

Not my dad. That's for sure.

'Whatever you want,' the officer said, then he stepped closer and unlocked the door.

The first part I saw of the woman was her boots. Tall

black boots, going up her leg, almost to the knee. She had a short black dress on and caramel-coloured skin. Maybe she was a lawyer? Except she didn't look much older than me. Too young to be a lawyer.

She didn't smile or give me any kind of a friendly greeting as her boots tapped their way into my cell. She just stood in front of me, arms crossed, waiting for the police officer to walk away. 'Listen up, junior. Here's the plan: I'm getting you the hell out of here and then we're going back to your apartment where you will explain your recent behaviour. I have a long list of questions. But not a word about anything inside this establishment, understood?'

'Um . . . who are you?' I asked.

'Miss Stewart,' she said with a smug expression.

'*Miss* Stewart? How old are you? Like, twenty?' She didn't look even twenty. Eighteen or nineteen, maybe. Something wasn't right, and I had no reason to trust anyone at this point. Even if it meant staying on this bench in jail. Like it mattered. 2007 was already a prison.

'I don't like to tell people my first name.'

'Where's my father? I left a message for him.'

She dug through her purse and pulled out a slip of paper, then handed it to me. It was a fax, but definitely my dad's writing.

Jackson,
Please do exactly what Miss Stewart tells you to do or you'll only make things worse. She works for me and has extensive knowledge in handling

confidential situations without getting media outlets involved. We will be talking later.

Dad

I stuffed the note into my bag, but she snatched it right out.

'What do you do for my father?' I asked.

'Secretary,' she said.

'Really?' I shook my head and stood up. 'Whatever.'

She walked out of the jail cell and didn't even wait to see if I followed. Like she just knew any halfway sane guy would tail her anywhere. Too bad for her I wasn't even close to halfway sane. But I couldn't ignore my dad's note.

I sighed and trudged down the hall behind the clacking stilettos, feeling the lead in my legs along with the grief in the pit of my stomach. One of the officers nodded and tipped his hat towards me as we walked past the front desk. 'Incredibly sorry for the misunderstanding, Mr Meyer,' he said.

I opened my mouth to respond politely, but Miss Stewart hissed in my ear, 'Don't answer him.' Then she stomped towards the door, calling over her shoulder, 'He'll be expecting a formal letter of apology. As well as the other conditions we discussed.'

Other conditions?

I started to turn around and say something nice to them, but my dad's 'secretary' grabbed my arm and pulled me out the door into the cool night air.

'That was rude. They were just trying to—'

She stuck a hand in front of my face. 'Did I not give you very specific directions?'

I rolled my eyes and followed her towards a car parked outside the police station. My car. Well, the one Cal, our driver, used anyway. Just as we approached the door to the car, I debated running from this woman, but then decided it wasn't wise right in front of the police station after being bailed out. Neither of us said a word all the way to my place.

I was too distracted by the idea that I was really going home. But a 2007 version of my home. In reality, I was never actually in my apartment on this day the first time I lived in 2007. I was in Spain. *I'm still in Spain*. The other me. Except I was here too.

Being this younger me was totally weird. The Jackson in Spain wasn't even legal yet. He couldn't vote, didn't know for sure where he was going to college. This was a completely different experience. And, so far, not a pleasant one.

But the hardest concept to grasp was the fact that I might be staying here a while.

At the apartment Miss 'bitchy secretary' jumped right out of the car after me and I spun around to face her. This was already weird enough without the strange chick following me. 'I don't need you to come in. I'll wait for my dad to get home. I appreciate your help.'

'Aren't you adorable?' She shoved past me. 'Sorry, I'm following orders. Besides, your father's been detained for several hours.'

Orders? Like CIA agents telling you what to do? Or just a bossy CEO? And detained? It was eleven o'clock at night. What pharmaceutical company situation couldn't wait a few minutes for a phone call, at least?

I caught Henry staring at me as he walked closer to open the door.

'Mr Meyer, we weren't expecting you today. Is everything all right?' He looked me over carefully, then glanced at Miss Stewart.

I forced a smile. 'Yeah, I'm home early. From Spain . . .'

He opened the door for me. 'Good to see you again.'

Miss Stewart grabbed my arm and yanked me inside the building. 'Let's go, junior. Don't you have a bedtime? Or a curfew?'

I jerked my arm out of her grip and walked quickly ahead, hoping I could get in the elevator before her. Maybe slam it in her face. But of course the elevator attendant heard her boots coming a mile away and turned to me before saying, 'Should we wait for the lady?'

'Yeah,' I mumbled.

I have to admit, seeing the inside of my home, the familiar furniture, brought a small amount of comfort. I collapsed on to the couch, wishing I was in better condition to argue. Miss Stewart seated herself in the big armchair and lifted her long legs up to the footrest. 'So how'd you do it?'

'What? Get arrested?' I asked.

She shrugged. 'Sure, let's start with that and move on to the bigger question.'

I racked my brain for excuses. What I needed was a role, and the best one was usually arrogant, inconsiderate, spoiled rich kid. I lifted my feet on to the coffee table and kicked off a tennis shoe before tossing it across the room, towards the mat in front of the door. 'Well . . . I have a friend who does a little side business and he made me some fake IDs, credit cards, that kinda shit, as a joke. All the years were messed up on purpose, and he must have switched them into my wallet.'

'Are you on drugs?' she asked me.

I wasn't sure how to answer this without ending up in rehab or throwing out a good excuse by denying it. 'Maybe . . . maybe not.'

'The police seem to think you are. Said you lied about being a diabetic to get out of trouble.'

'I'm not going to tell you anything I didn't tell them.'

She leaned forward, dropping her feet back to the floor and stared straight at me. 'How the hell did you leave a foreign country with no luggage, no passport, no money and virtually no identification?'

I sucked in a breath and held it for several seconds. *Maybe the other me isn't there. In Spain. But my passport is. Keep it together*, I reminded myself. *Don't let her see you sweat*. 'I don't know what you're talking about.'

Her face tightened. 'Yes, you do. The manager of your apartment in Spain said you disappeared several days ago, without taking a single possession. He thought you were dead. So did your father. He's been worried sick. Until you called from the police station.'

I rarely went anywhere in Europe without telling someone, getting permission. I certainly didn't in Spain in the 2007 I remembered. I was known in 2009 for pulling some stories out of my ass to cover up time-travel experiments, to lie to Holly, but this would have to be the ultimate story. The passport thing would be really difficult to get around. 'My buddy in Spain, the one that makes fake IDs—'

'Is he American?' she interrupted.

I shook my head. 'No . . . uh . . . British.'

Her forehead wrinkled. 'I wasn't aware of any UK foreign-exchange students within a twenty-mile radius of your location.'

OK, that's a little weird.

'He's not a student . . . just some dude I met. Actually, I think he got kicked out of his own country. His visa's probably not even legal.'

She relaxed back in her chair again. 'Sounds like you keep good company.'

'I try to. Anyway, I offered to test out one of his products. A fake EU pass. So I could go through the EU line at the airport. It's a lot faster than the other line.' I stared at her stone-cold face and stalled a little before adding on to my story, 'An EU passport. That's just a passport for people in Europe.'

'I know what an EU pass is,' she snapped. 'If you weren't an American citizen, what were you?'

'French,' I said.

She laughed a humourless laugh. 'Nobody would have believed you.'

I smirked at her and recited the French declaration of rights with the best accent I could muster. This was something else I had to learn in high school that I actually put to use.

Her eyes narrowed at me. 'Not bad. Go on.'

'So me and my friend, I'll call him Sam, made it to London with his fake passport. Then we got really wasted in this pub and I told him I could get on a flight home without a US passport. As Pierre, the French exchange student. He bet me ten thousand dollars. I wasn't sure I could pull off this big of a scam, but luckily I had just met these chicks who worked for Delta. I talked them into giving me a free ticket to New York.'

'And it worked?' she asked. 'You actually came here as a French citizen?'

'Obviously,' I said, holding out my arms.

'Where is this French passport?' she asked.

'I burned it after going through customs.'

'So you're trying to tell me that a straight-A student, with 1970 on his SATs, educated enough to be fluent in two foreign languages, no previous criminal record, not even so much as a traffic ticket, decides to get drunk and not only break a few federal laws, but foreign ones as well. In some countries you could be hanged for something like that.'

'Bullshit,' I said.

She leaned forward again. 'Wanna bet? I'll send you a list of every single country that would have your head, literally, for such an infraction. I'll even include the exact clauses that spell out your imminent death.'

'Pretty smart for a *secretary*.' I waited a second for some kind of reaction, but she didn't even flinch. 'Believe what you want, I don't really give a shit. I was there and now I'm here. Just like magic.'

She groaned and stood up before pacing the room in long strides. 'Cocky-ass seventeen-year-olds,' she muttered.

'Aren't clerical workers supposed to be polite? Good customer service and all that shit.' I grinned at her and it didn't go over well.

She glared so hard it was like laser beams shooting at me. 'You should consider showering before your father gets back. You stink worse than the bums outside this building.'

I had no doubt she was right. I'd been rained on several times and wearing the same clothes for the equivalent of three days. With no shower.

I got up and walked to my room without looking at her again. As soon as I shut the door I leaned against it, letting my heart and my brain catch up with the rest of me. I had a feeling I'd be doing this a lot if I stuck around 2007, and I didn't seem to have a choice.

And based on the facts from the conversation I just had, it seemed like my younger self completely vanished around the time that I landed in 2007. None of it made sense. None of it went along with the data Adam and I had gathered. Knowing the other me was gone made me feel like I was sinking deeper into this year, this home base, like quicksand.

My room looked nearly the same as it did in 2009, but all my jeans were two inches short. The only clothes that fit were a pair of gym shorts and a T-shirt.

After showering I went back to the living room. Miss Stewart was on the phone, but she stopped talking as soon as she saw me.

'Your father would like to speak to you.' She stuck the phone in my hand.

I tried to look the part of rebellious teenager who didn't care what his parents thought, but my legs were already shaking. 'Yeah, Dad?'

'What the hell were you thinking, Jackson?!'

I pulled the phone away from my ear a little and turned my back on Miss Stewart. 'Um . . . well—'

'Do you have any idea how many laws you've broken?! Or the hoops I had to jump through to get your ass out of this mess?'

He didn't wait for me to answer, but instead rambled on for at least five minutes and then fell silent, waiting for my great excuse.

'I'm sorry, I just . . .'

I just want to know if you're in the freakin' CIA. *And if you're going to lock me up in a cage.*

'You know what, Jackson? I can't discuss this now,' Dad said, and I could hear him letting out an angry breath. 'I'm replacing your lost documents as we speak. Miss Stewart should be able to get you on a flight back to Madrid by tomorrow afternoon. Assuming you can behave yourself.'

Not really the response I was looking for. 'Um . . . actually, I don't want to go back to Spain.'

'And why not?'

I glanced over at Miss Stewart, now sitting down and filing her nails. 'Personal reasons that I'd rather not discuss in front of the company you forced on me.'

'O-kay,' he said slowly. 'I'll call Loyola in the morning.'

I was resigned to sticking around 2007 until I could

figure out a way back to 2009, but I wasn't about to return to high school.

'I just want to take the semester off, if that's all right.'

'We'll talk about this later. I'll be home tomorrow.'

'Where are you?' *Somewhere super secret?*

'Houston,' he said. 'Business trip.'

'Fine. See you tomorrow.' I hung up the phone and handed it back to the chick invading my privacy. 'Thank you. You can go now.'

She stood up and snatched her purse from the arm of the chair. 'Nice chatting with you, junior.'

I made a quick decision to try to wiggle some information out of the only source I had. 'You know, my dad told me what you really do, that you're not his secretary. You don't have to pretend any more. Actually I think it's pretty cool that you're so . . . involved.'

She laughed really hard. 'Well, you got that right. If you want to know about corruption and secrets in a major corporation, ask the person who answers the phones. They know everything.'

'Even detailed information about foreign policy. I was impressed with that.' I took a couple of steps closer and lifted one eyebrow.

'We're very international, but I think you already know that.' She pulled a card out of her purse and handed it to me. 'Call me any time if you change your mind about going back to Europe. Or . . . if you want to discuss those foreign policies a little more.'

I just stared at her in disbelief. *Is she flirting with me?* I didn't know anyone that could switch gears that fast. Not an honest person, anyway.

I flopped on to the couch again the second she left. Sleep should have come right away. God knows I needed it, but the whole 'My dad's a secret agent' thing was really creeping me out, and bumping into Courtney and getting arrested had distracted me from looking for clues.

I half expected those men with guns to jump out from behind a door. I tossed and turned for hours, feeling the guilt, the heaviness of everything I had left behind in 2009 pressing down on me. Could I really just start over? Maybe that was the answer. Seeing or talking to Holly, in this year. Just to know she was OK. It was possible the 2009 nightmare would stop haunting me if I knew she was safe. Here. Now. Maybe I could change things that way.

I reached behind me and picked up the phone from the end table. She might have the same cellphone number in this year that she had in 2009. It was five minutes to six on a Monday morning. She would probably be up. My heart pounded as I dialled her number from memory.

After three rings I heard the crackling sound of papers being crumpled and then music blaring, followed by the one voice I needed to hear most at this moment.

'Hello?'

I couldn't speak or move.

'Hello?' she said again.

'Oh . . . um, sorry . . . wrong number,' I managed to spit out.

I heard her laugh a little. 'OK, no problem.'

I let out the biggest breath of relief, but I knew the second I hung up the phone that it wouldn't be enough.

I had to see her. As I stumbled towards my room, feeling more tired than I ever have in my life, I started to devise a plan to worm my way into not only Holly's life, but also Adam's.

chapter thirteen

I slept a few hours and then pulled out my journal to write some of the developments down. If I was able to get into younger Adam's circle, he'd need all these pages of notes. I knew him well enough to know that.

MONDAY, 10 SEPTEMBER 2007

Today is my first official day of assuming the role of my seventeen-year-old self. Damn, this sucks! I have a few goals formed already, even at this early hour.

1) Avoid a repeat of any form of high school.

2) Find out what Adam and Holly are doing in this year. I really need to see them. Both of them. Even if they don't know me.

Someone banged on my bedroom door, hard. It must have been my dad and he was probably still pissed off about last night.

'You have no consideration for the fact that I've been living in a different time zone since last May,' I said as I stuffed the journal under my pillow.

'It's almost noon – you've slept enough. I made you something to eat,' he shouted through the door.

I took my time showering and got dressed slowly, developing a story as to why a nearly straight-A student would suddenly want to drop out senior year.

Dad was waiting for me at the kitchen table with coffee and eggs, wearing his usual suit and tie, his dark hair neatly combed.

Part of me wanted to tell him everything, but I mostly just wanted to tell him that I'd seen Courtney, talked to her. He missed her as much as I did. Maybe more. Not that we ever talked about it. But I gave myself official orders: *Don't trust anything he says*.

'Jackson,' he said with a stiff nod.

'Dad.'

'I want to talk about you dropping out. I understand you have your reasons for coming back from Spain, but at least consider returning to Loyola.'

'No, thanks.' Not biting that bullet again. 'So, are you heading to work?'

He opened the newspaper all the way, concealing his face. 'Yes.'

I poured a glass of orange juice and took a long drink. 'What was going on in Houston?'

Killing people with your bare hands?

'Nothing interesting, just some meetings with politicians. Cutting off the FDA before they start dumping new regulations on us. All things a high-school dropout could never do.'

I groaned and stuffed a forkfull of eggs in my mouth. 'I'm not interested in going back to a school with a bunch of stuck-up kids.'

He folded the paper and looked at me. 'Huh . . . Europe has diversified you. Can't say I object to that . . . but your education shouldn't suffer. It's just one more year, and then you can go to college wherever you want.'

One more year. What the hell did that really mean for someone like me?

'I'll get back to you,' I grumbled.

He left me alone in the kitchen and took off for work. Several questions ran through my head, like . . . did he yank off his suit and turn into a spy the second he walked out the door? But if he really did work for the CIA, there was no way I could follow him without getting caught.

My dad never seemed like the government-worker type, but he had been closed off the past few years. I thought that was because of Courtney. Mostly I thought he wished it was me who had died instead.

Can't say I blame him, especially now that I was acting the part of pain-in-the-ass delinquent seventeen-year-old, too spoiled to finish high school.

The doorbell rang and I forced myself off the chair and trudged over to open it. Henry was standing on the other side holding out a large brown envelope. 'Delivery for you.'

I took the envelope from his hands. 'Thanks. Did you check it for explosives?'

His eyes widened. 'Oh . . . I didn't know . . .'

'I'm kidding, Henry.' I patted him on the shoulder

before closing the door and plopping back into my chair. I dumped out the contents of the envelope and found a new cellphone, passport, licence, credit cards, a couple of hundred dollars in cash and a note.

Junior,
Hope this helps you get around a little better today. I know how helpless you privileged kids can be. In fact, I even programmed my number into your phone. I'll be keeping an eye on you. Your father's orders.

- Miss Stewart

PS I already have the entire international security staff at JFK on the lookout for Pierre the French exchange student, so don't even think about pulling that shit again.

I forced a full meal down my throat, hoping my energy level would return to normal. I needed to get dirt on Holly and Adam in this year. Preferably without time jumping because it was only moving me backwards. I did know one guy who might be able to help, but it wouldn't be a pleasant experience.

I walked through the empty hall of an NYU dorm and knocked on the very last door. Music filled the hallway as a plump guy with greasy hair and food stuck in his teeth opened the door, grabbed the front of my shirt and yanked me inside. 'Don't say a word!'

'Um . . . OK.' I glanced around the small single room. It was covered in takeout containers and dirty laundry, and somewhere in there was a bed. I think.

He tightened the frayed tie of his blue bathrobe. 'How did you hear about me?'

'A friend from your sociology class.'

Dirty Leon (the only name I knew he had) was a senior at NYU when I was a freshman. The guy who could get answers. Apparently he was able to get them while sitting on his ass eating deli sandwiches and entire jars of pickles.

He lifted an eyebrow but nodded. 'Good. You're one of us now.'

God, I hope not.

'So . . . tell me how this works . . . ?'

Dirty Leon had to toss a few pairs of underwear on to the floor before sitting down in front of his computer. 'Well, basically, this is a business deal. Confidentiality is a must, but I've never had a problem with a customer ratting me out.'

'Because you're so charming?'

'I get some pretty risky requests for information. Some of it could send a lot of people to jail. Now, tell me what you need.'

'Just to find someone. I have basic information, address and school . . .'

He nodded. 'A girl, and you need a little more insight into her life. That's elementary work, unless she's a government employee or underwent a recent sex-change operation.'

'No to both of those.'

I gave him the information and waited a few minutes, leaning against the door because I wasn't about to sit anywhere in the room and take the chance of physical contact with Leon's tighty whities.

'She has a job, according to the IRS,' he said, still staring at the computer screen.

OK, now *that* was impressive. 'Where does she work?'

'Some place called Aero Twisters in Newark.'

'Is that like a smoothie shop?'

He typed away for a few seconds and a picture of Holly popped up on the screen. 'Recreational and preschool gymnastics instructor. Looks like you might be too old to join one of her classes.'

The future Holly mentioned to me she had taught gymnastics, but I never knew where.

I scanned the screen and then my face broke into a grin. 'They're hiring.'

'For a cleaning-and-maintenance position. Think you can handle that?'

Probably not. 'Maybe, if I thought it would impress her.'

Leon stared at the wall above my head. 'Depends on what angle you're going for. Hard-working guy willing to get his hands dirty . . . that's got winner written all over it.'

'Yeah, it does.' *If I could pull it off.*

He turned to face the computer again. 'According to an email from the owner of the gym, he had a plumbing issue this morning that made him, quote, "want to tear his hair out". Sounds like you should jump on this right away.'

'Thank you. Any chance you can whip up a fake résumé?' I asked.

He grinned, revealing green bits of pickle stuck between his teeth. 'I'll make you look like the best cleaning-and-maintenance guy in the entire state of New Jersey – for an extra fifty bucks.'

'Great. You can email it to me.' I paid Leon his money, jotted down my email address and then left before the bacteria crawling the walls of the room got anywhere near me.

This would be a good start, and then I could figure out the best way to approach Adam. Even though he had told me to find him if anything like this ever happened, it seemed completely nuts to walk up to him and say, 'Hey, I'm from the future!'

Getting this job would put me one step closer to forming a plan. If I could manage to get hired.

'You're the first applicant in two weeks who actually has experience in maintenance,' Mike Steinman said to me from across his desk.

'That's good news for me.'

I had just spent thirty minutes making up more lies than I could keep track of, and fortunately he was eating them up. I didn't see any other way to get into Holly's circle. We didn't go to school together. Our paths would never cross enough for me to gain her trust – some guy who lives in Manhattan keeps 'accidently' bumping into her in Jersey. It was either this or enrol in her school. I'd leave that for plan B. And I was going to avoid plan B at all cost because it involved high school. And yeah, I'd never been to a big public school like Holly's, but basic 'High School 101' rules applied everywhere. It wasn't easy to get into someone's social circle without common ground.

'All right, the job's twenty hours a week plus overtime. You lock up every night. We have nearly a thousand kids running through here each week, so nothing is consistent – gotta be ready for those surprises.'

'I'm not easily shocked.' *Not any more.*

'Great. Can you start today?'

It took me a second to respond. 'Seriously? I'm hired?'

He stood and walked towards his office door. 'Yes, I'm that desperate. We just had a light go out above the asymmetric bars, and the list keeps getting longer.'

'Thank you, Mr Steinman. You have no idea how much I need this job,' I admitted.

He opened the door. 'Sounds like we both win. And everyone around here calls me Mike.'

'Gotcha.'

'Come on. I'll show you the staff locker room and the maintenance closet.'

My pulse was already speeding up. She was here, somewhere. But it wasn't *my* Holly. Not yet anyway.

I followed Mike across the carpeted gymnastics floor and in between the balance beams. My legs were shaking and I barely listened as he opened an empty locker and listed off instructions and cleaning schedules.

Eventually he slapped me on the back. 'I've never had a maintenance guy, always had to contract jobs out to different companies. Or try to fix stuff myself. It's a pain in the ass.'

I swallowed hard and croaked out a thank-you. Hopefully I wouldn't get myself killed changing a light bulb.

'The place gets really crowded between four and seven, so you'll need to make sure you're out of the way of classes while you're working.' Mike tossed me a black polo shirt. The words 'Aero Twisters, Inc.' were embroidered across the front.

I pulled it on over my T-shirt and followed Mike out of the locker room, towards the lobby and the wall separating the parent viewing area from the gymnastics gym. He pointed to a dark-haired girl and a short guy leaning against the half-wall. 'This is Jana and Toby. They're both on the team here. They teach classes when it fits in with their practice schedule.'

'Hi,' they said together.

I had met the future Jana several times in 2009, and I vaguely remembered meeting Toby.

'Hey, Holly, come here,' Mike shouted.

Her long, blonde ponytail stuck out from underneath the table. 'Yeah, Mike?'

She crawled out, holding up the pen she must have dropped, and stood in front of us, next to the other two. My breath caught in my throat and then my legs went wobbly. She was so close. So real. How long had it really been since I last saw her? Five days. It seemed like months.

'Jackson is our new cleaning-and-maintenance guy,' Mike said.

'I can't believe you wrangled someone into fixing this place,' Holly joked.

Her light laughter rang through my ears and I had the sudden urge to throw her over my shoulder and run out of there. Make sure nothing bad ever happened to her. I took in a breath and tried to concentrate despite the ache I was feeling inside. She didn't know me. I knew she wouldn't, but it still felt like a hard kick right in the gut.

I shook my head, then forced a smile and a nod hello before walking in the other direction. Besides watching the older version of Holly getting shot, this was the most freaked out I had ever been in my entire life.

And I still had a light bulb to change – another scary thought.

The ladder shook as I reached my hand towards the giant light hanging near the set of asymmetric bars. I managed to replace the bulb without electrocuting myself and was heading down the ladder when I caught a glimpse of Holly handing out stickers to her class as the girls were leaving.

I climbed slowly down the final step. Heights had never been my thing.

A loose strand of blonde hair fell over her eyes and I watched it, forcing myself not to reach out and tuck it behind her ear. To see if it felt the same. If she was actually real.

Every muscle in my body ached to touch her, drag her out the door and tell her everything. Maybe she'd believe me, but she still wouldn't know me.

Don't be a dumb-ass, Jackson. She'd never believe me and would most likely run scared. Who wouldn't? Other than Courtney . . . and Adam. I pulled myself together and started folding the ladder.

Just as Holly was finishing, Toby approached.

'Hey, Hol, was that your last class?' he asked.

I kept my eyes on the white wall I had just returned to scrubbing with a dirty rag.

'Yeah,' she answered.

'You want to go get something to eat, maybe a burger?' he asked.

I laughed under my breath and shook my head.

'I can't. I've got—'

He chuckled and tugged on her ponytail. 'Never mind.'

'Seriously, Toby. I've got two advanced classes this semester—'

Toby put a hand up to stop her, then looked in my direction. 'It's Jackson, right?'

I stood and walked closer to them. 'Yeah.'

Toby leaned back against the wall, his eyes fixed on Holly. 'Jackson, what does it mean if a girl turns you down five times in two weeks?'

I dug deep to find my buried voice. I didn't need them thinking I was incapable of competent speech. 'Maybe she doesn't eat meat.'

Holly cracked a smile.

'She eats fake meat,' Jana said, walking up behind me. 'Do you go to Washington?'

'No.'

The three of them waited, expectantly. I went through a quick mental checklist of who I was. This time.

'I don't go to school.'

'You're homeschooled?' Toby asked.

'No, I dropped out . . . you know . . . got my GED.'

'So you're in college?' Jana asked.

'You're such a snob. You think everybody has to go to college,' Toby said to her.

'I might go. I haven't decided,' I said.

'Then you're eighteen?' Jana asked.

'Give him a few more days before you pounce on him,' Toby said.

'I'm seventeen,' I told her.

'So is Holly,' Jana said. 'She just had her birthday a few days ago.'

Holly rolled her eyes and pulled Jana by the arm. 'Let's go clear off the preschool area. Give the new guy some breathing room.'

Mike walked out of his office and I jumped back into my wall-scrubbing. 'Jackson, I'll show you how to lock up. I have to take off in a couple of minutes.'

'I can do it, Mike,' Holly shouted from across the gym. 'I'll show Jackson . . . so he can lock up tomorrow.'

Mike shrugged. 'Cool.'

The second he walked out the door, Holly, Toby and Jana headed upstairs to the fitness equipment. I watched Holly get on one of the treadmills before I turned back to my work.

The evening chore list was huge and it took me a while to finish, probably due to my lack of experience in cleaning much of anything. I was packing up my stuff when Holly and Jana came over and grabbed water bottles from their bags. Holly pulled her black polo shirt over her head, revealing a bright pink sports bra. Her ponytail whipped right in front of my face and I caught the scent of watermelon shampoo.

I knew it well.

Toby and Holly went back upstairs for an all-out treadmill battle.

'They do this all the time,' Jana said, sitting down next to me. 'I hate running.'

'I'm out of breath just watching,' I said.

One of them would up the speed and the other would do the same. This went on for at least twenty minutes until Toby jumped off.

'I finally won!' Holly said when they were back downstairs.

'Whatever,' Toby muttered. 'I'm taking a shower.'

'Someone's a sore loser,' Jana sang.

'Fine, Holly. I admit defeat.' Toby took a graceful bow in front of the locker-room door.

Holly laughed and sat down beside her bag, right next to me.

'Is he gone?' she whispered.

My tongue felt like it was covered in sawdust. All I could do was nod. I silently cursed myself for being such an idiot. *Say something!*

She collapsed on to her back on the mat. 'There's no way I'll be able to move in the morning. And if you tell him that . . .'

I leaned over her and mustered up a little confidence. 'What? Will you get me fired? Take all the screws out of the ladder?'

Laughter shook her whole body. 'No, I won't do anything. It was a pathetic attempt to intimidate you.'

I reached my hand out to help her up and she hesitated before taking it. I let go the second she was standing. Touching her was too much of a reminder.

'I better go. You work tomorrow?' I said as we parted ways later, having locked up.

'Yeah, I'm here pretty much every day.'

I nodded and left before saying anything I'd regret.

I walked several blocks to the train station, hating the distance between us more with every step.

chapter fourteen

MONDAY, 10 SEPTEMBER 2007

I walked in the front door of my apartment and immediately recognized my dad's voice, but he wasn't speaking English. It was something like Russian, maybe?

I leaned against the wall on the other side of the kitchen and listened as he rattled on for another minute or two before hanging up the phone.

'Jackson, is that you?'

So much for eavesdropping. 'Yeah, Dad.'

He met me in the hallway. 'Where have you been?'

'Uh . . . yeah, I was just out with . . . you know, people.'

He frowned. 'It's late. It'd be nice if you would call.'

'Sorry,' I mumbled, before switching subjects. 'Were you just speaking Russian?'

He turned his back to me. 'Turkish, actually. We're working on a new drug trial in Turkey. I like to be able to communicate without a translator as much as possible.'

Totally secret, CIA stuff.

Suddenly, I was reminded of another suspicious incident. One from the future. At the time I honestly thought Dad was just being a snob about me dating an average girl. Now I really wished I *had* continued writing detailed accounts of every moment spent with Holly. For clues and to alleviate my grief. Once we hooked up, it was all just pages and pages of experiments and crunching numbers. But I did remember this one strange evening pretty vividly. It was mid-July 2009. Holly and I had just come back from dinner and were walking into my building. She jumped on my back and we both saluted Henry at the door. He laughed and shook his head. 'Have a good night, Mr Meyer, Miss Flynn.'

'Why don't they ever use first names?' Holly asked.

'They refuse. Believe me, I've tried.'

She was already kissing the back of my neck before the door to my apartment was open. Both of us had been out of town for a long weekend. Five days apart and we were ready to jump each other. Sitting through dinner first had been a terrible idea.

'Do you want a drink?' I asked her, opening the fridge at the bar in the living room.

'I like that really fruity wine. Do you have any of that?'

I snatched the bottle from the fridge and decided against glasses. Since we had actually planned our dinner date, all I wanted right now was to dive back into the impulsive whirlwind we had been in the previous week. 'Let's get totally trashed tonight.'

'What are we celebrating?' Holly asked as we walked into my room and sat on the end of the bed.

Nothing . . . yet, I thought as I pulled the cork out and handed her the bottle. 'Us, of course. The two coolest people in the world.'

She took a swig of the fruity wine, as she called it. 'I can't believe you're not using glasses. How much is a bottle of this anyway?'

I examined the label. 'I don't know . . . maybe a hundred dollars.'

Holly choked on her last gulp. 'A hundred dollars! You can get wasted with a ten-dollar bottle of whiskey.'

I laughed. 'It was your choice. Besides, *you* could get drunk from two or three beers.'

She rolled her eyes, then smiled again. 'Tell me about Europe. Adam couldn't stop yapping about seeing the Alps and people in suspenders and lederhosen.'

'You first. What did you do in Indiana?' I asked, stalling so I could mentally edit my story a little.

'Jackson, it's the Midwest. Completely boring. I baked a lot of cookies with my grandmother and babysat my cousins.'

I gave her the rundown of my trip to Germany and Italy with Adam – minus the time-travel stuff. By then we had finished the bottle of wine and Holly was flipping through my music.

She finally made a selection and then crawled on to the bed next to me. 'So, I know we're being all cool and casual, but is it cool to say I missed you? Just a little, when I got really bored. Like when watching the corn grow was the only entertainment.'

'It's allowed.' *And I just decided we're getting completely naked tonight. There. I made a plan.*

Now all I had to do was convince Holly.

The two of us had had minimal time alone and so far I hadn't pushed the issue of removing clothing. Not that I would ever push her. It was more like persuasion or a really good sales pitch. She rolled on her back and I lifted her shirt up, revealing her stomach. Then I leaned over and touched my lips just above her belly button.

I watched her face carefully as I unbuttoned her jeans, and when I pulled them off from the bottom, yanking her all the way down to the end of the bed, she laughed really hard, releasing some of the tension hanging in the air.

'Nice, Jackson.'

I lay down next to her again and kissed her cheek. 'Are you making fun of me?'

'Yep.' She touched her lips to my neck and slid a hand under my shirt.

A while later most of our clothes were on the floor and Holly was lying on top of me, my hands all over her, when we heard someone cough loudly. We both lifted our heads and saw my dad standing in the doorway, his arms crossed.

'Oh my God!' Holly said and then she dived under the covers, pulling the duvet over her head.

'Dad, what are you doing home? I thought you were in South Africa.'

'South America. Put some clothes on, Jackson. I need to speak with you. *Privately.*' He walked out and slammed the door shut behind him.

I pulled the blanket from Holly's head. Her hands

covered her face, but I could see the rosy red colour between her fingers.

'I can't believe that just happened,' she moaned.

I laughed and pulled her up towards the pillows. 'It's OK. He couldn't care less what we're doing in here, trust me.'

'Jackson, your dad just saw me in my underwear. I'm allowed to be a little humiliated.' She flipped on to her stomach and covered her head again. 'Just go!'

I grinned at her even though she wasn't looking. 'I'm going to need a minute before I go parading around.'

Her body shook with laughter. 'Next time you're locking the door, even if you think your father's in Antarctica.'

'You are so damn cute.' I kissed her cheek. 'Don't go anywhere, OK?'

'Really? Because I had big plans for showing my panties to the elevator dude,' she mumbled into the pillow.

'He'd love that.' I pulled on my jeans and walked into the kitchen, where Dad waited, leaning against the counter.

'What's going on in there?' he asked.

I opened the fridge, pulled out the milk and drank straight from the carton – just to piss him off. 'Well, remember that talk we had when I was twelve?'

'Don't be a smart-ass, Jackson. Who *is* this girl? And why do you keep seeing her?'

'Her name is Holly, remember? You met her. And I keep seeing her because I like her. What's the problem, Dad?'

He moved closer and leaned forward. 'You don't know anything about her. She's had access to confidential information for weeks now. You fall asleep with some stranger in our home – who knows what she's doing.'

I pointed a finger at him and nodded. 'I think you're on to something. Industrial spy girl from Jersey. I've noticed her diary getting a lot thicker lately. Wait here while I go search her for evidence.'

'Real mature, Jackson.'

I let out a breath. 'You know what, Dad? I like Holly. We're both adults and what we do is our business.'

I walked away without looking back. I was acting all cool and shit, but inside I was shaking like a ten-year-old.

I slid into bed next to Holly and tried to figure out what the hell was going on with Dad. He had never, ever shown any interest in or concern for the girls I dated or brought home.

'Is everything OK?' Holly asked.

'Yeah, fine. You're not a spy, are you?'

She laughed. 'No, but I've always wanted to be one, since I was a little girl.'

Thinking about me and Holly, all casual and having fun in 2009, was so hard. My main goal right now, while stuck in 2007, was to find out as much about my father and myself as I possibly could. And to make sure there was never a repeat occurrence of 30 October 2009. If there was, it would be my fault because I would know what was coming.

As I fell asleep in my new present, in 2007, I tried to sort out the details of that night in July 2009 when my father had acted a little bit too much like a secret agent. Come to think of it, he'd been gone for nearly three weeks and yet he seemed to know Holly had hung around our place on several occasions. He knew a lot more than a normal parent would know.

It all came back to the real question I was too afraid to really ask . . . was it possible those men that shot Holly could work for my father or be on his side at all? At this point, I couldn't rule it out. I couldn't rule *anything* out.

chapter fifteen

FRIDAY, 14 SEPTEMBER 2007

OK, so I totally have a job now. In Jersey. As a janitor. If my father knew, he'd kick my ass. Or just yell at me a lot for dropping out of an expensive private school to change light bulbs. One week has passed in my new job, and so far I haven't killed myself. However, my co-workers have been nice enough to conceal some of my major screw-ups that happened late at night, after Mike left. Neither Jana, Toby nor Holly has ever said this out loud, but I think we have unofficially agreed to a vow of silence. They always stay late and play around on the equipment, despite Mike's constant grumbling about injury prevention and liability.

'Something nasty happened in the bathroom. Can you check it out?' Mike asked as he breezed past me on his way back to the group he was coaching.

I groaned to myself and grabbed a pair of rubber gloves. It couldn't be much different than cleaning a dorm-room toilet. I had been assigned bathroom-cleaning duties every other week during my one year of college and sharing a bathroom with two other guys.

When I went into the men's room and got a quick look at the clogged, overflowing toilet, I walked right back out and over to Mike on the floor.

'I think you might need a plumber.'

He laughed. 'Wouldn't that be you?'

'Yeah . . . sure. Just joking . . .' In other words, I was screwed.

Holly was watching me from over her shoulder. She was sitting on the floor with sheets of paper and a stapler spread out in front of her.

'You need some help?'

'No, that's OK. I got it.'

She got up and followed me anyway. 'I don't mind.'

'OK, but you're going to need this.' I handed her a surgeon's mask from the cleaning cart before opening the door.

We tied them on and stood in front of the clogged toilet.

'That's just nasty,' she muttered.

'Men are pigs, Holly.'

'I wouldn't know. I've never lived with one.'

'Then you're lucky.'

She pointed to the plunger next to the toilet. 'Maybe you should use that?'

I raised an eyebrow. 'Have you done this before?'

'Many times. Have you?'

I shrugged. 'Sure, every day.'

She laughed as I attempted to plunge the toilet. This

wasn't exactly what I had in mind for our longest 2007 conversation thus far, but at least it was something.

Holly reached over me and lifted the top off the tank, leaning it against the wall. Then she stuck her hand right in – nothing squeamish about this girl. 'See this little thingy? I don't know what it's called, but it's supposed to be up and that's why it won't flush.'

She moved her hand from the tank and the toilet flushed immediately.

'Nice!' I said.

She pulled her mask down and smiled. 'Do you think it's safe to breathe?'

I snatched the bottle of disinfectant from the cleaning cart and started spraying every inch of the toilet. 'It will be in a minute.'

Holly grabbed another pair of gloves and a sponge and helped me clean. When the two of us walked out of the bathroom, we ran right into Jana.

'Diving into boys' bathrooms with the new guy, I'm impressed,' she teased.

'You should be. We were doing really nasty things,' Holly said.

She walked away, leaving me standing next to Jana, who was dressed in a leotard and covered up to her elbows in chalk. 'She's probably not going to go out with you. Just so you know.'

'We were just cleaning a toilet, I swear.'

Jana laughed under her breath. 'I know. But somebody needed to fill you in before you get too attached.'

Too late.

'Does she have a boyfriend?'

'Nope. What about you? Do you have a girlfriend?' Jana asked.

'Um . . . kind of . . . well, no, not really.'

Toby walked up and stuck his head between the two of us. 'Mike's taking off early tonight and he'll be gone all weekend. I'm thinking we should do something?'

'Poker night,' Jana suggested with a devious grin.

'Exactly. Are you in, Jackson? You're the key holder now, so we kind of need you here.'

'You want me to risk the job I just started so you can play poker and screw around?'

Toby laughed quietly. 'All right, what do you want?'

I nodded towards Holly. 'I'll agree if you convince her to come, but you can't use me as a reason.'

'Are you moving in on my woman?'

'Toby, it's called unrequited love. Give it up, man,' Jana said, patting his head as if he was a little dog.

'I'm just curious, that's all. Plus, we had a moment,' I said.

Jana rolled her eyes. 'They cleaned a toilet together.'

'Romantic,' Toby said.

'Jackson!' Mike called. 'Need you to clean up the preschool floor. One of the kids got sick.'

Great. It was nice to know that the hundreds of thousands of dollars' worth of private-school education was being put to good use.

As soon as I finished removing the vomit from a stack of mats, Toby came over to me. 'OK, it's a deal.'

'How did you do it?'

He grinned. 'I can't reveal my methods, but it involves touching, lots of sweat, and possibly exploring the range of motion of her joints.'

I punched him lightly on the shoulder. 'You wish.'

Toby and Jana took off before Mike left and returned about ten minutes after his car had cleared the parking lot. I was mopping the front lobby when the door opened and they walked in with their arms full. Two more guys followed behind them and I dropped the mop to the floor with a loud clang as soon as I saw the dark-haired boy with black glasses.

'Adam!'

Uh-oh . . .

He stopped and turned to face me. 'Do I know you?'

Oh crap! Think of something quick.

'The county science fair last year – weren't you in it?' I said lamely.

'Yeah, me and about a thousand other people.'

All four of them stared. I forced out another lame cover-up. 'Your project was really cool. The whole . . .'

'Theory of Relativity,' he finished for me.

'Exactly.'

Toby rolled his eyes. 'OK, we got another science geek. You better not be able to count cards like Silverman.'

Holly bounded over to us, stopping in front of the guy next to Adam. That's when I realized who it was. David Newman. Holly's future boyfriend.

He smiled and handed her the brown paper sack he was holding. 'That'll be seven dollars. And I should add that I had to wait twenty minutes for them to make a fresh batch of guacamole.'

She placed a few bills in his hand. 'I love you, David.'

'She never says that to me,' Toby said.

Holly leaned closer to Toby. 'That's because you don't want me to. Admit it – those three little words frighten you.'

I can totally relate.

He laughed and moved his face even closer to hers. She backed up immediately. 'Maybe, but *makin'* love doesn't frighten me.'

David laughed and Holly shoved him out of her way, then walked off with Jana, muttering, 'Juveniles.'

'Real smooth, Toby,' David said.

'Don't tell me you've never made a game out of shaking her hard exterior,' Toby said to David.

'I refuse to respond to that,' David said, but he was laughing.

'But you've thought about kissing her?'

I shot a glance at Adam, who, like me, was listening in silence.

'Not really,' David answered.

'Well, I have,' Toby said, unashamed. 'Mostly when I've wanted to shut her up.'

They all laughed loud enough for Holly and Jana to dart their eyes in our direction.

I went back to mopping while the game started at the table they'd set up on the gymnastics floor. When it was obvious I didn't have any more work to do, Toby called me over.

'Aren't you going to play?' he asked.

'Sure, I could use a little extra cash.' I sat down next to Adam and across from Holly.

I really wanted to talk to him. But right now I needed to be cool. Get into character and be the mysterious new guy.

David dealt out the cards. 'Jackson, where did you go before you dropped out? Was it in Jersey?'

I nodded and said the name of another high school.

'That's why we've never seen you,' Jana said.

'So, why did you quit school?' Toby asked.

Jana elbowed him in the side, but I waved her off.

'I just got sick of it. My dad wanted me to work.'

'I can't wait to be done,' Holly said, throwing two cards in the discard pile and picking up new ones. 'AP English bites. I knew it would be tough, but a new novel every other week and a five-page paper every other day is a bit much.'

'What are you reading?' I asked Holly.

'We just finished *A Tale of Two Cities*.'

Aha, a door just swung open.

Toby and Adam both groaned.

'Couldn't stand Dickens,' Adam said.

David threw his cards into the pile. 'Really? Mr Perfect GPA? I'm surprised.'

'Literature is very different than math and science,' Adam said.

'So, you haven't read it yet?' I asked Holly.

'I have, but I'm not having any luck writing the paper. I started, then I got stuck.'

'All you need to say is, "It was the best of times, it was

the worst of times", the end,' Toby said in a very bad British accent. 'Who's in this round?'

'I got nothing,' Jana said, throwing down her cards.

David did the same.

'Toby, I'm starting to see why you have so much trouble with women,' Holly teased. 'Obviously you can't see the romance in a story like that. Unrequited love and personal sacrifice with nothing in return.'

He turned his eyes on her. 'You're incredibly sexy when you speak ze language of literature.'

Holly shook her head and looked at me. 'See what I mean? He has no clue.'

I threw another chip on to the pile. 'Enlighten us then, since you're such a wise woman. Save some other poor girls from our unromantic ways.'

She fumbled the cards in her hands and nearly dropped one. 'Um . . . I'm probably not the best person to ask. Jana, what do you think?'

Jana perked up in her chair. 'OK, I'll take a stab. Well, Toby's not sharing common interests. Maybe that's the problem. Holly loves to read, so her future man should too. Personally I'm into punk and ska music, so I'm going to look for someone who shares my love of bands nobody's heard of.'

'All right, you haven't tripped me up so far. That can't be everything,' I said.

'I couldn't date a guy who didn't at least appreciate sports. Gymnastics takes up more than half my life, so that's a given.'

'Well, what about Toby? He's a gymnast.'

Jana raised her eyebrows at me. 'He's also my cousin.'

How did I not know that? 'OK, that won't work.'

'Ya think?' Toby said, shaking his head. 'Come on, Holly, give us a little peek inside your head.'

Yes, please do. The truth was . . . I didn't know seventeen-year-old Holly very well at all.

'I don't know what I want. Maybe I'll figure it out some day, but for now I'll settle for school, work and saving money for college,' Holly said.

'Borrrrr-ing,' Jana sang.

Holly threw a handful of popcorn across the table at her. 'Fine, Jana, I want a guy who has read beyond the first few words of a Charles Dickens novel and can quote beautiful lines of prose while ballroom-dancing to . . . hmm . . .'

Jana rested her chin on her hands and sighed. 'What about "Come Away with Me" by Norah Jones? It would have to be a waltz.'

'This is a dude, right?' David asked.

Toby snorted back laughter. 'You've got to be kidding, Flynn. You are the *last* girl who I'd guess would fall for that shit.'

'It's not shit if it's genuine,' Jana said.

'Exactly,' Holly agreed. Then she tossed her cards down on the table. 'Full house.'

'Damn,' Adam muttered.

Everyone folded and I turned my eyes on Jana. 'Do you think she's bluffing?'

Jana looked bewildered. 'Bluffing? She's already shown her cards.'

'No, I mean about the perfect guy. Mr Shakespeare-quoting, tango-dancing lover.'

Holly leaned back in her chair and crossed her arms. 'Waltz, not tango, and I'm not bluffing. But he has to be straight.'

'Yeah, have fun finding *that* guy,' David said.

'Maybe he's sitting right across from you,' I said.

A flicker of nerves crossed her face, but she replaced it quickly with a confident smirk. 'No way.'

I grabbed the deck and started shuffling. 'Yeah, you're probably right. Besides, it's not like I want such a high-maintenance girl.'

'I am *not* high maintenance.'

David grabbed a soda from the pile of cans on the floor. 'Holly, you've got some fantasy guy waltzing around in tights, whispering *Romeo and Juliet* in your ear. That's as high maintenance as it gets. For guys our age, you're lucky if you can get us to stop spitting and scratching our balls when you're around.'

Holly smiled and pinched his cheek. 'You're such a charmer, David. And I never said anything about tights.'

Toby groaned. 'Well, the rest is bad enough. Who's filling your heads with this shit? That's why we can't get a date.'

'It's women writing romance novels starring men that would never exist. It sets unrealistic expectations,' Adam said.

Holly nodded. 'Nicely put, Adam. That could be true, but we can't help what we want.'

Jana nudged me in the shoulder. 'I believe Jackson was

going to give it a try, weren't you?'

'Yeah, right,' Holly muttered, reaching across the table and taking the deck from my hands. 'Are we playing poker or not?'

Toby's eyes darted between the two of us. Then he pointed a finger at Holly. 'You're scared he might charm you. Just admit it.'

'This I've got to see,' David said.

Holly put on her competitive poker face. 'Fine, do your thing, Jackson.'

I shook my head. 'No, that's all right, I'm not really in the mood for dancing. Besides, you've already got this whole "All men are created equal" mentality. It's obvious you don't have a very open mind.'

I kept reminding myself to keep it light, annoy her if I had to. Fawning never works with any halfway intelligent girl.

The flicker of anger hit her eyes and I fought back the urge to smile. 'OK, if you're right and you have the qualities of my imaginary perfect guy, I'll agree to go out with you.'

I scoffed at her. 'What makes you think I want to go out with you? I'm not seeing what I get out of this.'

Her cheeks turned pink and she dropped her eyes to the table, but raised them quickly. 'Sorry, that's not what I meant. I'll buy you dinner tomorrow night and I'll clean the bathrooms after I get done working. But you have to agree to something if *I'm* right.'

'Jackson, I'd take her up on that bathroom deal. After three birthday parties, it's gonna be bad,' Toby admitted.

'And if I'm right, you have to come in early and help

me with those three birthday parties of screaming kids and cake and wrapping paper up to your elbows,' Holly added.

'Deal,' I said.

'This is so much more entertaining than getting drunk,' David said.

'We can do that later,' Toby added.

'I'll pick the music,' Adam said, pulling an iPod out of his pocket.

'No, let's see what Holly has,' I said to her with a smile.

She forked over her iPod and I flipped through her playlist quickly, hoping I could find the perfect song. I did. After choosing "You Don't Know Me" by Jann Arden, I handed it back to Holly, who passed it to Jana.

I stood up from the table while Jana turned the music on by plugging the iPod into the stereo. I held my hand out to Holly.

She rolled her eyes. 'A kid from Jersey who cleans bathrooms knows how to waltz?'

I nodded. 'The question is, do you?'

I wasn't lying to her. I learned from attending way too many fancy parties.

'A little. Just from gym class,' she said.

As soon as I placed my arm around her waist, I knew this was going to be difficult, but I wanted an excuse to touch her, even if it was just for a few minutes. She placed a hand in mine and I could feel the nerves flowing through her. Her body was stiff and rigid, waiting for me to make a move.

'Relax,' I whispered.

Her shoulders loosened just a little as I drew her closer to me. I stepped back and she followed along. Her steps moved with mine and I let my nose touch her hair.

We stopped dancing at the far side of the floor as the song ended and she looked up at me, waiting for something.

Instinctively, I leaned my mouth closer to hers, then remembered what she was waiting for. It wasn't a kiss. I quickly moved my lips next to her ear and delivered a quote from the Dickens novel that was well past the first page. '"When you see your own bright beauty springing up anew at your feet, think now and then that there is a man who would give his life, to keep a life you love beside you."'

As I lifted my head she turned hers towards mine so her mouth just barely brushed along my cheek. I froze when her lips were an inch from mine.

Don't kiss her. It was too soon. She'd probably freak. Her eyes closed and I immediately dropped my arm and stepped back, plastering on a confident smirk.

'You were going to kiss him,' Toby accused.

'No, I wasn't,' Holly said.

'Looks like someone's going to be cleaning the bathrooms,' Toby sang. 'Jackson, I had no idea you were such a player. Do you have a manual on this stuff?'

I grinned at him and then looked back at Holly. Her face was bright red and she turned quickly, walking away from me. 'You win. I'll clean the bathrooms.'

'Holly, I don't really want you to—'

She put her hand up. 'Hey, you played to win. I'd do the same if the tables were turned.'

'You wouldn't have to do anything.' I blurted out without

thinking. She let out a breath. 'You can stop the playboy moves. I get it, you won.'

It was obvious she was angry and no one knew what to say, including me. I rubbed my temples with my fingers.

'I have to get home. My mom's going to freak if I'm late.' She grabbed her bag and headed towards the door.

David glanced at me, then jogged after her. 'You want me to come over for a while?'

'No, I'm tired and I have to work all day tomorrow.'

'You OK?' he asked.

'I'm perfect, David. Why shouldn't I be? I've been charmed by the perfect guy.' She was trying to make a joke of it, but the sarcasm and hurt seeped into her tone.

I sank into a chair and leaned my head against my hands. 'Damn.'

'Man, what did you do?' Toby asked.

'Isn't it obvious?' Jana said.

All of us stared at her, waiting. We were clueless.

'She practically asked you out, and now she thinks she got played.'

'Nice, Jana,' Toby said sarcastically.

'I didn't mean that he *is* a player; I'm saying that's probably how Holly sees it.'

I lifted my head and gave her a tight smile. 'Great.'

'I don't think asking guys out is something Holly does often,' Adam added.

'No, it isn't,' David said, returning to the table.

'I'm such an idiot,' I mumbled.

'Actually, I think you're a genius. What did you tell her anyway?' Toby asked.

'It doesn't matter. Are you guys ready to go?'

'I guess so, if you are,' Jana said.

'Yeah, I am.'

The night had been a complete failure. In fact, I might have done more damage than good. I locked up and headed for the train. I knew as soon as I sat down that I would make another attempt to get back to 2009. Being a part of *this* Holly's life was just too hard. And I really sucked at it.

chapter sixteen

SATURDAY, 15 SEPTEMBER 2007, 12.05 A.M.

Just seconds before I attempted another jump back to 2009, someone plopped down in the seat beside me.

'Hi, Jackson.'

I turned and looked right into my reflection in Adam's glasses. 'You followed me?'

He crossed his arms, glaring at me. 'What are you doing on a train to New York after midnight?'

'My dad works nights in the city. I usually help out.'

'Where?'

'Loyola Academy. He's a janitor.'

'Like father, like son.'

'That's right.'

'Bullshit. How did you know my name? Before anyone told you.'

'I'm from the future and we're friends in 2009.'

He ignored what he took to be a joke. 'You know what I think?'

I leaned my head against the window and closed my

eyes. 'What's your theory, Adam?'

'Government agent.'

No, but I might be the son of one. 'I see. So, I'm not a time-traveller, I'm an agent studying your science project because the government wants to steal your theories and use them to make weapons.'

'Well . . . not weapons.'

I laughed and sat up again to look at him. 'I don't work for the government. I promise. And I have no desire to steal your project or bust you for hacking.'

His face tightened. 'I didn't say anything about hacking.'

'Oh . . . right.'

'So you *do* work for the government?'

'Adam, I want to tell you the truth, but you probably won't believe me.'

He relaxed back in his chair. 'Try me.'

I took a deep breath. 'We'll take this slow. I don't want you to have a heart attack. First of all, I live in Manhattan.'

'OK.'

'Do you want to come to my place? I'll tell you the rest there.'

He nodded, slowly. 'Just so you know . . . I've got friends who know exactly where I am, in case I don't show up later.'

I rolled my eyes. 'Sure you do.'

Adam looked up at the building with wide eyes. 'You live *here?*'

'Yup.'

We took the elevator up. During our ascent Adam was twisting his hands and darting his eyes around like the hacker police were going to jump out at him any second.

'Who's your friend?' Dad asked when we walked past him in the front room.

'This is Adam Silverman. Adam, this is my dad.'

Adam shook his hand. 'Nice to meet you, sir.'

'Jackson, I'm going out of town for a couple of days.'

'For what?'

'Business in South Korea. I left you a message earlier, but you didn't return my call. Someone's picking me up in five minutes. Will you be OK?'

'Since when do you have business in South Korea?'

His eyebrows lifted as if to say he wasn't going to talk about this with a stranger present.

'See you in a few days.' I walked down the hall with Adam trailing behind me. I led him to my room and shut the door before pointing to the couch on the far side of the room. He walked over and sat down, watching closely as I pulled a silver lock box from my desk drawer. After sifting through a stack of pictures, I handed him a few. I had just made prints from my 2009 memory card yesterday, thinking they might seem more real like this.

'Is this . . . ?'

'Holly,' I finished.

He flipped it over and looked at the back, then a huge grin spread across his face. 'Nice. This is really elaborate. And it's kinda genius how you tie in my science project. Most people know about the Theory of Relativity part, but actually taking the next step and throwing time travel at me . . . very creative.'

'So . . . you don't believe your own research?' I knew a few pictures wouldn't be enough.

'Of course I do, in theory. How did you get these pictures of me? My parents' computer, maybe?'

'I took them myself. And what do you mean, "in theory"? Either you believe it or you don't.'

'I believe time travel is possible, but with a lot more research and probably technology that doesn't exist yet.'

'You're wrong,' I stated flatly.

'It's not possible?'

'It's very possible and I can do it.'

He laughed and shook his head. 'All right, prove it.'

'What can I say that won't make me sound like a carnival fortune teller? It's the future. You get into MIT and get a 2300 on your SATs.'

'Not a bad score. What else you got?' He leaned back and put his hands behind his head.

I flopped back on to my bed and yanked the journal from my bag before thumbing through the pages. 'It's possible I forgot what you told me to say.'

'Must not have been important.'

'It's not like I really thought I'd get stuck in the past.' I sat up and grinned before pointing at his chest. 'Your dog just died, didn't he? Like a few days ago?'

'Thanks for the reminder,' he grumbled. 'But that doesn't prove anything. Jana and I were talking about it tonight. You must have overheard.'

'Sorry.'

'How did you meet me, in the future?'

'We worked at a day camp together. Holly did too.' I watched his face carefully for any indication he believed me, but it was all calm and cool.

'But you must have proved that you could time-travel at some point, right?'

I nodded. 'Yeah, it started something like this conversation. Only we were supervising an all-night camp-out. The kids were asleep and it was just us. You came up with an experiment and made me jump back and forward again.' I opened my wallet and handed him the memory card. 'This has lots of experiment data on it.'

His flipped it between his fingers while I went back to the journal, trying to find the page with my description of that first experiment.

'That was all it took to fool me? My older self must be an idiot.'

'No, you made me do it ten times.' The scribbled cursive at the bottom of the 11 April 2009 entry caught my eye. 'Here, check this out! You wrote yourself a note.'

He snatched the notebook from my hand. I watched as all the colour drained from his face and he sank back on to the couch. 'How did you get this?'

'You wrote it. I don't even know what it says. Is it Latin?'

'Yeah . . . Latin.' His fingers froze on the corner of the page.

'What's it say?'

After a long silence he jumped into action, flipping frantically through the pages, then finally said, without looking up, 'Not important. Forget about it.'

I stared at the ceiling, waiting patiently for the questions that would inevitably follow. Of course Adam would know exactly what to tell himself. Something he would never doubt. I shouldn't have doubted him either.

'Jackson, wake up!' Adam stood over me, shaking my shoulders.

It was so bright that I could barely open my eyes. He must have turned on every light in the bedroom. 'What time is it?'

'Four.'

With all my excursions into different years, saying it was four meant nothing to me. I walked to the window and saw that it was still dark outside. That's when I took in the mass of computer parts piled on the floor. Extraneous pieces were strewn all over the room, and two monitors now sat on the desk.

'What the hell?!'

'Sorry, I borrowed two other computers from around the house to collate your most recent data. The hard drive wasn't big enough and didn't work with the memory card you gave me, so I kinda . . . made my own computer.' He shuffled around, picking up loose items and tossing them into the pile faster than I'd ever seen him move.

I studied his current state closely. His black hair stuck up in every direction, pupils dilated like a crack addict's, and he was doing the snapping thing with his fingers. I had seen him like this once before after a six-pack of Red Bull. He could probably be declared insane in this state. 'Did you have caffeine?'

He held up a thick stack of papers. 'I've got some notes to go over with you.'

'Let's eat first. Was it Red Bull or coffee?' I shoved him towards the door from behind. He didn't object, but he held the papers to his chest, probably so I couldn't take them.

'Ready for number one on my list of questions?' he asked, plopping down at the kitchen table.

I grabbed some turkey slices from the fridge and a loaf of bread and tossed them on to the table. 'All right, but eat while you talk. Soak up some of that caffeine.'

He stuffed a piece of bread in his mouth and chewed quickly. 'Wait . . . so, in 2009 you're nineteen and Holly's nineteen and you're both freshman at NYU?'

'No, I'm a sophomore . . . Holly's a freshman.'

'So this Holly is a Junior and the other one is in college . . . got it. How did you meet us in March 2009? We were still in high school, right? Or do we graduate early?!'

'No, you don't graduate early . . . we started camp counsellor training in March . . . it was just a few sessions until the summer officially started.'

'Dude . . . that's a little taboo, isn't it? College guy, hooking up with a high school chick? Oh wait . . . I guess that's what you're trying to do now . . . but worse . . .'

I sighed, fighting the urge to crawl back into bed again. This all made sense in *my* head. 'It's not taboo. That Holly is only four months younger than me. She's one of the older ones in her grade and I'm one of the younger ones . . . that's all. Is this really important?'

He ignored me. 'OK, so you commute from here to NYU? And Holly lives in the dorm? Which dorm? Maybe we should go scope it out?'

'Why?! You're making me really tired,' I said. 'Besides, I didn't commute from here . . . I lived in a dorm both freshman and sophomore year . . . a different dorm to Holly. But I lived at home during the summer and on breaks. You've been here . . . the older you . . . visiting. Holly's been here too . . . and to my dorm. Anything else? Need to know all of my professor's names or the path I took to class every day?'

Adam paused for a long moment, staring at the paper in front of him, then finally said, 'Nope . . . not now anyway.'

'Next question?' I prompted, rubbing my temples.

'So, what happens if you . . . for example . . . jump back thirty minutes, then stay thirty-one minutes. Then, technically, you'd be in—'

'The future,' I finished. 'I've never travelled outside the span of my own life.'

He nodded. 'That's what I figured. Do you even have to jump back? If you end up staying in the past until it's the same time you left?'

It was so weird being the one explaining shit to Adam. 'Sorry, in my typical disorganized fashion I have a few missing pages, but we did that experiment really early on. I just bounce back. Remember, it's different when I'm in the middle of a jump. I feel like I'm not all the way there, like I feel lighter, very little sensation as far as hot and cold. And nothing I do during my normal jumps affects my home base.'

'Right,' he said, stuffing more bread in his mouth. 'All those regular jumps are like some kind of shadow timeline. Or a . . . *mirror* timeline.'

'Yeah, like watching the same movie over and over, hoping eventually that the character you don't want to die will somehow make it. Or maybe if you shout a warning at them, it'll change something, but it never does,' I concluded. 'But how the hell did I end up here, in 2007? Not as a . . . shadow, but the real me?'

'And how did the other you just disappear?' Adam asked, shaking his head. Then he stared at me with his crazy, caffeine-addict eyes. 'I do have a theory.'

I rested my elbows on the table, trying to focus, even though it would probably be over my head. 'OK, let's hear it.'

'Well, first of all, it's obvious that there's only one version of you in any given home base.'

'Yep, but technically, I'm in the past right now.'

He leaned forward, over his papers, and slammed his fist on the table. 'What if this is another universe?'

I nearly fell out of my chair. 'OK, you are definitely insane.'

He scoffed at me and shook his head. 'Seriously? All the crazy shit that's happened to you and you think I'm insane because I mention parallel-universe theory?'

I laughed without even thinking about it. He was right. What the hell did I know? 'Let's tuck that one away for future analysis. What's the next question on your list?'

'There's a couple of times you noted that it felt like you were being forced back. I'll figure out a formula for this, but it seems you can't actually live in the past.'

I let out a breath. 'Apparently I can . . . if I move my home base.'

'Exactly. If only we knew how you did that. But I don't get why you can't go back to 2009. Or to that other universe, if we're going with that theory. None of the experiments indicate even the slightest possibility of getting stuck in the past. Although obviously I planned for it just in case. By writing the note. My older self did, anyway.'

I sat across from him and covered his paper with my hand. 'So you really do believe me? That I'm from the future?'

I needed to make sure it wasn't just the caffeine talking and he'd go back to logical, realistic thinking in a couple of hours.

'Yeah, there's no doubt in my mind. But did you leave 2009 because you thought those dudes with guns would kill you?'

'You read that part of the journal?' He nodded and I took a deep breath before spilling something I hadn't told anyone, future or past. 'Honestly, I don't even remember deciding to leave, but I know staying would have been too hard . . . You read about my sister, right?'

'Cancer, brain tumours, died in April of 2005,' he rattled off from his notes.

'I wasn't there when she died,' I admitted.

Adam lifted his eyes to mine, staring intensely. 'I thought the time-travelling didn't start until years after that?'

'I mean, I just wasn't there. Like, in the room with her.' I swallowed the lump threatening to form in my throat. 'You know how people always say they wished they could have been there, to say goodbye or whatever?'

He pushed the notes aside and rested his arms on the table. 'Yeah?'

'Well, I didn't want to be there. I was too scared. Not so much about talking to her, or being sad, but the actual act of watching someone go from living to . . . not living. I saw it in my head so many times, her chest moving, taking in deep breaths and suddenly it just . . .'

'Stops,' Adam finished for me.

'And then I was thinking all these things, like . . . when does she stop hearing us? Is it after her last breath? Because people hold their breath all the time, maybe she would still hear us or be processing thoughts.' I rubbed my eyes, ridding them of the blurriness. 'It's stupid . . . I know.'

'It's not stupid,' Adam said softly, 'but I'm not sure what your theory is . . . How does this have anything to do with leaving 2009?'

'Well . . . Holly was breathing and I didn't want to see her . . . stop. And that's probably why I'm stuck here . . . why I can't go back.'

His forehead wrinkled. 'I'm still not getting it.'

'Karma. Punishment . . . for leaving.' I picked at the slice of turkey in front of me, keeping my eyes on the table. 'But if I could do it over . . .'

He waved his hand to stop me. 'No need – I know that. It's cool. I just needed to wrap my head around your theory.'

'I'm sure that's the reason. People shouldn't get a second chance to do the right thing. And karma is probably going to keep kicking my ass, and Holly's never going to want anything to do with me. Like last night.'

'Yeah, you completely bombed.' He busied himself making another sandwich.

'I was such an idiot. And she's got guys like Toby asking her out all the time.'

'Well guys don't ask her out that often. She doesn't give off that vibe. That's how it works. And Toby isn't capable of looking at a girl without having some kind of sexual fantasy.' He crammed the corner of the sandwich into his mouth. 'Seriously, he's very open about what goes on inside his head, and I don't think he knows how to do the whole "friend thing" with a girl. So he flirts instead. Besides, he knows she'll say no.'

I rested my head in my hands, trying to get some grasp on the idea of this day . . . of this *year* as my new life. When would I ever stop wanting to be somewhere . . . some*when* else? And what was less selfish? Staying here or continuing on with more attempts to get back? And could I even save Holly if I did?

'You don't have to answer any more questions right now. I'm sure this is hard for you,' Adam said, breaking me from my thoughts.

I lifted my head and smiled at him. 'Honestly, you can ask me everything on that list. It's been forever since I could actually talk to someone like this – no lies or cover stories.'

He tried to hide the excitement on his face, but I wasn't fooled. Maybe it wouldn't be fun and games like it had been in 2009 . . . but at least I wasn't alone.

'I think we can be absolutely sure of one thing,' Adam said after sliding the notes back in front of him again.

'What's that?'

'You have *definitely* changed your home base, but I don't know how the hell you managed that.'

'Besides hopping over to another universe.' I grinned at him. 'Knowing you, you won't give up until you find out.'

chapter seventeen

SATURDAY, 15 SEPTEMBER 2007, 8.00 A.M.

I got to the gym around eight to get my cleaning done early so I could help Holly with the parties. I thought it might make a nice peace offering since she hated me now. When I opened the door the lights were already on and two people were in the gym: Holly and Toby.

She was swinging around the bars, with Toby standing on a block underneath her.

So this is the sweating and touching he mentioned yesterday.

Toby gave her a push on one of her swings and I nearly had a heart attack when she let go of the bar and flipped twice in the air before landing with a loud thud on the blue mats.

'Nice!' Toby said.

'That was pretty freaky,' I said.

Both of them jumped and then relaxed when they saw it was me, but Holly's face tightened immediately.

Damn, she's still mad.

Holly took off for the locker room to change. I gathered my supplies and started cleaning the front windows. After a while, Toby strolled over.

'I guess she's still pissed off,' he said.

My stomach twisted with grief, but I forced a grin. 'You're probably psyched.'

He laughed and picked up an extra rag to clean a smudge on the window next to me. 'Maybe, but I'm not going to fall apart because Holly Flynn turned me down for a date.'

'Sure you won't,' I said.

'Seriously, she's just fun to tease. Don't get me wrong – Holly's really cool. But a girl like that is a little more than I can handle.'

'What do you mean?'

'Too smart – I couldn't pull any shit with her. She'd see right through me.' He paused in his window cleaning and tilted his head to one side. 'I'd make out with her though.'

'So why isn't Holly on the team, like you and Jana?' I asked. 'She seems really good.'

'She hasn't competed in three years, since she moved from Indiana. I think it's injuries and maybe a money thing.'

'Money?'

'She's not in the poorhouse or anything. But it's an expensive sport.'

'Is she good enough to compete?'

'Yeah, that girl's got more talent than anyone on our team. She'd never believe me though, which is why I'd never tell her.'

'She'll just think you're trying to hook up with her.'

He laughed. 'Well, at least *I'm* not the professional player. Besides, I just met this chick last night at my friend's party. She's mega-hot and a total airhead.'

'Exactly your type, right?'

'Yeah, but only if the flakiness is genuine. Not that pretend-I'm-stupid shit. You know it's going to bite you in the ass later. Besides, I love messing with people who just don't get it.'

I had to stop myself from telling Toby how lame his dating philosophy was. 'She sounds like a blast.'

Both of us stopped talking when we saw Holly come out of the locker room wearing her staff shirt and tan shorts. Her hair was wet and braided. On the front of her shirt she had pinned a giant button that said 'PARTY HOST'.

I followed her to the party room. She was placing cups on the table in front of each chair. I grabbed a stack of plates and walked behind her, setting them next to each cup. She ignored me for several minutes, then finally stopped and turned to face me.

'What are you doing?'

'I'm just helping. You're obviously pissed off and I'm trying to smooth things over.'

She put her hands on her hips. 'Why?'

I tried to respond, but my tongue twisted, holding back words I couldn't say. What would *my* Holly have told me to do?

Jackson, quit being a chickenshit and outsmart me.

'I'll tell you why if you tell me why you're mad.'

She went back to setting the table with brightly

coloured spoons and forks. 'I'm not mad . . . just not interested.'

Ouch. 'Why not?'

'Because I know your type.'

'Which is?'

She grabbed a roll of string and a pair of scissors and started cutting long strips to tie to the balloons. 'You know . . . the type that's all charming just to get in a girl's pants.'

I attempted to look angry. 'First you assume I want to go out with you, and now you're assuming I want to get in your pants.'

Which I do and have.

She blushed again, just like last night. 'No, that's not what I meant . . .'

'If you're so sure, then tell me five things you know about me,' I said.

'You work here – that's one.'

I rolled my eyes. 'OK, what else?'

'You've read *A Tale of Two Cities* and know how to waltz, despite being a high-school dropout from Jersey.'

'Someone is very judgmental. Admit you don't know enough about me to make an accurate assumption regarding my alleged player status.'

'And what do you suppose we do about it?'

'You owe me dinner.'

'Fine, five o'clock. I'm driving and we're eating Thai food,' she said.

'Sounds good.'

*

The last party was out by five o'clock, and at quarter to six Holly was waiting at the door for me, wearing a denim skirt and a blue top. Her hair hung down and the ends were curled.

'You look nice,' I said.

She shrugged. 'I went home to change while you were fixing that broken shower head in the men's locker room.'

I locked the door to the gym and followed her to her car.

She had about a dozen library books stacked on the passenger seat. I moved them carefully to the back. 'This car is awesome.'

'It's a beat-up fifteen-year-old Honda and the air conditioning never works.'

'Classics are great.'

We were both quiet the rest of the ride, but she turned to me in front of the restaurant and cut the engine. 'Just so you know, I'm not allowed to date. Not that this is a date . . . but to my mother it will seem that way. So I invited a few friends.'

'Chaperones?'

'Exactly.'

'Who did you invite?'

'David and Adam. You met them yesterday.' I nodded. 'And Jana.'

'Great.'

Right before we walked into the restaurant, she spun around and was just inches from my face. 'I decided you were right. I was way too quick to judge you.'

'Are you apologizing?'

'No, but I'm giving you an opportunity to prove me wrong. Not because I think you need to impress me, but just to protect your reputation.'

I shrugged. 'Whatever.'

She smiled. 'Great, then I'm sure you won't mind answering a few questions over dinner. Like you said, I couldn't list five things I know about you.'

'OK,' I said, unable to hide the growing nerves in my voice.

'And Jackson?'

'Yes.'

'This won't be easy.'

My heart was already pounding. Holly was a very hard girl to lie to. I would know. I'd done it more times than I could count.

'What do your parents do?' she asked me as soon as we sat down at our table.

'My dad works at a school in Manhattan.'

'He's a teacher?' Jana asked from my other side.

'No, he's a janitor.'

She nodded but didn't say anything. I turned my eyes back to Holly.

'Siblings?' she asked.

I swallowed a big gulp of water from the glass in front of me before answering. 'One sister.'

'Older or younger?' Holly asked.

'We're twins actually, but she died a few years ago.'

Her eyes dropped to her hands and she muttered, 'I'm sorry.'

Hopefully the family questions would end there.

David's eyes darted between the two of us, taking in the uncomfortable air.

The waiter came over and took our order, and then David and Jana jumped into an in-depth analysis of how pathetic this year's football team was. Holly was silent, stirring the small bowl of sweet and sour sauce in the centre of the table.

'Are you done questioning me already?' I asked.

She lifted her eyes to meet mine and gave me a half-smile. 'Not even close. What's your favourite book?'

'Um . . . *Stranger in a Strange Land*,' I answered.

'I haven't read that. Is it any good?'

'Yeah, it's great. A human's raised on Mars and then returns to Earth.'

'Sounds interesting. Favourite song?'

'Hmm . . . I can't pick *one*. I'll give you my top five in random order. '"Somewhere Only We Know" by Keane, "Pictures of You" by the Cure, "Falling Slowly" by Glen Hansard, "Mad World", the Gary Jules version, and "Beast of Burden" by the Rolling Stones.'

I had managed to quickly rattle off not only older songs, but ones that brought up vivid memories of me and Holly.

'I don't know if I've heard any of those,' she said.

'I'm sure you'd recognize some of them.'

'Favourite movie?'

I went with really old again, just to be safe. '*Back to the Future*.'

Adam choked on his water, spraying some on me.

Holly laughed at him. 'OK, odd choice.'

'I'm sure your favourite is some sappy eighties movie

with a whiny girl for a main character.'

Something like . . . *Sixteen Candles*.

Holly rolled her eyes as the waiter set our food on the table. 'Not even close.'

'What's with the twenty questions, Hol?' David asked.

She picked up her fork and twirled noodles around it. 'I'm making new friends.'

'Interesting,' David said, the corners of his mouth twitching.

When the others were deep in conversation Holly started talking again. 'What was your sister's name?'

'Courtney,' I said, lowering my voice. You'd think after all this time it would get easier to say her name, but it never did. 'Now can I ask *you* something?'

'You can ask.'

'Why the early-morning training sessions, since you've obviously retired your leotard?'

'It's fun. No other reason, really.'

'Pure love of the sport. That's inspiring,' I said.

She laughed and tossed her napkin across the table at me. 'Go ahead and make fun of me. Jump on the trampoline for five minutes sometime and see if you don't get addicted.'

'Any other addictions I should know about before I take another ride in your car?'

'Just caffeine,' she admitted.

'Me too.'

'So you really don't mind hanging with kids that are still in school?'

I shrugged.

'Nope? OK, what about . . . your favourite spot in New

York?' She pushed pad thai around her plate, waiting patiently for my answer.

'Central Park.'

She narrowed her eyes at me. 'Well, we have that in common.'

'Does that mean you'll give me your number?'

For some reason, the other conversations at the table seemed to stop a split second before I said that. Really bad timing. Everyone paused for a second and then jumped back into eating. Holly kept her eyes on mine and I waited while she took a long drink of water. 'I'll give you my email.'

'Fair enough.'

'When are we going to be done with the bargaining thing?'

I shrugged. 'Personally I think it's fun.'

A smile lit up her whole face. 'Me too.'

Of course I already had her number, but I wanted Holly to give it to me.

I told Holly to drive back to her house and I'd walk to the train station from there, and to my surprise she didn't object. But we pulled up to her house just as her mother parked in the driveway. The blonde woman walked over to us as we got out.

'Hey, Holly. Who's your friend?'

She wasn't exactly smiling at me, but I stuck my hand out anyway to shake hers. 'I'm Jackson.'

Future Katherine didn't really like me too much, so I wasn't expecting a warm welcome.

'He works at the gym with me.' Holly stepped around

her mother and yanked the front of my shirt, dragging me behind.

'Nice to meet you, Ms Flynn,' I said.

'Suck-up,' Holly muttered.

I laughed and followed her through the front door. 'I'll write down my email and you can send me one first, OK?' I asked.

She handed me a piece of paper and a pen from the kitchen table and I jotted it down. 'See you Monday?'

She nodded and I grabbed my bag and left before Katherine could ask any more questions.

When I got home she had already sent me an email, but it was only one sentence long. An invitation for a little online chatting.

'*Do you want to hear a funny story?*'

I pulled up the instant messenger and typed my reply there since she was already online.

ME: *Does it involve me breaking things in the gym or falling off ladders?*

HOLLY: *You fell off a ladder?*

ME: *Not yet.*

HOLLY: *OK, here it is: my mom just spent twenty minutes drilling me with questions about you. She's sort of a freak when it comes to guys even talking to me. I think it's her Lifetime movie obsession.*

ME: *So she suspects I may be a bank robber/murderer/con artist?*

HOLLY: *Don't forget kidnapper and Internet porn addict.*

ME: *Lol! I admit nothing.*

HOLLY: *All I ever hear is shit like, 'Holly, you remember*

what happened in that one movie when that woman was talking to the nice guy online and decided to meet him in Aruba only to be kidnapped and held for ransom by Caribbean mafia.'

ME: *I've heard the Caribbean mafia hangs out in Jersey ALL the time.*

HOLLY: *I know. Totally. Do they even have mafia gangs in Aruba?*

My new cellphone rang and I saw that it was Adam calling. 'What's up?'

'Your dad's not your dad,' he spat out through the phone.

I leaned too far back in my chair and nearly fell off, knocking the laptop off my desk in the process. 'What?!'

'I stole some hair samples and there's no match. Unless another man is sleeping in your dad's bed.'

'How would you know? I mean . . . ?'

'I have connections at a private DNA lab,' he mumbled quietly. 'But that's just between you and me.'

My heart was pounding. 'There must be inaccuracies with those tests sometimes.'

'You can get a false positive with paternity tests, but a negative is a negative.'

I was silent for so long I'm sure Adam started to get worried.

'Do you feel like conducting an experiment?'

My hand shook so much I could barely hold the phone. 'Definitely. And I think maybe . . . my sister was right. I need to find out more about my mom.'

'That's exactly what I was thinking. But wait for me. I have to see this for myself. I mean . . . I know I already have, but . . . not really . . . uh . . . because—'

'I get it, Adam, I'll wait.' I slammed the phone shut and threw it on to the desk.

After a few minutes of pacing, then sitting in stunned silence, I remembered that I'd left Holly hanging. I picked up the computer from the floor and pulled myself together before responding.

ME: *Sorry, Internet problems. I would have called but . . .*

HOLLY: *Real smooth, Jackson. I'll tell you what – give me your number and then if I don't hear from you and I'm worried that you might be choking on a peanut or something, I can call you and verify that you're alive.*

ME: *And what if I'm worried you're choking . . .*

HOLLY: *Fine! You can have my number.*

ME: *I swear I'll only use it in life-or-death situations.*

HOLLY: *Deal.*

I had to end our conversation because Adam called again and said I needed to come to his house just in case the CIA had installed listening devices at my place. Not only did I agree with him, I made a promise to myself not to roll my eyes or dismiss what I used to call Adam's paranoia ever again.

Adam flung the door open seconds after I knocked. I followed him through the dark living room, where it looked as if his parents were cosy on the couch watching TV.

'You've been here before, right?' he asked as he closed his bedroom door.

'Yeah. So, can I ask what made you even think to do a paternity test?'

He was pulling items from his desk drawer. 'It was after those caffeine pills I took to stay awake. I pretty much thought of everything. Mostly I wanted to see if there were similarities in your DNA.'

'Why would that matter?'

'It answers some of the questions you've asked in your journal entries. If he does work for the CIA, wouldn't a time-travelling agent be a benefit to them? I can think of a million ways the government could make use of that.'

'You thought maybe he can do it too?' This was another theory we hadn't come up with before, but then again, Adam had read all the notes about his future self. Now he was taking the next logical step in his insane thought process.

He shrugged. 'Don't know. But it explains how he does the whole CEO and CIA thing. No reason to look further if there's no match. Do you know what date you're going to use?'

'Well, you and me had this plan, in the future, to steal my medical records. I still think we could do this, but what about my mother's records? Maybe she's the reason I'm this way . . . Do they even keep records for people who are dead?'

Adam's face took on a look of deep concentration and I could tell I'd just sparked something. 'If you could go back far enough . . . stuff like that was much less secure.'

'Like I could just walk into the hospital, talk a nurse into leaving her station and hijack her computer?' I was half joking, but of course Adam took it as a serious plan.

He sank down on to the bed and glanced up at me.

'OK . . . so, you and your sister were born at NYU Medical Center, which means your biological mother died there, right?'

'Right,' I said slowly, absorbing the weight of that conclusion. I hadn't really thought of it like that before. All those times I'd been in that hospital . . . never once had I thought about the fact that my mother and Courtney both died in that building. Over half of my family. Maybe all of my family, since my dad and I apparently weren't biologically connected.

'Jackson?' Adam said, waving a hand in front of my face. 'What we need is a date that you were there . . . in the past . . . preferably far in the past.'

'I visited Courtney a bunch of times,' I said.

He shook his head. 'No, sometime when you were a patient. Or there for a sick visit or a check-up with Dr Melvin. If you go far enough back, like when they used to cart around medical records in file folders rather than a computer, you could take a peek.'

It must have been the shock of finding out my dad wasn't my dad, but the most perfect plan formed in my head. I knew of one date very far in the past that would work. And there was something I needed to see. 'Twenty-four December 1996,' I said to Adam.

'Great, and I think you should take a stab at getting a look at your mother's file too if you can figure out how. At least give it a try while you're there.' He handed me a stopwatch and a small notebook. 'It still seems so strange that you can take stuff with you but not bring anything back. Like there's some kind of force field around you when you jump. Assuming your notes are accurate.'

'Well, you're about to get your own evidence to record.' I clicked the stopwatch on and off several times like the older Adam had always done. 'Do you think it would work if I was touching a person?'

'Not sure. But I don't want to be your lab rat for that one.'

'Good point – it's too dangerous.'

'We need to make sure the time you're actually gone is accurate. Tie the watch to your belt loop. As soon as you take in your surroundings, start it.' He opened his closet and pulled out a black ski jacket and then pulled a blue stocking hat over my head.

I knew almost nothing about my mother. The name on my birth certificate said Eileen Meyer. But I didn't know what colour hair or eyes she had. I'd never even seen a picture and suddenly I wanted to know. I closed my eyes and focused on a date much further than I'd ever travelled to.

chapter eighteen

TUESDAY, 24 DECEMBER 1996

The first thing I noticed – after waking up in a pile of snow and hitting the start button on the stopwatch – was the twin towers, standing tall in the distance. Like some giant up in the sky had just set them right back in place. I suppressed a shudder at the sight of them and stood up.

I zipped up Adam's coat and waded through the pavement. I remembered this Christmas Eve so well. At least six inches of snow had fallen and Courtney and I were home with Dad, watching it come down as we wrapped presents for the party our neighbours hosted at midnight. It was the most excited I'd been in my six years of life. All the money in the world couldn't buy a perfect snowfall on Christmas Eve. Adam would probably call me careless later, but I had to see this again. Relive it. And then I could return to the plan of hunting down medical records. In fact, this event would lead me right to the source.

Everything glowed white. It was almost blinding. I made my way across the park to one of the baseball fields. I only had to wait about fifteen minutes before I saw the two little kids, dressed like punk-rock marshmallows, dragging their dad by the hands. I leaned against the backstop of the baseball field so I'd have my back to them, and then I pulled the stocking cap further over my ears and slipped on a pair of sunglasses. There were a few other people around, so I didn't stand out too much.

'Jackson, why don't you start with the head?' Dad said.

It was hard not to react when he said my name, but I kept my eyes forward.

'No, I'm doing the bottom first. This dude is going to be huge,' the younger me said.

'You never do what Daddy tells you to, Jackson. Santa isn't going to bring you anything,' Courtney said in her know-it-all voice.

'He brought me a bunch of stuff last year.'

'Let him do the bottom, Courtney. Somebody has to.'

After a while, I shot a couple of glances in their direction and saw the snowman coming to life.

'Let's give him three eyes like an alien,' the younger me said.

'Ew! He's supposed to have a top hat and look like a man,' Courtney said.

'Fine, I'm making my own.'

I heard Dad laughing, but he didn't attempt to force me into working on Courtney's version.

'Daddy, why does Santa bring small presents to poor people?' Courtney asked.

'Duh, because their houses are smaller,' the six-year-old me said.

'Who told you that, Courtney?' Dad asked.

'Silvia.'

The babysitter from Puerto Rico. She stayed with us whenever Dad was out of town.

'What did she say?'

'Well, she told me her family always got fruit for Christmas, and Santa brought it because they didn't have enough money to buy any presents,' Courtney said.

From the corner of my eye I could see her wrapping her scarf around the snowman.

'Silvia's from a different country. Everyone has their own customs,' Dad said.

'I'm giving her half of my presents,' Courtney announced.

'Yeah, I'm sure she wants your Barbie car,' the little me said. 'Silvia's, like, a hundred years old. She can't drive a Power Wheels. She can have some of my stuff.'

'If you even get anything besides coal,' Courtney said.

'I wouldn't care if I got coal. You can make diamonds with coal. Right, Dad?'

'Right . . . and no one has to give their presents away. We can get Silvia her own gift.'

'Can we take a picture of the snowman to show her?' the little me asked.

My voice had grown more distant and I knew what was coming. I held my breath and waited.

'What are you doing over there?' Dad called to the younger me.

'I'm getting some arms for *my* snowman.'

I spun around even though I was risking being seen. I

had to watch. The younger me started to climb the tree, jumping to reach a twig above his head.

Dad took off running towards the tree. 'Jackson! Don't grab that branch!'

I almost shouted out to myself. The six-year-old version of me froze on a lower branch of the tree, watching the branch above his little head buckle under the immense weight of the snow on top and the tugging from a little kid who had just attempted to tear off a small piece.

Dad dived forward and grabbed the young me around the waist as he tumbled down, covering both of their heads with his arms. One of my younger self's hands had reached out to break the fall and hit the bare, frozen ground that the giant tree had shielded from the snow. I cringed and held my breath. Even from so far away, I could hear the bone snap. Or maybe I just remembered the sound so vividly. But it wasn't as loud as Courtney's scream. She ran to the fallen branch and stood over the little me. Her hands covered her face. 'His arm fell off!'

That's when the younger me decided it was time to freak out and start crying.

'It's just broken, sweetie,' Dad said to Courtney before carefully picking me up off the ground. He pulled my arm from the sleeve of my jacket and his face tightened. Courtney got one look at the bone poking through the skin and turned around and puked up the pound of cookie dough she had eaten earlier.

'I don't want to die,' I heard myself wail. 'Call Dr Melvin, please, Dad.'

'We just need to go to the hospital. You'll be OK, I promise,' Dad said.

From a distance I saw him turn his head to his sleeve and heard him say, 'Edwards, where the hell are you?!'

Seconds later a man ran past me.

'Excuse me, sir, do you need help?' he asked Dad.

'Yes, my son hurt his arm.'

The man picked up Courtney, who had finished vomiting and started wailing out her apologies in case I was, in fact, dying. 'I didn't mean that . . . about Santa, Jackson. He's bringing you lots of stuff. I'm *sooorry*.'

'That's a compound fracture. He's going to need surgery,' the man called Edwards said.

The younger me held his deformed arm across his stomach and continued to cry, much quieter than Courtney's ear-piercing wail. Dad carried young me through the snow, walking fast. I watched the back of their heads get smaller and smaller.

That guy Edwards was definitely some kind of agent. I remembered the man, but thought he had just come over to help. Dad would have never let some stranger pick up my sister though. I had been a little distracted at the time from the stabbing pain shooting through my arm, and probably too young to remember those details.

I pulled up the sleeve of Adam's jacket and ran my fingers over the scars from my Christmas Eve surgery, faded after so many years.

I took a cab to the hospital, where I knew Dad was headed. After reliving this day again, Dad didn't seem like someone pretending to be a father. His concern was genuine. It's possible *he* didn't know that we had no biological connection. Or he was just one of many adoptive parents who made the decision to keep that a secret.

Or it was something entirely different.

When the cab pulled up to the hospital I had to dig into one of the tiny pockets of my wallet to get the oldest dollar bills out. Luckily I had been collecting old money. Just in case.

I strode through the emergency-room doors, hoping to get a better glimpse of the man Dad had called Edwards. They were nowhere in sight, and from what I could remember of that night, I was awake for only a short time before they wheeled me into surgery and put screws into my arm. I just needed someone to give me access through the closed ER doors.

'Can I help you?' a woman at the desk in front of the emergency-room doors asked.

'Um . . . yeah, I'm here to see my . . . brother, Jackson Meyer . . . he just came in with my dad. Hurt his arm.'

'Name, please,' she said, glancing up from the stack of papers in front of her, probably because I was staring at her like she had just spoken Japanese. '*Your* name, not his,' she added.

Oops, hadn't thought about that little issue. 'Uh . . . Peter . . . Peter Meyer.'

She typed away at her computer. It had a thick monitor with one of those black and green screens. Something I hadn't seen for many years. Even the hairstyles of all the nurses I had walked past were so unusual. I would've laughed if the situation was different.

'Can I see some ID?' she asked.

Uh-oh, time to go.

'Yeah, I . . . uh . . . left it in the cab. I just called and the driver's on his way back. In fact, I should go down and meet him now. I'll be right back.' I spun around and nearly ran into a man in a blue suit. He was well over six feet tall with a shaved head and dark skin. He looked familiar. Very familiar.

'I think I can help you,' he said in this deep, booming voice. It had just a hint of a Southern drawl.

'Really?'

He nodded. 'Why don't you come with me.'

It wasn't a question. I followed behind him, feeling totally freaked, but also dying to figure out how all these people and events connected. Besides, it wasn't like I didn't have a way out of there.

I struggled to keep up with the man's long strides. He held the door open for the elevator and I stepped in. He swiped a card in a hole and a small door slid open big enough for his hand. I craned my neck, trying to get a good view. It was some kind of fingerprint scanner.

Was this normal security for hospitals? Especially in 1996? And why were we straying so far from the ER?

He kept his eyes straight ahead but answered my unspoken question. 'The government wing of this hospital is available only to those with security clearance, but I'm sure you knew that already.'

'Uh . . . no,' I said.

My voice came out like a scared child's, and yet this man was cool and calm. Like he brought people to his secret fingerprint-scanner place all the time.

I could feel the elevator moving down, but the numbers that usually lit up to tell you the floor you were on stayed dark. When the doors finally opened, I sucked in a breath. Four men with guns stood right outside the elevator. They all raised their weapons and pointed them at us. I froze on the spot, debating whether or not to push another button.

'You can't go back up without clearance,' the mystery man said.

It was at that moment that I tried to focus and get out of there, back to Adam in 2007. Of course, like that time when I was in my dad's office with his hands around my throat, I was too freaked to do it. One of the armed men grabbed me and started feeling my pants all the way up to my shirt.

'He's clean. No weapons.'

'Thank you. Follow me.'

I managed to put one foot in front of the other and took in my surroundings. It was some kind of underground tunnel. The first man opened a door and pushed me inside a room. Another man forced me into a chair, like the kind at the dentist's. He tied my arms with straps. I thought about fighting back but decided there was no point if these dudes had guns.

'I'm Chief Marshall,' the man who led me down here said. 'Who are you? We both know Jackson Meyer doesn't have a brother.'

I didn't answer and Chief Marshall nodded towards the other man. 'Test his blood.'

OK, totally creepy. I closed my eyes and tried to let the

room dissolve. To get the hell out of there. To avoid the one experiment Adam and I couldn't perform.

Yes, the dives into the past were like *Groundhog Day*. And the light feeling that I always had while in a jump (except that one time on 30 October 2009) kept pain at a minimum while in a jump. In other words, if I hurt myself in a jump, when I came back to the present I'd have a bump on my head or whatever, but never a bad one.

But still, what if they *killed* me in this year? One that wasn't my home base? I had no idea what would happen. If I would *really* be dead.

I barely felt the needle prick my arm, and seconds later I heard feet shuffling away.

'You can't leave from here, just so you know,' Chief Marshall said.

My eyes flew open again. 'You already told me that.'

'I mean you can't leave by *any* method. New security device Dr Melvin invented. An electromagnetic pulse.'

Um. What the hell was he talking about? And he knew Dr Melvin. Maybe Courtney was right about the connection. Was Dr Melvin trying to zap me – or whoever else they brought in this room – with electromagnets? Except Chief Marshall was in here, and the other dude too.

'Come on, tell me your name,' Chief Marshall said in his deep Southern voice as he sat in a chair across from me, arms folded over his chest. 'How do you know Jackson Meyer?'

I stayed silent, staring over his shoulder, trying to calm myself.

'He's not an enemy.' the other man spoke up.

'Are you positive?' Chief Marshall asked.

'Yes.' He walked over and stared closely at my face, then yanked off the stocking cap.

'An enemy?' I finally said.

'Don't act dumb,' Chief Marshall said. 'You see the resemblance?' he asked the man with the needle. 'To the others.'

Others?

The man put his face so close to mine I could smell the garlic he must have eaten for lunch. 'Yeah. I see it. But it can't be . . . Right?'

For the first time Chief Marshall's face lost its calm, collected expression. He hit a button on the wall and shouted, 'Edwards, get in here!'

More creepy connections. Seconds later, the man who had raced past me out on the baseball field came charging in. 'What's going on, Chief?'

'Get Agent Meyer down here right away,' Chief Marshall said.

Oh man. Too freaky!

'Sorry, sir, he's with the boy.'

'Fine. Melvin then.'

'Also with the kid,' Edwards said.

Chief Marshall turned slowly to face Edwards before saying, 'And so am I.'

Edwards opened his mouth, then closed it again. 'Do you mean he can . . . I mean, not yet, but eventually . . . ?'

I didn't get to hear the rest. The idea of my father coming down there and seeing me, older, after what had happened in his office in 2003, was enough to give me the ability to focus on my escape – electromagnets or no. The last thing I saw was Chief Marshall's face up close as he examined mine. I don't know what freaked me out more . . . the look in his eyes or the greedy smile that was snaking on to his face as I jumped out of 1996.

chapter nineteen

SUNDAY, 16 SEPTEMBER 2007, 12.30 A.M.

'Jackson!' Adam shouted into my ear.

I was lying on his bedroom floor, staring at the ceiling. 'What year is it?'

'2007,' he said slowly.

The room spun, and when I sat up and stared at Adam's giant DNA model on the desk, the blue and red balls swirled around like the birds that fly over a cartoon character's head. I grabbed the front of his shirt and shook him. 'I have to call my dad. Like . . . *now*.'

'OK.' He lifted me up and I slumped over on to him.

'I can't feel my legs,' I mumbled before collapsing on to Adam's bed. I lifted my hand in front of my face, turning it over, expecting it to fade away or turn transparent.

Then the spinning blue and red turned black, along with everything else.

The first thing I noticed when I woke up the next morning was the lump next to me, sound asleep. I rolled over and stood, happy that feeling had returned to my legs. But they were weak and my head throbbed, like a bad hangover.

Adam's eyes opened slowly. 'You're standing.'

'Barely.' I clutched my sides, putting pressure against the stabbing pain running up and down my ribs.

Adam pulled a shirt over his head and opened the bedroom door. 'Let's get you something to eat.'

Food was the last thing on my mind, but my lack of appetite in the last week had already caused me to lose at least five pounds. Pretty soon I really *would* disappear.

'Morning, Mom,' Adam said to the woman in the kitchen flipping pancakes.

'You're up early. I didn't know you had a friend over.' Mrs Silverman turned her back on the griddle and smiled at me.

I tried not to laugh because Adam's parents were a big joke for me in 2009. Lovely. But completely clueless about what their son was up to or capable of. It was all pancakes and sunshine.

'I'm Jackson,' I said.

Adam and I sat at the table and he slid my journal in front of me. 'Write down what you remember.'

'What was the time on my stopwatch?' I asked.

'A little over two hours.'

'And *your* stopwatch?'

'Four minutes,' he answered.

Even though I'd done this so many times with the older Adam, it was still weird to be gone that long and then come back and find only minutes had passed. Usually, it was seconds.

'What did I look like?'

'Just like the other times you recorded with m– . . . with the other guy. You were staring into space, completely unresponsive.' He tapped the page again with his finger. 'Write.'

The memory was choppy and jumbled, but once I started forming a list and Adam drilled me with questions, most of it seemed to come back.

'Wow, it sounds like you picked the right date. So now we know he's definitely an agent of some kind,' Adam said.

Mrs Silverman slid a giant plate of pancakes in front of each of us. 'Who's an agent, honey?'

Adam shrugged. 'It's just this TV show.'

She smiled at him. 'Orange juice, anyone?'

'Sure,' Adam said.

'No, thanks,' I said.

'OK, so you resemble these mysterious other people . . . or was he talking about you looking like your younger self? No surprise if that's the case.'

'He just said, "You see the resemblance?" Then he said something about looking like the others . . . or maybe he said "other" . . . which could be the other me,' I said.

Feeling nauseous from my wild adventure last night, I pushed the plate away from me, but Adam slid it back. 'Eat.'

I could only force down a few bites before running to the bathroom and puking it back up. While I was brushing my teeth I heard Adam talking to his mom. 'Probably bad sushi.'

'I've got Maalox,' I heard Adam's mom call through the bathroom door.

Adam was waiting for me outside the bathroom, holding a bottle of Maalox, when I came out. I chugged it straight from the bottle as we walked back to his room, where I promptly fell on to his bed. He shut the door behind him, balancing his plate of pancakes. 'It's the time travel that's making you sick. Based on your journal notes and your latest binge and purge, it's obvious.'

'Are you sure it's not psychosomatic? Guilt manifesting itself into illness? It never happened until Holly was shot.' I pulled the covers up to my neck, rolling myself into a shivering ball.

'Someone's taken Psych 101.' Adam sat in his desk chair and continued stuffing his face. 'I think it's all relative. Before you came back to 2007, the furthest you'd gone was a few days. It's a formula based on the number of years you travel backwards, along with the length of time you stay in the past. You know that part already because the formulae are in your journal.'

I nodded. 'But why don't I feel constantly sick in this year? Technically it's the past for me.'

He shrugged. 'I think it's because this is your home base now. Every other year is the one you *shouldn't* be in, so bad things are going to happen to you when you travel to those non-home-base time periods. And the longer you stay away from home base, the worse the symptoms are. It's like your body's actually being pulled apart and maybe you can only stretch so far.'

'I guess it makes sense. I just don't get *why*.'

'I think we can safely say there's a ton of shit we haven't figured out yet.'

'Agreed. But . . . I really need to call my dad. I can just ask him if he's a government agent. Tell him I overheard a conversation or something. It's not like he's the bad guy, right?'

Adam lifted an eyebrow. 'You positive about that? So he rushed you to the hospital when you broke your arm. Big deal. And even if he *is* good . . . what if it doesn't matter and he *has* to turn on you the second he knows you're not in the dark any more?

'Since the jumping around in time is kicking you in the ass, I think you have to limit your jumps to very important tasks. You need to recover, man. For now I think you should just play dumb around your dad. It'll be easier to get information. From what it sounds like, those guys in the underground hospital wing were not too happy to see you, and they knew your dad . . . like they're on the same side.' He stopped for a minute and I could tell his mind was racing.

I sat up and leaned against the wooden headboard. 'Damn. I feel like shit and I was gonna try to get Holly to go out with me today. She gave me her number last night.'

Adam turned his back to me and fumbled with a stack of papers on his desk. 'She's busy.'

'She is?'

'I told her I'd help her study for her calc test.'

'Great, then I have an excuse to see her. I can tag along on your little study session. Tell her we were hanging out.'

He grabbed a pair of jeans from his closet and pulled them on, still not looking at me. 'I don't think that's a good idea. She's really freaked about this test . . .'

'Adam, what are you not telling me? Did she say something to you?'

He finally looked at me, then sighed. 'I wasn't going to bring this up today, but obviously I don't have a choice. After reading all your notes, it seems like . . . you and Holly were just having fun. Nothing serious.'

'Do you mean 007 Holly or the other one?'

'007 Holly?'

'Yeah, it sounds much cooler than 2007 Holly.'

He shook his head and laughed. "Interesting way to decipher. But I meant the other one. From 2009. Anyway . . . other than guilt about leaving her to die . . . is anything really different now than it was in the future?'

I stared at him, not sure how to answer, feeling my face redden with unintended anger.

'Look, Jackson, I don't have anything against you. You've dealt with a lot of crazy, messed-up shit, and the fact that you want to keep her alive, make sure she's safe, proves you're a decent guy. But don't you think it's a little risky to be close to her . . . for several reasons? Holly's my friend and I don't want her to get hurt.'

'Do you think I'm trying to get close to her out of guilt?' I asked, because I really wasn't sure. This was uncharted waters for me. In fact, *serious* relationships of *any* kind were uncharted.

'It kinda seems that way . . . but maybe I'm wrong. Either way, you need to stop feeling guilty.'

Adam turned on his computer and I rolled over on my stomach, staring at the pattern on the sheets, absorbing his insightful message. *Was* pursuing Holly just about guilt or maybe even the thrill of chasing her again?

Then again, I could have walked away in 2009 that last night we were together. I'd been an hour late for dinner and then told her I needed to skip the movie because I had plans with Adam.

She had gotten up from her chair, picked up her purse and said calmly, 'Well, I have other things I could be doing, too, so I'll just go and do that now.'

I knew she was pissed, even though she didn't start shouting at me until I chased after her. But I did chase after her. That had to mean something.

I never dated girls from my high school or anyone who knew much about my personal life. Or people who knew my sister before she died. College was easier. Somehow I ended up telling Holly nearly everything about myself . . . but for once I was the only source. She wasn't picking up the gossip and rumours that had flown around my school.

What made it so easy to talk to Holly was that I could tell her half of what I meant and she'd fill in the rest. She knew what I was thinking. Like the first time I kissed her . . .

It had been my nineteenth birthday. 20 June 2009. My dad was ignoring it, just like he'd done every year since Courtney died. Holly had just broken up with David and reluctantly agreed to go out with the rest of the camp staff to a club. Of course I was thrilled about the opportunity to get her alone, but I could tell she had mixed feelings about being out.

Just like that, I ditched my original plans to lure her on to the dance floor.

'You want to get out of here?' I asked her.

She nodded. 'Are you hungry?'

'Famished.'

'Me too.' Her fingers landed inside my palm and I gripped on to them, leading her out into the warm summer air.

I dropped her hand before we started down the pavement. 'You don't eat pizza, do you?'

She shook her head. 'No. Milk allergy.'

'I know this amazing diner across town. Lots of non-dairy items,' I suggested.

'Sounds good.'

We hopped in a cab and headed far away from the club. The deli was almost empty and we took our time selecting one of nearly every dairy-free vegetarian item on the menu, then spread out our feast across the largest table. 'How long ago did you give up meat?'

She dipped a hunk of pita bread in hummus before answering. 'Just a few years. I'd eat it if I liked the taste, but I don't.'

'So it's not because you want to save a cow?'

'Not exactly.' She smiled and took a drink from her iced tea. 'Can I ask you something?'

'Go for it.'

'Was this your plan all along? To get me alone tonight? I've heard you . . . do this a lot.'

My tongue was tied for a minute. The usual retort wasn't right. I folded my hands over the table and stared right at her. Her jaw froze mid-chew. 'Honestly, I watched you dancing with Brook and I knew you felt guilty about enjoying yourself tonight. We have that in common.' This was the truth. I just wanted to be around her, but I didn't know exactly why. Which kinda scared me a little.

She dropped her eyes and pushed the fork around the container of fruit. She knew exactly what I was talking about. 'Yeah, we do.'

'OK, so here's what we'll do to alleviate the guilt.' I sat up straighter and watched her eyes lift. 'Only regular, everyday things are allowed tonight. Like eating, drinking, sleeping.'

Her mouth pulled into a half-smile. 'Sounds good. Only the mundane stuff permitted.'

'And talking?' I suggested.

'Mr Meyer, how are you this evening?' a voice said behind me.

I spun around in my chair and saw my father walking up to the counter. 'Dad, what're you doing here?'

Dad looked over and nodded. 'I'm working late. Just grabbing some dinner to take back to the office.'

'Doesn't your secretary usually do that?' I asked.

He shrugged. 'I sent her home.'

He wanted to be alone for the same reason I didn't. I jumped up from my chair and glanced at Holly, then back at my dad. 'This is Holly Flynn. We work together.'

Dad stuck out his hand to shake hers. 'Kevin Meyer.'

'Nice to meet you,' Holly said.

Dad grabbed the bag from the man at the counter and turned back to us. 'Are you in school in New York?' he asked.

'I'll be at NYU in September.'

'She's a freshman,' I told Dad.

He nodded before turning towards the door. 'You'll have a sophomore to show you around then, Jackson's good at that.'

I decided to give it one last effort. 'I'll probably be home really late, if that's OK . . . ?'

Dad didn't even look over his shoulder. 'No problem.'

I sucked in a deep breath and ran my fingers through my hair.

'That was awkward,' Holly said.

I snapped my head around to look at her. 'He works in the building across the street. He's actually the one who told me about this place.'

'That's not what I meant. I'm talking about . . . um . . .'

I dropped my eyes. 'Right.'

She must have caught on to my need to change the subject. 'So, what are we going to talk about?'

'What happened with Daniel or Donny? Whatever his name is.'

She hid a smile. 'David, but you already know that. And isn't it bad form to talk about exes while on a date?'

'Well, it's not a date, so you won't be breaking any rules,' I said.

This is not normally something I would ask for specifics about, but Holly was too hard to figure out without knowing what kind of guy she could spend a year dating. I couldn't even imagine being with someone for that long at our age. A month was my longest relationship and the girl had been out of the country for two weeks of that time.

'Nothing exciting. Typical "outgrowing the high-school boyfriend" story.'

'Is he . . . OK with it?'

She smiled a little. 'Yeah, but David's a nice guy. I don't know if he's just saying that so I won't feel bad.'

We changed subjects and chattered on for at least another hour before heading out. I kept the conversation casual and hoped she'd believe me about not having any 'big plans' for our evening.

'What now?' I asked.

'I guess maybe I should go home.'

No, no, no. 'Can we go for a walk first? Daily exercise is certainly allowed. Nothing fun about that.'

'Sure,' she said.

The tension that had dissolved during dinner had started building again. Holly obviously felt it too, and maybe she wanted something to happen, or else just the opposite – close the door on that idea as soon as possible.

'So is there anything good about your new-found freedom?' I asked.

'Everything. I guess that's why I feel guilty.'

'Makes sense.' I turned a corner, not even caring where we walked, as long as it didn't end.

Holly's hand went into mine and she stopped in the middle of the pavement. When I turned to face her she had this look on her face, and I knew the casual fun had just ended.

She stepped closer to me. 'I have to tell you something.'

Uh-oh. Here comes the 'friend' speech.

'Oh yeah?'

Her light blue eyes gazed right into mine. 'Happy birthday, Jackson.'

I opened my mouth to respond, but nothing came out. All I had wanted today was for my father to say those words to me. No expensive gifts or parties. Just one short statement. Maybe even something like, 'I know Courtney's gone, but she would have wanted you to be happy today.' That would have been more than enough.

Holly's forehead wrinkled and she dropped my hand. 'I'm sorry. That was the wrong thing to say, wasn't it? I just thought after your dad left . . .'

My brain went into high-speed mode, focused on one thing. I gently nudged her backwards until her shoulders touched the wall of the building behind us. Her eyes were wide open and pink crept up into her cheeks. I didn't even hesitate, afraid she would stop me. I leaned down and kissed her, pressing my body to hers. She tasted so good, like strawberries and peppermint.

Her arms went from up against the wall to around my neck, yanking me even closer. Fingers were in my hair, lips moving across my cheek, hearts pounding. I wanted to tear off our clothes and let her crawl all over me.

Then her hands were on my chest, pushing me away. I backed up immediately and watched as she leaned on the wall for support, her chest rising and falling rapidly, eyelids fluttering. Nerves coursed through me. Had I misread her signals?

Then her lips pulled into a smile. 'Wow.'

I sighed with relief and moved close enough to wrap my arms around her waist. 'I've wanted to do that for such a long time.'

She opened her eyes and looked up at me. 'I know what you mean.'

Of course, that wasn't 007 Holly and that kiss was totally hot.

Future Holly *got* me. And no one else seemed to. Maybe that scared me after a while, being *that* exposed to someone. I did push her away a little once school started and we were both so busy. It was easier to make excuses than admitting to her (and myself) how I really felt. I guess my life was pretty simple then. No reason to clearly define things like relationships because there was always time for that.

Until there isn't.

Back in 2007 Adam continued to type away at his computer, allowing me some private time to think and rest. Maybe the best thing to do now, with *this* Holly, was to let her get to know me. No more act. No more games. Just me.

Well, minus the 'I'm from the future' part. If that wasn't enough for either of us, then I could back off and just make sure she was safe from a distance.

'Hey, Adam?' I sat up when I heard his chair spin around.

'I thought you were asleep,' he said.

'No, just thinking about what you said. I don't really have an answer, but I promise to keep the risks in mind at all times and be careful with her.'

'Great. I'm glad to hear it, man.' Adam pointed at the desk. 'I wrote something in your journal, on the back inside cover.'

I looked it over. 'Is that more Latin?'

'Um . . . sort of.' He stared at me again. 'Now this is important: if you ever need to tell me something that you can't say in home base because it's too risky or you're not alone, you can always jump back a day or two and I'll teach you a way that we can communicate without anyone understanding, then you can jump forward and use it.'

'What are you talking about? You can't tell me now?'

He shook his head. 'This is one thing even the CIA won't be able to figure out and I'm not going to risk telling you in home base, when it actually has consequences.'

I nodded and stuffed the journal into my bag. 'I'm going to head home and let you get to your afternoon plans.'

'If you want to come with me, you can. Seriously, I'm sure Holly won't mind.'

'No, I'll wait till tomorrow to see her.'

I was really surprised when I got back to my computer at home and Holly had sent me an email. I'd figured she would play it cool for a while, even if she was interested. Holly had more patience than any girl I had ever met. It was annoying as hell sometimes.

HOLLY: *Just heard you've been hanging out with my friend Adam. Are you really a science geek?*

ME: *I'm a wannabe science geek. I'm not that smart. I just attempt to sound that way.*

HOLLY: *So basically you're full of it?*

ME: *Yes, but I'm trying not to be. I might even start attending a support group.*

HOLLY: *What's your greatest weakness?*

ME: *Steak, I really love a juicy New York Strip with that crispy fat around the edges.*

HOLLY: *Lol! And yuck! But that's not what I meant. What's your favourite load of crap to feed people?*

ME: *You have such a delicate way of putting things, but I'd have to say quoting Shakespearean sonnets in French to impress a girl. I'll need therapy to give that one up. It works really well.*

HOLLY: *Hmm . . . I'd love to say that wouldn't impress me, but I think it might. Of course you've ruined the surprise now.*

ME: *Of course.*

HOLLY: *Adam just got here. Time to cram for my calc test. Later.*

There. That was the beginning of honesty and a little bit of me exposed. It wasn't so bad. Yet. I fell asleep on the couch, writing as many 009 Holly moments as I could possibly remember. Just in case I forgot. There were so many I never bothered to write down. I always thought there'd be time for that.

When I woke it was dark and I had slept for most of the day. I spent nearly an hour keeping busy with random tasks, trying to decide if it was a bad idea to call or email Holly again. Just when I was ready to cave and send her a quick note, I saw that she had already sent me an email. Maybe seventeen-year-old Holly was a little less patient.

HOLLY: *I know I'm such a dork writing you yet another*

email after only six hours, but I was just going to ask you if you had any good tips for SAT studying?

I sent her an instant message instead of an email reply.

ME: *Yes, a ton. But what do I get out of it?*

HOLLY: *What do you want?*

ME: *Can I call you right now?*

HOLLY: *Why don't you try and see if I answer.*

I should have known she'd say that. I crawled into bed and flipped off the light before dialling her number.

'Hey,' she said.

'Hey.'

'So . . . ?'

'So . . . tell me something interesting about the world of school. I feel like I haven't been there forever.' Again, another true statement. So far, I was on a roll.

'Well . . . I have this new project for AP English and it's actually really cool. We have to keep a journal of song lyrics that represent our mood throughout the day, for a whole week.'

'What's your song right now?'

'"Vacation" by the Go-Gos. Do you know it?' she asked.

I sang the first lines. '"Can't seem to get my mind off of you / Back here at home there's nothing to do . . ."'

'Is that cheesy?'

'No, I love it.'

'Tell me yours.'

The tone of her voice relaxed and I closed my eyes, imagining her snuggled under her white comforter, head pressed against the light blue ruffled pillow.

'Hmm . . . "All Mixed Up".'

'Never heard it,' she said.

'It's by a band called 311.'

'You know a lot about music, don't you?'

'Yeah, I'm a music geek.'

'I have weird favourites. Stuff I'm embarrassed to say I like sometimes,' she said.

'Like what?'

'There's this one Billy Joel song called "Don't Ask Me Why".'

'"All the waiters in your grand cafe / leave their tables when you blink,"' I sang into the phone.

'I can't believe you know that song.'

'I can play it on guitar.'

'No way!'

'Seriously, I can. I'll show you sometime.'

'Cool.'

OK, so I cheated a little with the song thing, but I couldn't help it if I knew her favourite song and had already learned to play it on the guitar to impress 009 Holly.

I went to sleep that night feeling more like myself than I had in a long time. I'd let Adam wrap his much more capable brain around the new information acquired and do as he said, play along with my dad. For now I was stuck in this strange limbo, waiting for something or someone to tell me what to do next.

chapter twenty

SUNDAY, 7 OCTOBER 2007

I know I'm not supposed to time-travel for a while. Considering the fact that I felt like death for several days after the last time jump, Adam's orders needed to be followed. But this morning I woke up thinking about Courtney . . . things I wished I could fix . . . like seventh grade. Since we were not only siblings but also classmates, I knew everything that was going on with my sister. A lot of stuff I didn't want to know.

Like her nervous stomach issues . . . any time we had a test or band audition she'd get terrible gas and diarrhoea. I'd see her running off to the bathroom and know exactly why. I really didn't think much of it and never brought it up until one day my best friend, who had an obvious and unrequited crush on Courtney, watched her race out of the gym right before her presentation for the science fair. He asked me if she was sick, and without even thinking about it I blurted out, 'She's fine. She just doesn't like to fart in front of people.'

As soon as my friend snickered, I knew exactly what I had done and there was a second where I could have said it was a lie. Or taken it back. But I didn't. I just laughed with him and for several weeks Courtney had to deal with the nickname 'Hershey Squirts'. It was horrible.

It's hard to believe after everything that's happened to her, and to me, a stupid fart joke in middle school is causing me to feel like the world's biggest asshole. The worst part is, I never told her it was me that unintentionally started that rumour. We never talked about it. Almost like she knew I wasn't bold enough to stand up to my friends for her. Like she understood. But she shouldn't have and I shouldn't have been such a pansy.

I tried to put the key in the lock on the gym door, but everything was spinning so much that I couldn't get it to match up. After a few weeks of rest in my new home-base year, I'd broken Adam's rules and spent a full four hours with my sister in the year 2003. Now I was paying the price. I had only planned to stay a few minutes, but then I just couldn't leave. Adam had also prescribed daily workouts to build myself up a little in case that helped with the time-travel side effects. I'd probably reversed the three weeks of running and weightlifting in my four-hour excursion. At least, that's what it felt like.

Eventually the door appeared to open on its own and I stumbled through it, hearing a familiar voice.

'Jackson, what's up, man?' Toby said.

'Are you OK? You look really . . . pale.' Holly's voice, like it was coming from a distance.

Both of their faces spun in front of me and then I just closed my eyes and fell into nothing.

'You got any other shoes to wear home?' I heard Toby say.

'No, but I can drive barefoot,' Holly said.

I started to peel my eyes open and saw the grey lockers in the staff lounge and realized I was lying on the couch.

'Look who's awake. Are you hungover, man?' Toby asked.

'He doesn't smell hungover. I'm sure it's that flu going around. I had it a couple of weeks ago and barfed, like, every fifteen minutes for six hours straight.'

'Since you're conscious now, I'm gonna take off.'

'See you later, Toby,' Holly said.

I felt a wet washcloth on my forehead. 'What year is it?'

Holly laughed and sat down beside me on the couch. 'Do you mean what time is it?'

'Yeah, that too.'

'It's five.'

I tried to sit up, but she pushed me back down. 'Don't get up. You'll just fall over again and I'm not nearly as strong as Toby.'

'I've got to get my work done.'

'We took care of it.'

'Seriously? You guys didn't have to do that.'

'You should have called in sick,' she said.

No, I should have saved the time travel for my day off. 'Yeah, I guess. How did I get back here?'

Holly smiled and shifted the washcloth on my forehead.

'Well, you fell over on Toby, who caught you before your head hit the floor. Then, when he stood you up, you barfed all over my shoes.'

I covered my face and groaned. 'Sorry.'

'It's no big deal. Like I said, I had the same thing. All these kids in the gym wiping their snotty viruses everywhere, you're bound to pick one up.'

'I'm just glad you were here. Otherwise I'd be passed out in front of the door. Probably with a big bump on my head.'

She laughed and brushed her fingers over my right forearm. Just that small touch from her made me crazy. Three weeks of email exchanges, mostly about nothing – jokes or stories about the crazy 'gym moms' Holly had to deal with, but not one time had I seen her outside of work. I didn't exactly plan it that way, but Adam's words stuck in my head and I was afraid of being alone with her – starting something that was more than just friendly co-worker stuff. Besides, 007 Holly was only seventeen. In 2009 I would have never, ever considered hooking up with a seventeen-year-old.

Her fingers moved over my scar. 'What happened?'

'I fell out of a tree when I was six.' I reached out to touch her, just under her chin. 'How did you get that scar?'

'Parachuting off the kitchen counter. Eight stitches.' She grabbed my fingers and held on to them. 'Your hands are freezing.'

Her stare was intense. I knew that look, and as much as I wanted her to look at me that way, I wasn't sure she should. 'You're probably ready to go home.'

'Yeah, my last party left an hour ago. But what about you? Will you be OK?' she asked.

'I'll call Adam. He'll give me a ride.'

'I could take you home. Where do you live?'

Nowhere close.

'That's OK. Adam and I had plans anyway.' I pulled out my phone to call him.

Holly gathered up her things and sat next to me again. Then she did something that completely shocked me. She pulled the washcloth from my head and leaned forward, just barely brushing her lips over my forehead.

'You don't have a fever. That's a good sign.'

I didn't know if it was just a friendly gesture, but I didn't care. My arms went around her. I moved my hand over her hair and held her so tight.

Her head turned and I felt her breath on my neck, then she laughed lightly and said, 'What are you doing?'

I dropped my arms and leaned back. 'Just saying thank you, that's all. My family likes to hug.'

She stood and smiled. 'You're welcome. And I hope you feel better.'

Holly stumbled a little on her way out the door. Like she was dizzy or off balance.

Adam showed up a few minutes later with a sports drink in hand. 'I can't believe you did it without me!'

I took the drink and opened it. 'Sorry. It's been a few weeks and I had a moment of weakness. Obviously I'm paying the price now.'

He waved a hand in front of me. 'Forget it. I've got a really awesome plan. Well, it's more of an opportunity to pursue the medical-records task. And if that doesn't work out . . . maybe just get info from the person who's been recording all the notes in your records.'

'Does it involve a time jump? Because I'm pretty much spent.'

'And whose fault is that? But no, no jumping today. However, you're gonna have to let your dad in on your secret job, assuming the CIA people haven't been watching you this whole time. He'll probably sit up and pay attention if you mention certain symptoms.'

I knew exactly where he was going with this and was glad that he was skirting around the issue. Especially after I'd just spent several hours with Courtney. He wanted me to fake brain-cancer symptoms. Something my dad has been more than a little freaked about in the past few years. 'OK, what's the plan?'

My dad was alone when he came rushing into the gym.

Adam greeted him at the door. 'He just passed out and he said his head was killing him,' he said.

I slid down on the couch and left my eyes half closed. 'Dad, is that you?'

'Yeah, Jackson. Let's go. I've already called Dr Melvin. He's waiting for you in his office.'

'Really? On a Sunday?' I muttered as Adam helped me off the couch.

'You're a special patient,' Dad said.

Adam raised his eyebrows behind Dad's back as if to say, 'I told you there was something in those records.'

I was a little shocked when I found out Dad had driven

himself here in my BMW M6. Hopefully I could keep from spewing Gatorade all over it. I buckled my seat belt and Dad took off, driving way too fast. 'Don't you think you should slow down?'

'Don't worry. I have plenty of friends in the New Jersey State Police.'

Yeah, I'm sure you do, Agent Meyer.

'We *will* discuss this new job later. It's the reason you dropped out, I assume?'

'I thought we were discussing it later?'

He muttered a string of profanities under his breath before making a sharp right turn, sending me flying into the window. 'Is this because we have money? You want to feel normal for a change?'

'Not really. I just want to hook up with a girl who would never date a rich kid from Manhattan.'

He glanced sideways at me. 'What?'

'Kidding, Dad.'

We were silent the rest of the trip, mostly because his crazy secret-agent driving was honestly freaking me out. He must have diplomatic immunity or some shit like that. Or he knew he could outrun the cops. It would be all Adam's fault if I ended up on TV in some crazy-ass police chase, with helicopters flying over us.

He screeched to a halt in front of the hospital. 'Wait for me inside while I park the car.'

He returned in record time and we headed for the elevator. He rocked back and forth on his heels while I pushed the button for Dr Melvin's floor. 'I thought they had some kind of lower level here. I don't see it anywhere on the map. Something underground . . .'

I had been doing this for a few weeks now. Dropping little hints and testing his reactions. So far I'd gotten nothing useful. He was good at covers. Damn good.

'No idea. I'm sure you can ask someone at the information desk if you really need to know.'

An old man with wild grey hair and a round belly met us outside the elevator. 'How are you, Jackson?'

'Not great, Dr Melvin.'

'We'll go right to radiology and get an MRI, see what's causing those headaches . . . and the fainting spells,' Melvin said.

His voice held the same friendly tone it always did, like a grandpa or a favourite uncle. Courtney and I had loved coming to see him. We were showered with presents and candy every time.

'I would prefer you did a full-body scan,' Dad said.

'OK, we can do that.'

The machines in radiology were nothing new to me. Even the tunnel didn't scare me any more. I lay there patiently while the machine clicked over and over. When I was done, I got dressed in the MRI room. Through the glass I could see Melvin and Dad in the observation area, and right after I pulled my shirt over my head, I saw the doctor drop the clipboard he was holding.

Dad picked it up, his face tight with concern. I turned my head when they looked in my direction and then waited a good five minutes until Melvin finally came in and we walked to his exam room. Dead silence hung in the air. Lots of secrets they probably wouldn't tell me, but if I could just get a little bit of info, the trip here would be worth it.

I sat on the exam table and watched as Melvin displayed my brain images on a large flat-screen computer monitor. 'Something's wrong. I saw you guys in the observation room.'

Melvin turned to me and faked a smile. 'Nothing serious. No tumours or contusions.'

'Then why did you look so wigged out?' I asked.

Dad paced the floor, then stopped to look at the pictures. 'We're not exactly sure what's wrong.'

Melvin had hooked up the blood-pressure thing to my arm and had the stethoscope in his ears. 'Your blood pressure is low and you're dehydrated.'

'*That's* why you flipped out?' I totally wanted answers to all of my (and Adam's) questions, but right now they were really freaking me out.

He tucked the stethoscope into his lab coat and glanced sideways at Dad, who nodded slightly. 'I need to ask you a few questions before I make a diagnosis.'

'OK,' I said slowly.

Melvin pointed to the right corner of the first brain image. 'This section showed activity on the scan. That might indicate . . . maybe . . .'

'What?' I asked, hanging on his words.

'Well, it's unusual and might explain some of your symptoms.'

Like getting stuck two years in the past? Is that considered a medical symptom?

'Unusual, like . . . different than the other pictures you've taken of my brain?'

'Yes,' Dad answered.

'Maybe it's because I'm older.' Like . . . a *lot* older.

'Have you experienced any . . . *memory loss*?' He seemed to choose those last two words very carefully. 'For example, waking up somewhere and you're not sure how you got there?'

'OK, you guys are scaring me.'

'What about a photographic memory? Can you recall pages from a book word-for-word or possibly directions or maps?' Melvin asked.

'*Should* I be able to do that?'

'It's possible with your genetics—'

Dad cleared his throat loudly.

'Sorry, I meant, it's possible with that section of the brain showing activity,' Melvin corrected.

It would have been nice to be completely calm so I could plan my words carefully, but that just wasn't happening today.

'What part of the brain is it? I'm not a complete idiot. I did take anatomy and physiology.'

'When?' both of them asked.

Oops, in college. 'Um . . . actually it was more like a seminar. A one-day workshop. Honestly, I only went so I could get out of this algebra test . . .'

Dad turned to look at me and his face was intense. 'Look, Jackson. You . . . You're adopted. Courtney too, of course. I'm sorry I never told you, but there was never really a reason. Until now.'

Faking this kind of shock was tricky and I was nearly positive he dropped this bomb to distract me from the little slip about my genetics Melvin had made. He was really good at this secret cover thing and would probably recognize that I was lying. I decided on a different course than fake shock. 'Um . . . yeah, Dad. I kinda guessed that a long time ago.'

'You did?' Melvin asked.

'Well . . . we don't look anything alike and, well . . .' I couldn't come up with a good excuse because another question dominated my thoughts. 'So, that story about my mother dying in childbirth . . . is it even true?'

Dad shook his head. 'Not exactly. I'm sorry I never told you.'

Now it felt like I had moved backwards. I already knew my dad wasn't my dad, and now it seemed I actually knew less about my mother than I'd thought.

Melvin sat down next to me on the table, putting his arm around me like I was a hurt little kid. I half expected him to open his drawer of lollipops and hand me one. 'Jackson, what you have to understand is . . . we have no family history for you. As a physician, I generally draw on medical history of family members when making a diagnosis.'

Hearing Melvin say out loud that I had no real family was tough to swallow. Was there anyone else that could do what I could do? Or was I just some crazy mutant someone found on the side of the road. 'So . . . you think whoever I came from had weird brain activity like me?'

'Not exactly like you, but similar.'

To my surprise, Dad slipped right out of his careful

cover and glared at Melvin, then said, 'No, he's *nothing* like them. I've been telling you that for years.'

He walked out and slammed the door behind him. Melvin stared at the door for a minute before turning to me with wide eyes.

'He knows my real parents?' I asked.

Melvin shook his head. 'He's just upset about . . . your sister. It's my fault for bringing up the bad memories. Her cancer was so aggressive and rare, and with your real parents being dead, no family history, you having the same cancer gene is a possibility that we can't ignore.'

What a perfect story. Too bad something was missing. The underground people knowing me, Dad, and Melvin didn't fit anywhere into this plot they were feeding me. What my father and Melvin just did was a technique I had used many times. For example, when I was accused of doing something really bad at school or at home, I'd admit to a lesser crime to distract from the original accusation. It always worked like a charm.

'My biological parents are dead?'

Dr Melvin nodded grimly. 'Yes, I'm sorry. We don't have any information other than the fact that they're deceased.'

'But when . . . when did they die? Right after me and Courtney were born? How long have I been adopted? Did I live with them?' I drilled, not able to hold back.

Dr Melvin glanced nervously at the door again, but I didn't know if he was hoping Dad would come back or that he wouldn't and maybe he could tell me something. Finally he took a deep breath and said, 'All I know is you've lived with your father since you and Courtney were eleven months old.'

Eleven months. So for almost a year of my life, the first year, someone else raised me. It didn't really change anything, but it seemed like it should.

My head was spinning with questions and I suddenly had to lie down. 'I'm not feeling very well.'

Melvin filled a cup with water and handed it to me.

'No lollipop?' I asked.

He smiled and grabbed a red one from his drawer. 'Why don't you rest here while I go and talk to your father?'

'Sure.'

The second the door closed I grabbed my cellphone and started texting Adam.

Later, when Dad and I were headed home, his defences were back up and he apologized. 'I'm sorry the fact you're adopted had to come out like that. I overreacted. Dr Melvin just gets so deep into scientific details sometimes, I think he forgets he's dealing with real people. Anyway, it was more about your sister than you.'

'It always is,' I said, realizing how much I probably sounded like my seventeen-year-old self.

He gave me a long searching look before getting out of the car and handing the keys over to Henry. 'You're right, Jackson. Courtney may be gone, but you're not. Sometimes it's hard for me to pick up where we left off without feeling that grief. But I'll try harder. I promise.'

Was this another tactic? Create all this sympathy so I stop digging for answers and trust the man who's been lying to me my entire life? 'OK, Dad.'

'So, tell me about this girl you're trying to impress. I could tell you weren't lying about *that*.'

Holly's safety and Adam's message about not wanting her to get caught up in any of this weird shit ran through my mind, dominating my thoughts. I strode through the front door, keeping my back to Dad. 'You wouldn't like her, trust me. And it's nothing, really. I just like having a job.'

'If you say so.'

In other words, he didn't believe me.

My phone rang, and it was Adam of course. I walked to my bedroom and shut the door before answering. 'Hey, what's up?'

I filled him in on Dad's sympathy act. 'You can play that game, too, Jackson. Let him feel some guilt about whatever the hell he's hiding.'

'Smart. Who knows . . . maybe he'll crack.'

'All right, now you can tell me what was so important you had to break the one rule I gave you?'

I wasn't exactly ashamed of wanting to visit Courtney, but I knew it was wrong for several reasons and I didn't want to go into details with Adam. 'First of all, you've given me a lot more than one rule. And second, it wasn't anything, really. Just a short visit with someone, then I lost track of time.'

He groaned into the phone. 'You seriously need to be way more responsible than that. Just don't let it happen again. I'm going to type up a new list of theories based on today's data.'

'OK.'

'Oh . . . and Holly asked me how you were doing,' he said, the sound of high-speed typing coming through the phone. 'She called about an hour ago and then a second time five minutes ago.'

For just a few seconds every aspect of my crazy, messed-up life dissolved and I was just me, Jackson Meyer. A normal guy, elated that the girl I liked might actually be interested. Even though I wanted to be careful with Holly, not get too close, it still felt good to hear. She made me happy . . . and right now, that wasn't an easy task.

chapter twenty-one

FRIDAY, 12 OCTOBER 2007, 10.00 a.m.

Crowds of people zipped by me as I stood in front of the stained-glass windows in the Metropolitan Museum of Art. I was starting to get more than a little pissed at Adam. After all *he* was the one who woke me up by sending a text at three in the morning that said: 'Meet me at Met 9.30 a.m. Big physics experiment. Super secret. Science geeks rule!'

'Do you know how hard it is to spot you when you have a hat on?'

I spun around and was face to face with someone who definitely wasn't Adam. 'Holly? What are you doing here?'

'Field trip,' she said with a smile, then her eyes darted around the large open space. 'But I'm sneaking out, and you're going to be my accomplice.'

I must have looked totally confused because she laughed.

'I can't . . . I'm meeting Adam.'

Holly shook her head. 'Adam is currently snoring in third-period trig.'

'No, he's not. He's meeting me here,' I said, even more confused.

Her face suddenly filled with alarm and she yanked my arm and pulled me behind a statue. 'Sorry. Mr Orman, my drama teacher, was looking this way.' She looked at me again and her cheeks turned a little pink. 'Adam didn't text you . . . I did.'

That shocked the hell out of me. Holly initiating this impromptu adventure . . . ? 'You sent me a text from Adam's phone at three in the morning?'

'Uh-huh,' she said. 'He was helping me study and it turned out to be an all-nighter, but he fell asleep and . . . then I remembered what you said about Central Park being your favourite place . . .'

If this had been 009 Holly, I would have kissed her right then. But she wasn't 009 Holly, so instead I drilled her with more questions to fill the sudden awkward silence. 'Your paranoid mother let you sleep at Adam's? And aren't you afraid of getting in trouble for sneaking out?'

She rolled her eyes. 'I told her I was sleeping at Jana's. Besides, we were just studying. And my mom never lets me come to New York by myself. This is my only chance. Are you in or out?'

I watched her walk towards the exit and felt myself grinning. 'I'm in.'

She glanced at me from over her shoulder and smiled again. 'I was sure you'd figure out it was me who texted you.'

I laughed. 'The "science geeks rule" part should have tipped me off . . . but I thought maybe he was drunk.'

Holly spun around to face me, walking backwards down the pavement now. 'This is so awesome. I can't believe I pulled it off. Toby's covering for me, and Mr Orman isn't even riding the bus back with us. Basically, I have all day.'

'You should be a spy or a detective,' I teased.

She sighed. 'I wish. My foreign-language skills would really have to improve if I wanted to go into espionage.'

We walked around the outside of the museum and under the bridge that led us into Central Park. I pulled her bag off her shoulders and slung it over mine. 'This thing is *packed*. What have you got in here?'

'A blanket and three different books, in case I feel like lying out in the sun and reading for hours,' she said. 'Oh . . . and lots of snacks.'

'Sounds like you really planned this. How did I manage to win the part of accomplice?'

She laughed but kept her eyes on the trees in front of us. 'Well . . . I figured if I was going to drag someone along, then maybe it'd be smart to pick someone who wouldn't actually be cutting school.'

'Oh . . . so, it's not my potential for rebellious-bad-boy behaviour?'

She flashed me a grin. 'That too, of course.'

We found a great spot in the grass near a playground. Holly tossed her blanket on to the ground right beside the swings.

'I used to have a swing set like this in my backyard, but I hardly ever used the swings.'

'What did you do with it?' I asked.

'Watch this.' She climbed up the side of the red metal pole and shimmied across the top bar. She pulled her chin up to the bar, then turned her body upside down and suddenly she was above the bar.

'Nice. Let me try that.'

'Go ahead.'

I did a pull-up just like she had and then turned myself over. 'Not as hard as I thought it would be.'

'You're pretty good. You should have Toby teach you some high-bar skills.'

I jumped back down on to the grass and waited for Holly to do the same. Instead she swung one leg over the top bar and stood sideways.

'Holly, I don't think you should—'

'Relax, I've been doing this since I was five.' She turned with ease and started to walk the length of the swing set, her toes curling around the edge. All I could think about was her head smashing on the hard ground.

'You're really freaking me out. Can you please come down?' I pleaded.

'The first time I did this, my mom was standing at the kitchen sink, washing dishes. When she looked out the window and saw me, she ran outside so fast, screaming at me to come down. Which I did, and then spent the evening in time-out.' She returned to hanging again and swung a few times, then did a back flip in the air and landed lightly on her feet.

I let out a sigh of relief and she laughed.

'You just gave me a heart attack. You're like a wild

monkey.' She moved closer and as soon as she was within reach I grabbed her hand and dragged her towards the blanket. 'Sit. Please.'

She rolled her eyes, but sat down anyway. I stretched out across the blanket, staring at the clouds through the trees. Holly stretched out next to me. 'Are you feeling better?' she asked. 'That stomach flu totally sucks.'

'Yeah, pretty much. But that was a really bad day for me.' I turned on my side to face her. 'Can I ask you something?'

'You can ask.'

'What if you could have a do-over? Like . . . a time when you screwed up or maybe just to make a great memory. Would you do it?'

She turned to face me. 'Where is this coming from? That's just a really vague question so it's hard to answer.'

I propped myself up on my elbow. 'I had this dream the other night. It was about this one time I was a total jerk to my sister.'

'What did you do?' she asked.

'I told my friend a really embarrassing story about her, and he told pretty much the whole school. I think we were twelve and I was trying to impress the guys.'

'What kind of embarrassing story? If it was like . . . telling someone she wet her pants when she was three, that's no big deal.'

I wrinkled my nose. 'It involved flatulence and was very recent . . . like, days.'

Holly covered her mouth. 'Wow. That's pretty bad.'

I smiled at her. 'I know. Anyway, in my dream I was

there like I am now, this age. I knew I could keep it from happening, but then it wouldn't change anything, not today or even the day after it happened.'

'Your sister wouldn't know you had a change of heart?'

'Correct.'

'But you would know?'

'Exactly.'

Holly was quiet for a minute before answering. 'I think there's some nobility in trying to fix it.'

'I wouldn't really be fixing it.'

'But doing the right thing is hard sometimes. The more practice you have, the easier it gets. Even if it's only in a dream.'

I rolled on to my back again. 'I think you may be right.'

She scooted closer to me, but then started twisting her hands together like she was nervous.

I kept my eyes on the clouds and reached over and pulled her hands apart. I set one of them in between us and put mine right next to hers. Seconds later her fingers brushed my palm. I squeezed them and closed my eyes. 'Hol?'

'Yeah?'

'Relax, OK? Just being here with you . . . it's more than enough. I don't have any other plans.'

And that was the truth. My thumb made tiny circles on the outside of her hand as I breathed in the scent of crisp fall air combined with burning wood.

'You're so different than I thought,' she said quietly.

I smiled to myself. 'You're exactly how I thought.'

She leaned her head against my shoulder. I felt her lips

touch my cheek and a warmth spread through my whole body. I reached my other hand over, resting my palm on her cheek. I could stay like this forever. It didn't matter what year it was.

It was like that the first time we slept together (of course that was 009 Holly, the one that was legal). I had these crazy ideas in my head right before it happened, some really big plans. But what I remember loving most had nothing to do with the main event.

It was the middle of July 2009. A couple of days after the little incident with my dad catching us.

Finally we were alone in my apartment. Bedroom door locked. Great music blaring. Nothing stopping us from doing whatever we wanted.

Holly pulled her dress over her head then crawled back across the bed on her knees. I touched the waistband of her pink panties and started to slide them down. My mouth followed my hands.

Her fingers combed through my hair and then she whispered, 'I've never done this before.'

My lips froze just above her hip. There were so many ways to translate that statement. 'Never done what?'

'Had sex.'

Not what I expected to hear. I guess with all my fantasies, I had never once pictured Holly a virgin. I stood on my knees again so I was eye-level with her. 'Never?'

She shook her head and covered her face with her hands. 'I should have said something sooner.'

'Holly, it's no big deal. We don't have to—'

'No, I want to.' She dropped her arms and flopped on to

her stomach, face pressed into the pillow. 'I can't believe I just said that.'

I lay down beside her, resting my hand on her back. 'It's OK.'

'If I tell you something, do you promise not to make fun of me?'

I held up my right hand. 'Scout's honour.'

She smiled and then sat up, crossing her legs. 'I *almost* did it once. David and I had this big plan, like forever, to rid ourselves of the big V on prom night.'

I tried not to smile and Holly rolled her eyes. 'I know, it's not very original. Anyway, we had a hotel room and everything, but David had a little issue and broke all the condoms he brought.'

'I thought you said you'd never—'

'No, he broke them before I had even taken off my dress. I'll spare you the details.'

I laughed loudly, then shut my mouth after she glared. 'Anyway, we decided to go to the store and buy another box.'

'A bigger one, I hope.'

She laughed and nodded. 'The whole time we're shopping, both of us are looking around the aisles, making sure we don't see anyone we know. Anyway, we get up to the register to pay and David realizes he doesn't have his wallet. I didn't bring my purse, so we tell the lady to cancel the sale. But she gets on her microphone and calls the manager over. At that point me and David just want to get the hell out of there, and she's trying to talk the manager into giving us free condoms.'

I rolled with laughter and Holly joined me. 'OK, so what happened?'

'I just said no thanks and then dragged David out the door and told him it was a sign that we shouldn't be doing it. At least not that night.'

'So, did you go back and laugh about it?'

She returned to lying beside me. 'Not exactly. David's ego was a little bruised. He fell asleep as soon as we got back to the hotel, or pretended to so we didn't have to talk.'

'And you never tried again?'

She shook her head. 'Nope. And not because he screwed up with the whole condom thing, but mostly because, that night, all I could think about was . . . is David the last boy I'll ever kiss? And I wasn't sure I wanted him to be and then the doubts just kept piling up. Knowing we were going in such different directions, it just didn't feel right.'

I wrapped my arm around her waist and pulled her close. 'Everything is so deep with you, isn't it?'

She rested her cheek on my chest. 'You're deep too. You just don't want to recognize it. What about all that classic literature that you secretly read?'

'That's for school.'

'But you chose your major. And Jackson?'

'Yeah?'

'I really *do* want to do it,' she said.

I touched my lips to her shoulder and closed my eyes, not responding. I knew that had to be a hard thing for her to admit, but I had my own concerns.

'Jackson?'

I sighed heavily, then rested my head back on the pillow. 'Maybe another time.'

'Like one that's more perfect than tonight?' She loosened her hold on me and started to move away.

'I just don't want to hurt you,' I said, barely above a whisper.

The idea that she might not enjoy this was turning me in the other direction. I couldn't remember the last time I had been with a virgin, even just messing around. Maybe never.

She started kissing every inch of my body while I was deep in thought. Her hands were doing things that made my brain completely void of logical reason. I groaned and covered my face. 'Holly, what are you doing?'

'Think about it this way, Jackson. Are you saying you want me to go find some other guy?' Her voice was light, teasing.

'No.'

'Then you want to dump me for some loose chick?'

'Of course not.'

'I see no other way forward, unless you're OK with celibacy.'

'Of course not.'

She laughed and then put her hands on the sides of my face. Her forehead touched mine. 'I want it to be *you*.'

'Why?'

She kissed my lips. 'Because . . . I just do, OK?'

I had a pretty good idea what she had almost said. The three words that neither of us had uttered. 'You have to tell me if I hurt you. Do you swear?'

My hands were already shaking. She picked one up and placed it over her heart. 'I swear.'

'All right.'

She kissed my cheek. 'I don't think I've ever seen you this nervous.'

I *was* nervous. And I've never done anything so slow in my entire life. She teased me about being an expert at putting on a condom, so I told her I practised when I was younger, which was true when I was, like, fourteen. Somehow, Holly and I managed to make a scary and awkward moment incredibly funny.

As far as the actual sex part – to me, it was great. I think mostly because Holly is never fake. And she has this way of making me feel like I'm part of something important. Like we're always making a memory. One you'd never be able to erase. Me, I'm all impulse. Whatever the hell I feel like doing at any given moment, I do it. But I had a feeling Holly had thought this night through and played it out in her mind for a long time. The fact that she was willing to include me was beyond cool.

We hopped into the shower together, later on, and she stood on her toes and wrapped her arms around my neck, squeezing me so tight. Her face was buried in my chest, the water running over us, and I thought that she might be crying, the way she hid her face. But I was too afraid to ask. We stayed like that, holding each other, for a while. Then she finally whispered, 'Thank you.'

That was the first time I ever even *thought* about saying it . . . *I love you.* It would have been perfect, just melting into the moment. Not like some overplayed drama. But my tongue tied up just thinking it, not knowing if it was really true or not, so instead I said, 'Did you know you have a freckle on your—'

She put a hand over my mouth. 'Yeah, I know.'

Then we were laughing again, and it set the tone for the whole night. Holly sat on the kitchen counter, listening to my jokes, while I made scrambled eggs. She looked so gorgeous, wrapped up in my blue bathrobe, her hair wet and her cheeks still flushed.

Looking back on it now, I could have stretched that moment out for weeks and been completely content. Maybe even months.

Nothing went exactly right. And yet it was perfect.

I was so engrossed in my recollection of 009 Holly, I hadn't even noticed that 007 Holly was breathing deep and drooling on my sweatshirt. I released her hand and put my arm around her, bringing her closer so her head wasn't on the hard ground. She stirred for a minute, then lifted her head.

'I fell asleep, didn't I?'

I smiled when she wiped the slobber from her face with her sleeve. 'Might as well get a nap in while you're cutting class, right?'

She sat all the way up and her cheeks turned pink. 'Sorry. I'm one of those people who could sleep in the middle of traffic, honking horns and everything.'

'Lots of homework last night, I guess?'

'Yeah, and studying for the SATs. I'm going to take them in a few weeks.'

I sat up across from her. 'I did OK on mine. I'm still willing to help you.'

'Define "OK".'

'Nineteen-seventy.'

Her eyebrows arched up. 'That's a really good score. I need a nineteen-hundred to get into NYU and I'd like to do better than that so I can get a scholarship, hopefully.'

'I'm sure you'll do great. In fact, I'm nearly positive.'

'A little extra help couldn't hurt,' she said with a smile.

She started leaning forward like she might try to kiss me and I wanted to dive in with both feet, but something inside me tensed up. Something different than Adam's warning. Was it possible to cheat on Holly *with* Holly? Was she too young to be kissing someone my age? Would it be the same as kissing *my* Holly?

I chickened out of making a decision and stood up, holding my hand out for her. 'Let's go for a walk. Maybe that'll wake you up a little.'

She got up from the ground after tossing the blanket into her bag. 'Where are we going?'

I smiled when she didn't release my hand. In fact, she gripped it even tighter as we strolled towards the pavement. 'Have you ever been to Shakespeare's Garden?'

'Nope.'

'It's not far from here.'

When we arrived, Holly walked up to the first plaque to read the writing, and as I moved towards her, a short man with red hair brushed past me and said in a low voice, 'Nice to see you again, Jackson.'

I sucked in a breath, trying to focus despite the blood pounding in my ears as he slowly turned around to face me. It was *him*, looking exactly the same as he had two years from now when he charged into Holly's dorm room. Then he was walking away. His pace picked up with longer and faster steps, and without even thinking about it I took off after him.

Instinctively I reached for my pocket knife and clenched it in my fist. His fast walk turned into a light jog and I ran after him, not saying a word as he led me off the path, towards a different part of the park, thick with trees.

My pulse raced, matching the beat of my steps. Without any indication he had been aware of my presence behind him he froze, right in front of a tree, and lifted his hands in the air as if he was giving up. 'I was *hoping* you would follow me.'

I took a step closer. Maybe this was a trap and maybe he had a better weapon than an old pocket knife, but I was too furious to care. He turned and I nearly had a heart attack when I saw the gash above his left eye, fresh blood still streaming from it. And the red mark. A shoe print. Holly's shoe print.

009 Holly's shoe print.

It couldn't be a coincidence. Could it? 'How did you . . . ? I don't . . .'

My voice faded as the man held my gaze with an expression far too calm compared with the roiling emotions I felt.

'Jackson . . . what are you . . . doing?' Holly sputtered out from behind me, her breath coming out jagged, probably from running after me.

I glanced quickly over my shoulder and then back at the man, trying to figure out a way to word my question.

'How did you . . . get *here*? From there?'

His eyebrows lifted and a slow grin spread across his face. 'Interesting. Why don't you tell me how *you* got here?'

I wanted to punch the grin right off his face, but then Holly gasped behind me and I spun around to see a tall blonde woman with one of her arms locked tightly around Holly's throat.

Nausea swept over me. *God, this can't be happening again.* And where the hell did that woman even come from?

'Rena, I thought you'd be here sooner,' the man said, like she was late for dinner or a dentist appointment.

'Things were a little different than we expected,' she said.

My eyes darted between the two of them and then rested on Holly's face. Tears streamed down her cheeks, but the panic in her eyes, as she squirmed to get out of Rena's grip, sent me over the edge. She tried to kick free. I had to do something.

I snapped my pocket knife open at the same time the man behind me shouted, 'Watch out, Rena!'

But it wasn't me he was worried about. In a blur, a man flew out of the bushes, landing hard on Rena's back and putting her in the same choke hold she had used on Holly. Suddenly Rena's eyes rolled into the back of her head and she fell over sideways on to the ground, taking her victim and her attacker down with her. Holly pulled herself free and stood. She let out a breath of relief and bent over, resting her hands on her knees.

'Don't even think about pulling one of your little tricks,' a female voice said from behind me and Holly.

We both turned around and my jaw dropped open when I saw my father's secretary, Miss Stewart, execute a perfect round-house kick. Her knee-high leather boot connected with the red-haired man's face, sending him stumbling backwards into the woods. Fashionable women's shoes: 2. Red-headed man: 0.

She took off running after him.

I turned back the other way. Holly raced over to me and my arms immediately went around her. She looked just as stunned and confused as I felt. My dad was pulling himself off the ground and I quickly let my thoughts catch up and realized he was the man who had just saved Holly, moving so fast I never even saw his face.

'What the hell . . . ?!' I started to say to Dad, but he was mumbling something in another language into his sleeve.

He rested a hand on Holly's shoulder. 'Are you OK?'

Her eyes were huge as she backed away from him. One hand still clutched her chest, the other reached into her pocket and pulled out the bottle of pepper spray she always carried with her.

Dad held up his hands. 'I'm not going to hurt you,' he said.

I didn't know who to believe and I had the sudden urge to snatch the bottle from Holly and spray him with it, just in case.

'Are you all right, Jackson?' he asked me.

I stared down at the woman lying in a heap on the ground and then at Holly, who seemed to be putting two and two together and coming to the conclusion that I knew these people, and that I was involved. She lifted the bottle of pepper spray and pointed it in my direction.

'Easy, Holly. I only know as much as you do,' I said. She eased the pepper spray to her side.

Miss Stewart returned, followed by a man close to my dad's age.

'The target got away,' the man said.

'It's not like he outran us. What the hell are we supposed to do if he just—'

Dad put up a hand to quiet her, and then pressed his finger to his ear, holding perfectly still for about ten seconds. 'Deal with our sleepy blonde friend,' he said to the random guy who had just shown up.

The guy hoisted the blonde woman over his shoulder and took off.

'Don't move, young lady,' Dad said firmly to Holly, who was backing further away, towards an escape.

Fresh tears ran down her face and she looked so scared. Her fingers moved over the keypad of her cellphone.

'Stewart, clear the area and we'll meet at the designated location,' Dad said to his secretary. The second she was out of sight, he snatched the phone and the pepper spray from Holly's hands. 'I'm sure you have a lot of questions about what you just saw, but we can't discuss them out in the open.'

Dad placed his hands on her shoulders and turned her around, towards a path that led to the street.

'What are you doing?' I asked him. I didn't want him touching her.

'Just making sure she gets home safe and sound.' He continued to walk her towards the pavement. 'We've already made quite a scene here and I'd rather not have any more slip-ups.'

Holly cooperated for a few seconds, then she stepped on his foot, hard, and jabbed him right in the groin with her elbow. Dad didn't even wince from Holly's pint-size torture. He was now holding tighter to her shoulders and steering her towards a car parked on the street.

'Please, just let me go and I'll . . . I won't say anything . . . please,' she said quietly.

'I promise, no one is going to hurt you,' Dad said, then he removed his wallet and flipped it open, revealing a badge with his picture on the top and the letters 'CIA' down the side. 'I'll explain everything in just a minute.'

We had reached the long black car and I debated grabbing Holly and making a run for it, but this was our car, with our driver, Cal, who had driven me to the Met just this morning.

'Oh God,' Holly muttered as Dad opened the door. 'Please, just let me go.'

'Everything will be much easier if you get in on your own,' Dad said. 'Trust me.'

'Why does she have to get in the car?' I asked desperately.

He gave me a sharp look that basically said to keep quiet. So that's what I did because I didn't see any other option.

Holly's lip trembled a little, but she discreetly wiped the tears from her face and slid into the car. The back two rows faced each other, and Dad sat right across from Holly. I moved in next to her, and the sound of my heart pounding felt twice as loud inside the confined space.

'Who . . . are you people?' Holly managed to say.

Obviously she wasn't convinced by the CIA thing and she seemed to think Dad and I were partners in crime rather than father and son.

'This is my dad,' I said to Holly.

'OK,' she said slowly.

He hesitated for a second, his eyes on me. 'And I do work for the CIA.'

Holly shook her head and sank back into her seat with a sigh of defeat. 'This is beyond creepy . . . You're never letting me go, are you? . . . I'm going to die, or be one of those disappearing girls you hear about on the news.'

'Stop,' Dad said, pointing to the car window. 'Look where we are.'

I glanced out the window at the same time as Holly and saw that we were parked in front of the same museum we had left a couple of hours ago, right behind a big yellow school bus.

'See, just like I promised. We got you back safe and sound.'

'But . . . what about those people . . . and—'

'The people we were chasing are terrorists.'

'Terrorists?!' Holly asked.

'Look, I think it would be best if we had a chat with your family, just to let them know about the situation today,' Dad said in this smooth voice that could probably calm someone in the middle of a war zone.

Holly shook her head vigorously. 'I wouldn't exactly recommend that . . . My mom is a total nut case about stuff like this . . . she'll completely freak. I'll never be allowed out of the house again.'

'If that's what you want.'

I had a feeling that was exactly what Dad wanted. He seemed to know how Holly would react. What else did he know about her?

'Yeah, that would be best.' She looked longingly out the window. 'Can I go now?'

Dad nodded and put a hand on the door handle, preparing to open it. 'Holly, agents almost never reveal their identity. When we do, it's documented, and if anything leaks, we know *exactly* where it came from, trust me.'

'I get it,' she whispered, but her breath caught in her throat.

'Good.'

I hated the way she was looking at me. Like she didn't know me all over again. 'I'll walk in with you, Hol.'

'No, really, I just . . . want to go on my own.'

'I guess I'll see you at work later?'

'Yeah . . . work,' she said, right before jumping out and slamming the door shut.

I sat there and watched her walking away until the car started moving again, and then I turned to Dad. 'If anything happens to her . . .'

'Nothing will happen. You have my word,' he said. 'But I have to ask you . . . how old are you right now, Jackson?'

He knows. Because of my hints? The tests?

My heart pounded harder than ever. But I kept my focus, knowing whatever information I gave him could be used against me.

'Did you know my real parents?' I asked him, hoping the quick change of subject might catch him off guard.

He shook his head. 'Not exactly . . . no.'

'Who did Courtney and I live with for the first eleven months . . . Dr Melvin told me that part?'

He turned his eyes to the window, but his face remained completely unreadable. 'Just someone who wasn't able to continue caring for two children. That's all I know.'

OK, obviously he wasn't going to tell me those details. 'Why am I like this?'

He turned away from the window and back to me, his face very businesslike. 'I can't answer that without asking a few questions of my own. Your abilities – I'm guessing you can use them freely?'

I so badly wanted to lash out at him. He'd been lying through his teeth the other day with Melvin. How was I supposed to believe a word he said? I sank back in the seat as an idea formed in my head.

'Dad, I'm not going to fork over all the secrets you want to know without getting something in return.'

'Like what? You have everything.'

'First of all, no more talk about high school, and I'm not quitting my job.'

He shook his head and stared at me for a minute before speaking. 'Is the job part for Holly? Because that just seems extreme for someone your age.'

'And what age would that be?' I sighed, knowing I'd have to reveal a little. 'Something happens to Holly, two years from now. She's my girlfriend in the future. Now I'm stuck here and there's no way I'll let that happen again.

But I don't know how to prevent it as well as you probably do. I want to learn whatever you secret-agent dudes know. That's my second request. You have to teach me some spy stuff.'

'What happened, Jackson? You can tell me,' he said.

Part of me still saw my dad, not someone I had to keep hiding stuff from. And I really wanted to ask how that red-headed man had been in the future, two years from now, but also, here, in 2007, with the same cut on his face. The shoe print. Like it had just happened. But it was too risky – I still didn't know whose side he was on.

'Not now.'

He let out a breath, but nodded. 'OK. I've got plenty of ideas for beginners, also some manuals you can look over. I'm actually training a group of agents right now.'

I laughed a little, despite the tension still in the air. 'You mean your secretary?'

Dad cracked a smile. 'Yes, she's one of them.'

'How old is she?' I asked. I'd been dying to know ever since she told me to call her Miss Stewart.

'Nineteen.'

'The CIA recruits teenagers?' I asked.

'In certain unusual cases, yes,' he said, choosing his words carefully. 'Jenni Stewart is fairly new. If you do run into her again, you can't tell her your real age or how you got here.'

I laughed a little because I knew she didn't want me to know her first name. 'I'm not telling anyone. I'm not an idiot.'

'So you haven't told Holly?' he asked.

'What do you think?' I rolled my eyes. 'She thinks I'm a high-school dropout from Jersey.'

The first sign of worry crossed Dad's face. 'She doesn't think that any more. I already told Agent Stewart to check on her and . . . invite her to a company party at our place.'

I rubbed my hands over my eyes and groaned. 'Great. Now she's freaked out and she's going to hate me for lying . . . Seriously? A company party? That should be interesting.'

'I'm sorry, I thought it might smooth things over,' he said with a sigh. 'If she saw we were just normal people.'

'Even without the CIA, she'd never think we were normal.' I changed the subject so I wouldn't end up yelling at him. 'What about your CEO office that I've seen a thousand times?'

'It's a government-run company made to look like a normal corporation. My involvement in the day-to-day operations is limited.'

Hearing him say this so casually was infuriating. 'OK, so first I find out you're not really my father, and now you're in the CIA and everything I knew about your work life is fake. A complete lie. What do I actually know about you?'

'It's complicated, Jackson. People could lose their lives if agents like me don't take every precaution to conceal what we do.'

I leaned back and crossed my arms, staring straight at him. 'Then tell me what exactly you do. Fight bad guys that can somehow be two years in the future and then here, wearing the same clothes, with the same cut on their face?'

'I think we should go talk to Dr Melvin,' he suggested.

'Not yet. You can take me later, but I'm not going to tell you anything else.' I turned my eyes to the window and saw big raindrops hitting the pavement at an increasing rate. 'I have to go to work and see how much Holly hates me.'

Probably more than I could make up for, which made me feel more alone than ever.

chapter twenty-two

FRIDAY, 12 OCTOBER 2007, 2.30 p.m.

When I got to the gym later, I had several versions of conversations worked out in my head to get Holly to not hate me, but Mike had his own plans for me.

'I want to touch up all the red paint on the sign behind the gymnastics floor. Since Friday's a light day, I figured we should do it now.' He stood facing the back wall of the gym, pointing up at the word 'Twisters', which was painted in red against the white wall. The red was peeling and chipping in places.

By the time I spread plastic all over the carpet and set up the ladder and paint trays, Holly and Jana had arrived to teach their classes. I jumped down from the ladder the second I saw her and walked over.

'Hey, Jackson, how's it going?' Jana said with a friendly smile.

This was a good sign that Holly hadn't said anything to her.

'Good. How about you? Glad it's Friday?' I asked, faking calm.

'Totally.' She elbowed Holly in the side and Holly finally looked up at me.

'Um . . . yeah, Friday's . . . good.' She chewed on her thumbnail and shifted from one foot to the other.

Jana's eyes darted between the two of us and she shook her head and walked away, as if she sensed we needed privacy or something. Holly glanced quickly at Jana and it looked like she might run after her, but I put my arm out to stop her.

'I'm so sorry about this morning. I had no idea anything like that would happen.'

She stared at my fingers, now gently curled around her bicep. Her whole body stiffened. 'I'm fine. Seriously, it's no big deal . . . I won't tell anyone, I swear.'

She ducked under my arm and took off before I could respond. Mike came out of his office and clapped his hands loudly. 'Get painting, Jackson! I can't wait to see the finished product.'

I had no choice but to return to working. The whole time Holly was teaching I kept looking over at her, and I could tell she was a bundle of nerves. I just wanted to be lying in the grass with her again, feeling more relaxed than I'd felt in such a long time. My eyes stayed focused on the wall in front of me for the rest of the evening.

'Hey, Holly, you want to come to my parents' party tonight?' Jana shouted from across the gym as they were putting away mats at the end of the night. 'You can come, too, Jackson.'

I started to climb down so I could respond. 'Sorry, I won't be done for a while, and I'm really beat. I'll probably just go home and crash. Thanks for the invite though.'

'I might come,' Holly said after Jana had walked closer to her.

Jana dug through her purse and pulled out her keys. 'Awesome. Just head over whenever you're done.'

'You're leaving now?' Holly asked, and I heard panic creep into her voice. 'I still have my skill sheets to fill out. I promised Mike I'd leave them on his desk.'

Jana already had her back to us and her cellphone up to her ear. 'So finish and then come over. I gotta go. My mom's already pissed that I'm not home yet.'

The second Jana left us alone in the building Holly raced across the gym and busied herself by sitting under the balance beams, scribbling furiously on the top sheet of a large stack of papers.

I sighed before climbing up the ladder again. Getting back in Holly's circle wouldn't be an easy task. Basically, I'd lied to her about almost everything.

I barely glanced over my shoulder at her as I reached again for the large bucket of red paint hanging on the side of the ladder. Too much of my weight shifted to one side and seconds later I went tumbling down. I landed flat on my back with the ladder across my stomach and the bucket of red paint tipped over at my feet and splattered everywhere.

'Oh my God!' I heard Holly say and then she was beside me, lifting the ladder upright again. 'Are you OK?'

I nodded, but the wind was completely knocked out of me and I couldn't speak.

She leaned in closer, scrutinizing my face. 'Can you sit up?'

Slowly I pulled myself up, trying to take in a few short breaths. 'We all knew I'd fall off a ladder eventually, right?'

She cracked a smile before glancing around me and frowning. 'Mike's gonna have a heart attack.'

I used the bottom of my shirt to wipe the splattered paint from my face so I could assess the damage. It looked like a bloody massacre. 'Shit, you're right. Good thing I used plastic on the carpet.'

Holly stood up. 'I'll get some paper towels from the supply closet. A *bunch* of paper towels.'

Both of us worked in silence for at least thirty minutes, scrubbing the walls, rolling up the sheets of plastic, and laying out new ones. At least she was willing to get within a few feet of me. It was a small amount of progress.

'Thanks for helping, Holly,' I said after a while.

She wiped sweat from her forehead with her arm and ended up streaking red paint across it. 'It's not your fault you suck at this job.'

'What do you mean, I suck at this job?' I asked.

'That chick who kicked the crazy dude in the face . . . she talked to me right after your dad dropped me off. She told me about your community-service hours,' Holly said with a shrug. 'For getting arrested or . . . something. What did you do, anyway?'

So Jenni Stewart had made up a cover story for me. How nice of her, except now I was 'spoiled rich kid caught breaking the law', which is even worse than just spoiled rich kid.

'This,' I laughed and picked up the small paintbrush,

lifting it to her cheek. Then, before she could stop me, I swiped it across the side of her face.

Her eyes shut immediately. 'You did *not* just do that.'

'What are you going to do about it?' I teased.

She opened her eyes and darted around me, diving for the big roller in the paint tray, then held it up, ready to attack. 'Go ahead and come a little closer, Jackson.'

I put my hands in the air. 'OK, OK, I surrender.'

'Fine.' She lowered the roller so it hung at her side.

The second I reached down to pick up a wad of paper towels, I felt the wet, sticky roller running down my back. The paint brush was still in my hand. I straightened up slowly and came face to face with her, grinning at her smug expression. I quickly swiped the paintbrush from her forehead down her nose. She ducked under my arm and pressed the roller down the back of my hair.

This went on for a couple more minutes until finally, after we were both covered in paint, I dropped down on to the plastic floor covering. 'I gotta take a break.'

Holly laughed and sat down beside me. 'Truce?'

'Truce,' I agreed.

After a few seconds of silence she was nervous all over again, pulling her knees to her chest and chewing on her nails. I fiddled with the anklet around her leg, testing the waters a little. When she didn't jump or move away, I took the next step.

'Just so you know, I've never actually been in trouble before. It was just a stupid mix up with a credit card and a fake ID.'

She nodded and then rested her cheek on her knees.

'So . . . you really live in Manhattan?'

'It's true.'

Her eyebrows arched upward. 'Let me see your licence.'

I tugged on her arm until she was lying next to me. Then I handed over my wallet. She dug through it and pulled out my driver's permit. 'You were born in 1990, just like me. But you would be a senior, right? If you didn't drop out.'

'Yeah, summer birthday. I started school early.'

'So, where did you go to school?' she asked.

'I went to a very snobby private school on the Upper East Side,' I answered with a sigh.

Holly wrinkled her nose. 'Yuck.'

'Tell me about it.' I turned on my side to face her. 'I like working here. Getting away from all that crap I had to deal with in high school. And I swear, I had no idea anything would happen today. That was *so* freaky.'

'But you've been around it all your life, haven't you?'

I wiped some of the paint from under her left eye. 'Actually I only just found out about my dad's real job. A couple of months ago, anyway. I'm still getting used to the idea.'

'It's hard to believe he does stuff like that every day. I don't think I've ever been more scared in my entire life,' she admitted.

My insides twisted with guilt. 'I'm so sorry, and if it helps any, my legs are still shaking. That's probably why I fell off the ladder.'

She smiled a little before sitting up. 'Should we finish cleaning?'

I reluctantly got up from my comfortable spot. We both carted the trays and brushes into the guys' locker room.

'Maybe we should run the hot water over them and come back in a few minutes,' I suggested.

'Yeah, that's probably best.' Holly took off her tennis shoes and rolled up the bottom of her pants before turning on one of the showers.

'I hope this comes out of my hair,' she said as she dropped her paint tray on to the floor, under the hot water.

'I think it looks good like that,' I joked. Her arm was within reach and I couldn't resist the temptation. I grabbed the brush clutched in her hand and pulled hard enough to drag her under my shower. The water poured on to her head.

'I can't believe you just did that,' she spluttered.

'I thought you should rinse the paint out of your hair before it dries.' I moved under the water with her and she looked up at me and smiled, like she'd forgotten all about this morning, even though I knew she hadn't. Even though I knew how scared she'd been. And yet she was here. Now.

And then before I could even try to stop her, Holly stood on her toes and kissed me lightly on the mouth. I instantly tossed the moral debate from earlier today out of my mind. Just the thought of us being closer sent my pulse racing, bringing me to life. The second her lips were against mine both of us stepped closer, hands reaching out for some part of each other to grab hold of. My hands were on her face, her mouth moving with mine, fingers curling around the back of my neck, the stream from the shower running over us like a waterfall.

It was just like the first time . . . a couple of years in the future.

The water suddenly turned from steaming hot to icy cold and we jumped apart. I reached for the knob and shut off the shower. Holly was shivering and dripping wet. I snatched a couple of towels from the shelf above the sink and wrapped one around her shoulders.

'You still have paint in your hair.'

She laughed again, a nervous laugh, and then stepped around me, sitting down in front of one of the lockers. 'I wonder if Toby's got an extra shirt in his locker.'

I picked up the paint tray again and dropped it on to the shower floor and watched Holly yank on the lock. 'Damn, it's closed.'

Suddenly I had a flash of an image in my mind: Toby spinning the lock earlier today while I stood at the sink, washing my hands.

'Twenty-two, sixteen, five,' I said without even thinking about it. Then it hit me – Dr Melvin had said something the other day about a photographic memory . . . When had I started being able to remember things like this, and what did it mean?

She turned the numbers perfectly and the lock popped open. 'I hope there's nothing I don't want to see in here.'

She didn't seem in the least bit concerned that I knew his combination, but it wasn't exactly a safe full of money. It was a gym locker, probably filled with sweaty socks and possibly deodorant. I pushed the questions aside and added them to my list for Adam, when I finally got a chance to fill him in on everything.

'You're not going to . . . uh . . . tell anyone about this, are you?' Holly asked while her head was half stuffed in the locker.

I had to assume 'this' meant us kissing and not the paint incident. Or maybe both . . .

'Not if you don't want me to,' I said.

She sighed and plopped down on the bench that was pushed up against the wall. 'I'm just imagining all the shit Toby and David would give me.'

'For getting in a paint fight?' I sat down next to her, and both of us leaned against the wall.

'Not about the paint.' Her cheeks turned a little pink.

'Your friends are teasing you about me?' I asked.

She nodded. 'Ever since the poker game . . . And *teasing* is an understatement.'

I leaned forward and kissed the side of her neck, just below her ear. I could feel goose bumps rise on her skin. 'You don't have to tell them anything. It can be our secret.'

Holly smiled and laced her fingers through mine. 'Well . . . then we have to have a secret meeting place, so no one knows.'

I stared at her face for a minute, taking in the youthful, dreamy expression. 007 Holly *was* different than the older one. The girl I met in 2009 was deep and analytical like this girl, but a lot more serious and realistic. She didn't spend her free time climbing things and turning upside down. She didn't take nearly as many risks. It was almost like we had switched places.

I kissed her again, then put an arm around her shoulders.

'Let's see . . . Well . . . There was a great make-out spot at my high school, under the third-floor stairwell. Lots of scandals happened there.'

'Jackson?' someone called from outside the locker room.

Holly and I both jumped up and walked out the door back into the gym. Dad was wandering around, taking in the mess we'd made with the paint.

'What are you doing here?' I asked him.

I could feel Holly stiffen and move behind me.

'What the hell happened?' Dad asked.

'I fell off a ladder,' I answered.

He had his phone out and punched button after button. 'We've got some . . . family business to take care of, right now.'

'Now? What about the gym?' I asked.

'I can clean up,' Holly said, barely louder than a whisper.

Dad shook his head. 'I've got someone coming. It'll be good as new in a couple of hours.'

'I guess I'll get going then,' Holly said, heading towards the staffroom.

I followed behind her and grabbed my stuff. 'Thanks again . . . for staying. You didn't have to.'

She glanced sideways at Dad through the open staffroom door, then back at me before kissing me quickly on the mouth. 'Oh . . . and Jackson, there's no good stairwells at my school, and you can't get in without a student ID. So, I'll have to tell my friends the truth.'

'If that's what you want,' I said, smiling at her.

I'm pretty sure she just declared herself my girlfriend. Again.

'I'll wait for you outside,' Dad told me before heading out the front doors.

Holly smiled at me again and leaned her shoulder against the wall. 'He's a little bit scary, I'll admit that.'

'What about me?' I asked.

She took a step closer and reached for my hand.

'Mostly you just make me nervous, but in a good way.'

I kissed her forehead and then moved my mouth to her cheek, drifting closer to her lips. My phone was clutched in one hand and it buzzed. I groaned before flipping it open and reading Dad's text: *Outside now.* 'I gotta go. I'll see you tomorrow?' I ran outside.

Dad was waiting for me.

'Get in.' He pointed to a black car parked on the street.

I slid into the back seat, and the second I saw the tall man beside me, blending into the dark, the fear from earlier today returned. It was the blue-suit guy with the secret fingerprint scanner, dragging people to the underground place in the hospital. I reached for the door so I could jump out, but Dad was already flying us down the street.

'What the hell is he doing here?' I moved all the way over, gripping the door handle.

'You know Chief Marshall?' Dad asked.

'Yeah, we've met.' I barely had the words out when the crazy tall dude pressed a towel to my face.

Not good. I slumped over against the cold window and everything faded.

chapter twenty-three

SATURDAY, 13 OCTOBER 2007, 2.00 A.M.

The first thing I noticed after peeling my eyes open was the old man leaning over me, shining a tiny light in my face. The smell of whatever chemical they used to knock me out was superglued to the inside of my nostrils.

I was lying on a couch in what looked like a normal living room. I covered the light with my hand. 'Dr Melvin? What are you doing here? Where am I?'

Dad came up behind me and flipped on the lamp sitting on the end table. 'This location is confidential. That's why we had to knock you out.'

'Confidential, as in no one will find my dead decaying body?' Melvin came at me with the light again and I shoved his hand away. 'Cut it out.'

'He's just checking your vital signs,' the deep voice boomed from the other side of the room.

He was here. I hadn't imagined it. And what exactly was the significance behind the 'Chief' title? Dad was just

Agent Meyer, so Chief Marshall must be in charge of . . . something.

I didn't know what to believe at this point. I needed a plan, and maybe some serious help in the form of advice from Adam. I rolled into a ball, clutching my stomach and moaning. 'Bathroom, quick!'

Dad pointed down the hallway to my left. 'Second door on the right.'

I glanced in Chief Marshall's direction for a second before heading down the hall. He looked cool and calm, just like he had that day in 1996.

I locked the bathroom door and tried to remember what I was doing a couple of days ago and, more importantly, what Adam was doing. I closed my eyes and jumped back in time about forty-eight hours. This was the plan we had come up with. Find a method of communication while in a time jump, so no one in home base would have any knowledge of it.

chapter twenty-four

WEDNESDAY, 10 OCTOBER 2007, 4.32 P.M.

I ended up sitting in the parking lot of the gym. Lack of focus on my ideal destination, I guess, although my accuracy had improved tremendously since leaving 2009. But Adam's house wasn't too far from work. I ran all the way there and was panting a little by the time I rang the doorbell. I only had to wait a few seconds before Mrs Silverman let me in.

'Hi, Jackson, how are you?'

'Um . . . OK. Is Adam home?'

'Yeah, go on in. He's in his room.'

I walked down the hall and knocked on the door.

'Mom, I told you I'm not hungry!'

'It's Jackson,' I said through the door.

He flung it open and stared at me, taking in my paint-spattered, slightly damp clothes. 'What happened?'

'Remember when you told me to ask you about the Latin stuff or whatever?'

Adam yanked me into his room and slammed the door shut. 'Spill.'

'Am I supposed to show you the message again?'

'I know what it says. That was only for if you jumped back to before I wrote the note.'

I paced around the room, telling him everything, starting with the incident in the park.

'This is so weird,' he mumbled. 'You're from the future and this isn't your home base, so that means I won't remember anything. Maybe this has happened lots of times . . . of course, I wouldn't know and neither would you, if it's your future self who jumps back to see me.' He spun around and looked at me, his eyes bugging out. 'I wonder how many times we've had this exact same conversation!'

'Focus, Adam! Crazy CIA dudes are waiting for me to come out of a locked bathroom two days from now!'

He shook his head like a swimmer emerging from a pool. 'Sorry. The message is just a code. One I made up years ago that no one will be able to decipher. I can teach it to you.'

I nodded slowly. 'That way, in my present, I can tell you what's going on without my father and his colleagues knowing.'

He grinned. 'Exactly. And Jackson, I've never told anyone about this. I've only written messages in my code twice. The first time was nearly two years from now, which hasn't happened yet . . . and the second one was a few weeks ago. I created the whole system in my head. They're not going to figure it out easily.'

'I think the real question is . . . can I figure it out, and quickly?'

He nodded. 'I think so.'

We dived into a major cram session. Adam was right.

His spy language wasn't *that* hard to decode with him there to explain it.

'OK, what now?' I returned to pacing. 'I don't know who I'm supposed to be more worried about – the CIA or the people they were trying to take down today. The red-headed dude from 2009 . . . he didn't seem to have good intentions then or today, and my dad and his team went after him, so does that make the CIA good?'

Adam wrinkled his nose. 'They *did* knock you out without your permission. Not exactly nice-guy behaviour.'

'Do you think they want to kill me?' I asked.

His momentary silence reflected the many arguments I had gone through in my mind, and his answer matched mine. 'They would have done it already. Of course, if you give them everything they need, then maybe—'

'What's my plan for when I go back? My dad already knows I'm from two years in the future. So that secret is probably out in the open.'

Adam shifted in his chair. 'OK . . . tell them you jumped once.' He paused. 'No, once is a dead giveaway that you're lying . . . Say it's been three times and the last time you ended up here and now you can't do it any more.'

I nodded in agreement. 'Which is sort of true. I can't go back to 2009.'

'Exactly, and since your dad knows something happened to 009 Holly, then he knows you're not just hanging out two years in the past for fun. That you're actually stuck.'

I was so relieved he said that because giving Dad that information had been an impulsive decision and I had been worried it wasn't the right one. 'Glad I did something right.'

'I think it should help,' Adam said. 'I've read tons of government documents . . . just for fun. The more truth to your answers, the better. CIA agents are incredibly well trained in identifying liars. Give them some real details and see if you can get Dr Melvin to accidentally slip again, like he did with the genetics thing, and help fill in some of the pieces we're missing.'

'I accidently let it slip that I'd seen Chief Marshall before,' I remembered.

'Yeah . . . but none of them know how or when. Don't tell them about *that* dive into the past. The one with the secret underground hospital wing. But if you're too secretive or guarded about everything, they'll know you're up to something.' He stared at me and lifted his eyebrows. 'I'm sure your dad and the other CIA people expect you to be scared about finding out you can time-travel, and the weird brain-activity thing. You played that up pretty well with your dad and the doctor the other day.'

I took a deep breath and nodded. 'This is going to be tough, fooling those guys.'

'Good luck.'

I didn't waste any more time in my little excursion. I jumped again, hoping I could pull off this act. Chief Marshall was a very intimidating guy.

chapter twenty-five

SATURDAY, 13 OCTOBER 2007, 2.07 A.M.

I leaned against the sink, turned on the water and splashed some on my face. I waited another couple of minutes before leaving the bathroom and returning to the living room.

'Are you OK?' Dad asked.

I sank into the couch. 'Yeah. False alarm.'

Chief Marshall spoke from the armchair he occupied across the room. 'You recognized me, earlier, in the car,' he prompted.

I glanced quickly at Dad and Melvin, leaning against the wall, before answering. Then, as quick as fingers snapping, an image popped into my head, like it had with Toby's lock. 'You were in a bathroom . . . at a restaurant and you handed me a paper towel, right?'

How did I remember that now and not when I jumped back to 1996?

'Correct. I was checking up on you after you disappeared from Spain. Is that the only time you've seen me?' His eyes beamed into mine like he could read my mind.

'Well . . . not exactly.' *Just make something up*. 'You were in my house once. In the future. I came home and you were sitting at the table with Dad. I remember thinking you looked familiar then, but I didn't say anything.'

'Jackson, when was the first time you time-travelled? Do you remember the date?' Melvin asked.

I turned my eyes back in his direction. This was an opportunity to tell the truth. '12 November 2008. I was eighteen. It just . . . happened in the middle of my French-poetry class. One minute I was falling asleep at my desk; the next I was standing outside my dorm. It took me a while to figure out what had happened.'

And that I wasn't completely insane.

Melvin shook his head. 'Amazing.'

'What's amazing about being stuck two years in the past?' I asked.

'Not that part, but these abilities of yours and you're not even—'

Dad elbowed him in the side. 'Let's not throw too much at him tonight.'

'How did you know what I can do? The time-travel part?' I asked Dad.

Melvin and Dad exchanged a long look, and then Melvin answered for him. 'You carry a rare gene. We refer to it as the Tempus gene. It's been known to produce certain symptoms or abilities.'

'What do you mean, "it's been known"? Like . . . there are others?'

Like the man in the park today? One of the last people I saw in 2009.

'Time jumpers have been traced throughout history, for centuries. But it's been kept a secret,' Marshall said.

They all waited for me to respond, probably thinking I was in shock. And believe me, I was, but mostly I needed time to plan my words carefully. 'So, that guy at the park and that woman . . . are they time-travellers too? Can they just do it whenever they want?'

'That depends on the individual,' Dr Melvin said. 'Based on the information we've been able to obtain, ability levels vary. What kind of control do you have over this skill?'

'I can't do it any more . . . it happened twice before this last jump . . . but those were very different.'

Dr Melvin straightened up and strolled over quickly, then sat on the coffee table in front of me. 'You said you're stuck two years in the past, right? But what about those other jumps? How did you keep from getting stuck during those?'

I explained the details of jumping up until the point where I got stranded here. I tried to put as much real detail as I could into the two jumps I told them about.

'Do you ever see yourself when you jump into the past?' Melvin asked. His face had this intense look I'd never seen before.

'Once. The second jump . . . I ran into myself at work . . .'

Somehow that one statement caused both Marshall and Dad to slip from their composed selves. Marshall came over and sat next to Melvin. Then Dad said, 'Could be a hallucination of seeing himself. The actual memory colliding with the dive into the past.'

'Maybe, but why don't I have another self here? The other me totally vanished from Spain.'

'He hasn't been making full jumps!' Melvin said suddenly. His face had the same look of greedy excitement that the man called Edwards had had in 1996. 'The irony is just incredible. Half-breed makes half-jumps and—'

'Melvin!' Dad said sharply.

'Half-breed?' I asked. 'Half-jumps?'

Dead silence. Then Dad and Melvin both started talking at once.

'Well . . . the gene isn't identical to the others,' Melvin stammered.

'Not identical?' OK, this was getting really weird.

'In documented history. Melvin knows a little–'

'Enough!' Marshall said before staring straight at me. 'Dr Melvin is an expert in this gene. Probably more knowledgeable than anyone in the world. The CIA has no choice but to closely monitor anyone carrying the Tempus gene. I think what we're dealing with is a simple matter of evolution. This is why you're different than other documented cases. Change over the course of time.'

Yeah, right. More missing pieces. Melvin's slip with the 'half-breed' comment, and then I remembered Dad's slip the other night when he stormed out of the office.

He's nothing like them.

Maybe he just meant I wouldn't use my abilities to destroy the world. But other people would? Everyone except me?

'Technically he did jump all the way once,' Melvin said, looking over my shoulder. 'He probably could—'

'Dr Melvin, I think Jackson's heard enough for today.' Dad stared at him and it was almost like his eyes were pleading with Melvin. 'He's just a kid. You heard him, he said he can't do it again.'

I hid my reaction to what Melvin had just said, like I didn't even get it. But I did. He was talking about what I had done when I left Holly.

A full jump. Changing my home base. That's why it was different. And saying I *could* do it again.

'So the CIA is watching all these other time-travelling people? And they're all bad? Like, destroy-the-world bad?'

'It's complicated,' Dad said. 'The ones we know of are all working against us. We call them EOTs.'

'EOTs?'

'Enemies of Time.'

So the bad guys had a nickname. 'What makes them so bad?'

'It's hard to explain in such a short time, but mostly it's a power struggle we deal with constantly,' Marshall said. 'Something an average citizen like yourself would have no knowledge of. Try to understand what might happen if past events were altered. Or if future events were revealed.'

They can go to the future? *They can alter things?*

'I think we've already established that I'm not an average citizen,' I said.

'And you're not a highly trained special agent for the CIA either,' Marshall snapped.

If Chief Marshall was trying to convince me that the CIA were the good guys, he totally sucked at it. 'Fine, if you're not going to tell me anything else about why I'm a crazy freak of nature, then I'm ready to go home.'

'There's not much else to tell,' Dad said, trying to use the good-cop tone with me. 'Maybe if we knew more about you, and if Dr Melvin could . . .'

It was just like Adam said. They would try to dig for as much information as they could get. This was one game I knew I could play well. I'd spent nearly a year time-travelling and covering it up. Making up stories. Of course, fooling 009 Holly was probably a little easier than fooling these dudes. But I had kept it from my dad in 2009 too.

'I'm done talking for tonight,' I said.

'Fine,' Marshall snapped.

Melvin handed me a tiny red pill and a glass of water. 'This will make you sleepy,' he said to me, like I was a child about to have a tooth pulled.

'What, no poisoned rag?' I asked bitterly.

'This location is only known to myself and Agent Meyer. Even Dr Melvin requests to be kept in the dark. For his own safety,' Marshall said.

Yeah, because he's an old, round doctor with a drawer full of lollipops. Not exactly someone who could strangle a man with his bare hands.

'Also, to anyone outside of this room, you are Jackson Meyer, a seventeen-year-old kid whose father is a CEO, understood?' Marshall said.

'Yeah, I get it.'

I stared down at the red capsule and reminded myself that if they wanted to kill me, they would have done it already, and probably would have used a more exciting method than swallowing a pill.

Thirty more seconds of this secret location was all I remembered. My mind faded into a state of black nothingness. And for the first time in weeks I truly wanted to be back in my old home base. 2009. My true present day. Pretending to be this other me, maybe forever, totally sucked.

chapter twenty-six

SATURDAY, 13 OCTOBER 2007, 9.00 A.M.

I woke up safe and sound in my own bed. The only damage I had left over from the night before was a pounding headache. After showering and getting dressed, I grabbed my journal and started writing every detail I could recall from the day before. I'd been slacking on writing for the past few weeks, but things were a little different now.

Apparently I'm a genetic freak of nature. Not just weird time-travelling genes, but one that has somehow evolved so my method of time travel is so weird it even freaked out Dr Melvin. Basically: half-jumps don't change anything; full-jumps either change the past or send you to this alternate universe in the past. Assuming Adam's theory is correct. Or the future? Assuming what Marshall and Dr Melvin said was true. Great.

If Dad and Melvin knew about my messed-up brain and genetics, then why didn't they just tell me what might happen so I could have been prepared? Is it possible Dad knew in 2009 and didn't say anything? The so called Enemies of Time knew in 2009 if they ended up in Holly's dorm room. And I find it very interesting that my father happens to work for people who fight evil time-travellers and he also happens to have adopted a child who is a time-traveller. Coincidence? Somehow I doubt it.

If I can get some more information out of Dr Melvin then maybe there's a way for me to get back to 2009 and actually change things.

I left my room and wandered towards the kitchen. Jenni Stewart was sitting on the couch in the living room, with a laptop and a pile of papers spread out all over the coffee table.

'Is this your new office?' I asked her.

She continued to stare at the computer screen. 'I've been assigned to keep an eye on you, make sure there were no damaging side effects to whatever they drugged you with last night.'

She was speaking with a heavy Southern accent today, something I hadn't noticed before. 'What's with the accent? Or is this the real you?'

'You have to know me very well to find out which is the real me,' she said. 'I specialize in undercover operations.'

That I believed. I'd seen her change gears so fast I could hardly keep up. 'So, my dad's not home?'

'He'll be back later, I think,' she said.

I plopped down beside her and leaned over to look at the computer screen. 'Is that something super secret you're working on?'

She rolled her eyes. 'It's a ten-page paper on disease in African countries. For Anthropology 108.'

'You're a college student?'

She shrugged. 'Sometimes. It's a cover I can do fairly well.'

'Probably not nearly as well as your bad-ass secretary role,' I said, and she cracked a smile. 'Do you have evil time-travellers in your anthropology class or something?'

That was my attempt at casually opening up the dialogue for me to ask questions. But her fingers froze over the keyboard and she leaned back against the couch before turning her eyes on me. 'I can't believe they told you about Tempest.'

'What's Tempest?'

Her face twisted with confusion. 'That's my division . . . of the CIA . . . your dad's too. We're sort of the bottom layer. People know about us, they've heard the name Tempest, but unless you're in this division, you don't know what we do. Not even the agents with the highest level of clearance.'

Maybe I wasn't supposed to tell her that I knew. Chief Marshall and Dad had had little choice but to tell me. Obviously I already knew about time travel. But how could I justify that to Jenni Stewart without telling her about me? 'Um . . . I saw one of them . . . the Enemies of Time or whatever . . . I saw one disappear.'

'Wow,' she said. 'I'm still surprised they didn't use memory-modification drugs or something. Security is beyond tight in this division.'

The questions were flooding in because Jenni Stewart

wasn't nearly as intimidating as Chief Marshall and I could actually concentrate on what I still needed to find out. 'The dude with the red hair that you kicked in the face . . . he vanished, didn't he?'

'Yeah. His name is Raymond and he's a pain in the ass.'

'What about the blonde chick that passed out? What did they do with her?' I asked.

Jenni shook her head. 'I don't know. I imagine they'd try to get more information out of her, for the list.'

'The list?'

'Marshall's list.' She grabbed a cushion and put it behind her back, before stretching out her legs across the couch. 'He drags information out of them about the future, like people the opposition might try to assassinate, so we can prevent it. It's mostly political figures or scientists. Sometimes it's just an event that we need to stop.'

'It's so crazy that people can time travel to the future?' I said, but the more I thought about it, the more vague the concept seemed. What exactly was the future? To me it was any date beyond 30 October 2009. But if one of the other time-travellers was born after me or before . . . just thinking about time that way made my head spin.

'Marshall and Dr Melvin think it's possible some of them can travel outside the span of their own lives, but of course—'

'You have no idea what years that involves,' I finished. Her explanation of calling it the span of their own lives was much easier to understand than *past, present, future*. 'If time-travellers have been around for centuries, like

Marshall said, maybe they came from way in the past.'

'It's hard to say. We just show up when we're told to,' she said. 'At least that's what I do, but then again, I'm new.'

'So that's what Tempest does . . . follow Marshall's list.' I sank further into the couch, deep in thought. 'But how do you fight off people who just pop in and out like that?'

She leaned forward a little and lowered her voice. 'I've read every bit of Dr Melvin's research. It's some crazy shit. But basically, time travel doesn't work how you think it works.'

I wasn't sure if she was going to provide me with new information or not. 'What do you mean? Do you think they change stuff all the time?'

'It's unlikely,' she said.

'Why?'

'Basically, before they jump for the first time–'

'The first time ever? How old are they?' I drilled.

'Melvin's data says most have jumped by seven or eight years old, but it's not controlled for a while, meaning they don't know what they're doing or where they're going. It differs, depending on the person. Some are better. Some are worse. Like anything else.'

Wow. Seven or eight. I couldn't even imagine being a freak for that long. And were there little time-travelling junior EOTs popping up in random places?

'Anyway,' Jenni continued, 'before that first jump, think about their life as one long, thick tree branch. When a jump happens, a piece of the branch splinters off and keeps growing in a different direction.'

'And they can stay on the new piece of the branch . . .

They can live there, right?' That's what I had done. *What I'm doing now.* My jump from 2009 to 2007 had caused my branch to split off and grow a new arm. The other jumps didn't seem to do anything.

'Yeah, that's right,' Jenni said. 'It's kinda like a parallel universe.'

Not this again. Adam still clung to this theory, and for some reason I hated it. It made the world seem less valuable. More lonely.

'Can they go back to another timeline once they've made a new one?' I asked.

'Some can,' she said. 'Most of the ones we run into can. But the one thing very few can do is jump forward or backwards within the same branch or timeline.'

'Which is why they can't mess with too much shit in our world,' I added. 'Except if they can just jump to another timeline and then jump right back to our world, couldn't stuff be changed?'

'We don't know for sure, but we think there're some kind of physical repercussions for excessive time jumps.'

Yep. There sure are. 'Really . . . I didn't know that.'

'Yep, and we don't think they *want* to make these other timelines, but when they try to jump along the same one, it just happens.'

'But why wouldn't they?' I said sarcastically. 'More choice. Like having a summer house in Aspen and a timeshare in Florida and an apartment in Manhattan.'

She smiled. 'Do you want to hear Melvin's craziest theory? I only know because I sort of . . . hacked into his computer.'

'OK.'

'He believes that if they keep making all these new stems off the same branch, they could eventually collide, which may cause the world to end . . . or it may just cause the EOT's brain to explode.'

'Wow . . . that's a lot more than I can handle right now,' I said, half joking, half serious.

'Yeah, I'm hoping for the brain-exploding option,' she said.

'So if they all have different levels of what they can do, there's really no way to predict or prepare?' I asked.

'Agent Training 101 – don't make assumptions about anyone. Same basic rules apply to evil time-travellers.'

'It's possible one of them could just jump by accident as a little kid or whatever and then get stuck in some other timeline?' I asked.

'Yep.'

I didn't ask any more questions. The last one was hard to swallow and I needed time to let it sink in. Maybe that's why 2009 still felt like home to me. Or maybe it was guilt that made me think about getting back. Guilt for leaving and guilt for any happiness I'd had in this timeline.

And I wanted to be face to face with those men in Holly's dorm. Find out who they were. I could picture the red-haired, shoe print guy – Raymond – perfectly, but the other one, the taller dude, I couldn't remember what he looked like.

'Having a nice chat?'

Jenni and I both looked over and saw Dad leaning against the mantel. He stared straight at her, his eyebrows lifted. She tossed the couch cushion back in place and returned to her computer.

'Can I speak with you privately, Agent Stewart?' Dad asked.

Her face was immediately stricken with fear. 'Yes, sir.'

I would almost have felt bad for her, if she hadn't been such a pain in the ass the first time we met. I stared at her neglected computer resting on the coffee table.

The temptation was too much to resist, but the second I hit a key to pull the last image on to the screen, she was right behind me, like some kind of ghost.

'I wouldn't touch that if I were you.'

I jerked my hand back from the keyboard. 'Sorry.'

She stood in front of me, arms crossed, game face on. 'How about we make a deal? You write a Spanish term paper for me, and I'll teach you to kick some ass like a real agent.'

'Did my dad put you up to this?' I asked, and she nodded. 'How many pages is this paper?'

'Ten.'

I guess Dad was willing to keep his promise to teach me some stuff. 'Single or double spaced?'

'Double,' she said with a grin.

'Deal.'

She sat down in front of the computer again. 'Your dad wants me to show you the step-by-step diagrams of silent defence.'

'Silent defence?' I scooted closer to get a better look at the screen. I hadn't realized, until the opportunity was presented to me, how badly I wanted to learn this. How much leverage I could have if I didn't need so many people helping me out, telling me which side to join.

'It means the most amount of force with the least amount of reaction. No sound, very little movement,' she said.

I watched carefully as she clicked through image after image of basic attack diagrams. 'Are we only going to look at pictures?'

She shrugged. 'I'm just following orders. Your dad seemed to think the diagrams would help. Personally I prefer a more hands-on method.'

I laughed. 'Maybe he didn't think I was ready for that.'

Or maybe he knew I'd remember this. Like Toby's combination. Isn't that what Melvin had asked me in his office the other day?

'What about a photographic memory? Can you recall pages from a book word for word or possibly directions or maps?'

I hated that Dad and Dr Melvin were able to get further inside my head than I was, but if I could use this photographic memory to stay alive, and to keep Holly safe, then I had no reason to complain about my recently acquired freakish ability.

'Honestly, I'm surprised he hasn't taught you at least the basics of self-defence, given his position and everything. I guess yesterday was a wake-up call. It's not like we couldn't have predicted someone would use you as a target. Leverage to get to your dad.'

Have I always been a target?

Was that why the EOTs were after me in Holly's room?

I laughed nervously. 'Definitely a wake-up call for me.

If they hadn't knocked me out, I doubt I would have slept at all last night.'

'Wimp,' she muttered. 'And what the hell were you planning on doing with that pocket knife?'

'I have no idea. Exactly why we should get started now.'

She nodded her agreement and returned to explaining every diagram, in depth. And I listened, as if it was life-or-death information. It *was* life or death.

'What you have to keep in mind is . . . it's not about strength,' Dad said, walking up behind us. 'Take Agent Stewart, for example. She topped everyone on the last trial run. She's light on her feet and has the ability to reduce her sound levels more than the others. Walking through a mission unheard is a huge advantage. And it helps that she never misses the exact point of attack. If you get that right, down to the centimetre, strength doesn't matter.'

Jenni Stewart looked absolutely elated by Dad's compliment, but tried to hide it. 'Take a second to look at the picture and then let's try it.'

I studied the man on the screen hitting the other man behind the knee and squeezing the throat at the same time. The attacker's weight falls on to your foot, making less sound, and the squeezing of the throat keeps them from yelling or even talking.

After shoving the coffee table aside, I did it perfectly on the second try. 'Junior's got a little secret agent in him after all.'

'This is just basic life skills,' Dad said to her. 'Things every teenager should know, right?'

'Sure,' she said.

'Why don't you try the same move with me instead,' Dad said to me.

I hesitated long enough to get a laugh from Jenni, which made me determined to succeed in attacking Dad. 'All right.'

I focused on his face, imagining Holly standing behind him, or Courtney, and then on the frustration of his keeping secrets from me, lying. Pretending. All of it made my temper flare and something just snapped into place. Seconds later he was sinking into the carpet, gasping for air.

'Not bad, Jackson. Not bad at all.' His expression showed that he was impressed, but I could see the hurt flicker in his eyes, just for a second.

I reached out a hand to help him up. 'Let's do it again.'

Dad nodded, and this next time he got me on the ground before I could react. We spent another hour, back and forth. He won, then I won, until we had gone through every single method of attack in the diagrams, several times each.

'What else do I get to learn?' I asked him.

Dad actually smiled a little. 'I can show you how to search for listening devices.'

'OK,' I said, following him into the kitchen.

'Don't forget about the party tonight,' Jenni called after us. 'Your girlfriend already confirmed she was coming.'

I stopped and turned around. 'Holly's coming over here, tonight?'

'That's the plan,' she said.

'I thought you were kidding about that,' I said to Dad.

He was digging in a kitchen drawer now. 'Seeing a few CIA agents mingling and having dinner like normal people will help alleviate any anxiety she might have. All we've done so far is expose her to a terrorist attack and then stuff her into a car and tell her not to tell anyone.'

'I'm surprised you didn't modify her memory or something,' I said bitterly as the memory of the poisoned rag being pressed to my face returned.

'I thought you wouldn't want that.'

'I don't,' I said, trying to make my feelings very clear.

Dad nodded. 'OK, and we'll leave Adam Silverman alone as long as he stays quiet.'

My stomach dropped. They knew about Adam. 'Um . . . he's completely harmless. Seriously, it's not his fault that I told him all this shit . . .'

Dad held up his hand. 'I just said we'll leave him alone. But it's possible he could be a good resource for you, if you want to learn some new skills. Just a thought.'

Yep, Adam could teach me all kinds of science-geek stuff. I just had to get a minute alone with him so he could hear the whole story from yesterday up until now.

Dad placed a small flashlight in my hand and opened the cabinet under the kitchen sink. 'The CIA has a million devices to help find bugs, but I like to start old school. Pretend you're stranded somewhere with nothing but the contents of the average man's pockets.'

'Yeah?'

He stuck his head under the sink and I did the same. 'Your recent plumbing and maintenance experience should come in handy. I once found an explosive inside a pipe at the Plaza, when I was assigned to search the President's room. Either one of the Secret Service agents planted it, or I caught something they missed.'

OK, my dad was officially much cooler than I'd ever imagined. Even if he was a big fat liar.

chapter twenty-seven

SATURDAY, 13 OCTOBER 2007, 6.00 P.M.

Not only did Holly actually show up for this staged party, she also brought Adam along.

'I really didn't expect you to come,' I whispered to her after taking her coat. 'I thought my dad scared you?'

She smiled but still looked fairly nervous. 'You can be scared and curious at the same time.'

'Don't I know it,' Adam muttered under his breath.

When I had had a few minutes this afternoon, I emailed Adam several scanned pages of handwritten code, explaining how I learned his highly secure method of communication. It took a while to give him the full update without screwing up his process and telling him something completely wrong. It's possible he was more scared than Holly was after hearing the details that I couldn't tell her.

'I can't believe you live here,' Holly said, glancing around the foyer. 'Do I get a tour?'

'Sure.' I took her hand and led her through the living room, where at least twenty people wandered around, drinking wine or cocktails. The only guests I recognized were Dr Melvin, Chief Marshall and Jenni Stewart. I had no idea where the other people came from.

'Dude, are these all agents?' Adam asked quietly so no one would hear.

I shrugged and continued to walk Holly through the house while Adam struck up a conversation with Dr Melvin.

I saved my room for last, not sure if she would be comfortable going in there. 'Do you want to see my room?' I asked tentatively.

'Oh yeah,' she said with a smile. 'I'm immensely curious to get a look at the room of a rich, delinquent teenager.'

I laughed and flung the door open. 'I already told you, I'm not a criminal.'

Just a guy who's already seen the future you naked. Nothing creepy about that at all.

'I know. I'm just teasing you.' She glanced around the room before turning to face me. 'Nothing too exciting in here.'

'Of course not. I keep all the psychopath stuff in a different room.' I picked up one of her hands and laced my fingers through hers. She blushed and took a step back from me. 'I was kidding.'

She smiled. 'I know, it's not that. It's just . . . something else.'

'What?'

'OK,' she said, diverting her eyes away from mine. 'Jana has this theory . . . She thinks second kisses are weirder than first kisses because . . . you're expecting them, but not really comfortable with the person yet.'

I tried not to laugh, but it didn't work. This was her problem? She gave me a little shove and I laughed even harder. 'Sorry, Hol. I just figured it was something bigger you were worried about. I'm glad it's an easy one.'

'Easy for you, maybe,' she said with a hint of amusement in her voice.

'I'll make it easy for you, Holly. I expect nothing. Do whatever you want to because *you* want to. No other reason.'

'You could just . . . kiss me now and get it over with?' she said quietly. Unsure.

I shrugged. 'Nope, sorry. Intimidation is not my style. Your move, partner,' I said, imitating Jenni Stewart's Southern drawl, which had turned into some kind of British accent this evening.

Holly's cheeks turned from pink to red and she pulled my hand towards the door. 'Let's go see what Adam is doing.'

'So you're not afraid to walk on a swing set ten feet above the ground, but you're scared to kiss me?' I teased.

The whole idea was amusing and made me realize how much of a journey she would take between now and 2009.

'Later,' she said with a smile.

'Like I said, only if you really want to.'

She turned her back to me and headed down the hall. 'I do.'

'When do you need to be home?' I asked Holly after the

last party guest had left. We were alone in the TV room. Adam had hit the champagne a little too hard, and Holly and I had carted him to my room and tossed him on to the bed.

Her cheeks turned a little pink. 'I kinda . . . told my mom I was staying at Jana's. I figured since Adam passed out here already . . .'

'So . . . you want to stay here tonight?' I asked, lifting one eyebrow.

'Sorry, I was just planning ahead. I can go home if you want.' She started to get up, but I pulled her back down next to me.

'Or . . . you can stay.'

'It's OK?' She rested her palm against my cheek. I only had a second to nod before she kissed me, leaning further forward, forcing me to lay back.

My mind went completely blank for a few minutes until I had to pause and take a breath. Holly was lying on top of me, her fingers in my hair, her lips on my neck, and my hand drifting under her dress. That's when I forced myself to remember that this was 007 Holly. Not the eighteen-year-old girl who was far too responsible to do anything on impulse. In other words, I could never talk her into something she wasn't one hundred per cent sure about. But 007 Holly . . . she might be a different story.

What I did next took way more effort than any of the defence techniques Dad had thrown at me today. I slid her over and stood up from the couch. 'I'm gonna get a drink. Do you want something?'

She sat up and wiggled her dress back down so it

was just above her knees. 'Water.'

Dad stood in the kitchen with the refrigerator wide open, surveying the contents. 'Having fun?'

I reached around him and grabbed two bottles of water. 'Yeah. Could you do me a favour?'

'What's that?'

I spat out the words reluctantly. 'Just find some excuse to walk in on us in about five minutes.'

Dad pulled out the carton of milk, then closed the fridge. 'Why?'

I groaned to myself. 'Because apparently I've turned into a morally decent person who feels guilty about going too far with a seventeen-year-old girl.'

He smiled a little. 'But she wasn't so young when you dated her in 2009?'

'Exactly. It's not the same as it was . . . before . . . in the future . . . however you want to look at it.' I started to walk away, then turned quickly. 'Maybe ten minutes, OK?'

He laughed. 'Sure.'

Holly was standing in front of the bookshelf, scanning the movie titles, when I returned. She tugged at the straps on her dress and shifted the top into place.

'Do you want something to change into?' I asked, looking for any excuse to leave the solitude of this room and cover a little more of her skin.

'I should have brought a bag. I was in such a hurry after work.' She took the water from my hand.

I nodded towards the door and Holly followed me down the hall. My hand hesitated on the knob before entering Courtney's room. Holly's steps were much slower than mine as I walked towards the closet. Dad still hadn't gotten rid of anything. The room was spotless – no dust, nothing. The cleaning lady came in here every day and vacuumed, shook out the lavender comforter on the bed, picked up the trinkets lying on the dresser and dusted them.

Holly ran her index finger along the surface of the white vanity. She was tentative, like she might break something, or maybe she felt the impact of staring at a room full of stuff that would never be touched again by its owner.

I walked into the closet and scanned the racks, took my time searching through Courtney's clothes. I spotted the pink and green tennis shoes she was wearing when I first talked to her during a jump, in 2004, after she turned me into a self-defence lesson.

When I finally emerged with a pair of sweatpants and a long-sleeved T-shirt, Holly was staring at a card lying on the vanity. There were at least two dozen Get Well cards still standing upright. I crept up behind her and glanced over her shoulder. The acid in my stomach churned the second I saw which card she was reading.

In December of 2008 Dad had finally mustered up the courage to let go of Courtney's things – something he had needed to do. I came home for winter break and the room was bare. Everything was gone and this card was the one item I was desperate to keep. Not just in the house, but here, in her room. I hadn't even thought to come looking for it in this year.

I stared at my own writing, feeling the grief consume me. Not because of the actual words, but because she never got to read them.

Courtney,
To my favourite sister who is way cooler than I've ever been willing to admit. In fact, I made a list of a few more secrets I've been keeping from you. Show this to anyone and I will pull out the naked-baby pictures and let them circulate through the school.

EVERYTHING I'VE NEVER TOLD MY SISTER
(well, maybe not everything)
By Jackson Meyer

1. You don't really smell bad.
2. I was the one who stuck gum in your hair last year, when you had to get six inches cut off just to get it out.
3. I lied about showing the picture of you with your headgear on to my friends. I only said I did because you told Dad about those movies under my bed (and no, they weren't mine and I never watched them).
4. I thought it was nice when you helped Miss Ramsey teach Spanish songs to those little kids at the hospital.
5. I HATE when guys talk about how 'hot' my sister is . . . but despite what I've told you, you're not ugly.
6. Even though I always make fun of it, I think it's kind of sweet that you cry at the end of 'Titanic' (Every. Single. Time.)
7. Occasionally I stay home on the weekends and tell you my friends are busy even if they're not because I'd rather hang out with my dorky sister.
8. I'm scared I'll be different if you're not here. I won't be as good.

9. Sometimes I can't fall asleep at night because I'm so afraid you'll be gone when I wake up. Like if I just keep moving, you will too.
10. I can't help thinking it should be me, and I can't help thinking . . . what if you've thought the same thing? What if Dad has too? Does everyone look at me and say, 'You got lucky' or, 'Your sister's the good one'?
11. My greatest fear is saying . . . I love you. Even if it's true. I'm scared to say it because it's so final. Like goodbye. But I'm not saying goodbye. Not ever.

Maybe you could just try and stay longer, for me. Because I don't know if I can be me without you.

Love always,
Jackson

I reached around Holly and picked up the card. She jumped like I had startled her, then wiped her eyes with the back of her hand. 'Sorry, I didn't mean to read—'

'It's OK.' I folded the card and held it between my fingers.

'What's going on?'

Both of us looked up at Dad, standing in the doorway. He smiled just a little. 'Holly, take whatever you want from here. I've been meaning to donate some of this stuff . . . I just haven't . . . gotten around to it.'

Holly's eyes moved from Dad to me. I set the clothes in her arms. 'I think these should fit.'

Her gaze locked with mine. 'I'm so sorry. I shouldn't have been looking . . .'

'Don't worry about it.' I leaned down and kissed the top of her head. She gave me one last fleeting look before taking off down the hall towards the bathroom.

I started to leave but Dad plucked the card gently from my hands, then opened it up to read. 'I used to look at this every night after you went to sleep,' he said.

'You did?'

He nodded. 'Do I manage to get rid of anything . . . in the future?'

This was one of the first personal questions he'd asked me about 2009. 'Yeah, you got rid of everything. Including this card.'

He smiled and handed it back to me. 'Well, now you can keep it.'

I flipped it over in my hands. 'I never gave it to her. I wanted to . . .'

Dad's hand rested on my shoulder. 'She knew. I know she did.'

But I wasn't nearly as sure as he was. I lifted my eyes to meet his. 'I've seen her, Dad. I wasn't going to tell you but . . .'

His face filled with both grief and fascination. 'When? I mean . . . what year?'

'A few different ones. I talked to her when she was fourteen, and then when she was twelve. She snuck out of school and we spent the day together.'

Shit! I had just contradicted the story I told Chief Marshall and Dad yesterday. The part where I had only jumped two times and only short ventures to the recent past. Basically, nowhere near the year 2003. I stared at

Dad waiting for his reaction. There was no way to take it back now.

His mouth hung open but he managed to close it, then speak, 'You talked to her? She knew about—'

OK, maybe I'd distracted him with the mention of Courtney. *Not likely.*

'I explained everything and she believed me. She freaked out at first but . . . then she just accepted it.'

Dad leaned his head back against the door frame and closed his eyes. 'I miss her so much.'

'I know.'

His eyes opened and he held his arm out to stop me from leaving. 'It's not true, Jackson . . . what you wrote. I don't wish it was you. I could never choose between the two of you. You know that, right?'

I patted him on the arm. 'I do now.'

As I walked down the hall back towards the TV room, I couldn't help thinking that I might have witnessed the greatest cover by any CIA agent . . . or maybe, just maybe, I had seen my dad truly emerge from the carefully composed agent shell for the first time in years.

Holly jumped when I opened the door. All I could see was her back as she stood in front of the shelf again, but I didn't miss the quick, discreet way she wiped her face with the sleeve of Courtney's shirt. I strode quickly across the room and turned her around to face me. 'Hol, I'm not upset with you. I swear.'

I touched her face with both hands and she closed her eyes and nodded. 'I know. It's just . . . that was . . . a really nice letter.'

I wiped her cheeks with my fingertips, remembering the effect her tears had on me in 2009 after our last big fight. I was so used to 009 Holly's rock-solid composure . . . Seeing 007 Holly fall apart like that – it felt like the world was out of whack.

'I wasn't trying to make you sad,' I said to Holly.

She held on to one of my hands and pulled me over to the couch, then stretched out next to me. She touched her mouth to mine and I closed my eyes and sighed. Her body pressed against mine, then she whispered, 'I don't mind hearing your secrets, even if they're sad.'

I dived into kissing her again, slipping my hand under the back of her shirt, hoping Dad remembered his promise to walk in on us before I got too lost in the moment. Before I forgot which Holly I was kissing.

Just as I was moving my mouth along the front of her neck, Dad stumbled into the room. 'Sorry, forgot you were in here.'

As predicted, Holly turned bright red and nodded when I asked if she wanted to watch a movie. She fell asleep with her feet across my lap about fifteen minutes into it. I covered her up with a blanket and left the room. The weight of tonight pressed against my chest and I knew sleep would be difficult without some help.

I headed straight for the bar. Just as I was pouring a glass of Crown Royal, Dad walked in.

I stashed the bottle under the counter, but I knew he'd seen. 'I was just . . .'

He nodded before I even finished. 'You can pour me one too.'

Silently I filled another glass. He sank down on to one of the stools and downed his generous portion in one gulp.

'Dad, can I ask you something?'

'Sure.'

I took a long drink of the whiskey, hoping it would give me some confidence. 'How did you end up with a kid like me? I mean, considering you happen to work for this secret squad that knows all about freaks of nature like myself.'

He set his glass down on top of a coaster. 'I figured you were going to ask that soon enough.'

'Was it just a coincidence?'

Dad shook his head. 'You and your sister were my assignment.'

'An assignment?' I asked.

'Yes. One that I volunteered for and was very happy to take on indefinitely.'

'So you never wanted to have children . . . like, you didn't plan for it?'

'No, not really, but I'm sure you can understand why. With my job, there isn't any room for a personal life.' He stood up and smiled. 'Unless it becomes your work . . . or *they* become your work.'

'What about Agent Edwards?' I called to him as he walked away. 'Wasn't he protecting us or something . . . ?'

Dad stopped but didn't turn around. 'How do you know Agent Edwards?'

The change in his tone pushed me to tell the truth. 'I saw him . . . in the past.'

'You've been that far back?'

In other words, he's not here any more.

'What happened to him?'

Dad took a couple of steps closer. 'He was murdered . . . Ten years ago.'

My stomach dropped. 'How?'

'By others . . . the EOTs.' He shook his head.

He walked away before I could ask any more questions. Had he already told me more than he was supposed to? Or had he slipped back into agent double-speak? There was no denying the fact that I wanted to trust my dad. So much so that I might be ignoring signs pointing in the other direction.

chapter twenty-eight

SUNDAY, 14 OCTOBER 2007, 5.00 A.M.

I woke up suddenly, without any trigger other than a bad feeling, or maybe I had been dreaming and didn't remember what it was about. The recliner nearly tipped over when I shot up, my eyes darting around the room. Holly was still curled up on the couch, right where I'd left her hours ago. I pulled the blanket over her shoulders and walked down the hall to my room.

Adam was passed out sideways across my bed, probably feeling the beginnings of a hangover after all the champagne he drank during the party. The second I closed my bedroom door and took a few steps down the hall, I heard voices coming from the kitchen.

'I don't see why we have any reason to push him.' Dad's voice.

I stepped as quietly as possible towards the kitchen. The hall-closet door had been left open and I slid into the crack of space behind it.

'He's lying to us. What reason would he have to lie if

he hasn't been recruited by the opposition?' That voice belonged to Chief Marshall. It was impossible not to recognize the deep authoritative tone. Had Dad told them about my slip-ups last night? When I mentioned visiting Courtney several times in time jumps, and seeing agent Edwards. Why wouldn't he tell Chief Marshall . . . he told him every other damn thing. 'We've spent years letting you play the father so he'd trust you, and for what? He didn't even trust you enough to come to you when he first discovered his abilities.'

My whole body was completely frozen, waiting to hear if it would get worse.

'He's from a different timeline,' Dad said. 'You can't hold me accountable for another timeline or future events.'

'We are *all* accountable for future events,' Marshall boomed.

'It's possible he's just scared.' Dr Melvin's voice. 'Suddenly, his world has gone from small and insignificant to something much greater.'

Why weren't they concerned I'd be listening in?

'Your job is to find the glitch and fix it, Melvin,' Marshall snapped. 'I will not have this agency wasting time analysing the poor boy's feelings. We could be using him by now.'

Using me? My stomach turned over and over.

'Wait a minute, Chief,' Dad interrupted. 'We never agreed on any specific missions.'

'That's because all we had to work with was a malfunctioning experiment that Dr Melvin spent half his life creating. Things are a little different now,' Marshall said.

Malfunctioning experiment? This was getting worse by the second.

'Just give him time. If you could have seen how quickly he responded to the planned stimulation . . .' Dad said. 'Today is out of the question.'

Today? I literally felt sick to my stomach trying to absorb everything they were saying. Then I just couldn't take it any more. My feet moved of their own accord, towards the kitchen. The three men were sitting around the table with mugs of coffee when I entered.

'What experiment?' I asked immediately.

They all stared at me and finally Dad spoke up. 'It's a confidential project we were discussing. Nothing you need to worry about.'

Seriously? Did they think I was five years old or just a complete idiot? 'Maybe you should take the grown-up talk somewhere else if you don't want me to listen.'

'What exactly did you hear?' Marshall asked.

My hands balled up into fists. 'All of it . . . and someone needs to explain this experiment. *Now.*'

Dr Melvin jumped up from his chair and walked over to me, staring at my eyes like I had a concussion or something. 'Do you understand what I'm saying?'

I glanced over his shoulder at Dad and Marshall. 'Is he OK?'

'He's fine, but he's a little surprised that you were able to eavesdrop on our conversation, given the fact that we were all speaking Farsi,' Marshall said.

'What?' I asked, backing away from Melvin. 'Farsi?'

'It worked in one night! This is incredible,' Dr Melvin said.

Marshall lifted his eyebrows in Dad's direction. 'Finally. Millions of dollars spent on Axelle and we might actually be able to benefit from it.'

Axelle?

This time I heard the difference in sound. He wasn't speaking English. My palms were sweaty and I had to wipe them off on the dress pants I still had on from last night. 'What the hell did you guys do to me? Some kind of weird brain-frying electromagnetic shit?'

Dr Melvin rummaged through a drawer and pulled out a pair of tweezers. He came closer to me, pointing them right at my eye. 'Hold still for one second.'

I froze in my spot and he stuck the tweezers into my ear and pulled out a tiny piece of metal. I stared at it like he had just removed a cockroach from my ear. I felt dirty. Tainted.

'It plays sound in your ear while you sleep. I programmed it to play foreign language lessons. Nothing but audio copying,' Dr Melvin said in the calm voice I knew so well from years of childhood memories with this man. 'This is just like the picture diagrams you looked at yesterday . . . the photographic memory . . . only it's auditory.'

'But . . . how can I understand a language I haven't been taught? I can't say anything in Farsi. It didn't even sound different until you told me it was.' I ran my fingers through my hair, trying to focus on getting information. Absorb now, process later. *Panic later.*

'You can't speak the language because speech is a motor

skill. You have to practise forming words just like you practise throwing a baseball, or riding a bike,' Melvin said.

'It just means you can absorb the information, like a sponge. You can't learn things you haven't been taught. You have above average intelligence, but not a genius IQ or even close,' Dad added. 'There's a difference.'

'That's a relief,' I muttered. 'So, is that the experiment – Axelle or whatever you called it? You just play stuff in my ear?'

Melvin glanced at Dad, who was staring at Marshall, who looked at his watch before saying, 'We don't have time for this. Let's watch and see if he worms his way out of this situation.'

'Who? Me?' I asked. 'What situation?'

Dad jumped up from his chair. 'I heard something coming from down the hall.'

I took off running before any of them had a chance to move, but I heard several feet pounding behind me. Holly came stumbling out of the TV room, rubbing her eyes. She stopped when she saw all of us. 'Oh . . . I was just going to see where you went,' she said to me.

Something about her expression didn't look right. She felt around with her hand until it landed on the wall in front of her, then she rested her forehead against it. I put my hands on her shoulders. 'Holly, are you all right?'

'Huh?' she mumbled.

'It's the drugs,' Melvin said.

'What drugs?' I demanded, tying to turn around, but Holly tilted sideways and I had to hold her in place.

'This is just protocol for her protection,' Marshall said.

'I don't care if it's protocol!' I glared right at Dad. 'I can't believe you let them do this.'

I scooped Holly up off the ground. Her eyes were barely open and she was still feeling around with her hands. Her fingertips brushed over my face and eventually stayed pressed against my cheek.

I turned my back on them and walked towards the couch with Holly.

'She's the next name, Jackson,' Dad said so quietly I barely heard. 'The next name on Marshall's list.'

I felt as if the wind had been knocked out of me. Slowly I turned around. 'Someone wants to hurt her? Why Holly?'

'We just found out . . . That's what we were discussing when you walked in,' Dad said.

Marshall spoke up. 'The girl is just a device to get to you. One device. I'm sure there will be other methods. My theory is that you set them off in 2009. One of your time jumps revealed your abilities. Before that, we had them convinced that you had turned out completely insignificant . . . normal.'

My legs turned to Jell-O and I stumbled towards the couch to set Holly down before I dropped her. She mumbled something and then curled up with her face against the cushions.

I sank down on to the floor beside Holly's head. *It was my fault.* Getting stuck. Everything that had happened to Holly. Not Karma, but an actual, concrete reason. If I hadn't kept doing those stupid experiments with Adam, if I had told someone . . . I could barely speak but I forced out a few words. 'Why did they ask me to come with them . . . if any government people had approached me . . . ?'

I stopped talking and stared at Marshall, still calm yet nodding like he knew I had just answered my own question.

'They want me on *their* side,' I croaked. 'The Enemies of Time.'

Dad spoke up next. 'Yes, but we're not going to let anything happen to you, Jackson . . . or Holly. Now that we know what's going on.'

Melvin's eyes got really big all of a sudden and Dad and Marshall both whipped out guns and pointed them behind the couch. I jumped up from the floor and came face to face with a woman. The first thing I noticed was her hair.

Flaming red . . . just like Courtney's. She was like a middle-aged version of my sister. For a second I lost hold of my surroundings, the danger, and nearly said Courtney's name aloud. Could she be time-travelling, too?

Then I had to remind myself that Courtney had never reached her fifteenth birthday.

I shook the thought from my head and saw the man to her right. Shoe-print guy. And a tall dark-haired man stood on the woman's other side.

None of them had weapons out like Dad and Marshall.

'We didn't come for a fight,' the woman said, holding up her hands. 'Just a message from Thomas.'

Dr Melvin tugged on the back of my shirt, pulling me closer to him and further from the five people facing off. Marshall and Dad both walked around the couch, forcing the three intruders to the far side of the room.

'You have five seconds, Cassidy,' Marshall said.

Cassidy. I tried to etch the name and her face into my head so I wouldn't forget.

'We're here to take the boy back to where he came from,' shoe-print guy said.

'That's not happening,' Dad answered.

'He's drifted from his main path, and Thomas believes this could be detrimental to all of us,' Cassidy said.

Who the hell was Thomas? CEO of the Enemies of Time?

For the first time ever I watched Marshall's face falter a little. Fear. He believed them. The theory Jenni Stewart had told me about timelines merging and the world ending or brains exploding came swimming back into my head. Somehow I doubted Marshall was too worried about my brain rupturing. But the other option sent my heart into a full-out sprint.

And could they really take me back there? To 2009? Without thinking about what the hell I was doing, I pointed right at the shoe print guy. 'What were you doing there . . . in Holly's room? Why did you . . . ? I mean, why did that other guy . . .'

I couldn't say what had happened to Holly out loud. The shoe-print dude nodded from across the room. 'All of us were under the impression that you were a threat. We realize now that her death was a mistake. That you were unaware of our existence.'

The room had become so silent I heard Dad's finger move over the trigger.

'Agent Meyer, you will work under my orders only,'

Marshall said quietly but firmly.

Shoe-print guy kept his eyes on me and very slowly pulled something from his pocket. I walked closer to him as I stared at the image of Holly and me, in our swimsuits, sitting by the camp pool.

Me and 009 Holly.

'Where did you get that?' I demanded.

'I took it myself,' he said. 'I thought you might need a reminder. This is where you belong.'

It scared me that he wanted the same thing I did. Like I was already on their side. But honestly I wasn't sure I wanted to be on either side. Maybe it wasn't good and evil, but a whole bunch of grey area. Like gangs fighting gangs.

'But—' I started to say before the man interrupted me.

'Don't believe everything you hear about us. We're not so bad. I thought maybe you would come looking on your own, but I guess Dr Melvin's little Frankenstein only knows what he's been programmed to think.'

I stepped closer and lunged for the photo in his hand. For some reason I hated that he had it. He blocked my attack so quickly I didn't even see it coming.

'They don't want you to know how to jump for real. That would make you a threat. I can show you how to leave any time you want. I can tell you when and where you can be with her, safely – both of you.' He stuck the picture of Holly right under my nose.

He was probably just as capable, if not more capable, than Dad and Marshall of killing someone fast and easy. But he wasn't doing anything like that. Just making an offer.

'I believe I have a say in his well being, given the circumstances,' Cassidy said, turning her eyes on Dad. 'Much more than you ever will.'

Dad's face twisted with anger, but the dark-haired man who hadn't spoken a word dived forward and wrestled the gun from Dad's hand before getting him to the ground. I immediately jumped over the back of the couch and landed on Holly, covering her completely. I lifted my head for a second and watched Cassidy and the shoe-print dude vanish.

I couldn't breathe or think for several seconds, realizing what they had just done. Marshall fired his gun into the empty space they had left behind but the bullet just tore into the wall. I pressed myself further over Holly and heard another gunshot, followed by a man's loud cry of pain.

'Damn it!' Marshall shouted.

I slid off Holly, not sure if I could even stand. The sound of the gun was all too familiar. Dr Melvin pulled himself slowly off the floor, and Dad stood over the dark-haired man with a gun pointed at his chest. The mysterious man had been shot in the leg. Blood seeped through his pants and all the colour had drained from his face as he moaned in agony.

The thought running through my head was: *Why isn't he jumping?* Then I remembered that time in 1996. I had been too scared to focus on getting the hell out. I assumed the pain was clouding his ability to concentrate.

My stomach turned over and over as I got closer to the man and his bloody leg. Marshall looked up at us and nodded. 'Agent Meyer, would you please question the witness?'

Dad kicked the man in the stomach, forcing him on to his back.

I just stood there, my arms hanging lifeless at my sides.

Dad leaned over the man and shouted, 'What year did you come from?'

No response.

'What's your name?' he asked.

'His name is Harold,' Marshall answered. 'One of Dr Ludwig's spawn.'

Who the hell is Dr Ludwig?

'OK, Harold, what timeline did you travel from? Give us one main event.'

The man laughed this dark, insane cackle. 'You're all dead. Every one of you. But I'm not going to tell you when.' He lifted his head and looked at me. 'Except you, Jackson, you're not dead. Think about that. Don't listen to them.'

My whole body froze. *What did he mean?*

Marshall let out an exasperated sigh. 'He's useless. I'm done with him. Agent Meyer?'

Dad raised his gun and fired two shots right into the man's chest. I threw my arm over my face as blood spattered on all of us. My survival skills kicked in again when I saw his chest still moving. I dropped to the ground beside the man.

This guy didn't even have a weapon. He didn't do anything wrong except try to take Dad's gun. Maybe to keep Dad from shooting someone. Now he was dying. Right in front of us.

I yanked off my sweatshirt and pressed it to the front of his shirt. My fingers went straight for his jugular and felt his faint pulse. 'Dr Melvin! Help me. He's still breathing!'

Dr Melvin didn't move any closer. 'I'm not sure we should—'

'What's wrong with you? You're a doctor. He's not dead.' I pressed more firmly on the sweatshirt, which was already soaked with blood. The whole scene brought back images of Holly in 2009.

'Jackson,' Dad said, 'back off . . . *now*.'

I couldn't look at him. How could he do this? Like it was no big deal. He grabbed my arm and I yanked it away. 'Don't touch me!'

Seconds later Marshall was forcing me up against the wall. He towered over me, his dark face twisted with rage. 'I was trying to give you a chance to prove to your father what you and I both know you can do. Only you could have kept them here – or gone after them. Not only did I not get to prove my point, we've also missed a chance to kill two very important enemies.'

I saw Dad say something to Marshall, but I couldn't process it. The blood pumping in my ears drowned him out. The computer images flashed through my mind and in three quick motions, I had Marshall flat on his back, right next to the dying man. 'Tell me about Axelle!'

Marshall sprang up from the floor and in one swift motion had his hands closed around my throat. 'Perhaps if I threaten your life, you'll prove you're lying about what you can . . . and can't . . . do.'

From the corner of my eye I saw Dad moving behind Marshall. I couldn't look at him, only at Holly lying on the couch, helpless, and then at Marshall again. His calm, calculated face just inches from mine, his fingers constricting the air from my lungs. I fought to get out of his hold, but it was no use. My gaze locked with Dr Melvin's. The man with all the answers, the brains behind this mysterious Axelle project, and probably the only one in this room who couldn't kick my ass. If I could just get him alone . . .

A plan formed immediately. If I could finally do it. A full jump back to 2009, the same timeline I'd left. I'd keep Holly from getting hurt. Get all the information I needed about this supposed experiment from an unsuspecting Dr Melvin.

I wasn't going to be used as some kind of weapon. That much I knew for sure. But when I attempted to jump, the shouting coming from Dad and Melvin distracted me and I felt myself pulling apart. A half-jump. And what if Marshall continued to strangle me while I stood there like a vegetable in home base?

Too late now.

chapter twenty-nine

I shook out my arms and legs, feeling the relief of being free from Marshall's grip, before taking in my surroundings. My apartment. Home. I had magically appeared exactly where I left, but it looked different. The living-room furniture had completely changed. Not only was this not a full jump, it wasn't 2009. The reality hit me hard. And at this very moment 007 Holly was passed out in a room full of people I didn't trust, and I was standing there like a vegetable, probably about to get strangled or shot . . . But time would move slower there and if I could just form a plan before I jumped back . . . *Something better than another failed attempt to reach 2009.*

I glanced at the time on the cable box: 7.05

No light streamed in from the window behind the couch. *Evening*. But what day? *What year?* The sound of feet shuffling against the wood floor came from down the hall. I pressed my back against the wall and poked my head around the corner. It was me. A younger me, walking towards Courtney's room.

The second my eyes dropped to the younger me's hand I knew exactly what day it was. My heart thudded and nausea swept over me. I had avoided this date in every time jump. And when I first arrived in 2007 and attempted the failed jumps to 2009, I always had this overwhelming sense of dread that'd I'd eventually end up here. Now.

The younger Jackson entered the bedroom and I crept closer to the door. This was me at fourteen.

On the day my sister died.

I could see halfway into the room, enough to watch the younger me take the card and set it upright on her dresser. I didn't really need to watch; the memory hadn't faded, even after all these years, and I knew exactly what he was going to do next.

Actually I had forgotten some of it until I met 009 Holly. A conversation that I once had with her took over my thoughts.

'It's like you don't have normal family things to talk about, like the crazy drunk aunt you have to put up with or what salad to bring to the next family reunion,' Holly had said, teasing me.

I laughed. 'Just because I'm not middle class like you doesn't mean I don't have normal family issues money can't solve.'

Holly smirked at me. 'Fine. Give me one Average Joe family secret that you couldn't buy your way out of and I promise I'll never bring it up again.'

I dug for the perfect true story to prove her wrong. 'OK, I've got one . . . Courtney was petrified of thunderstorms. The second she saw lightning, she'd race down the hall and drag me out of bed. She made me sleep on the floor in her room.'

'And you went along with it?' Holly asked.

I shrugged. 'It was the only way to get her to shut up.'

'Such a typical brother thing to say. Sorry I doubted you.'

The day that Courtney died, this day, I just had a feeling that it was happening. Like something inside me was fading. And without thinking about it, I had walked right into her room and lain down on the floor. I remember pressing my face into the carpet and breathing in the scent and realizing that she'd never ask me to stay with her again. Never wake me up at two in the morning to leave my comfortable bed and sleep on her hard, cold floor. And I think I might have decided, at fourteen, that I never wanted to end up alone with my face in someone else's carpet again.

I patted my left front pocket. My own copy of that card was folded into a small part of my wallet. Two copies and still neither reached the owner.

My heart nearly leaped out of my throat when the Beatles song came blaring out of the younger me's phone. He jumped too, then sighed after looking at the number. He turned it off and tossed it into the hallway, and then kicked the door shut.

It was Dad calling, and Courtney's room was the very last place he would have looked for me. I had wanted to hide from him. Hide from everyone.

I leaned against the wall, squeezing my eyes shut and fighting the urge to jump back. It wasn't a coincidence that I ended up here, and this was my chance to do it right, even if it didn't matter. If it didn't change the future.

Luckily the doormen ignored me as I wandered out and grabbed a cab to the hospital. On the ride there I pulled out a tiny newspaper clipping, crumpled and yellow from five years of being stuffed away. There was one piece of information I couldn't remember.

IN MEMORY OF COURTNEY LYNN MEYER

Courtney Meyer, 14, of Manhattan passed away 15 April 2005, at 10.05 p.m., after a three-month battle with cancer.

10.05. Less than three hours away. I still remembered the floor and room number. I had come to visit her plenty of times, but it was mostly in the beginning. I didn't know how she'd react, seeing me five years older, or if she was even coherent.

I crept past the nurses' station when they weren't looking, but the sound of my dad's voice stopped me. I hid behind a large trash bin and watched his feet stomp towards me, his phone pressed to his ear.

'Jackson, where the hell are you?!' He stopped right in front of the trash can and I held my breath. 'I'm sorry . . . I didn't mean to shout . . . just please call me, so I know you're OK.'

I watched him take off running out the doors of the ward and realized for the first time, that he might not have been there at the end either. She was alone. I stood up and slipped into Courtney's room, unnoticed by any hospital staff. It was the largest patient room in the hospital and the entire place was covered with flowers, cards, and gifts. I closed the door behind me and already I felt the urge to run. Knowing what was coming, the weight was so heavy, like a truck sitting on my chest.

Courtney was lying on her side, curled up and so pale. If it wasn't for the red hair, she'd have just blended in with the sterile white sheets. The monitor above her head ticked like a clock, counting the minutes.

Somehow I managed to put one foot in front of the other and made it to the chair next to her bed. The one I'm certain my father had just abandoned to go find me. Her eyes peeled open and then squinted as if trying to focus on my face. 'Jackson?'

All I could do was nod and force back the tears.

'You look so different . . . must be the morphine,' she said.

Just hearing her voice, seeing that little bit of life still clinging to her body, it was too much. I started to get up, but she slipped her cold fingers under mine. 'Please don't go. I haven't seen you in forever.'

I scooted my chair closer and squeezed her hand. 'I won't.'

She smiled and her eyes fluttered but she forced them open. 'I hate this place too. No wonder you never want to come.'

That's when I lost it. I leaned forward and pressed my forehead against the cold white sheet and watched the tears drop from the end of my nose on to the bed. 'I'm sorry, Courtney. I'm so sorry.'

Her cold fingers moved through my hair, rubbing my head.

'No, that's not what I meant.' She patted the empty space next to her. 'Come up here with me. I'm freezing.'

I wiped my eyes on the sleeve of my sweater and rested

my head on her pillow. Courtney scooted closer and my heart pounded. This was almost like seeing a ghost.

She lifted my hand and rested it against her cheek. 'You're so warm . . . and you're scared to be here, aren't you?'

I stared into her green eyes, still bright as ever. 'Yes, but I won't leave. I promise.'

'Close your eyes,' she whispered. 'It helps me when I want to be somewhere else. Now tell me something great, but no hospital or sick-people or medicine stuff.'

I closed my eyes and forced my voice to come out even and told her the same thing I'd told her in 2004. 'I have a girlfriend now.'

'No way!' she said, only a faint whisper. 'Who?'

'She's from a different school.' I moved my hand to her back and rubbed it gently.

'How did you meet her?'

'It's a great story. Do you want to hear it?'

'Yes, please.'

'You know the big doors in the front of the YMCA? With the steps leading up to it?' I asked.

She nodded.

'Well, I was walking up the steps almost to the big doors when this girl comes barrelling into me. Apparently she was reading a book while walking—'

'What book?'

I brushed the hair from her face and smiled. 'I knew you'd ask that. It was some John Grisham book. Anyway, she knocks right into me and her giant pink smoothie falls on top of my shoes. So we're sliding around in frozen strawberries and the first thing I notice are her pale blue eyes.'

Courtney laughed lightly. 'So romantic . . . but I don't believe you looked at her eyes first.'

'No lie. I totally did. Then I reached for her book to save it from the smoothie flood and saw she had written her name on the inside cover: Holly Flynn, with a big curly loop in front of the H. Of course I thought it was really cute, but I couldn't tell her that. I mean, who actually writes their name inside a book?'

'I do,' Courtney whispered. 'So, then what happened?'

'Well . . . I handed her the book and she smiled at me. And all I could think was how much I wanted to kiss her. Just to see what it felt like. Somehow I knew it would be different with Holly. Everything would be different.'

'My brother's in love . . . never thought I'd hear that,' she mumbled with a smile.

I touched my lips to her forehead. 'You're so cold.'

'Jackson, promise me something, OK?'

'Anything.'

'Marry the girl with the smoothie and have lots of kids. At least six. And you can name one Courtney and another one Lily. I've always loved that name.'

'I know. You named, like, five of your dolls Lily. But I'm only nineteen, a little too young to get married . . .'

Her eyes flew open and I could see her brain reeling with theories, and then panic flooding in. She gasped before saying, 'You're not really Jackson, are you?'

I pulled her closer, wrapping both arms around her. 'Shh, it's OK. It's really me, just older.'

'But we never meet here. I usually go to see you.'

'Yeah . . . I know,' I said, even though she wasn't making any sense. I hated that she was so calm after what I just accidently told her. No punching me or screaming in the middle of coffee shops. It meant they were giving her a lot of morphine and she was dangling by a thread.

She yawned and relaxed her muscles again. 'I'm so . . . tired.'

I glanced up at the clock on the wall. It was only 8.45. Watching her eyes close again, knowing she would drift off soon, sent *me* into a panic. Even though I knew what was coming. I mean, I'd already seen my sister lying in a casket . . . but still, I wanted to stop it. Or at least delay it. Give her a little more time.

'Courtney! Stay awake . . . please. Please.' I shook her shoulders lightly, then pressed my forehead against her hair. 'Just a little longer.'

She touched her hand to my face and wiped the tears off my cheeks. 'You have hair on your face . . . it's prickly.'

I laughed. 'I love you. You know that, right?'

'I love you too.' Her hand slid to my neck, like she didn't have the strength to hold it up. 'You still haven't promised me . . . marry the smoothie girl, have six kids and maybe a dog.'

'I promise,' I whispered right in her ear, so I knew she'd hear. Her face broke into a huge grin. 'What should our wedding song be?'

'Hmm . . .'

'I know what you'd pick,' I teased before singing her

favourite song, '"I see the bad moon arising / I see trouble on the way . . .".'

'Yep,' she said. 'Not really a wedding song though . . .'

I could already feel the shallowness of her breath. I wanted to be brave. To keep talking and hold it together for Courtney, but I couldn't. She was headed somewhere far away from me and I felt more alone than ever.

I wiped my nose with my sleeve and lifted her chin to make sure her eyes were still open. 'Courtney, does it hurt? Anywhere?'

'I'm OK.'

She was lying. I could see it written all over her face. 'Courtney, tell me the truth.'

Her eyes filled with tears and she finally nodded. 'Yes . . . It hurts . . . everywhere . . . and trying to stay . . . that hurts the most. Like holding on to the edge of a cliff and my fingers keep slipping.'

That's why she'd hung on for two more hours the first time. She was waiting for us. For someone. I squeezed her tighter and felt the tears falling twice as fast. 'I'm sorry. It should be me. It should be me.'

'No, Jackson. Don't say that, ever.' Her voice came out with more life than it had all night.

I drew in a deep shaky breath and forced myself to stop crying. 'It's OK, Courtney. You can sleep now. It's OK. No more pain.'

'Thank you,' she whispered.

And I could almost see it, a clear picture in my mind: her knuckles white, fingers gripping around a rock, and then the instant relief of letting go. Free falling, feeling nothing but air, no weight. No pain.

I combed my fingers through her hair and watched with silent tears until her breath came in short spurts and then it just . . . stopped.

The beeps turned to one long beep. Several pairs of feet pounded against the tile floor of the hallway. I whispered one last goodbye and closed my eyes, thinking of nothing but Holly, lying on her doom-room floor, bleeding and alone. That's where I needed to be.

I heard Dr Melvin's voice just before I jumped as he uttered a loud but confused, 'Jackson?!'

I didn't even open my eyes when I tagged up in 2007. I felt myself being pulled back together. Chief Marshall's hands had dropped from my throat. Nothing but air surrounded me, but I was sure they were all still close by, ready to make a move. I heard my dad's voice just before I attempted the full jump back to 30 October 2009 again. *Please let it work this time.*

chapter thirty

Icy water splashed over my face. I coughed and sputtered, tasting chlorine. The air was thick and humid and dissolved the chill I had gotten from the hospital.

And that jump. It felt like nothing. No pulling-apart sensation. A full jump. I finally did it again. But to where? And it totally felt too hot to be 30 October.

'Maybe he's drunk,' a voice said.

'No, it's swine flu, I know it is,' another voice said.

I opened one eye and was nearly blinded by the sun. Then the six or so pairs of little eyes leaned closer.

'Why are you dressed for winter?'

I shot up and all the kids jumped backwards. 'Oh no,' I groaned.

'Jackson? Are you OK?' a little girl asked.

I stood up from my chair and nearly walked backwards right into the pool. 'Um . . . what year is it?'

All the kids giggled and then one spoke up. '2009. Yup, he's drunk.'

2009. I did it. I actually made it back here. Well . . . at

least I hoped it was the same timeline I left.

'Hunter, nobody's drunk,' a familiar voice said from behind me.

I spun around and came face to face with Holly. I clutched her shoulders. 'What year is it?'

Her forehead wrinkled as she looked me up and down. 'What are you wearing? When did you change clothes?'

'I don't know,' I answered slowly.

I was still wearing the thick sweater and dress pants I had worn for my dad's fake party in 2007. I could already feel the sweat running down my back. The temperature had to be at least ninety degrees. Adam walked up behind Holly and his eyes were huge. 'Uh-oh.'

'Adam, thank God! What year is it? How long have you known me?'

Holly laughed, but there was a hint of nervousness. 'Is he OK?'

'Um . . . must be the heat.' He grabbed my arm. 'Let's get you in the shade. And it's thirteen August 2009. You've known me since . . . March.'

OK, it's the right timeline. He doesn't remember meeting me in 2007. I got the year right too. Just not the month . . . or the day . . . but if this worked like it did when I jumped to 2007, the slightly younger me should have disappeared. Which meant that I might have time to fix things. Or more importantly, *to prevent things.*

I followed him away from the pool and under the protection of a tree. I fell on to the grass and laid down, looking up at the swaying branches. Holly knelt down beside me and pressed her hand to my forehead. 'Do you need water?'

I grabbed the front of Adam's shirt. 'I don't know if I'm really here in . . . you know . . . home base.'

I heard his breath catch. 'You mean it can change?'

'Oh yeah.'

'We should get some help,' Holly said, panic filling her voice.

'No! It's just these . . . vitamins I made with herbs from the greenhouse. Jackson offered to test them out. I think he's having hallucinations.'

'Lots of them. Like weeks' worth of hallucinations,' I said.

'Damn,' Adam mumbled under his breath.

Holly shoved him, hard. 'Are you crazy?! You can't just make stuff and give it to people. What if you poisoned him?'

Adam pulled me up so I was standing. 'He'll probably be fine. It's all natural ingredients. Maybe we should go to the hospital just in case.'

He was pulling me further from Holly and I couldn't stand the thought of having her out of my sight. 'Wait! I just need—'

'You need to come with me, now!' Adam said.

I pushed him out of the way and dropped down in front of Holly, who was still sitting in the grass. I wrapped my arms around her and squeezed tight. 'I missed you so much.'

'Seriously, Adam, what did you give him? He's really messed up.'

I released her and held her face with both hands then touched my lips to hers. 'I'm so sorry I left.'

She gently prised my hands from her face and stood, glancing at Adam. 'I'm going to round up the kids. Help him, OK? Use Mr Wellborn's car.'

I flopped back on to the grass and closed my eyes. A minute later Adam shook my shoulders. 'She's gone.'

'I had no idea you were so puny at sixteen.' I shot up like the building was on fire. My plan . . . Dr Melvin's experiment. 'We've got to do something . . . go somewhere.'

Right now, in this timeline, no one in the CIA knew about time-travelling Jackson. They were completely unsuspecting and I had to act fast, before that changed.

I quickly filled Adam in on Marshall's mention of the experiment, which I thought would fascinate him, but he couldn't get past the CIA stuff and being stuck in 2007 to ask the most important questions.

'I can't believe your other self just disappeared in 2007. That's so freaky! Never in any of my time-travel research did I expect to hear that,' he said.

'The weirdest part is that they totally freaked when I told them about seeing my other self . . . in the half-jump or whatever. It was like they'd never heard of that, and Dr Melvin's supposed to be some kind of expert on this messed-up gene or whatever.'

Adam shook his head in disbelief and then let out a huge breath like he'd been holding it in for the last few minutes.

'We should go,' I reminded him.

'I've got extra shorts and a T-shirt you can change into. You'll die of heatstroke in those clothes,' Adam said, already heading in the direction of the camp office.

'Wait!' I said. 'Where was the other me . . . before I ended up here? We should make sure he's *really* gone . . . what if going forward or sideways or whatever is different? I can't have two of me running around.'

Adam stopped and turned around to face me. 'You were by the pool watching your group during swim lessons.'

Just to be sure, Adam radioed every single counsellor in the camp to see if they'd seen the other me, the one that was actually dressed for work . . . and for August weather. We couldn't take a chance not knowing for sure, but I had never left my group of kids alone during swim lessons, and my other self's bag with wallet was abandoned by the pool. Something else I wouldn't have done.

After we convinced the camp director my condition required medical attention, but not in the form of an ambulance, and we were on the road headed to Dr Melvin's office in the hospital, I finally explained things in more detail.

He took my story with a lot less shock than most people would, but that's totally Adam.

'So, here's what I'm thinking,' I said as my plan formed in more detail. 'Since we know Dr Melvin did some kind of wacky experiment that involves me, and let's say the data is stored in his computer somewhere, could you get it out? Copy it or whatever genius computer hackers like you do? I'd like to do this without a time jump, if we can pull it off. I don't want to risk exposing my abilities.'

Assuming I hadn't already.

'If it's in there, I can get it. There are very few networks I haven't been able to breach,' he said.

'Damn, the CIA would love to get their hands on you.' I grinned at him and then remembered the most important part. 'They called it Axelle – I don't know if the file would be named that or not, but Dr Melvin is bound to have done more than one experiment in his life.'

'Got it,' he said with a quick nod. 'I think the real question is . . . can I do this without somebody killing me?'

'And without my superpowers.' I thought about this for a minute before answering. 'I need to fake an injury.'

'You could run into a pole, get a big bump on your head,' he suggested.

'No, nothing that might require brain scans of any kind.'

'Right . . . forgot about that. When was the last time he did an MRI?'

I let out a breath. 'June. Right before my birthday.'

'So . . . you think . . . he knows?'

I looked out the window. This was something I thought about a lot in 2007. 'He knows something. He has to. Maybe it doesn't mean he did something bad with the information, but the signs sure point in that direction.'

'So, basically, you have no clue who's good and who might want to kill you?' Adam concluded.

'Yep,' I said. 'From now on, I'm on my own side.'

Adam nodded and his expression was full of sympathy. 'I think you've always been on your own side.'

He meant that in a good way, I was certain he did, but to me it just reiterated the fact that I was alone in my own universe. My own timeline.

The elevator ride up to Melvin's office was like that day in 2007 when Dad and I went to see the doctor. I decided on faking a back injury because lots of people have that without anything a doctor can physically see.

Melvin came right out of his office to meet me. 'What happened, Jackson?'

'He fell off . . . um . . . a diving board,' Adam said.

'Actually it was more like I fell *on* a diving board,' I added.

Dr Melvin hurried me into an open exam room. 'You're still walking – that's a good sign.'

'Do you mind if my friend waits in your office?' I asked.

'No, not at all,' Melvin said.

I nodded to Adam, who ducked into the office and closed the door.

'So, how did you even know which one it was?' My stomach dropped just thinking about the rest of my question. 'Or did you read it already?'

We were driving towards my apartment in Mr Wellborn's car and Adam was practically giddy with excitement at this big scam we'd pulled off. Before I left 2009 I would have thought this was pretty big too, but after the many life-threatening experiences in 2007, fooling Melvin was like kindergarten to me.

'I was able to log on to his computer and find a bunch of encrypted files. According to the computer, they haven't been accessed for at least a month. I copied the files over to a ThumbDrive. I might be able to decrypt them once I get home.'

He pulled up to the circle drive in front of my building and turned to face me, the amusement dropping from his expression. 'I know you want to go after your dad and try to get answers or whatever, but I think you need to be careful. Give me some time to decrypt these files, and in the meantime get Holly out of town, go somewhere and stay there until we know more. It's kinda freaky that the EOT dude in 2007 had her picture from 2009.'

I took a deep breath and nodded. 'I'll have to convince her.'

'She'll go – I know she will.' He glanced at his watch. 'You've got, like, ten minutes before the camp bus gets back to the Y, and then she'll head home in a little while. It's better if you catch up to her now.'

I jumped out of the car with my bag from this year. The one that hadn't made the journey back to 2007. But at least I had a cellphone and credit cards from this year. I didn't need a repeat of my arrest in 2007. In the wallet I brought with me when I jumped, I also had false FBI and CIA badges that 007 Adam had made for me. To me, they looked pretty authentic. At least enough to fool an average person or the state police.

The doorman greeted me after Adam drove off. 'Can I get the spare key to my car? I'm gonna go for a drive.'

'Yes, sir,' he said, putting his own key into the lock box.

Holly was just getting off the bus when I pulled up to the YMCA. I left the car running and walked up to wait for her by the doors. As soon as she reached me I pulled her into a hug. 'I'm sorry.'

'Are you . . . OK?'

'I think so . . . listen, Hol . . . can we get out of here?'

Her eyes travelled to the kids pouring from the bus and into the building. 'What about dismissal?'

'Adam will cover for us. He's parking Mr Wellborn's car right now.' I brushed my fingers over her cheeks and smiled. 'Please?'

She nodded, but there was something guarded in her expression. I took her hand and led her to the passenger side door.

'You drove here?'

'I just picked up my car for the occasion.'

Since I'd never done a full forward jump of any kind, it was uncharted waters. I wasn't taking any chances. This was *my* Holly and I had to tell her everything I'd never said. Just like with Courtney. And I needed the time and space to do that.

'I've never seen you drive. You *can* drive, right?' she asked.

We both got into the car. 'I'll manage, don't worry.'

'You think it's OK to operate heavy machinery after Adam tried to poison you?'

I had forgotten that 009 Holly didn't trust my ability to do anything responsibly. I took one of her hands and held it on my lap. 'I'm fine, I swear.'

'Where are we going?'

I smiled at her as I drove away from New York City. 'Somewhere far. Do you have a passport?'

She laughed. 'Are you *ever* serious?'

'OK, maybe a place we can drive to. Is five hours too far?'

'When are we coming back?'

'Um . . . Sunday night?'

The amusement dropped from her face. Now she believed me. 'Like a weekend trip?'

'Yes, just you and me. No distractions.'

She shook her head. 'This is so crazy.'

'Exactly why we should do it, Hol.' I turned the full force of my eyes on her.

'OK . . . what the hell,' she said with a smile. 'I'll think of something to tell my mom.'

She leaned her head on my shoulder and I squeezed her hand. 'Take a nap and I'll wake you up when we get there.'

Holly didn't fall asleep. Instead she drilled me with questions about where we were going.

'Martha's Vineyard?' she asked after at least twenty clues.

'Correct. I know you like the beach and there's this great resort me and my dad stayed at a few years ago on vacation.'

After we checked into the hotel, I handed her one of the room keys. She pressed her hands against her temples, rubbing them. 'I can't believe I'm doing this.'

'I'll take you home early, if you want,' I said, leading her down the hall towards our room.

Before she put the key card in the door, she turned to face me. 'Tell me what's going on. Are you running away from something?'

This was an opportunity to tell the truth . . . sort of. I

took a deep breath and nodded. 'Yes. I had a fight with my dad. I needed to get away and I didn't want to go alone.'

OK, so maybe 'fight' was a huge understatement and it happened in a different year and timeline, but it was true that I didn't trust my dad and being in the same room with him right now didn't seem like a good idea.

She stood on her toes and kissed my forehead. 'Next time just tell me that so I don't get so freaked. I've had to run from my mother before. Though, for me, I just spend the weekend with Jana . . . it's not quite this elaborate.'

'Aside from that, it's basically the same, right?'

She nodded and finally opened the door. 'Might have been nice to pack a bag.'

I nudged her forward into the room. 'When you're a spoiled kid like me, running away, it's part of the rebellion to charge massive amounts to your parent's credit card. If we need something, we'll buy it.'

The door shut behind us and Holly took in the nice-sized suite. 'Lots of charges, huh?'

My phone rang, and when I saw that it was Adam, I answered it. 'How's it going?'

'I'm close to cracking the files. Just wanted to make sure you were OK,' he said. 'You are feeling OK, right?'

'Yes, I feel great, Adam. I'll call you if anything changes.' I hung up the phone and Holly kicked off her shoes and flopped on to the bed. 'You want to see the beach? Maybe go for a walk?'

'I just took my shoes off,' she said.

I grabbed her hand and pulled her off the bed, then scooped her up in my arms. 'No shoes needed.'

She laughed and put her arms around my neck. 'I'm just going to pretend this is real.'

'I know exactly what you mean.' I turned my head and kissed her arm. 'Sometimes I have trouble separating reality from . . . other things.'

I set her down again once we were on the sand. It *was* beautiful here. If I'd had time to actually *plan* a special weekend with Holly, it's possible this is exactly what I would have chosen.

'I love the beach at night,' she said.

'Me too.' I didn't want to get too far from the well-lit hotel with people milling around, so I stopped after a few minutes and we sat in the sand.

'Thanks for letting me tag along on your strange act of rebellion.'

I turned myself so I was facing her. 'You were mad at me earlier, weren't you? When we were by the pool.'

She shook her head. 'No . . . not mad.'

I held her hands in mine. 'Just tell me what was bothering you.'

'You said something before lunch, when you were high on Adam's drugs or whatever . . . it's no big deal.'

I didn't know what I had said to her before I landed in this year, but I knew we were right around the point where I started ditching her for more and more time-travel experiments.

I lifted her hands, held them to my face and took a deep breath. 'I don't know how to say this without freaking you out . . .'

Her face filled with alarm. 'Too late. You can't say

something like that and expect me not to freak.'

'I love you,' I blurted out the second she finished talking. I didn't do anything but stay perfectly still and watch her face change from fear to shock.

Her eyes were teary and she turned them towards the water. 'You don't have to do this . . . I'm happy just being here with you.'

'Holly, look at me.'

She didn't move, so I turned her face towards me. Tears were running down her cheeks. She wiped them away quickly with her hand. Her eyes closed, probably so she wouldn't be forced to stare into mine. 'I'm sorry.'

'For what, Hol?'

'For making you feel like you had to say that. I wish I didn't care what you thought, that I could just . . . *not* want more . . .'

'I love you,' I said again, moving my face closer to hers.

'Just stop,' she whispered. 'This is my fault for –'

I touched my finger to her lips, stopping her from talking. 'I love you so much and I've never said it because everything's always so great with us and I don't know if you can really mean it until . . . it's not great.'

Her eyes opened and I could see she might actually believe me this time. 'You're serious?'

I laughed. 'Yes. I'm seriously, completely in love with you.'

Her arms went around my neck. 'Me too . . . I mean . . . I love you too.'

I pulled her down in the sand with me, kissing nearly every inch of her face.

'Ew!' a voice said from behind us.

Holly pulled away from me and we both saw two little kids being hurried off by their parents. She laughed and kissed my cheek. 'I hate that you made me cry.'

'Cry all you want, just as long as you're still happy.'

'I'm happy,' she said.

And so was I. In spite of everything.

I jumped out of the shower and tied a towel around my waist. When I walked back into the room Holly was lying flat on her stomach in the middle of the bed, sound asleep. The white hotel robe had shifted over, exposing the Japanese character she had tattooed across her shoulder blade. I didn't really have any doubts *which* Holly this was. But still, it was nice to have her marked somehow. Maybe I could talk her into getting 009 tattooed right below the other one.

She had crashed in the six or seven minutes I was in the shower, but it was almost midnight. I shook the sand out of my clothes and put them on before leaning over her. 'I'm gonna run to the store. What do you need?'

Her eyes opened halfway and then closed again. 'I'm awake. I'll go with you.'

I pulled the blanket over her. 'Just sleep.'

'Underwear,' she mumbled.

I glanced over at her orange swimsuit lying on the floor. Of course she would have had that on under her work clothes. 'I guess we really were unprepared. I'll see what I can find. Holly?'

'Yeah?'

'I have my key, so don't open the door for anyone, OK?'

She nodded and I left the room quietly. The gift shop in the lobby stayed open twenty-four hours. Holly and I were about to become the hotel's walking advertisement, because nearly everything for sale had their logo written on it. The lady at the counter jumped when she saw me enter the store. She had been dozing in her chair.

'Can I help you find something?'

'Um . . . yeah. The airline lost my girlfriend's suitcase. She needs some clothes, underwear and stuff . . .' I flipped through a stack of T-shirts and pulled out a small and a medium.

'What size?' the woman asked me.

From the corner of my eye I spotted a little person with red hair snatching a business card from the front desk across from the gift shop.

'Um . . . I'm not sure. Just give me one of each size,' I said to the woman. 'I'll be right back.'

I walked towards the front desk in just a few quick strides. The child turned around and headed for a hall to the right. Either I was going crazy or this was the same little girl I had seen at the zoo that day back in June of this year. But this child looked smaller. Younger, by a couple of years. She stepped into the little room with the vending machine. I leaned against the wall, waiting for her to come out. It was after midnight. What was a little kid doing wandering around alone at this time of night?

I waited another minute and didn't hear any sound, so I peeked around the corner. I scanned the soda machine, the ice maker. She wasn't there. She couldn't have gone anywhere without passing me.

I walked away, shaking my head. Sleep. I needed sleep, or just something normal. One regular day to stop the insane thoughts . . . because I was obviously seeing things at this point.

The man in the lobby pacing back and forth, wearing a staff uniform, glanced up at me when I approached the gift shop again.

'How are you tonight, sir?' he asked me. The name on his tag read 'John'.

'Did you just see a little girl with red hair in the lobby?'

'No. Are you looking for someone?'

I shook my head and tried to look calm. 'Nope, just thought it was strange to see a kid wandering alone at night. Are you the manager?'

He grinned. 'Assistant manager, but I'm covering the night shift on my own.'

I pulled out the fake FBI badge and flashed it in front of him for a second before stowing it away again. Just my one day of secret-agent training with Dad and Jenni Stewart had given me several ideas for methods of protection, and more importantly, prevention. Or maybe I had always been good at being undercover . . . good at concealing things. 'Listen, John, I'm going to need to see a floor plan of the entire place and a guest list, updated daily if possible.'

'Is everything . . . OK?' he stammered.

'For now. Let's make sure it stays that way. I'll be in the shop waiting for those floor plans. And remember, I'm undercover, so we never had this conversation. Got it?' I said, channelling a cliché Hollywood version of intimidating 'secret-agent-speak.'

He nodded and turned his back to me, shuffling quickly towards the front desk. I returned to the woman in the shop, who was holding several hangers in one hand and sifting through a rack of dresses with the other.

I grabbed toothbrushes, toothpaste, dental floss, deodorant and a pair of sandals for Holly. I piled everything on the counter, adding a few things for myself, and finally John returned and handed me a stack of papers.

'That's every map I could get my hands on. And I've put a note in for the morning manager to get you those updated guest lists.'

I studied the first-floor map and then looked up at him again. I wasn't sure exactly who I was looking for on the list, but it had seemed like the right thing to ask for. 'Thank you, John. Room 312, OK? Slide them under the door.'

'Would you like me to charge this to your room?' the woman asked me.

'Yes, please.' I grabbed several paperback books and added them to my already large purchase. 'These, too.'

I had six full bags to cart back to the room while I tested the parameters of my photographic memory. I attempted to follow the staff-only routes through the first floor and leading up to the third. I already knew twelve different exits. Methods of getting out quick seemed like a good thing to know.

Holly was sound asleep when I slid into bed next to her. I grabbed one of the books and opened it, keeping the small desk lamp on. I only looked at the book for about thirty minutes before Holly rolled over and ran into my legs.

'Did you find some underwear?'

'Yes, but it has the resort name written across the ass.'

'Underwear is underwear.' She threw her arm around my waist and rested her head in the crook of my shoulder before closing her eyes again.

I set the book aside and watched her breathing in and out perfectly. I knew right then that I'd do just about anything to make sure that perfect rhythm never stopped. That was the only thing I wanted. I didn't care about Tempest or the Enemies of Time. None of them could ever give me something more valuable to defend or to fight for.

I watched Holly sleep until my eyes simply wouldn't stay open any longer.

chapter thirty-one

FRIDAY, 14 AUGUST 2009, 6.30 A.M.

I woke up the next morning feeling fingers combing through my hair. When I opened my eyes, Holly was propped up on one elbow, wide awake, her mouth close to mine.

I lifted my head just enough to kiss her. 'Can you do this every morning?'

And then just for a second her face fell, but she pulled it together and smiled. 'I already peeked out the window and it's beautiful outside.'

'Hol, what did I say yesterday at the pool?' I attempted a smile. 'Before I changed clothes.'

She shook her head. 'Nothing, really. It was stupid for me to even mention it.'

Her expression contradicted her words and I started to get worried and a little pissed off at my slightly younger self for being such an asshole. I rubbed the back of her neck with my fingertips. 'You can tell me. It's OK.'

Her eyes dropped to my chest and she traced a finger slowly over my skin. 'You know how I went to orientation to meet my roommate last weekend?'

The God-awful Lydia. 'Yes, I remember.'

'Well . . . there's a guy from my school staying on the floor above me.' She started talking faster, maybe hoping I wouldn't catch everything. 'I don't know him that well, but his roommate changed dorms at the last minute and if he doesn't find a replacement he has to pay the single rate and . . . I just thought . . . since your dorm is so far from mine . . .'

'You want me to move in . . . to your building?' Not at all what I expected, and I couldn't remember her ever asking this.

'It was just an idea. I mean . . . why would you want to move when you already have a place, and it's a lot bigger?' She rested her head on my pillow.

'Now the real question is . . . what did *I* say?'

'You said you hated that building and . . . that I would get sick of seeing you every morning.'

'But you thought I really meant something else? That I would get sick of *you*?'

'Yeah,' she said, barely above a whisper.

'Not a chance.' I grinned and kissed her before standing up. 'I'll move wherever you want me to. But I think you need a new roommate.'

'You've never met her,' Holly said.

'Yeah, but I know her type.' I grabbed a few of the bags, dumped the contents on to the bed and started digging for some clothes.

'What are these?' Holly asked, holding up a pair of underwear so giant they covered her whole head.

I cracked up. 'We could go sailing with those. Or jump out of an aeroplane.'

'Go take a shower. I'll find the smaller ones.' I grabbed her hands and pulled her off the bed, then brought my mouth to her ear. 'I'd still love you even if you fit into those giant panties.'

'I'll work on it. It's gonna have to be a big breakfast,' she said with a laugh before closing the bathroom door.

I called Adam while I dug for smaller underwear. 'Hey, Adam. Any luck with the project?'

'Damn, I just went to bed ten minutes ago,' he mumbled sleepily. 'But no luck yet.'

I sighed to myself, then I switched from English to French so Holly wouldn't understand just in case she overheard me. 'OK, well then, the way I see it, I have a couple of options. If I somehow managed to slip into a date before I exposed my abilities, then I won't do any time jumps and just keep searching for information.'

'And what if someone knows?'

I found a razor and shaving cream in the pile of stuff and set them aside. 'Then I have to choose a side.'

'Wow, so it's almost like join or die,' Adam said.

Those words didn't hit me as hard as I thought they would. I guess part of me knew it would come down to this eventually. 'Yeah, I imagine it's something like that.'

I could hear Adam suck in a breath through the phone. Then he finally spoke again. 'Just because you choose a side doesn't mean you're *on* that side . . . do you understand what I'm saying?'

He was right. There were loopholes in this game. Ones

I could use to my advantage. 'Good point. Let's just hope Plan A works out. My life would be so much easier if I could keep everything a secret from those Tempest people.'

'Somebody's got their head on straight,' Adam said. 'What happened to you?'

'Too much. Way too much.' The bathroom door opened so I switched back to English. 'Talk to ya later, Adam.'

I tossed the phone on to the bed and turned around. Holly gripped a towel with one hand and the other she held out to me. 'Any luck or should I get some safety pins?'

'You're such a good sport.' I pointed to a pile of clothes that were non-giant size and she sifted through them.

'You were talking about me in French again, weren't you?' she asked, lifting her eyebrows suspiciously.

'Maybe . . . but we only said good things.'

John was still in the lobby when we went down for breakfast. When Holly walked in front of me, I turned around and saluted him. He gave me a small nod. I could only assume he'd be off duty soon and I might be in the hands of someone a little more suspicious. Someone not as easy to manipulate. At least I already had the floor plans memorized.

After breakfast we went shopping and bought clothes that didn't have the hotel logo on them, then sat by the pool, dangling our feet in the water. It was nice, since I hadn't done anything remotely relaxing in weeks. Not that I wasn't keeping my eyes open for trouble.

'Why is this place so deserted?' Holly asked.

'It's Friday. Lots of people will check in tonight, for the

weekend.' I slid off the side and into the pool.

She got in the water and sat next to me on the steps. 'Did you mean what you said earlier, about changing dorms? You don't have to. Your room is so much nicer. I took a tour of that building before I applied.'

My arms snaked around her waist and I pulled her so she was sitting sideways on my lap. 'Yes, I meant it. If that's what you want.'

'Well . . . let's see . . . no Katharine Flynn around objecting to us closing my bedroom door. No doormen writing everything down in those secret spy books.' She touched the side of my face.

I leaned down and kissed her. Just as I was debating luring Holly back to the hotel room, I caught a glimpse of a very familiar man in a blue suit and black sunglasses making strides in our direction.

What did he know? Just that I'd left town without calling? Or something more . . . I groaned and moved my mouth to Holly's neck. 'How long can you hold your breath?'

I didn't let her answer before I pulled her underwater for about five seconds. She was laughing when we came back up. Dad stood at the edge of the pool, arms crossed, sunglasses pushed down to the end of his nose.

Holly's eyes went wide. She put her feet back on the bottom of the pool and walked towards the steps. 'I'm going to . . . uh . . . get a drink from the bar.'

'Would have been nice to hear about your little vacation,' Dad said.

'Sorry, forgot to call.' I climbed out and grabbed a towel

from the chair, keeping my eyes on Holly. 'What are you doing here?'

'I was worried about . . . What are you doing with this girl?' he asked.

'Her name is Holly.' I rubbed my hair with the towel.

'I know her name—'

'Then maybe you could try using it,' I suggested, trying to sound like an annoyed spoiled teenager.

Another man wearing a suit slid into a chair next to where Holly stood at the bar. I couldn't see his face, just his dark hair and his build. The bartender set two glasses of ice on the counter and then held up a pitcher of iced tea and filled them to the top.

Holly looked over her left shoulder at a noise in the distance. It was just long enough for the man to drop something into her glass. Before all the recent life-threatening events I never would have noticed that, and the thought scared me to death.

I ran towards them, hearing Dad's footsteps behind me. I came up behind Holly and covered her glass with one hand, then turned my head to whisper in her ear. 'Let's get out of here. We can get a drink somewhere else.'

'Um . . . OK.'

I forced down the fear that was building inside me. It was obvious that their intent was not good. I grabbed Holly by the hand and started walking away from Dad, fast.

'Jackson! Where are you going?' he shouted at me.

Holly glanced over her shoulder and started to slow up. 'Maybe you should talk to him.'

I shook my head and pulled her along more quickly. We

headed for the back of the building and away from hotel patrons.

I didn't even see anyone when we ran past the dumpsters, but suddenly an arm hooked around the front of my neck and my brain snapped into full defensive mode. No pounding heart. No shouting. No sign that I was even in the least bit startled. Just perfect silent defence emerging from some locked-up part of my brain.

Holly leaped backwards, and in just a few seconds, I had the attacker flat on his back, staring down the barrel of his own weapon. I finally got a look at his face. I had seen him before, for a split second while jumping, that time Courtney snuck out of school to meet me in 2003.

Now I was breathing hard, shaking a little, trying to figure out what to do next. Dad ran up beside me and took in the situation. 'Freeman, what the hell happened?'

'Will someone tell me what's going on?' Holly stuttered out while staring down at my attacker, who was still lying on the ground. 'Jackson . . . how did you . . . *do* that?'

I didn't have time to answer anyone. The guy named Freeman hooked his foot around the back of my leg, attempting to force me to fall forward. I stumbled a little intentionally, to get him to stand, then forced him back on to the ground, face first this time, arms pinned behind his back. I had performed this manoeuvre several times on Dad in 2007. I pressed my foot against his spine to make sure he couldn't move, then dropped his gun into my swimsuit pocket. I didn't know how to use it, but I didn't want him to have it.

'OK . . . how did you do *that*?' Holly asked.

Plan A was officially demolished. No hiding now. But who was the real enemy?

'Just basic self-defence,' I said to Holly before turning to Dad. 'What the hell do you want?'

Dad managed to wipe the shock from his face and he kept his distance while Freeman squirmed under my foot. 'We caught your friend . . . We know what he's been doing.'

I glanced around the corner and saw a very pale Adam Silverman being escorted by Dr Melvin.

Yep, cover blown, big time.

'Adam?' Holly said. 'What are you doing here?'

Adam didn't answer. His eyes moved from Freeman to me to Holly.

'Mr Silverman stole confidential CIA documents, and Dr Melvin believes you assisted him,' Dad said before lifting one eyebrow at me. 'We know what you can do, where you've been, *when* you've been. All of it.'

I glanced at Adam, and his weary expression silently answered my question. I hated to even think about what they'd done to him to get him to talk. I should have never dragged him to Dr Melvin's office yesterday. It's a good thing I didn't tell him everything.

'Wait a minute . . . CIA?' Holly asked.

I finally looked at her face and knew we'd have to tell her something. I thought of Agent Stewart in 2007 being only nineteen. Holly might believe this lie. 'I'm training . . . to be an agent. Like my dad . . . actually me and Adam are both joining.'

'Is that what you guys are always doing together . . .

when you're off acting like idiots?'

'Adam and I like to do different research projects . . . we just started the training thing. He's mostly hacking into computers.'

'Obviously,' she said. She looked at Dad. 'Is that true?'

I couldn't believe she'd trust his opinion over mine.

'Yes, it's true,' he said, not missing a beat. Maybe he thought we'd get to the point faster if he went along with my lie. Obviously we were going to have to make up a story for Holly anyway. It's not like we could tell her about time-travellers.

I stared at my dad's face and put every ounce of intensity I could muster into my voice. 'Since you stopped Adam from getting the information, you're going to give it to me. I'm tired of lies and bullshit. Whatever it is, I just want to know.'

'I'm not sure that's a good idea, Jackson,' Dad said slowly.

'Fine.' I released Freeman and reached for Holly's hand again. She clutched on to it instantly, which surprised me a little, considering what she had just found out. I grabbed Adam's arm and started to drag him along with us too. After we got a few feet away I yelled over my shoulder, 'I guess I'll do this my way. I hope you know what you're getting into. There's no way Adam told you everything . . . especially since even *he* doesn't know everything.'

Dad was right in front of me in no time. 'Hold up a second . . . all right . . . you win. Maybe we can tell you. I didn't realize how much you already . . . guessed.'

'Great, just me and Dr Melvin.' I turned to Adam. 'How

about you and Holly go back to the pool and you can brief her . . . on the rules.'

'The rules?' Adam asked, looking puzzled.

'Yeah, you know . . . having knowledge of an agent's identity . . . remember?' I prompted.

'Oh . . . those rules.' He slung an arm around Holly and she glanced over her shoulder at me.

'I'll be right back, I promise.' The four of us watched them retreat, then I turned back to Dad. 'You better make sure nothing happens to them. And keep this jerk from dropping things in people's drinks.'

'What the hell is going on?' Freeman asked Dad.

'I'll explain later.'

'Let's go, Dr Melvin.' I pointed towards the far exit door of the hotel and then we walked in silence up to my suite.

Dr Melvin sat on the couch in the front room and waited for me to talk first.

'Is Jenni Stewart still alive?' I asked. 'She's still an agent and everything?'

Melvin balked a little but then answered, 'Yes, she's in New York.'

I pulled the chair over from the desk and sat right in front of Dr Melvin, then I removed Freeman's gun from my waistband and held it in my hands. 'Now, tell me about Axelle.'

'Why don't you tell me how much you know first and maybe I can fill in the blanks,' he said, talking to me like I was five.

I had to laugh and then raise the gun a little, even though I'd never used one. But Dr Melvin didn't know that. 'Nice try. I visited a really interesting place once – this underground wing of the hospital, and I'm curious what exactly goes on down there.'

His eyes were the size of golf balls and then he nodded and sank further into the couch. 'OK, I'll explain . . . Axelle is a project designed to use a combination of my research on the Tempus gene and future technological developments we've obtained from various sources. The actual application of Axelle began in 1989, when we successfully implanted a fertilized egg into a surrogate mother. My team used the eggs of one of the female EOTs.'

'Wait, so you stole some EOT woman's eggs?' I asked. 'Is that why they're so mad?'

'They aren't happy about the experiment, if that's what you mean. And yes, we took the woman's eggs. But we used the sperm of a normal man. An anonymous donor.'

'Did you kill her?' I asked. 'The EOT chick.'

Melvin shook his head. 'No, she escaped.'

My heart pounded twice as fast. 'Is her name Cassidy?'

'How do you know that?'

If I had been standing, I would have fallen over. The woman that tried to take me back to this timeline was biologically my mother. No wonder she looked just like Courtney. And what had she said to Dad? '*I believe I have a say in his well being, given the circumstances. Much more than you ever will.*'

It was already too much and I almost told Melvin to stop, but hiding from the truth didn't appeal to me nearly as much as it used to. 'We might have run into each other. Go on with the story.'

'Axelle's purpose was to mix the genetics of time-travellers with that of normal humans to see if any abilities developed and, if so, how they differed from the pure-breeds.'

It felt as if the wind had been knocked out of me. Another missing piece of the puzzle snapped into place.

'Half-breed . . . Frankenstein . . .' I muttered under my breath. It made perfect sense now. 'Why would you want to create more of them?'

'Honestly, Jackson, I had no idea you would even be able to time-travel. Of course we hoped for it. But we at least wanted to bring someone into the world with similar brain activity. The capacity they have to hold information is fascinating. I've been far more interested in that than in their ability to travel through time.'

Yeah, like that made me feel better. 'Why the half-mutant experiment? Why not go for the full deal?'

He nodded slowly. 'This part is the hardest to understand. It's the main reason Tempest has to fight this constant and sometimes near-impossible battle. I can certainly try to explain, but you might lose trust in our organization.'

'Um . . . it's a little too late for that,' I said. 'You might as well use everything you've got. I doubt my impression of Tempest could get much worse.'

His face fell, but just for a second. 'The EOTs lack normal emotions. The ability to grasp concepts like fear, love or grief.'

I groaned and tried to refrain from rolling my eyes. 'You're right, that's a lame explanation. So basically, the Enemies of Time are evil sociopaths, and Tempest agents are the equivalent of Mother Teresa. Not very original.'

He sighed and attempted to flatten his wild grey hair. 'I never said evil. This is completely different. Perhaps they lack emotions because they don't see any permanence in time. For me and most people, losing someone you love is devastating because that person is gone and you can't go back to a time when they were still around. If I could, maybe death wouldn't weigh so heavily on my life. The fact that they can jump around and potentially recreate history is dangerous. It's the same for you, fooling around with time-travel experiments. But the biggest threat isn't what they can do, it's the lack of humanity behind their decisions.'

Well . . . I could go back and see Courtney any time I wanted, and her death still had the same impact on me. Maybe even more. I was so absorbed in Dr Melvin's explanation I forgot about the gun and the fact that I was practically holding him hostage. 'None of them seemed evil. They even apologized for . . . well, for something that hasn't happened yet . . . something that won't happen any more,' I said firmly.

Even Dr Melvin's composure had changed. I was the student and he was the teacher. 'This is why it's hard to explain. We live in a world with people like them. Not actual EOTs, but those who make every decision through logical and calculated risk.'

'Again, that doesn't seem so bad.'

Dr Melvin lifted his eyebrows. 'Really? Then think about war. Someone is in charge in every country. One man or woman has to make a decision to send soldiers off to fight. Young people who have loved ones that need them, men and women with children waiting at home. Whoever gives the orders to risk those lives is making a calculated decision. Weighing the benefits of losing a few lives in the hope of saving more. We need people like that in our world, yes, but imagine if everyone was like that. That's what they want.'

My shoulders slumped further down as the weight of his words pressed down on me. 'Do you think I'll be like them? I was normal until I was eighteen. What if I just keep changing and eventually I'm the same as them?'

Melvin smiled a little. 'I've known you since before you were born, Jackson. You could never be the one sending people off to die, no matter how many lives it saved. Their methods are mathematical and yours are heartfelt, though impulsive at times. It's a wonderful quality. But it's also a weakness.'

'They view it as a weakness, or you do?' I asked.

'Both,' he said immediately. 'Doctors fight the same internal battle. There are times when you have to set aside your compassion for a patient and use only medically driven facts to make a diagnosis or treatment. Other times, connecting emotionally with a patient has amazing benefits, but often it's hard to turn one part off at the right time.'

I didn't miss the sadness that washed over his face. 'Like with Courtney? You tried to keep her alive longer than you should have?'

'She was in a lot of pain. I knew that and I still didn't want to give up.' His eyes were misty but no tears fell. 'I don't know if it was right or not. For her, I think the change was starting earlier than for you. One month everything was clear, and the next, her brain was covered with inoperable tumours. There's no way I could ever have predicted that happening as a side-effect.' He sighed and focused his eyes over my shoulder. 'We had the best brain surgeons and oncologists in the entire world studying her case. But no modern medicine could change what happened to her.'

'So it's possible she could have been like me . . . if she hadn't gotten sick?'

'Yes,' he said. 'I'm just not sure telling you all of this will do anything but make you more miserable.'

'I wanted to know.' I shook my head and stared down at my hands. 'But now it's a little difficult to feel connected to anything . . . to my father . . . when I'm just some experiment.'

The words were out before I could stop them. At least it was just Melvin in the room. My dad told me in 2007 that Courtney and I were his assignment, his job. But I wanted to be his son. 'I don't know how to convince you otherwise, but I can tell you for sure, your dad's side is the right one.'

I remembered something Marshall had said in 2007, when we were standing over Harold's body. '*He's one of Dr Ludwig's spawn.*'

'Who's Dr Ludwig?' I asked.

Melvin's eyebrows lifted. 'A scientist, like myself. Someone with a similar fascination with the time-travellers' minds. Only, his products are pure-breeds, but not originals. Copies.'

'Are you talking about cloning?' I asked.

'Something along those lines. Genetic mutation as well.'

My mind painted an image of rows of Harolds, Cassidys and the shoe-print guy, all lined up in giant incubators. Creepy.

'Wait – I'm not a clone . . . am I?'

Melvin shook his head vigorously. 'Absolutely not. You and your sister were developed in the same way many children are brought into this world. No different than for a woman who has difficulty getting pregnant.'

I sighed with relief. Science experiment was bad enough, but actually being made by some machine or however it worked was far beyond what I could grasp and still maintain sanity. 'So, where is this Ludwig guy? Is Tempest going to take him out or stop him or something? I mean, he shouldn't be doing this "making people", shit . . . Wait – he's not on the CIA's side like you, is he?'

'No, he's not on Tempest's side,' Melvin answered firmly. 'And Dr Ludwig is not alive.'

'Someone got to him already?' I asked.

'Something like that.'

He had given me the information I wanted. It filled in the missing pieces perfectly and yet I felt I still couldn't trust my father, or the EOTs. Maybe they were pissed off because Melvin stole some lady's eggs. It kinda made sense. I believed Dr Melvin cared about me and Courtney. I had gotten good enough at reading faces to know that, but he wasn't calling the shots. Chief Marshall was, which meant I couldn't rely on Melvin.

I stopped thinking it over because Dr Melvin was staring at me so intensely I was worried he could read my mind. Earlier today Adam had given me the answer I needed. I could choose a side without selling my soul. 'OK, tell me the truth – is Chief Marshall lurking around here somewhere? I'd like to speak with him, alone.'

Dr Melvin's face tightened, but he nodded and pulled out his phone.

'I'm going to check on my friends. He can find me when he's ready,' I said, heading out the door.

As I was walking out towards the pool again Adam sent me a text that said, 'You can thank me later.'

I had no idea what that meant, but the second I spotted them, sitting in lounge chairs scooted close together, Holly jumped up and threw her arms around my neck. She had changed back into her dress from earlier, not that I expected them to be swimming and having fun while I had my little life-altering chat with Dr Melvin.

'I'm so sorry,' she whispered. 'Adam told me everything.'

My arms went around her and I looked at Adam over her shoulder, trying to converse silently. He lifted his eyebrows as if to say, 'Just go with it.'

I racked my brain for theories about what he might have told her and then settled on. Dad not being my dad as the most likely, given the reason for my escaping on this weekend trip. He could have said the information was on the hard drive. A little far-fetched, but it's possible she believed him.

'How come you're taking this government stuff so well?' I asked Holly.

She laughed a little and we both sat, facing each other on the one lounge chair. 'Promise you won't get mad at me if I tell you something?'

I smiled at her. 'I doubt I could ever be mad at you.'

'I have an entire diary of theories about you, and most of them were a lot crazier than son of CIA agent.'

'Like what?' Adam and I said together.

This was total news to me.

'Um . . . well . . . I considered money embezzling. I thought maybe Adam was helping you hack into computers of foreign banks. Then there's you being a mobster, of course.'

'Of course,' I said. 'And how exactly would Adam be involved?'

She leaned closer to me and I was honestly intimidated by the excitement on her face. Apparently her little-girl fascination with espionage didn't fade as she got older.

'Adam could have been your source for false identification, like if you wanted to hire illegal immigrants for your construction business and you needed documentation. He makes some kick-ass fake IDs.'

And fake FBI badges.

'Holly, why is it you're dating Jackson again?' Adam asked.

She shook her head and smiled. 'God, you have no idea how many times I've asked myself that same question.'

I leaned forward and touched my lips to hers. 'I don't blame you.'

'The mobster thing is a really good idea,' Adam said. 'We could totally pull that off.'

Holly cracked up. 'Adam being in the CIA surprises me a lot less than you being a secret agent. There's not a single member of our senior class that doesn't think Adam will either become some super-hotshot software programmer or some kind of government code breaker. Personally I thought he was probably already working for someone, playing the average high-school student by day, and by night . . .'

Adam let out this evil cackle to punctuate Holly's story. 'I just wish I could kick some ass like Jackson. That was totally sweet.'

'I'll teach you sometime.'

'And you'll teach me, or I'll tell everyone your secrets.' Holly stood up and snatched her purse from the ground. 'I'm going to get snacks for all of us.'

I waited until she had reached the bar, where Dad and Freeman sat watching us, before saying anything to Adam. 'What did you tell her?'

'Aside from our CIA recruitment? Just the "he's not my father" story. I figured she'd go for that, especially if I made your dad seem like an asshole.'

'So . . . did you get to look at the Axelle stuff?' I asked. He dropped his eyes and nodded. 'Pretty freaky, huh?'

'Yeah,' Adam said with a sigh.

'I'm sorry you had to get involved . . . What did they do to get you to talk?' I asked.

The colour drained from his face. 'A combination of threats against most of my family, you, Holly, and then eventually your dad took over the interrogation and said he'd bring me along to find you, to make sure nothing happened to us. He wasn't exactly nice about it, but at least he didn't threaten me, like the other dudes.'

Holly returned with food for all of us, but I saw Chief Marshall walking towards Dad. 'Save some nachos for me, OK? I've got another . . . meeting.'

Holly nodded and I could feel her eyes following me as I walked towards the man who, last time we saw each other, nearly strangled me to death. This should be interesting.

I stopped right in front of him and made sure to have my game face on. I had to crane my neck a little to make eye contact with him. 'Mind if we chat for a few minutes?'

His face stayed cold and distant, like always. 'Of course.'

Dad started to follow us but I turned around and held my arm out. 'This is just between me and Chief Marshall.'

Dad looked like he might object but gave in quickly, which only increased my suspicions. I turned to Marshall. 'No earpieces or communication devices.'

He hesitated, but removed the small piece of plastic from his ear and dropped it on the ground before smashing it with his shoe. Then he took off his watch and handed it to Dad.

I led him all the way to the very back of the building. My room was probably already bugged by Dad or that Freeman guy. I took a breath and focused on sounding as assertive as possible. 'I want you to make me an agent.'

As expected, he had no facial reaction. 'Why? To convince your girlfriend? I think Adam Silverman could produce authentic enough identification to convince her. You don't need my help with that.'

'I'm talking about actual agent training.' I ground my teeth together, trying to control my anger. Chief Marshall wasn't exactly my favourite person. 'I know about Jenni Stewart. You let her in when she was nineteen.'

'I don't think your father would be very happy with me.'

'He's not my father, and why do you think I left him out of this conversation.' I ran my fingers through my hair, trying to come up with something more convincing. 'I know Agent Stewart has a couple of months left of training. You can throw me in with that group.'

'As a time-traveller, right? That's your contribution?' He had that same greedy look as in 2007. 'You could add some more assets to the list, since you've been to October of this year. You must know something about the next few months.'

I shook my head. 'No, I'm not gonna let you use me for that. I don't want anyone to know. I'm sure my family connection will be convincing enough.'

He crossed his arms and I could see the ideas and theories whirling around in his head. 'I won't agree unless I know your motivation.'

I snorted back a laugh. 'Wanting to kill some EOTs isn't enough for you?'

'Not if it's a lie.'

I let out an exasperated breath. 'Fine, the reason is simple: I have to choose a side. That's my only motivation right now.'

He nodded and stuck out his hand, and I took it, tentatively. 'Exactly what I wanted to hear. I'll talk to your father, but you do realize everything about your life is about to change, right?'

'Hasn't it already?' I said with a shrug.

I left him and returned to Holly and Adam. I intentionally avoided eye contact with Dad.

'I'm totally beat. I was up all night,' Adam said a little while later, when the sun had started to set. 'Your dad got me a room already so I'm gonna crash.'

'See ya later, Adam,' I said.

Holly nodded towards the poolside bar where Freeman and Dad were still sitting. 'So, you're still mad at him?'

'It's complicated.'

Her forehead wrinkled. 'Explain then . . . he *is* still the man who raised you, right? That has to count for something.'

She waited patiently and I had a feeling this was the kind of information she wanted most from me. More than the CIA secrets. 'Yeah it counts for something . . . but I'm still not sure I can trust him.'

'Maybe you will . . . eventually. You won't have as many secrets now.'

'I hope so.' I moved my hands to her face, looking into her eyes. I wanted so many things at that moment. Things I'd never wanted before. But mostly, I didn't want to lose this memory. Or for her to lose it. 'You ready to go inside?'

She smiled. 'Definitely.'

We left the bar and walked quickly back to our room. The second I turned the lock on the door, Holly was right in front of me, unbuttoning my shirt.

'Look who's lacking patience today,' I teased.

Even in the dim light I could see her cheeks turn pink. I loved that I could still make her blush.

My fingers found the zipper on the back of her dress and I slowly brought it down and nudged the shoulder straps further down her arms until the dress fell to the floor next to my shirt.

'Just so you know . . . I haven't done this in a while.' I picked her up off the ground and her legs wrapped around me.

She laughed loudly as I dropped her on to the bed. 'Seriously? What crazy world are you living in? It's only been –'

I touched my fingers to her lips. 'Let's pretend it's been a long time . . . weeks.'

'Like you were lost at sea?'

'Exactly.'

Around midnight, the sound of my phone buzzing jolted me awake. Holly was curled up against my side but barely stirred when I reached under the pillow to pull out my phone.

'Dad?'

'Sorry if I woke you. Think you could meet me downstairs at the bar?'

No hiding out now. If I didn't go, they would just come in here and put a rag over my face or something.

'Give me five minutes.'

'Take as long as you need,' he said.

I shook Holly a little and rolled on my side to face her. 'Hol? Holly?'

Her eyes peeled open. 'Huh?'

'My dad wants me to meet him at the bar, OK? He wants to talk or something.'

She flipped over on her other side and pulled the covers up to her chin. 'Sure.'

'I won't be long.' I moved her hair from her face and touched my lips to her cheek. 'I love you.'

Her fingertips rested on my face and she smiled. 'Me too.'

I got dressed quickly, making sure to grab Freeman's gun.

When I walked into the bar it was completely empty except for Dad and the bartender, who was laughing at something Dad had just told him.

'Are you alone?' I asked him.

He turned to the bartender. 'We'll take our drinks over to the booth, if that's all right?'

'Sure thing.'

I followed him across the deserted room to a booth. He slid a beer in front of me and I could tell by looking at his face that he'd already had quite a few. Not typical for an agent on duty.

'I'm alone,' he said. 'Freeman and Melvin are . . . detained.'

'OK . . .' I said slowly.

'Melvin told me everything you talked about. Look, Jackson, I've been going over this for hours, and you shouldn't be forced into this life just because you think there's no other way.'

'You wanted to teach me stuff in 2007,' I pointed out.

He chugged the rest of his beer then shook his head. 'I don't know. Maybe I thought you would be safer under our watch or that you needed training.'

'And now?'

'I'm sure you have a good grasp of the sacrifices it takes to devote your life to something you can't tell anyone about. Not even your own children.'

For a few seconds he had me. The intensity in his eyes. I wanted to believe every word, to tell him I loved him, but I couldn't be one hundred per cent sure he wasn't still playing games. 'I can't help people I don't trust. I don't want to be tricked or fooled into things.'

He leaned back in his seat and drew in a deep breath. 'We were just trying to protect you. It's a lot to accept all at once.'

'I get that. But now I'm at the point where I'd rather you just told me. No matter how bad it is. Killing people or whatever.' The horrible memory of Chief Marshall giving Dad orders to shoot that Harold dude came flooding back. 'How do you even do this . . . kill people and go on living, not feeling any guilt? Is everything an act to you? Even being a father? It was your assignment, right?'

I expected him to get angry, like I was. But he just nodded and looked down at his hands before meeting my eyes again. 'There's something I want you to see. Something in the past. But you only have to watch, no tricks. It will answer a lot of your questions. Just do the half-jump. The one that won't affect history.'

'I guess Adam told you about half-jumps?' I asked and he nodded. 'When am I jumping to? What's the date?'

'Second October 1992,' he said. 'About three in the afternoon.'

'That's further than I've ever gone back. It's going to make me sick. Really sick. And I don't know how long I'll be able to stay.'

'I know. It's up to you if you want to try or not.'

All I could see in his expression was pure grief and exhaustion. This wasn't the excited energy that 007 Marshall, Melvin and Dad had when I had given detailed accounts of the past or the future. He pulled a pen from his pocket and drew a little map of Central Park, circling an old playground. Then he handed me what looked like an MP3 player, but I knew it magnified sound from a distance. Jenni Stewart had shown me hers that day I wrote a Spanish paper for her in exchange for secrets.

I closed my eyes and let the warmth of the room dissolve.

chapter thirty-two

FRIDAY, 2 OCTOBER 1992, 3.00 P.M.

I stood in the middle of the baseball field, not far from the tree I would fall out of and break my arm in four years. From a distance, I could make out one of the playgrounds I remember spending a lot of time at as a kid. Either with Dad or whatever nanny we had at the time.

As I walked closer a man about my dad's size pushed a little person with a bright pink sweater on the swing. A little boy with brown hair attempted to climb the slide, while a woman with lighter brown hair shoved his rear end up every time he slid back down.

Courtney and I would have been two years old on this day . . . it had to be us. I sat down at a picnic table and turned on the little device Dad had just given me. Then I slipped my ear buds into place.

Dad was definitely the man pushing Courtney in the swing, but he looked so young. Maybe twenty-four or twenty-five. The map Dad had given me was folded up inside my back pocket. I pulled it out and laid it on the table so it looked like I was studying something.

He took the red-headed toddler out of the swing and carried her towards the sandbox. Then the woman picked the younger me up and joined them in the sand. It was so weird to see myself, still in diapers, toddling around, trying to climb up the steep slide like Spider-Man.

Dad sat on the edge of the sandbox, Courtney at his feet. I could hear her singing. It sounded like gibberish at first, but then I realized she was singing in French while chewing on a shovel covered in sand.

A woman's voice joined in with Courtney's song and it was familiar.

Or maybe just pleasant enough to feel familiar. She must have been a nanny or babysitter. She looked almost young enough to be a college student. Maybe she worked for Dad while going to school.

She sat on the bench next to the sandbox. My toddler self jumped into the sand and continued to hop all the way across.

'Do you want a bucket?' Dad asked Courtney.

She nodded her head, shaking little pigtails that stuck out sideways, and kept on singing. Dad set the blue bucket in front of Courtney and then glanced at the woman and smiled. It wasn't the kind of look you'd give your hired help or even a secret-agent partner.

It was something more.

The little me hopped right behind Courtney and grabbed a fistful of sand, then sprinkled it on to her head. 'Raining, raining.'

She slapped her chubby hands over her face and screamed, 'No!'

For a moment I was captivated by my two-year-old self's ability to produce the most innocent yet devious look ever. It was as if I lived to make Courtney shriek like that.

'No, Jackson,' Dad said.

Courtney turned around and pushed my face away with both hands. 'Stop!'

She pushed the little me so hard I fell down on my butt. Little me stood up right away, grabbed a dump truck and started driving it over the mounds of sand.

'Let's make a castle for Princess Courtney,' Dad said.

I rolled my eyes. *So that's how it started.* My entire childhood, it was always, 'I'm the princess, so I'm in charge. Daddy said so.'

Dad filled a bucket using Courtney's shovel, but I could see him scanning the trees beyond the park, checking for something. Working. Courtney grabbed handfuls of sand and tossed them into the bucket. She patted the top and then pointed to Dad and said, 'Kevin.'

Only it sounded like, 'Kebin.' But she wasn't calling him Dad. I didn't have a chance to contemplate that because the woman on the bench got up and sat right in the sand. 'Jackson, you can decorate me. I don't mind.'

She had a Scottish accent. The little me grabbed some sand to sprinkle over the woman's head. She just laughed and leaned her head back, eyes closed. I could see her face clearly now from where I sat. She was very pretty, radiant in a way, but also plain. Maybe she was just happy. Happy about a little boy dumping sand over her head.

The woman snatched the little me in her arms and started kissing my face while the younger me laughed this loud giggle that rang through my headphones.

'We can make sand angels,' she said.

I watched with fascination as she lay back in the sand next to little me, spreading her arms out and flapping them like she expected to fly away. Courtney looked up from her castle and giggled, then crawled over next to me to make her own sand angel.

'You'll be shaking sand out of their heads for days,' Dad said, turning over Courtney's bucket. 'This is just like the finger-paint that never made it to the paper.'

His voice was filled with affection, not annoyance.

'But ten years from now, all they'll remember is this part. Not the sand we'll dust out of their beds for a week,' the woman said.

Then she sat up suddenly and grabbed Dad by the front of his shirt, pulling him down next to her. 'Come on, get down here.'

Dad laughed loudly but he didn't get up. 'Eileen!'

Eileen. The name on my birth certificate. The one I had thought was made up.

He reached out and took her hand, sliding it under his leg, concealing his fingers, now laced through hers. Who was he hiding it from? Surely not the oblivious two-year-olds taking a bath in sand. And what a great photo moment this was: four people lying in the sandbox like it was a giant water bed.

'You look so different when you laugh,' the woman named Eileen said to Dad. She turned her head just enough for her forehead to touch his cheek and I saw her lips barely touch his face and he smiled.

'Jackson,' Dad said, 'tell your mother the funny joke I taught you.'

'Knock, knock,' the little me said, still flapping his arms in the sand.

Eileen laughed. 'Who's there?'

'Knock, knock,' little me repeated.

'That's as far as we got,' Dad said.

Then they both laughed.

The sandbox activity wasn't the only noise I was picking up. The sound of leaves crunching came from the trees in the distance. Dad must have been more observant than I realized because he jolted up suddenly and stared through the trees. Courtney sat up too, and the little me stood and started stomping on Courtney's angel.

I heard the familiar click of a trigger before I even made out the man hiding behind a tree. The gunshot was loud, but all I saw was Dad diving over Eileen and grabbing me with one arm and pulling Courtney underneath him with the other. The little me got slammed hard on to his back and immediately started crying.

Dad shouted to someone but I couldn't see another agent or anyone except the man behind the tree. Dad pulled a gun from the back of his pants and fired a shot in that direction. He was covering the two little ones, giving him minimal ability to aim well. The hiding man darted towards another tree and that's when I saw his face and his red hair.

Shoe-print guy.

I don't know what made me even think to do what I did next. It was instinct took over. My heart stopped pounding and slowed to a normal rate and images flashed in my head so quickly – the area, the distance between me and the shoe-print guy – I could see all of it clearly. Then I pulled out Agent Freeman's gun and fired. I had never even picked up a gun until today, but I still knew without a doubt it would hit him right in the chest.

And ninety per cent of my brain wished I would have missed.

He fell to the ground and I took off running in that direction. I slowed down as I approached his body. He was lying on his back, staring up through the trees, eyes still open, but his chest was frozen. I dropped down beside him and pressed my hands over the blood seeping through his sweater.

Gasping for air, I dropped the gun right on the man's chest and couldn't bring myself to pick it up again.

I could see Dad from where I sat. He was squeezing the little me so tight and mumbling, 'You're OK.'

Two other people ran over, a man and a woman. They must have been agents because Dad nodded to them, and the woman picked up Courtney and Dad handed me over to the other dude and they took off. Dad flopped into the sand on his back and Eileen leaned over him with her hands covering her mouth. 'Oh God, Kevin, you got shot!'

Then his body shook with laughter and he reached up and pulled her down so their faces were close. 'It's just my shoulder. I'll be fine.'

She laid her head on his chest and I could hear her sobs

loud and clear even without the aid of fancy electronics. 'They could have killed you.'

'Shh, it's OK. Don't worry about me. I've been shot before.'

'What about the kids? Where are they?'

'Relax. They're already in the bulletproof car. That's where you should be right now. I could kill Freeman for scaring the shit out of me. Where the hell was he?' Dad asked.

Eileen lifted her head and then grabbed his face and kissed him, like she was taking advantage of his inability to use one of his arms. He used his free hand to run his fingers through her hair, and then a couple of seconds later he pushed her away, just a little.

'Marshall's coming,' he whispered.

She nodded but kissed his cheek again, then said very quietly, 'I love you.'

'Don't move!' Chief Marshall's deep voice came from behind me.

I closed my eyes and jumped before Marshall had a chance to get his hands on me again.

chapter thirty-three

SATURDAY, 15 AUGUST 2009, 1.20 A.M.

'Jackson!'

My forehead was pressed against the wooden table. 'Huh?'

This was the worst I'd felt after a time jump by a mile. It was like having a fever of a hundred and five.

'Let's get you out of here,' Dad said.

He lifted me from the booth and put one of my arms around his shoulders. We made it down the hall and into the elevator, then stumbled into Dad's room. I fell back on to the couch, closing my eyes, unable to move a single muscle.

'Damn, this is bad,' he muttered. 'What do you need? Food, water?'

'No,' I moaned. 'I'll just puke it back up.'

He flipped a light on. 'What's wrong? Why are you staring at your hands?'

I hadn't even realized I was staring until he said that. My hands were perfectly clean, but it was like I could still feel the sticky blood between my fingers. 'I touched the wound. The man was bleeding . . . I can't believe I did that.'

'What man?'

'The man I shot. He's dead. Actually, he's not really dead, but I did it anyway.'

'But . . . did you see what happened? With . . . her?' He choked on the last two words and dropped his eyes.

'What was supposed to happen? When I wasn't there?' It hit me right away. I have no memories of Eileen, and Dad asked if I saw what had happened to her. 'She was killed? In the real 1992?'

Dad nodded slowly and released my hands. He sat all the way down on the floor.

So when that event really happened, when I wasn't there, the red-haired guy didn't have anyone to stop him from shooting her.

'Dad, it was the same guy . . . one of the guys that was there when Holly got shot.' I couldn't stop looking at my hands . . . Where the man's blood had vanished. It wasn't real, but it *felt* real. 'I'm sorry . . . I couldn't let him go and not –'

'Do something?' he asked, before standing and sitting in the chair across from me.

'It was stupid. It didn't change anything.' I pushed the thought from my mind and dug for another question. 'Who was she? Eileen, I mean.'

He was quiet for a minute, collecting himself. 'A scientist. Completely brilliant and working with Dr Melvin. She's also the woman who carried you and your sister. Though you're not biologically connected. She called herself your mother.'

'I heard that. But we were just a project for her? An assignment? Dr Melvin explained about the surrogate mother for the experiment.'

He shook his head. 'Maybe at first, but the second she felt you two kicking . . . then, later, when she could hold you . . . you were her children. Two amazing babies who would change the world with their brilliant minds. That's what *she* wanted from the experiment.'

'What was your job? Protecting her?'

'My job was to protect you and your sister. Agent Freeman, not the one you attacked today but his father, was assigned to protect Eileen. I joined the project when you and Courtney were maybe . . . eleven months old.'

'After I shot that man, you were mad at Agent Freeman . . . said you didn't know where the hell he was.'

The colour drained from Dad's face. 'That's not what I meant for you to do. I just wanted you to see what happened, to know why I do what I do.'

'You don't have to explain.' I held up my hands, even though the blood had vanished, and he nodded. 'You loved her, didn't you?'

'Yes.' His voice cracked and he turned his eyes towards the TV. 'If I could change anything, it would be that day. Fifteen seconds and I could have covered her.'

'You almost did, but you grabbed me and Courtney instead,' I said, barely above a whisper.

'I know what you're thinking. It's not like that, Jackson. People always talk about resentment, like it happens all the time. If I'd saved her and let something happen to you or Courtney, she never would have forgiven me. Ever.' He smiled a little, but it was more of a grimace, filled with grief. 'To me, she left something she loved. Two somethings. A part of her that I could keep. Even before she died I wanted to be your father. To marry her and be a family. It was frowned upon, of course, but it was a line I was willing to cross once I figured out the best way to tell those above me.'

'I'm so sorry, Dad,' I said, then sighed heavily. 'I've been wondering who raised me before you came into the picture. Now I know.'

'I know you don't want to trust me, but I've already lost the only woman I've ever loved and my daughter. I don't want to lose you too.'

'And you lost your partner?'

He nodded. 'Agent Freeman senior was my mentor. He was brilliant. He died the same day as Eileen. And then having his son join as well, knowing he'd lost his father in this job . . . it's not easy. But there's a reason why agents are so young in Tempest . . . most don't last long.'

'They quit?'

'No, nobody quits. Ever,' he said, then changed the subject. 'Here's the thing, Jackson. There are ways around this system if you're good, and, fortunately, I'm that good. I've concealed a number of things from Marshall and from Tempest to protect you and Courtney. You don't have to give up your life for this.'

I was still trying to catch up with my latest dive into the past. 'But . . . why is her name on my birth certificate? With your last name?'

'She was the closest person you had to a mother, and using my last name helped with the cover story I gave you and Courtney about your mother dying in childbirth.'

'What was her real name?'

'Covington. Her family was extremely wealthy . . . they're Scottish. I'm sure you guessed that already from the accent. That's where our money comes from. She left her entire trust fund to you and Courtney. We live in her apartment. I gave you the life I thought she would have wanted you to have – very different than the way I grew up.'

'How did you grow up?' I asked.

Dad patted my shoulder. 'That's a story for another day. Remember what I told you . . . Marshall knows what I'm capable of, and he's constantly on guard. It's unlikely he'll let me have much involvement in your training.'

'Why?'

'He knows who I'm really working to protect.' He grinned. 'Besides, they want you to be good, but not good enough to work alone.'

'Or against them,' I added.

A loud dinging noise came from the radio on the bathroom counter and Dad's head snapped in that direction. 'Shit!'

'What?!'

'The sensors I put in your room.' He spun the dial on the safe and pulled out a gun. 'Someone may have gotten in.'

Despite the fact that moments ago I could barely move, I jumped up from the couch and beat him to the door.

Both of us charged down the hall and up the emergency staircase. I flew around the corner and smacked right into Holly, standing outside the door to our room.

Holly gasped but stayed on her feet. I was too weak to hold myself up and fell back on to the carpet. It must have taken her a second to realize it was me barrelling into her. All the CIA stuff had probably made her a little edgy.

'God, Jackson, you scared the crap out of me,' she said. 'I was just going to find you . . . What's wrong?'

Dad reached out a hand and helped me to my feet. 'He's a little sick. Might be food poisoning.'

'You look really pale,' Holly said before putting one of my arms around her shoulder. She opened the door to the room and I crawled on to the bed as soon as I walked in.

'I'll get some water,' Dad said.

Holly untied my shoes and pulled them off before sitting up on the bed and leaning against the headboard. 'Move closer and we can share the blanket.'

I moved over just enough so my head rested on her lap. She tossed the blanket over me and ran her fingers through my hair.

'Thanks, Hol.'

'Do you need anything else?' she asked.

I shook my head right before drifting off to sleep.

'I know – the first time I told my little first-graders I was taking the subway home, one of them actually cried,' Holly said, laughing.

'The crime rate on subways or any public transportation is far lower than most people think,' Dad said.

'I blame Hollywood. Too many movies about exploding buses and chasing bad guys on a subway,' Holly said.

'Was it strange for you? Supervising kids who have personal servants and no knowledge of any other way of life?' Dad asked.

Holly laughed again. 'At first maybe. When I taught gymnastics I used to bribe the kids with pennies to try a new skill. I knew after the first day of camp, pennies wouldn't get me anywhere. But I think every kid is sheltered from something.'

'Yes, that's probably true,' Dad said.

I finally opened my eyes. Dad sat in a chair across from the bed. I turned over and looked up at Holly. 'How long was I asleep?'

'A couple of hours.' She rested her hand on my cheek. 'How do you feel?'

'Better.' I sat up slowly and leaned against the headboard next to Holly. 'Dad, how come you're still here?'

He stood and handed me a bottle of water. 'Just wanted to make sure you were OK. And Holly is good company. I didn't even realize two hours had passed.'

'She's very good company.' I put an arm around her and pulled her closer. 'Whatever he told you, it's not true.'

Holly laughed and shook her head. 'So, you didn't really date one of the girls from *Legally Blonde, the Musical?*'

'OK, that's true but only for, like, two weeks.'

'She had to be the most obnoxious girl I've ever met,' Dad said.

I nodded. 'Agreed.'

Dad got up from his chair and headed towards the door.

'I think I'll go get a few hours' sleep before we make plans for today.'

'Dad?'

'Yeah?'

I glanced sideways at Holly, then back at him. 'I'm sticking with my decision to join the family business.'

His face fell. Then he nodded towards the door, indicating he wanted to speak privately. Holly caught on to the hint as well and gave me a nudge off the bed. After we were on the other side of the door and Dad had darted his eyes around the hallway several times, he finally spoke in a low voice. 'Let's talk about this some more tomorrow . . . but not here. Security's an issue in such a large building. I can't possibly check every corner.'

'OK.'

'We can go sailing . . . Freeman can keep an eye on your friends.'

I shook my head right away. 'Not a chance. I mean, I'll get on a boat, but Adam and Holly are coming with us. And I want you to tell me everything, but I already gave my word to Marshall and I'm not changing my mind about that part.'

He let out a breath. 'Are you sure that's what you want?'

I nodded. 'I'm not going to let history repeat itself.'

'I know what you mean,' he said. 'But we should still talk before someone else has a chance to glorify this job . . . fill your head with big ideas.'

He sighed and walked away towards the stairwell. Right now he was the only person that knew how many ways that history statement could be translated. 30 October 2009 might be the future in this timeline, but to me, it was history. And what happened to Eileen was *not* going to happen to Holly. I was determined to do anything to make sure of that. As I crawled back into bed, the reality hit me: I was officially in the CIA. Not just a made-up story. I slid Holly down so she was lying beside me, then leaned over her and kissed her. 'You are so pretty . . . Can I tell you a secret?'

'Yes, I like secrets. Especially yours.'

'I wanted to kiss you the first time I saw you.'

'Really?' She lifted her head and kissed my nose. 'Tell me another secret.'

'I promised my sister I'd marry you.'

Holly laughed. 'Was this one of your hallucinations induced by Adam's special science project?'

I ducked my head and touched my lips just below her collarbone. 'Yep, exactly. Oh . . . and we're having six children.'

'Six?!'

'Uh-huh. So keep those giant panties – you'll need them.'

Holly was laughing so hard she was near tears. Then her smile dissolved and she just stared at me for a minute, a hard, knowing look. 'Is that what you meant when you said . . . ?'

I knew where she was going with this. 'That it's hard to be sure until things aren't great?'

Her hands reached out to my face. 'What happened?'

'Just a really bad dream.'

'You can tell me.'

I rested my head on her pillow. 'Have you ever watched someone die?'

'No,' she answered, turning towards me so our faces were just inches apart. 'Never.'

The whole story about visiting Courtney in the hospital just spilled out of me, but I told her it was a dream or a hallucination. 'For a long time I thought my dad resented me for being healthy . . . for living.'

'I don't think that's true,' Holly said, and the second the words were out of her mouth tears trickled from her eyes on to the pillow. She wiped them away quickly.

'I'm sorry. I shouldn't have dumped all that on you.'

'No, it's OK. You can tell me anything. I mean that.' She picked up my hand and brought it to her lips. 'I just wish I knew what she looked like.'

'But you've seen . . .' I stopped myself, remembering that 009 Holly had only seen an empty room and a few pictures of me around the apartment. 'I mean . . . do you want to see a picture? I have one.'

She nodded and I reached over and dug through my wallet, pulling out the card I never gave Courtney with a picture of the two of us in Central Park on Christmas Eve, just a month or two before she got sick. Holly's eyes travelled from the picture to the words on the other side. And I let her read them because 007 Holly had and it only seemed fair.

She wiped away the tears that fell and handed me back the card, looking determined to retain her composure. 'I couldn't have done it either. Watch someone I love die. I would have been so scared.'

'I know you could, Holly.' I brushed my fingers over her cheek.

'Now, maybe, but when I was fourteen . . . no way.'

I smiled at her still-teary face. 'Enough with the sad stuff. It's torture making you this upset.'

'No more talk about me having six children either. Just thinking about that gives me the urge to cross my legs and leave them that way.'

That was exactly what we needed to shake us from our subdued mood. 'I love that you have no problem saying shit like that to me . . . So, can you tell me a secret? Actually, it's more of a question.'

'Maybe . . . ?'

'How did you end up hooking up with a guy like David Newman?'

'What's wrong with David?'

'Nothing, but what's the appeal? How did it start?' I asked.

She raised an eyebrow. 'You really want to hear this?'

'I'm just curious, that's all.'

'We got drunk one night and made out at a party in front of a lot of people and since we were already good friends, they just assumed . . . that was our special moment. David was so wasted he didn't even remember it. Still doesn't.'

'That's it?'

She shrugged. 'I think when I was younger, my vision was that the perfect guy was out there somewhere and then I just decided to—'

'Settle?'

She smiled, sheepishly. 'Yeah, but it's not like I knew that. I didn't know any different.'

I scooted closer and slid my hands around her waist. 'I know what you mean.'

'For a while, I hated you for making me doubt what I had already decided on. With David, I didn't feel . . . he didn't . . .'

'Light your fire?' I asked with a smile.

'No, he didn't.' She kissed me and rolled on top of me, tangling her fingers in my hair. Then she pulled away to yawn. 'Sorry.'

I pressed gently on the back of her neck until she laid her head on my chest. 'Go to sleep. You look exhausted.'

'You want me to move over?' she asked, laughing a little.

I tightened my arms around her. 'Nope, stay right here. It's very warm.'

She lifted her head. 'You've always been good at this.'

'At what?'

'You've always held my hand at just the right moment and kissed me with the most perfect timing. Like it was your way of saying what you couldn't say. I knew the words would come eventually.' She pressed her cheek against my shirt again.

'Sorry I ever doubted your patience.'

Sleep never came to me the rest of the night. I just lay there, feeling the warmth of Holly's presence spread through me, and I thought of my dad and everything he'd lost. He wouldn't betray me. Even if it was his job to save someone else. I knew that now.

I'd seen the scar before, on his shoulder, from the bullet

he took for me seventeen years ago, but didn't know how he'd gotten it. How could I have sat there in 2007 and whined about having to see a younger Holly, one that didn't know me, when my father had no chance of seeing Eileen alive again? Ever.

And hearing she was like a mother to me, I wanted to know so much more about her. Everything. If only it weren't so far back in time. I watched as the sun peeked through the curtain and knew things would never be as easy as they were at this very moment. But I didn't let myself think about anything else. Not yet.

chapter thirty-four

SATURDAY, 15 AUGUST 2009, 12.00 p.m.

'Wow,' Holly said, looking up at the giant white sailboat. 'Do we have a captain for this monster?'

Dad walked up behind us. 'That would be me.'

'You know, I think maybe . . . I'll sit this one out, lay out on the beach or something,' Adam said, looking longingly at the people on the beach, stretched out in the sand.

Dad clapped Adam on the back, a little too hard. 'Nope, you're coming with us. Can't leave you on land with all that access to technology. Not on my watch.'

I had a feeling Dad was joking, but Adam's face filled with fear. He leaned towards me and whispered, 'Mobsters use this technique all the time. Take the suspects out on a boat, shoot them, then toss their bodies into the ocean. By the time they wash up in some foreign country or Caribbean island, the evidence is gone.'

Holly heard Adam and rolled her eyes. 'Seriously? There's much better ways to erase evidence than that.'

Dad helped Holly on to the boat and I muttered to

Adam, 'What happened to the real Holly Flynn?'

Adam grinned at me. 'She's not so different than you. Holly's never wanted to be ordinary.'

He was right. It's not that Holly hadn't been herself around me, she just held back a lot because she didn't think I could handle it. Future plans, passion . . . commitment, all of that stuff would have sent me running.

I gave Adam a shove towards the boat. 'I got your back. Besides, most of the mobster murders happen on motorboats.'

Dad was hard at work getting the sails untied. I jumped in to help him, while Adam and Holly sat on the bench at the bow and watched.

'Is this part of agent training?' Holly asked. 'You guys look like you know what you're doing.'

I glanced at Dad and smiled. 'No, actually it was part of our family vacations. Something completely normal.'

'And we can't say that about much, can we?' Dad said.

A few minutes later we were off, staring out at the open waters. I immediately felt a sense of relief at being far away from a hotel full of people. Now I could understand why my dad wanted to escape.

'So, when are we going to discuss spy secrets?'

'When we get a little further out of range,' he said quietly. 'Have you learned how to check for listening devices?'

'Yeah, you showed me.' I began my search, starting with the lower level, then I scanned over the deck carefully. Dad was having a whispered conversation with Adam and I couldn't help listening in.

'There's a division I started in years ago, when I was

about your age. Anyway, headquarters are in the basement of the New York Public Library and there's very little risk involved. Mostly reading books, computer programs and websites, and looking for spy code,' Dad told him. 'I could get you in.'

'Cool,' Adam said.

They dived into an in-depth conversation about this particular department of the CIA and I left them alone and sat at the opposite end of the boat. The sense of urgency Dad had had last night seemed to have dissolved. Maybe he just wanted to spend some time together, now that we didn't have any more secrets.

Holly returned from the lower deck, handing me a drink, and then sat between my legs, leaning back against me.

'This is the first sailboat I've ever been on,' she said.

'Sailing was always my favourite part of vacation.'

The sun beat down on us, but the splashes of ocean water hitting us every few minutes made it perfect. I tightened my arms around her waist and rested my chin on top of her head. Both of us sat in silence for a while, then I felt Holly's eyes on me, and when I glanced down she was staring at me, her face intense.

'What?' I asked.

She shook her head. 'Nothing . . . just . . .'

I leaned down further. 'What is it, Hol?'

Her lips touched the side of my neck. Then she said in a low voice, right in my ear, 'I love you. I really mean it. Not like when I said it to David . . . Much more than that.'

I squeezed her tighter, feeling so warm. I don't know

what made me say what I blurted out next. Maybe it was the intensity in her eyes or the guilt of holding back for so long. Or maybe I wanted to say it because I knew my dad never got to.

I kept my eyes on Dad, but brushed my lips to Holly's ear and whispered, 'Marry me.'

I immediately felt her suck in a breath and hold on to it, but I didn't look at her. I didn't need to. Asking her was my only goal. The rest wasn't important . . . yet.

She turned my face so I had to look at her, then said, 'I will . . . some day . . . I promise.'

'You don't have to promise. I only wanted to ask.'

'I promise,' she repeated with a smile.

I wanted to just bathe in the perfection of this moment, but too much had happened for me to allow my mind to relax. Today was 15 August. Would Holly's life be in danger again on 30 October? Or sooner?

The worry on Dad's face as he steered the boat around jerked me into full-blown observation mode.

'Something wrong?' I asked him.

He pointed behind me and I quickly turned. Dark charcoal clouds were charging towards us, a complete contrast to the rest of the sky.

'Crap,' Adam said, standing up to get a closer look.

I got up and walked over to Dad. 'So we turn around, no big deal, right? It'll probably move over really quick.'

'Right,' he repeated.

Dad and I raced around, securing the sails, figuring out our coordinates in case we lost visibility. Ten minutes later the sky was completely covered with thick dark clouds ready to overflow on us.

A bolt of lightning lit up the sky, turning everything pink for a few seconds, then the rain came down in giant sheets.

'Lifejackets!' Dad shouted over the rumbling thunder. 'And get off the deck!'

Holly and I flipped open the seat of the bench and pulled out lifejackets. I tossed one to Adam and threw another over Holly's head, tying it tight. The rain was pounding so hard I could hardly see her face, but I heard the shriek that escaped from her mouth as she looked over my shoulder. I spun around quickly.

A dark-haired man with a long black raincoat stood at the very front of the boat. *Oh God, this was not happening now.* My first instinct was to shout for Holly to go below deck, but if someone had appeared up here . . .

'How did he get here?' Holly asked.

And who did he come for?

The sound of my heart pounding was louder than the rain. The man grabbed Adam around the neck and the boat tilted sideways, throwing Holly into the railing. The man holding Adam stumbled a little and I used my elbow to give him a hard blow to the side of his head, forcing him to release Adam.

Adam fell forward, then jumped up and grabbed Holly from the edge of the railing, pulling her towards the other end of the boat.

A second later I was tossed on to my back on the deck. When I leaped up, the man wrapped his hands around my throat and shoved me against the post in the centre of the boat. I didn't recognize his face, but I could see the rage written all over it. I grabbed his wrists, trying to prise them from my neck. I couldn't breathe. Black spots were appearing in front of my eyes.

'You killed her,' he sputtered at me.

Killed who?

'Holly!' I heard Adam shout.

I tried to kick the man, but my legs had turned to Jell-O. Running feet pounded all around me. Or maybe it was the blood throbbing in my head. A blurred figure appeared behind the man and a loud crack followed, then his grip loosened and he fell to the ground. I gasped for air and the black spots disappeared. Holly stood in front of me, a fire extinguisher in her hands.

She jumped back when the man stood up and stumbled around the rocking boat. It was like he couldn't see. His hands felt around for something and then he stood up on the bench. A second bolt of lightning blasted through the sky, revealing the confusion on his face. Then two shots went off and the man tumbled over the railing into the ocean.

I clutched my chest and turned around to see Dad poised at the far end of the boat, holding his gun. Perfect aim. He ran over to me and grabbed my face. 'Are you OK?'

All I could do was pant and nod.

'Sorry, I put all the guns down below,' he shouted, then he dropped a handgun into my palm.

I stared at it for a second and then tucked it into my pants, even though I hated the idea of using it.

'Somebody needs to explain . . . *that*, now!' Holly said,

pointing in the direction of the floating body.

The thunder was so loud, none of us could speak over it. Finally I found my voice and shouted at Dad, 'What the hell was that? Did you know? The next entry on Marshall's list, right? Why did you bring us out here if you knew someone might attack us?'

'If I knew about this, do you think I would have put my gun away?' he said. 'I've never seen that man before, and I've seen nearly all of them.'

The boat tilted further sideways, throwing us towards the railing. I caught Holly around the waist and covered her head with my arm as we crashed into it.

Dad stumbled back up and shouted to Adam, who was now attempting to steer the boat.

'Jackson, tell me!' Holly demanded as we struggled to stand upright again. 'Where did he come from? He appeared out of nowhere.'

I ignored her question and turned around to shout at Dad, 'Should we go below deck?'

Dad slid back towards us. 'No, Freeman's coming. ETA is two minutes.'

I stowed the gun and scanned the water, checking for another boat.

'Jackson?' Holly said again.

I could hear the hurt in her voice, like that time at the zoo when she knew something was wrong and I didn't tell her what. I looked at Dad and he nodded before heading back towards Adam.

When I turned around, Holly was sliding again. I grasped the sides of her lifejacket in between my fingers and leaned my face close to hers.

'Tell me,' she said again.

I pushed away the wet hair clinging to her face. 'He's a time-traveller.'

'What?'

'A time-traveller,' I repeated.

'But . . . but . . . then how did he just appear . . .'

The wind alone was strong enough to knock someone Holly's size over. I pulled her closer and held the rail with one hand. 'Erase everything you've ever heard about time travel because it will just confuse you.'

'Yeah, that helps a lot.'

Just that little bit of sarcasm from Holly as we were clinging to a boat threatening to sink gave me the confidence to tell her the rest. 'I can do it too.'

'Do what?'

'Travel through time.' No response, so I added to my explanation. 'When you saw me Thursday, in different clothes, I had been gone for weeks.'

More lightning. Bright enough so I could see the shock on her face. 'What? You didn't see me for weeks?'

Should I tell her? 'I saw you, but you were younger.'

'That can't be true . . . Why don't I remember?' she asked as we both turned at the sound of the motor from Freeman's boat. He also had a giant light that he shone right on us. 'What did I tell you, Holly? Erase everything you know about time travel.'

'Let's go!' Dad yelled to us.

He grabbed Holly's lifejacket and lifted her right on to the railing. 'I'll go first and help you across.'

The lights from Agent Freeman's boat shone on her face and I could see the mixture of confusion and hurt, but something else . . . like she really *wanted* to believe me.

The other boat was pulled alongside ours, but there was still quite a gap. Holly shook her head at Dad's offer of help and jumped before anyone could stop her. She rolled sideways to cushion her fall when she hit the deck of the other boat, then stood perfectly on her feet.

'Silverman, you're next,' Dad shouted.

Adam climbed up and jumped like Holly had, except he landed hard, on his knees. I knew he'd be hurting later on. Water rushed up the side of the motorboat as the waves rolled from every direction.

Dad and I both stood on the railing and jumped at the same time, landing on our feet.

'Who was it?' Freeman shouted to Dad.

'Never seen him before.'

'He said I killed someone . . . a woman,' I yelled, before pulling Holly down in one of the seats with me.

Freeman and Dad both looked at me, and then Freeman said. 'Maybe it hasn't happened yet.'

'I know it hasn't happened yet.' I hadn't killed anyone except the shoe-print guy – Raymond. But that was a half-jump, so he wasn't really dead.

'If you're a time-traveller, then why can't you just go back in time a few hours and make sure we don't get on the boat?' Holly asked.

'You told her?' Adam said from my other side.

'It doesn't work like that, Hol.' I picked up her hand and squeezed it. 'Sometimes I wish it were that easy.'

Suddenly Holly jumped up and grabbed Freeman's shoulder. 'Stop! There's someone else out there!'

Adam, Dad and I were at the edge of the boat in seconds, trying to see through the rain. Sure enough, a small figure stood on a dock that was close to shore.

'It looks like a kid,' Freeman said, turning the boat.

We all hesitated, even Dad. He was a government employee fighting evil time-travellers, not rescuing kids from storms. And yet none of us wanted to leave. I looked back at the shore. No frantic parents were standing on the beach, screaming at the child. Most likely they already went in for help.

'It's the opposite direction of the harbour,' Freeman shouted, but he was already starting to turn in the direction of the swim dock.

A giant wave crashed over the side of the boat, tossing water on top me, Adam and Holly. A loud grinding noise came from the motor and Adam and I both looked at it, waiting to see smoke rising.

'The damn thing won't turn!' Freeman said.

'I'll swim out there,' I shouted so all of them could hear. 'Just go without me. Get help from the harbour.' I jumped off the back of the boat before they could say anything. Waves crashed over my head as I swam. When I reached the swim dock, I could already tell it was a little girl, maybe nine or ten, arms wrapped around the pole in the centre of the platform. But I couldn't figure out why she was fully clothed: jeans and long-sleeved shirt, and tennis shoes.

I pulled myself up and walked closer. The light from the

distant boat shone on her face and her long red hair. 'Do I . . . know you?'

She shook her head and clung to the pole.

'Are you OK?'

'Yes,' she answered. 'Will you come with me?'

I knelt down in front of her. 'Where? Back to the shore?'

She shook her head again and an eerie feeling washed over me. I was just starting to figure out where I had seen her before when she released the pole and grabbed my hand. I felt the splitting-apart sensation immediately and knew we were jumping. Both of us. A half-jump. But to where?

chapter thirty-five

The first thing I noticed was the silence. No sound of rain or thunder. I opened my eyes and looked around.

'Is this . . . a subway station?' I asked.

'Yes, there's no one here,' the girl said in this formal, adult-like tone.

I knelt down in front of her again, looking her over. She was thin, frail, but looked so much like Courtney. She turned her head and stared at me. Her eyes were blue . . . not green.

'Wait a minute . . . I've seen you, haven't I? At the zoo?'

Water dripped from the end of her nose and she wiped it away. 'Yes.'

'Who are you?' I asked.

'I'm like you.'

'What's your name?' I glanced around the empty station, half expecting a train to come barrelling though any second.

'Emily,' she said.

'You're just like me?'

She shook her head. 'Almost, but not exactly.'

'So you're like the others?' I backed away from her a little, remembering the vanishing child I had seen in the hotel the other night, wandering around. Looking two years younger.

'Almost, but not exactly,' she said again, smiling a little bit.

I shook my head in disbelief. 'I fell asleep, didn't I? Or hit my head? You look just like my sister.'

'We all look alike. Most of us. Similar DNA, right?'

'I don't know . . . I guess,' I said.

Emily held out a small hand to me. 'Just come with me.'

'Why?' But I took her hand anyway.

'I have to show you something.'

She was leading me towards a set of stairs, probably leading up to the street. I used my free hand to pull out my gun. 'What do you know?'

She shook her head. 'I'm not going to hurt you.'

'It's not you I'm worried about. It's whoever told you to find me.'

'No one told me.' Then she turned to me and smiled. 'Actually, *you* told me.'

That's when I stopped in front of the staircase and froze for a second, then lowered myself so we were level. I forgot my question when I looked into her swirling blue eyes. 'You have my eyes . . .'

She smiled again. 'Yes.'

'Why? How?'

She frowned and shook her head again. 'I can't tell you that. Please let me show you something.'

But before she took the first step she spun around again. 'I almost forgot.' She reached into her pocket and put her hand over mine before dropping something into it. 'I'm supposed to give you this.'

I stared down at the tiny object in my open palm. The sparkle of a diamond reflected against the flickering lights above us. I turned the ring over in my hand, thinking that it must have some significance beyond what I had just asked Holly today. Either way, this other version of myself had really bad timing. It hardly seemed necessary to tell Emily to find me and drag me to a subway station in some other time to give me a ring, especially in the middle of a storm that nearly killed us.

I followed Emily up the steps and could see light peeking in from above. It was daytime. 'Is this New York?'

'Yes.'

When we reached the top step, I expected to hear the familiar sounds of the city – horns honking, engines running, people talking on cellphones. But it was silent. We emerged from underground completely and all I could do was stare with my mouth hanging open.

This was New York, but like nothing I'd ever seen. A few buildings remained completely upright, but they were covered in a sand-coloured dust, probably a result of the surrounding buildings having crumbled.

My legs felt so weak I could hardly stand. This was my home. The place I grew up. But no one was around. Nothing. I turned slowly in a circle and saw the street filled with so much debris that I couldn't even see the road.

I snapped back to reality when I heard Emily coughing beside me and realized I was coughing too. Everything above ground was covered in the sand-coloured dust. No wonder we were choking on the air.

'Emily . . . is this . . . the future?' I asked. It couldn't be the past . . . at least not any past I had studied in history.

'Yes,' she said through her coughing.

'What happened? What year is it?'

'I can't tell you that.'

'But how did it happen . . . ? Is it a war or . . . something else?'

'All I can say is . . . some people are fighting to keep this from happening and some people are going to . . . *make* it happen.'

I gave her a long searching look and saw the truth in her eyes. So it wasn't just gangs fighting gangs. This place – this year – was very bad. Someone needed to prevent this destruction.

'I . . . I've never jumped outside the span of my own life lived to date,' I said.

'It's because you're with me,' she spluttered while coughing.

'You're different than me, I get that. But how are you different from *them*?'

She covered her face with her hands, wiping away the dust. 'I have everything they could ever want.'

She didn't seem pleased with this at all.

I heard barking from far away. The first sound I had heard since we arrived here. Seconds later a pack of brown dogs came barrelling around the corner, snapping their mouths at us. Emily and I backed up against the building and she grabbed my hand. I expected us to jump back, but she just stood there, frozen.

'Emily, let's go!'

Her eyes closed for a second and I could see that she was trying, but nothing happened. 'Oh no . . . I did something wrong. They're not supposed to be here!'

Her eyes were monster-sized, but the dogs suddenly turned their heads and took off in the opposite direction they came from. I had about half a second to sigh with relief before three men came around the same corner the dogs had emerged from.

At least I think they were men. All of them had shaved heads and indistinct features. Their eyes were almost all white and their skin was practically transparent. The blue and pink veins running under their skin were clearly visible, as if a few layers were missing.

'He was right! I don't believe it!' one of them shouted with triumph.

I could practically feel the anger and vengeance rolling off the three men, and I knew they weren't here to have a friendly chat.

Emily still wasn't moving so I tugged her hand and pulled her in front of me as we started to run along the side of the crumbled building. This was panic of the worst kind, and there was no chance my dad would show up here to rescue me like he had on the boat.

The pounding of my feet matched my heartbeat. Emily's hair flew behind her as we ran and more dirt rose from the ground, landing in my eyes and mouth.

She glanced frantically over her shoulder at me. 'Jackson, running won't help . . . we've got to –'

Both of us practically screeched to a halt as the three men magically appeared right in front of us.

'I'm shocked the two of you even considered running,' one man sneered. 'Why run when you can jump?'

Emily backed up and I shifted her behind me and against the building. Her chest rose and fell so quickly there was no mistaking her fear. Probably the reason she couldn't get us out of here.

Jenni Stewart's diagrams played in my mind over and over, and it was as if the rest of me just knew what to do without even thinking about it.

One of the attackers lunged for Emily, and just as he was about to get his hands around her I kicked him hard in the stomach, sending him flying backwards. The back of his head cracked against the pavement. I jabbed the second man, who had approached from my other side, in the face with my elbow. He staggered backwards as Emily slid down the wall as if her legs were giving out.

'Can I do it?' I asked her frantically. 'Can I jump us both back if we're in the future?'

Her huge eyes searched mine and she opened her mouth to answer and then let out a scream. 'Jackson, look out!'

The third guy had his arms around my neck from behind. I used his own weight to throw him over my body and he smashed into the ground. He hollered in agony and I quickly pulled Emily up by her arms and lifted her off the ground. She squeezed me tight and pressed her face into my shirt. She was trying to block everything out. To get us the hell out of here. I had never been so happy to feel the awful sensation of a half-jump as I was right then.

chapter thirty-six

SATURDAY, 15 AUGUST 2009, 3.30 P.M.

The storm had picked up even more, which I didn't think was possible. Rain whipped me in the face. Emily was still gripping me tight, her face hidden, but I could feel her shaking. I was too. I attempted to set her down, but she wouldn't let go of me and her shaking had turned to sobs. I hugged her back, assuming she must be comfortable enough with me in the future, whatever year she came from.

Finally she released me and took in a deep breath. 'I didn't know it would be . . . like that.'

'Are you OK?' I asked her.

She nodded and then reached for the pole again, gripping on to it. 'I didn't exactly aim well . . . did I?'

'Were you trying to end up on a swim dock in the middle of a giant storm?'

'No, but things change . . . Sometimes it's hard to get it right.'

The wind picked up and rocked the swim dock. My

stomach turned over and I gripped on to the pole above her hand, trying to focus my eyes on the now distant boat. I could see it retreating further, towards the harbour docks.

'I have to swim back,' I said to Emily, pointing towards the shore.

'Me, too.' She cringed when another roar of thunder cut her off.

'Can't you just jump? Like, to another day?'

She shook her head, flinging rain everywhere. 'No, let them see us swim back and then I'll jump. You can't tell anyone about me. About what I can do. I'm just the kid you rescued from the storm, OK?'

That's why she did a half-jump, so everyone would still see us here, though I doubted the visibility would stretch that far. 'What's going to happen?'

'You have to let me go, no matter what, promise?' Pink and blue lightning brightened her face and I could see she already doubted my ability to take orders from a little girl.

'You took me to the future . . . Does that mean . . . ? Have you even been born yet?' I asked her.

'I can't tell you.'

I knelt in front of her and looked her straight in the eyes. 'How old are you?'

'Eleven.'

'Do you know Dr Melvin?'

She wasn't floundering in this unannounced staring contest. 'I know *of* him.'

'Then he's not the reason you exist?'

Her defences crumbled and she took a step back. 'We have to go!'

I grabbed on to her hand. 'Not yet.'

'You told me not to answer questions. Not many of them anyway,' she yelled through more thunder.

'That was the other me. He's, like, really old, right? Nobody listens to him.'

'Oh, really? So you don't trust your future self, even though he obviously knows more than you?'

I knew she was right. It was irresponsible to force anything out of her. 'I'm sorry. It's just . . . right now there's something that might happen and I've got to make sure it doesn't. It's hard to think about anything else.'

'I know you feel like you have to change everything or fix it, but don't over-think. Trust yourself to make the right choice. It's not as hard as it seems.' She pointed to the shore. 'We need to go.'

We both jumped in and I helped pull Emily along. Waves came flying over our heads, but finally we reached the shore and walked the rest of the way up the beach. I nodded towards the hotel. 'Run in that direction and I'll say you found your way in, OK?'

She started to turn and then hesitated for a second. She kept her eyes down but wrapped her arms around my waist and squeezed tight. 'Bye, Jackson . . . good luck.'

I watched her run towards one of the side doors and felt a giant weight pressing on my shoulders. It wasn't just about saving Holly. There was more to it. Much more. No wonder Dad wanted to keep me away from this.

Too late now.

I turned and jogged towards the harbour. Adam, Holly, and Freeman were already heading in my direction.

'Everything OK with that kid?' Adam asked.

'Yeah, she's back inside,' I said, waving off any more questions by changing the subject. 'Where's my dad?' I asked Freeman.

'Over by the front doors.'

Holly threw her arms around me and I hugged her quickly, then pointed towards the hotel. 'Should we get inside?'

Everybody took off running. Dad ushered us in and the chill of air conditioning hit us the second we walked into the lobby. We were all dripping wet, shoes squeaking across the marble floor, and yet everyone around us was so calm. It took every ounce of self-control I had to not announce the end of the world to the entire hotel. I couldn't even tell Tempest what I had seen without telling them about Emily.

Dad nodded towards the hallway on our left and we followed. But I sucked in a breath when I saw him draw his gun; Freeman did the same.

'What's happening?' Holly asked.

'They're here,' Freeman said.

'What do they want?' Adam asked, desperately.

'Jackson,' Dad answered. 'At least that's what Melvin thinks. Possibly to replicate the experiment. We've kept them away for a couple of months now. I let them get close, against Marshall's orders, two years ago, so they could see you didn't have any abilities. It went quiet for a while then, but not any more.'

'Why wouldn't they just kill me anyway?' I asked.

'They don't murder needlessly. Only to gain power,'

Freeman said, poking his head around the corner before leading us that way.

'Power for what?' Holly asked.

'They believe the world would be a better place if we were all like them,' Dad said. 'But Tempest believes time travel by mass population would be utter chaos.'

'Totally,' Adam said.

'Dr Ludwig's on their side,' I added. 'With all his cloning or whatever.'

'They think Melvin's creating a counter-army.' Dad said, turning towards me. 'Don't do anything stupid, Jackson. Just try to stay close and keep your distance from them. Freeman and I have done this many times. We can handle it.'

Freeman froze in the middle of the hallway. Then, about twenty rooms down, a blonde woman and the man named Raymond appeared out of nowhere.

The man who killed Eileen. I couldn't imagine what Dad went through, having to see him over and over again.

'Damn, that's freaky,' Holly muttered. 'I kinda didn't believe you about that time-travel thing . . . Totally believe you now.'

Dad immediately shoved me behind him and I did the same with Holly.

'What the hell are we supposed to do if they just appear and disappear?' Adam asked, fear gathering in his voice.

'They can't do it much, trust me,' Dad said.

'Except Thomas,' Freeman muttered.

Thomas again. His name kept coming up at very important moments.

Holly screamed when Freeman fired at them. They shot back at us and I yanked her further behind me. If they could pop in and out, she wasn't going anywhere out of my sight.

Adam yelled this time because another man had appeared right behind us.

The first two EOTs took off running, away from us, and I yanked Holly in front of me as we ran away from the man behind us and towards the two up ahead. Freeman followed them through two doors into a big dining room. The room was filled with people dressed for a wedding. The second we came bursting through the doors with our guns, screams erupted and everyone started running about.

The whole place was full of innocent bystanders. They needed to get out. Quick. I scanned the walls and spotted something to help clear the building.

'Go set off the fire alarm!' I shouted at Holly.

She ran over to the wall behind us and smashed the glass case with her elbow. The alarm sounded and water started spraying down from the sprinklers on the ceiling. More screams. The room emptied in about thirty seconds. Crystal glasses were on every table. A giant grand piano sat in the centre of the dance floor. Not exactly a great place for a gun fight.

The shoe-print guy, Raymond, sprang up on top of the piano and aimed his pistol right at Freeman. Holly gasped as we both watched Freeman drop his weapon from ten feet away and raise his hands in the air. The surrender lasted about two seconds, before Dad jumped up behind Raymond and kicked him so hard he fell on to the table behind the piano and then slid on his back, sending the plates, crystal and silverware soaring in all directions.

The other man suddenly went from thirty feet in front of me to right behind me. I moved out of the way and grabbed a chair from the one of the tables and threw it in his path. He tumbled over it and sprang back to his feet.

The blonde woman fired at the ceiling and Holly screamed again when the massive crystal chandelier shattered. She dived under a table as pieces of glass flew everywhere. I slid under with her and pulled her next to me. I could feel her heart pounding even harder than mine.

'Stay with me, OK?' I said. 'Don't run off or anything.'

She nodded.

Dad's feet raced past me and then the woman followed. I aimed my gun at her leg, but it was too close to Dad and I couldn't risk it. Holly reached out and grabbed the woman's ankle, causing her to fall right on her face. Adrenalin rushed through me and I rolled out from under the table, stood up and then stepped right on the woman's back, pointing my gun at her head.

'No, Jackson! Don't touch her!' Dad shouted, but I didn't know why.

The last thing I saw was Dad pulling Adam to the ground as a bullet soared over their heads.

The room dissolved and I had no idea where I was headed.

chapter thirty-seven

A full jump. We just did a full jump. *Duh.* That's why I wasn't supposed to touch her.

Despite the life-threatening situation and the fact that both me and this blonde EOT chick were armed, the first thought to cross my mind as my eyes opened was, *Holly just watched me disappear!*

If she didn't believe that I was a time-traveller before, she sure as hell would now. I heard several people gasp and I turned my head to look at a group of teenage girls standing on the pavement, dressed in weird argyle skirts and socks up to their knees. Like Jackie Kennedy or something. That's when I realized what exactly they were looking at. My foot on a woman's back, pointing a gun at her, and both of us dripping wet. And this day was clear and sunny.

I quickly tucked the gun into my pants and glanced at the street. Old-model Cadillacs were parked all over Fifth Avenue, except they weren't old. Most of them looked brand new. Weird-ass hippy buses lined up against the curb, and I was half expecting the cast of *Hairspray* to burst into the streets singing, 'Welcome to the Sixties'.

The EOT chick tossed me off her and I landed on my back and also on one of the prissy girls' shoes. All five or six of them screamed as loudly as possible and I sprung up from the ground and ran after the blonde woman.

If she jumped, would I be able to get back? And was this the same timeline that we left, but in the past? My guess was no, because I knew how hard it was to jump in the same timeline. I could see her head bobbing and I shoved past people to get closer.

My new observational skills never turned off, and as I ran I took in everything – the hippy guy singing a Bob Dylan song outside a store, the buildings that were missing from the skyline.

Finally I reached the woman and grabbed the back of her shirt. My arms went around her, squeezing tight. 'You had better be able to get us back . . . exactly where we left.'

She jabbed me in the stomach with her elbow, but I felt her pulling us back. Or somewhere else.

chapter thirty-eight

SATURDAY, 15 AUGUST 2009, 4.30 P.M.

My feet slid and I felt myself falling down a slanted surface. Rain. Thunder. Again. My eyes flew open and I nearly shouted after seeing that I was on the roof of the hotel. I sprawled out flat on my stomach and dug my fingers into the shingles. The EOT chick laughed an evil laugh. She had easily wormed herself at least three feet away from me. I would have liked to knock her teeth out, if it wasn't for the fact that I was too scared to let go of anything.

'Damn. Off by a few minutes. Maybe they had time to kill your dad by now,' she sneered. 'He's really good at getting in the way.'

Intense fury pulsed through me, giving me the courage to release one hand and reach for my gun. The EOT woman was still trying to get to her feet . . . she wouldn't even see it coming. But I couldn't do it.

Just as my fingers moved from the trigger and reached for a piece of the shingles to grip on to, a loud boom came from below, nearly causing me to tumble to the ground.

A bolt of lightning exploded through the sky at the same moment a bullet ripped through her chest. *Whose bullet?*

I watched in horror, unable to do anything, as the woman fell against the roof, then tumbled down and landed below with a smack. I heard shouts and sirens going off everywhere. I flipped over so my back was pressed against the roof and attempted to shimmy upward. I pulled the images of the hotel maps up in my mind. There was a roof access door where the roof levelled off above me.

When I reached the top I started to stand and made the mistake of looking at the ground below. My stomach turned, dizziness swept over me and I was on my back again, panting and trying to force the fear away. I was pretty sure they didn't let acrophobic join the CIA.

I heard a door burst open and voices.

'Just tell me what happened to him,' Holly said. 'Can he come back if he . . . vanished?'

I sighed with relief. She was OK. But who was she talking to? I didn't want to draw attention to myself yet, not until I knew it was safe

'I have a feeling we'll find out very soon, now that you're here,' another voice said.

A very familiar voice. One I had heard on the very worst day of my existence. I had to see his face . . . The other man in Holly's dorm . . .

Slowly I stood up, forcing my eyes to stay on the sky and not the ground.

The man had Holly pressed against a pole. It was the same man who fired his gun and shot her on 30 October 2009. *It hasn't happened yet*, I forced myself to remember.

'Jackson – just the person I was looking for,' he said. 'I'm not sure we've officially been introduced. I'm Thomas.'

'Thomas,' I spat, jumping down to the eight square feet of flat surface by the door. Of course it was Thomas. The EOT who could keep doing this over and over again until the fight turned out exactly how he wanted. Maybe I'd have to give him what he wanted right away, so he wouldn't try and do it over again. All I had to do was pretend to be on his side.

Easy, right?

I couldn't look at Holly or I'd deviate from my plan. Screw it up. But I could feel her eyes burning into the side of my face.

'Was that Rena flying off the roof?' Thomas asked casually.

'Um . . . who? The blonde chick?'

'Yes, that's her.' He turned to face me. 'I'm not here to hurt you, Jackson. That was never the intent. We'd be happy to leave your father alone if he hadn't killed so many of us.'

I sucked in a breath and tried to calm down. *Dad is a survivor. He makes it out alive all the time,* I repeated to myself. 'What is it you want from me, Thomas?'

He leaned closer to me, still gripping on to Holly, and I could see the slightest bit of resemblance between him and me. He was probably fifteen years older, but still, we looked alike. 'I just want you to hear my side. You've been influenced by others. Others not like you . . . they don't understand us. I want you to see what you could have. The perfect life. We've tried to get you alone, and now the only solution seems to be threatening the life of this girl. Look how you discovered your full abilities when she was shot. Amazing progress.'

I could feel my face hot with rage at the mention of what happened to Holly . . . but the other dude – Raymond – said it was a mistake. Did he mean that?

'What's he talking about?' Holly asked.

Thomas looked at her. 'Just the future, dear – nothing you need to worry about. The future's always changing.'

'Yes, it's changing already,' I said, jumping into my plan before I got distracted. 'A lot of time has passed since that event. For me, anyway. The more I use my abilities, the more I want to learn. Everything else is nonessential.'

A grin spread across his face. 'Now, that's *exactly* what I love to hear.'

'Like Rena. You don't care that someone just killed her because she's alive somewhere else. Another timeline, right?'

'Ah . . . I see you haven't been taught everything. When someone like myself –' he pointed at me – 'or yourself is killed, we cease to exist anywhere else, forever. Not in the past. Nowhere. But this young lady, and ordinary people in general, may be perfectly fine when creating another timeline. It's one reason EOTs and ordinary people don't interbreed, and it's why we were against Dr Melvin's experiment.'

'I don't understand,' I said. From the corner of my eye I could see Holly's chest moving up and down as she took in heavy, fearful breaths.

The rain was slowing to a light drizzle, but the sky was

still as dark as the middle of the night. I had tunnel vision right now, ignoring the turmoil I knew must be happening down below.

'Well . . . creating multiple timelines could lead to the destruction of the world. Time-travellers driven by emotion will never stop saving loved ones. You'll act the part of complete idiot, regardless of the power you have. It won't matter to you, and pretty soon . . . well . . . world destruction.'

Like what Emily showed me? Could I have caused that in the future? Or could another time-traveller?

'What if I fixed things without making a new timeline?' I asked.

He smiled this patronizing smile. 'Yes, that would be excellent for you, but only I can do that. Others have tried. So much that they rotted their minds and died. Besides, changing one event often creates a chain reaction, and if you haven't carefully considered each alteration, if you act impulsively, the results could be disastrous. It's a responsibility few can handle.'

'I get it. Well . . . I do now anyway. Now that I'm more *experienced*,' I said, channelling Jenni Stewart and her ability to dive into a role so completely. To pretend. 'So, tell me then . . . tell me your side.'

He smiled and released Holly, then wrapped his fingers around my arm. We were jumping. Together.

chapter thirty-nine

I shook Thomas's hand off my arm the second I felt the ground underneath me.

'It's Times Square,' Thomas said. 'What do you think?'

The buildings I knew so well surrounded me, only they were painted in soft earth tones, reflecting perfectly the sun's rays.

And this version of New York had people everywhere. Their clothes matched the earth tones of the buildings. A woman walked by us and smiled, then said hello. My eyes dropped. The ground was covered in greenish-brown brick that extended in every direction. No dividing lines between pavement and street.

'Where are all the cars?' I asked.

'No cars. Just teleportation devices for travelling lengthy distances,' Thomas said. 'Notice the air. It's perfect – always clean, never too hot or to cold.'

Not like the air in the destroyed New York Emily had taken me to. I wouldn't have lasted a day breathing that in. What was she trying to tell me?

'Some people are fighting to keep this from happening and some people are going to make *it happen.'*

'Is this where you're from?' I asked Thomas.

'Don't you mean, *when* I'm from?' Thomas asked, then he laughed. 'That's the wonderful thing about being one of us, you can call anywhere home . . . any time. Why not choose a world that makes the most logical sense?'

OK, so obviously he isn't going to tell me what year he was born. Not that I expected him to.

Behind me there were kids playing on a playground. At least I think it was a playground. But they were almost silent. Nothing like the kids I had in my group at camp. All the equipment seemed to be moving or electronic. This beam ran in between two poles and shifted from side to side and the kids walked the length of it while it swayed.

The small climbing wall leading up to the main structure revolved so kids just climbed in place. They all moved like little spider-men, practically leaping tall buildings.

'All solar-powered,' Thomas said, turning to face the playground next to me. 'Here, in the future, we don't do anything that damages the Earth.'

But somebody did damage the Earth in the future. Or at least New York. I saw it with my own eyes. Or maybe that already happened and they fixed it. Or . . . it's just a different timeline?

He started walking towards a light brown building and I followed.

'We've improved the quality of life beyond what anyone could have imagined. Eliminated obesity, improved vitamin supplements, increased brain function.'

Vitamins that gave everyone superhuman strength? That would explain the amazing spider-children. 'When does this happen?'

More importantly, what kind of drastic measures did it take to achieve this type of success?

'That, I can't tell you.' He spoke in this formal yet calm tone, as if he was a guide giving me the four o'clock tour of the perfect future.

I continued to take in my surroundings and they truly were beautiful. No trash anywhere, nothing out of place. The colour schemes were brilliant. Like city and country blending together. Unbelievably perfect . . . exactly why I didn't trust it. Emily showed me the other future for a reason. I really wanted dates. For both worlds.

'Time's up,' Thomas said, grasping my arm and pulling me back.

chapter forty

SATURDAY, 15 AUGUST 2009, 5.00 P.M.

Thomas did have skill. We were exactly where we left. I bent over, panting and trying to orient myself. Obviously, time travel had a different effect when I went with them. Going two years into the past had weakened me quite a bit and the half-jump to 1992 had beaten the shit out of me. But I felt fine now.

'So, were you impressed?' Thomas asked me.

'Yeah, it was . . . incredible,' I said.

He walked towards Holly, who must have only been standing there for a second or two because she was still in the same place. He grabbed her by the elbow and tugged her closer to the edge.

'What are you doing?' I asked him, not sure if I should make a move yet.

'Your speech earlier about nonessential items was very convincing, knowing what you've been through recently, but unfortunately I'm a little too smart to allow myself to be fooled.'

'You don't believe me?' I asked, keeping my voice perfectly even.

'That is irrelevant. Facts. Tangible proof. That's what I rely on.'

Thomas wrapped his arms around her, in a hold too tight for Holly to escape. I could see her face twisting with anger as she attempted to wiggle her way out.

I held on to my cover, waiting to see where Thomas was going with this little diversion.

'I've thought a lot about you, Jackson,' Thomas said calmly, ignoring Holly's attempts to break free of his death grip. 'I've recently learned the expression "kill two birds with one stone". We don't say that where I'm from. There's a way I can find out if you're lying about dismissing emotional attachments, and learn just how valuable you might be to my team.'

'What's that?' I asked, hearing the nerves leak into my voice.

'It's a well thought-out plan, and, as I said earlier, that's very important for people like us. The only problem is, if you do, in fact, show incredible talent, it will also prove you're lying to me. That you're not capable of dealing with the responsibilities that go along with this power you've been handed.' His eyes met mine and I could almost see remorse in them. Or disappointment. 'None of us wants to hurt you . . . or stop you from living your life, but we might not have a choice. Not if you're too much of a risk. We can accept your being on the other side, but not your being flighty and impulsive. We might consider Tempest our opposition but we don't dismiss how careful their leader is when dealing with time. Do you understand?'

I could feel the sweat trickling down the back of my neck. My heart thudded like a freight train. He was looking at me and reading it *all*. 'What do you . . . ? What are you talking about?'

He pinned Holly's arms to her sides and walked even closer to the edge. I finally let myself look at her face and I saw the panic creep into her eyes. She guessed the same thing I did.

Thomas moved his arms to her waist and lifted her from the ground, dangling her upper body over the ledge. I sucked in a breath as he leaned further over the edge.

'Wait! Don't!' I shouted, but it didn't matter.

Thomas hoisted her up higher and with incredible strength tossed her over the edge. Her scream was deafening and my brain went into machine mode as I jumped. Not through time, but an actual jump.

Off the roof.

The very millisecond I felt some part of Holly between my fingers, I forced my mind to focus as we were freefalling. *Think about where you want to be,* I told myself. Beautiful . . . wonderful . . . *solid* places.

chapter forty-one

A second ago I had felt Holly's wrist between my fingers. Now I could feel her weight on top of me. Soft grass around us. Her heart pounding against mine.

'Holly?' I mumbled. My eyes were still squeezed shut.

Both of us were breathing hard, panic flooding out.

'Oh God, are we dead?'

I stared into her light blues eyes, seeing the sun reflected in them. Sun, not rain. 'No, we're not dead . . . damn . . . I don't know what I just did.'

She looked at me for one more second and then she was kissing me, hard, tears flooding out of her eyes on to my face. I squeezed my arms around her so tight I don't how she kept breathing.

When I ran out of air I released her and let my arms flop down into the grass. 'Holly?'

'Yeah?'

'Did I really just jump off a freakin' roof?'

'Yes.' She pressed her face into my shirt and started crying harder.

I rolled us both over sideways so I could see her face better. 'It's OK, Hol. You're OK.'

She finally lifted her head and wiped the tears from her face. 'You can time travel with regular people?'

'Apparently. But I had no idea. It hasn't happened before. Honestly, the thought never crossed my mind . . . I saw you falling and it was just . . . instinct. I didn't even think.' I touched my forehead to hers and closed my eyes. 'I should have never let it get that close. I didn't know what he had planned and . . .'

'It's OK . . . I knew you were trying to stall . . . I would have done the same thing.' She rested her hands on my face and kissed me again. 'Is this Central Park?'

I finally looked around for the first time, not even thinking about the fact that we had just magically appeared out of nowhere. Nobody had screamed or anything . . . definitely a good sign. I recognized the location within a few seconds. It was the upper east side of the Great Lawn, near one of the baseball diamonds. Two girls were sunbathing about fifty feet from us. They had shades on and looked oblivious to anyone around. Everyone else was even further away.

'Yep, Central Park,' I said to Holly before pulling her up off the grass. 'The hard part for me is usually not where I am, but when.'

'You don't know when we are?' Holly asked.

I smiled at the shock on her face. 'We just have to find a source.'

Before we started walking I pulled her into my arms again, reluctant to let go. My face was buried in her hair and I took in a deep breath, trying to compose myself.

'Once we figure out what the hell we just did, I might have to drag you to some island a hundred years in the past.'

'And I might have to let you,' she mumbled.

We walked quickly towards a bench where a young woman sat reading the newspaper while a little boy kicked a soccer ball around in front of her. I walked behind the lady and Holly and I both glanced at the newspaper over her shoulder.

12 August 2009. 'Three days in the past,' I muttered to myself. 'But what timeline?'

'What are you talking about?' she asked.

'There he is!' someone shouted.

Both of us spun around at the same time. Raymond and Cassidy, the woman whose DNA was in me, stood about twenty feet away, guns pointed at us. I nearly fell over when I saw who was hiding behind Raymond.

Holly. Another Holly?

Like a different timeline Holly? Shouldn't my Holly make this Holly disappear?

I didn't have time to consider this. Not while my 009 Holly was staring at another version of herself.

'Holy shit!' the Holly beside me said.

Both Hollys stared at each other, completely shocked.

'Jackson?' the other Holly said.

'We have to go back,' I said to the Holly next to me. '*Now.*'

'No kidding,' she whispered before burying her face in my shirt.

'I'm aiming for the ground this time,' I mumbled before pulling us back.

chapter forty-two

SATURDAY, 15 AUGUST 2009, 5.30 p.m.

OK, so maybe I don't have perfect aim.

'Shit,' Holly said into my ear.

She was still on top of me and we were sliding down the slanted part of the roof. Again. She grabbed on to the hunk of siding like I had before, then clutched my wrist. I turned over quickly and climbed up.

'I thought climbing on ladders was bad . . . but hanging on a slated roof . . . eight storeys high, totally sucks.' I could feel my chest tightening and knew passing out here on the roof was a possibility.

Holly smacked my cheek lightly. 'Jackson! Look at me.'

I lifted my head and stared at her through the rain. 'I can't do this. I just need . . .'

'You can. I know you can.' She put a hand under my arm and tugged until I continued to climb.

'Sorry if I don't walk across swing sets like you. You're like a crazy circus performer,' I mumbled, slightly annoyed that I needed her help with this.

'Wait, when did you see me climbing swing sets?'

'The other you. 007 Holly.'

'Oh, of course. Makes perfect sense . . . Did I even like you in 2007?' she asked.

'No, then yes, then no again, then yes again.'

'So it's just like this year?' she teased.

'I guess it's possible we were just looking at *that* Holly, but older maybe,' I said, still not believing it.

'I'm trying not to think about what we just saw, but I have a feeling therapy is in my near future,' she said.

I realized then that we had reached the top, near the flat part of the roof. Holly had creatively distracted me from the height thing.

'Do you think that evil dude is still up here?' she asked.

'I guess we're gonna find out.' Right now my anger overpowered my fear and I wanted to seriously kick Thomas's ass.

We climbed over the edge and Thomas *was* still there. His head snapped in our direction and a grin spread across his face.

'Maybe we should jump off the roof again,' Holly said from behind me.

I shook my head. 'He's not going to touch you. I promise.'

'Amazing! Your abilities exceed those of ninety-nine per cent of the other time-travellers,' he said.

There was no sarcasm or anger on his face, just pure amazement. *Doesn't mean he won't kill us.*

My fists balled up as I approached him. 'I thought you

people didn't believe in careless murder? What if I hadn't been able to jump?'

'Yes. The poor girl. But she's disposable. She'll *always* be disposable,' Thomas stated in a flat tone.

I ground my teeth together and forced myself to focus. The only thing I really wanted to do was to toss this freak off the roof and watch his bones break into a million pieces.

Holly gasped as Thomas drew a pistol and pointed it at us.

'I think it's too risky for me to let you go anywhere alone. Maybe people like *you* are the real danger.' Thomas stared at my face like a curious child eyeing someone in a wheelchair. Emotions were crippling. That's what he had to be thinking.

I easily knocked the gun from his hand before he could even react. Adrenalin rushed through my veins after hearing the sound of the weapon hit the hard ground and slide out of reach.

From the corner of my eye I watched Holly dive behind the pole she had been pressed against earlier.

I grasped the front of Thomas's shirt. 'You're not going anywhere without me. Go ahead and try if you want.'

His forearm made contact with my face and I felt a wave of pain rush through me. His fist made a quick jab into my stomach, knocking the wind out of me. The second I doubled over, he was free again. *Free to jump to the future and figure out his next move*. I sprang forward and wrapped my arms around his legs. It should have thrown him face first into the ground, but he twisted mid-air and ended up right back on his feet.

My fingers barely gripped his wrist. But I just had to keep holding on to him, so he couldn't go without me. I used all my strength to pull on his arm and get him to the ground in a hold tight enough to keep him from getting out.

I had him pinned to the ground, was staring right at his face, but I had no clue what to do next. Reach for the gun and shoot him? I wasn't sure I could . . . but the image of Holly being flung off the roof replayed in my mind again and my fingers were already reaching for his weapon.

'Fine, we'll do this your way,' he said with a devious grin. 'Hope you don't mind the intensity my kind of jumping can bring on. Your head will feel like it's ready to explode, so much that you'll wish you were dead.'

'Jackson, just let go of him . . . please,' Holly said from behind me.

I shook my head at her and stared down at Thomas again. 'I'm not letting go.'

In one swift motion he headbutted me. I squeezed my eyes shut as my vision blurred. My fingers loosened from him and he lifted his leg enough to kick me hard in the stomach. Holly screamed as I flew back and hit my head against the metal pole.

Thomas leaned over me and grasped the front of my shirt. 'You asked for it,' he said.

I winced, preparing for the pain he had described so vividly.

The confidence in his face faded. 'What are you . . . doing?'

Me? I wasn't doing anything but waiting for intense pain.

His fingers tightened around my shirt, but he closed his eyes and his whole face scrunched up. It was at that moment that something occurred to me: maybe he can't do it if I don't want him to . . . or if I want to be here, *now.*

I only hesitated for a second before mustering up every ounce of energy to get him on the ground again.

He let out a cry of pain even though I wasn't doing anything but pinning him down.

I sat right on top of him as he lay on his side, gasping for air. The barrel of the gun was now pressed to his temple.

'Wait! Don't shoot,' he said in a strained voice.

I pushed the gun harder into his skin, feeling my anger thicken. 'Why shouldn't I?'

Dad burst through the door on to the roof, breathless. 'Jackson, thank God!'

I turned my head for a split second and Thomas reached up and yanked out a chunk of my hair. I jerked away from his hand. 'Seriously? I have a gun to your head and you pull my hair?!'

'This is plan B.' A slow, careful grin spread across his face as I stared at my brown hair between his fingers.

Shit. DNA.

Dad's footsteps barely distracted me from piecing together a load of clues acquired in the last twenty-four hours.

'Jackson, get up. I'll do this,' Dad said.

'You know, don't you?' Thomas said to me, lifting one eyebrow.

'Jackson! Get up!' Dad said again.

But all I could do was stare at my hair in this horrible

man's fist. They weren't trying to make *me*. They wanted to make something completely different. Something even better. Everything they could ever want.

Emily.

Sweat trickled from my palm to my index finger, causing it to slide a little on the trigger. I couldn't kill him. He can't die. Or she wouldn't exist. Emily's words came back to me then.

'Trust yourself to make the right choice. It's not as hard as it seems.'

And I knew then that I had already made the decision because she had come to me. She existed. Whether it was right or wrong, I could never erase that child or prevent her life from forming.

I stood up from my seat on top of Thomas, but stepped hard on his stomach in the process, feeling a small amount of satisfaction about his loud groan. Dad looked at me questioningly as I stood in front of him, blocking his shot.

But he didn't get a chance to ask me anything because Raymond, the shoe-print guy, who killed Eileen, appeared on the ledge right behind him, gun pointed at his back.

'Dad! Look out!' I dived forward and knocked Dad to the side just as the man on the ledge fired. I barely felt the sting of the bullet hit my arm. I watched the man fall from the ledge after getting hit by Dad's perfectly aimed return shot. Seconds later, the thud of Raymond's body slamming into the ground reached us through the rain.

Dad immediately spun around, looking for Thomas,

who now stood on the ledge like the other man had.

'We'll see each other again, Jackson.'

Then, just like that, Thomas turned and jumped, milliseconds before Dad took another shot. No thud followed his jump and I knew he had vanished long before his body hit the ground. He was free of my hold and his powers were intact again.

Dad swore under his breath, then rushed over to me, forcing me to sit. 'Damn it, Jackson! Do you *ever* listen to me?'

I smiled a little and leaned my head against the wall. 'At least we got three of them. Progress is progress, right?'

Holly crawled out from her hiding place and ran over to us. 'Oh my God . . . Someone shot you!'

She dropped in front of me and started unbuttoning my shirt.

'He'll be fine. I promise,' Dad said.

'Who shot the blonde chick from the ground?' I asked Dad.

'Agent Freeman.'

'He got away, didn't he?' Holly asked while gently pulling my arm out of my sleeve. 'The evil dude?'

I nodded and closed my eyes as stabbing pain ran down my arm. I rested my good hand against Holly's cheek. Her eyes met mine and I impulsively whispered, 'I'm sorry, Hol . . . I'm so sorry. This should have never—'

Her fingertips touched my lips and she shook her head. 'Stop. You do not get to apologize for saving my life. That's completely twisted. I still don't know how the hell you did that roof-jumping, time-jumping thing . . .'

She choked up a little at the end of her jokey response and then leaned closer and rested her cheek against mine.

I kissed the side of her neck and said, '*Amor vincit omnia.*'

'Latin?' Holly asked, touching her forehead to mine. 'What does it mean?'

'Love conquers all,' Dad answered as he pressed a torn piece of my shirt against the bleeding wound.

Holly brushed her mouth to my forehead. 'I can definitely live with that.'

A few minutes later Adam and Melvin came bursting through the roof door.

Another sigh of relief. But part of me knew Dad would have never let anything happen to Adam, not on his watch. Holly jumped up and hugged him.

He grabbed her shoulders. 'Why did I see you jumping off the roof? Do you realize I actually went into cardiac arrest?'

She leaned against him and I could tell the day had caught up with her. She looked as if she might pass out. Adam set her down on the ground next to me and she curled up against my good side, shivering like it was twenty degrees outside instead of eighty.

Melvin turned his eyes on me and spoke quickly in Farsi. 'You jumped with her?'

'You saw?' I asked, glancing at him, then at Dad. They both nodded. 'I didn't even know that was possible.'

'We call it Displacement.' Melvin leaned closer and the intensity on his face scared me. 'Listen to me – yes, you can take someone, if you're skilled enough. But the part of the brain *you* use to jump isn't even accessible to a normal person. If you jumped with her again, right now, there's an eighty per cent chance it would kill her. A third jump after that would have a hundred per cent chance of death.'

I swallowed hard, wishing I had known, but knowing it wouldn't have changed the outcome. I still would have tried to save her, no matter what.

I heard the sound of a helicopter coming closer and closed my eyes to keep the dirt from flying into them as the wind churned everything into the air. I forced myself to think only of the little girl whose eyes were bright with tears as she left me on the beach. Whatever she was heading back to wasn't pleasant and somehow I needed to help her. Though I had no idea when we would meet again. Sometime in the future. That's the only clue I had.

Dad lifted Holly off the ground and waited for me to climb in before lifting her inside. Adam helped him buckle Holly into the seat next to me. Her eyes opened again at the loud noise of the helicopter and she sat up. I leaned my head back against the seat, trying to keep my mind off the pain. Holly's hand slipped into mine.

As soon as we were in the air I looked down at the hotel. One entire side had collapsed. Emergency vehicles were everywhere.

Then a man in a paramedic uniform had an IV in my hand quicker than I would have thought possible, considering the sharp turns the helicopter was making. Whatever he put into my arm dissolved the pain and a hazy fog took over my brain. But just before I nodded off, Thomas's words played in my mind again: '*She's disposable. She'll* always *be disposable.*'

Holly would never be safe. Not as long as she knew me. And the pain came roaring back, but it was a different kind of pain. The worst kind.

'You were pretty lucky. This is one of the cleanest gunshot wounds I've seen,' the resident stitching me up said for, like, the tenth time.

'Yep.'

'Will he need a sling?' Dad asked.

'Yeah, probably for a few days,' the man said. 'But we'll have you out of here in less than an hour.'

'What time is it?' I asked Dad.

We had been here all night. Holly and Adam had been returned safely home.

He shifted in the chair he sat in beside me and looked at his watch. 'Eight o'clock. I promised Holly you would call her as soon as you woke up.'

I nodded slowly, feeling the worry and fear sink back in. I waited for the doctor to finish stitching and putting on a bandage before answering Dad. 'I don't . . . know if I should.'

Dad stood and peeked around the curtain, watching the doctor shuffle down the hall away from us. He sat on the end of the bed and spoke in a low voice. 'Did he threaten to hurt her? Thomas?'

'Not exactly, but I know he'll do whatever he needs to get to me.' I hadn't told Dad about my DNA theory. I didn't plan to tell anyone. Not just because Emily said not to. The CIA would try to stop the experiment from happening and I had already sacrificed so much just to let it happen. I had allowed Thomas to escape. Probably for all the wrong reasons. But I wasn't like Chief Marshall. I couldn't always look at the bigger picture, not when I had seen the little pieces.

'We can double the protection we have now . . .' Dad stopped talking when I shook my head.

'It won't be enough. You've seen how they just appear and vanish. We can't fight that off. Not forever.'

'But if you distance yourself from Holly, they'll have no interest in killing or harming her. Remember what I told you about their philosophy of only killing for power. They won't understand the sacrifice you'll be making to stay away. They'll just assume she's no longer good leverage.'

I could hear the desperation in his voice. This was the choice he wanted me to make. It's the choice he would have made with Eileen. Let her live and be safe, but not be in the CIA life. That's real love. But what if I wasn't as strong as Dad?

'It's hard, isn't it . . . being alone?' he asked.

I stared down at my hands and nodded. 'Yes.'

'But if it keeps her alive,' Dad prompted.

'I know.'

What was I supposed to tell her? I have an incurable disease? No, she'd hold my hand and wait for me to die. Should I tell her I never really loved her? Just the thought of watching her face as she absorbed those words was worse than getting shot again.

But what choice did I have?

Just a little while later the doctors released me, and Dad and I took a cab home. When we pulled up to our building I got out first and told him I was going for a walk. My arm rested in a sling and pain medication ran through my veins, so I only walked a little way before finding a bench in the shade to plop down on.

'You don't even have to tell her.'

I looked up and saw Dad standing in front of me.

'Just disappear and not say anything to Holly?'

He sat down next to me. 'I know what you're thinking . . . either stay with her 24/7 or break her heart. But I think there's a compromise.'

I turned to face him, desperate for any solution. 'What?'

Dad took a deep breath before speaking. 'You can never tell Melvin or Marshall about this . . . or anyone.'

He reached into his pocket and handed me a tiny memory card. I flipped it over in my hands. 'OK . . . ?'

'Adam Silverman isn't the only one with his own spy code.'

'I'm still not getting it.'

Dad did a quick sweep of the area with his eyes before continuing. 'This is for me. I want to update my slightly younger self with these recent events. Remember how your timeline works. Think about it. It wasn't *that* long ago that Holly didn't even know you. And if she doesn't know you . . .'

I stared at him, unable to form any words as his plan sank in like a heavy weight pressing on my chest. 'I'm not even sure I can move my home base again.'

He nodded. 'You've done it at very important moments. And this is a smaller move. It's completely your decision but I understand what it feels like . . . to watch someone die.'

My cellphone sat on the bench next to me. Dad picked it up and slowly placed it in my hand. 'Call her, just don't say goodbye. Then she won't feel anything but good things.'

He walked away and I opened my phone, staring at the picture of Holly and me on the beach just a couple of days ago. My throat tightened as I flipped through the phone for her number. It took a couple of rings for her to answer.

'Hey, are you still up for coming over this morning?' she said.

I forced my voice to come out calm. 'Yep. I'm leaving now. I should be there soon.'

She sighed with relief. 'Great!'

Just hearing that little bit of excitement, the longing in her voice, hurt so much. I had to clear my throat before saying anything else. I stared out at the trees in front of me and focused on the idea of life. Of Holly's life being long and happy. 'Hey, Hol?'

'Yeah?'

'I love you.'

Tears stung my eyes, but I could practically hear her smiling through the phone. 'I love you too. I'll see you soon.'

Not if I can help it. 'Bye, Holly.'

I closed my eyes and attempted a full jump back to one of the most important days of my existence. I immediately felt the weight of my entire body going with me and knew Dad was right. I *could* choose to do it.

chapter forty-three

SUNDAY, 15 March 2009, 5.38 p.m.

My new home base. And I managed to land exactly where and when I needed to be. I entered the 92nd Street Y and walked up to the receptionist. 'I need to leave a note for Mr Wellborn.'

'Sure.' She handed me a piece of paper and a pen.

I jotted a quick note explaining my resignation from the summer job I should have started on this day. I left right away, but stood next to a street light quite a distance from the front doors. I *had* to see her.

A few minutes passed, and then far down the pavement I saw the blonde ponytail swinging back and forth, the big pink smoothie in one hand and the book hiding her face in the other. I thought my emotions would win and I'd rush over to her, but instead I leaned against the pole and watched Holly get closer and closer.

Right now, she was happy and safe. I hadn't let her down yet or broken her heart . . . Or caused her death. I remembered the words she spoke to me so long ago:

'It's like you have this whole other life and I can't be in it.'

But it was just the opposite now.

I sucked in a breath as Holly approached the steps, not even looking up from her book. But my feet stayed firmly planted the whole time she walked up the stairs. This was the exact moment our lives had collided. Two paths that would now likely never cross. I felt a mixture of relief and crushing grief as Holly Flynn stepped through the doors, completely unharmed. History was changed forever. She and I had never met.

I dug inside my pocket, wrapping my fingers around the ring Emily had given me. She must not have known the choice I would make , or maybe . . . just maybe . . . she *did* know. I pushed that small glimmer of hope out of my mind as I turned around and walked in the opposite direction to Holly.

The further I got from her, the more it hurt. A bitter ache I didn't think would ever dissolve.

Without thinking about it, I stopped right in front of the playground where 007 Holly and I had spent one morning lying in the grass. An unexpected peaceful feeling swept over me, just like it had that day. Seconds later I was stretched out in the same spot, staring up at the clouds, hearing her voice like she was right beside me again.

'Jackson?'

'Yeah?'

'You're so different than I thought.'

'You're exactly how I thought.'

And I knew, without a doubt, I had finally done something right. Completely right. After all, pain and grief are nothing compared to regret.

I retrieved my journal from the bag lying in the grass and wrote only four words. A reminder for days even more difficult than this one. Because the truth is . . . even though I have no idea what comes next . . . at least for today . . .

I have no regrets.

acknowledgements

So, many individuals contributed to the success of this book. I realize every author says this, but now I actually understand how much each and every one of them truly means it. Nothing about this process was a solo effort and I hope that I can properly recognize every single one of my supporters in these pages.

i'd like to thank:

My husband, Nick, whose opinion and words of encouragement I value above all others (even if I don't always admit this to him), and who was and is the sole inspiration behind my main character's unwavering love and loyalty. He deserves more than half of any success this book gets because if there's one thing harder than *being* a writer, it's *living* with one. Thanks for never giving up on me, waiting up late at night for me to finish working or writing so we could spend time together. And most of all, thanks for being the kind of man that makes it nearly impossible to properly acknowledge in a single paragraph.

My older sister, Jenni, for her candid approach when reading versions of this book and for her constant encouragement and support all through this gruelling process. So many additions and edits were a result of her top-notch advice from a true reader's perspective, not to mention the moral support only a close family member can give.

My grandfather, Elm, one of my favourite people in the entire world. Also a fantastic writer and my earliest supporter once I decided to pursue publication. When all the rejection letters began to pile up, I'd get the most beautiful, inspiring emails from him telling me how proud he was, how much I was improving and growing as a writer, and I've never been able to delete those emails: nor have I forgotten their impact.

My mom, Colleen, because she's always proud of me, whether I'm writing an article for a small magazine or a three-book series for a major publishing house. She's never, once, told me I couldn't or that I wasn't good enough – quite the opposite.

My dad, Tom, who has given me not only the writing gene, but also the discipline to put that gift to use, and the daily reminder that loving and worry about your children continues far beyond their childhood. **And my step-mom, Joyce**, who has always treated me like her own child and is one of the most generous people I've ever met.

My mother-in-law, Marcia, who has been of fan of this book from day one. Both Marcia and **my father-in-law, Tim**, have provided me with a great example of love that lasts years and years, when life is great, but also when it isn't.

And of course, **my babies – Charles, Ella, and Maddie** – who are growing up way too fast. I hope some day, when they're old enough to read this book, they discover little bits of their childhood sprinkled throughout, dinner conversations where I discussed plot or characters, and they'll be able to put the story together with those memories and it will be that much more special for all of us.

Jamie, my little sister for her fangirl encouragement, and **Jacob, my youngest brother**. And my other **little brother, Ryan**, who I just know is going to write some amazing songs for *Tempest*. Assuming he hasn't already by the time this book is released.

Tracy, Kathy and Dawn, my favourite aunts and three women whose support and encouragement goes back as long as I can remember. Each of them has been a big reason I've worked so hard to produce something that I knew they'd be proud of.

My grandmother, Maureen, the backbone of our family and someone who has always shared my love of books and stories.

Rhiannon, my cousin and 'almost sister', for her willingness to read the unedited versions I've sent her way and for all the wonderful book discussions we've had.

I can't forget all my younger cousins. Each of you has read and influenced something I've written with your invaluable teen perspective. **Kevin Robbins**, one of my earliest readers; his helpful comments had direct influence on the final version of this book. And the rest of the little cousin clan that I've roped into being test readers long before my writing ever resembled something clean and publishable: **Lauren Robbins, Kelsey and Kayla Wilson, Grace and Sarah Geehan**.

Shannon Slifer, a long-time friend and the very first person to read the very first novel that I wrote back in the summer of 2009. **Laurel Jukes**, my most devoted teen reader. She's also sifted through the best and worst of my artistic journey. Our 'workout chats' have been invaluable to me all through this process. **Sarah Thorman**, my good friend for so many years now, who shares my love and passion for the sport of gymnastics and is someone I can always count on when I need to vent or spill good news. **Amanda Koba**, my oldest friend, for holding on to several pieces of my childhood, especially those early teen years, and bringing them out at just the right moments. We have enough memories to create a twenty-book young-adult series. My old neighbours and good friends **Justin and Tori Spring** . . . who I'm nearly positive were the first people I ever told about my desire to write a book.

My fellow management-staff teammates at the Champaign County YMCA for all the kind words and encouragement, but most of all for the daily reminders of where I came from, the thick roots the Y plants in its key staff, lessons I hope I never forget. My story was born under that roof and my children have grown up being a part of the CCY family.

Roni Loren, one of my first online writer friends and critique partners and my 'release-day sister'. It has been amazing having her support, having someone walking through the exact same process at the exact same time.

Suzie Townsend, my agent, who shares my true love for young-adult literature and someone who always knows exactly what I need to hear in moments of stress or excitement. She keeps me grounded and focused and is forever patient with my endless questions and story ideas. And her love for *this story* and my characters is apparent in every bit of feedback and critique I receive. I look forward to many, many years of working together.

Also, the entire team at **FinePrint Literary Management**, some I've met and some I haven't, but I'm sure all of them have done something to support this book or me as an author and I'm so grateful for the wonderful publishing team effort that comes out of a top-notch agency like FinePrint.

Brendan Deneen, my editor, my friend (to whom I've dedicated this book), for taking a chance on a newbie author and for believing not only in *Tempest*, but in me as a writer. Because of him, I've enjoyed the process just as much as the product itself. Developing this story together was truly an unforgettable experience. He's the equivalent of my Olympic coach, and I wouldn't be the same writer without him.

Some of the great guys at **Thomas Dunne Books – Pete Wolverton and Tom Dunne** – for also taking a chance on a newbie author and believing in this book enough to let me write two more.

All the awesome people at St. Martin's – so many of whom I haven't even met or heard of, but they're behind the scenes or on the front lines making my dream come true, an everyday task for these folks. I have a feeling that when it's time for book-two acknowledgements, I'll have met many more of them. But no matter how many hands *Tempest* falls into, I'll never forget sitting in **Matt Baldacci's** office, during my first visit to New York, and hearing him quote a line from *my book* and admitting to shedding a few tears while reading that morning. That was probably one of the greatest moments for me, as a writer, and proof of the entire publishing house's passion for the books and the authors they represent.

Summit Entertainment, for its continued effort to help bring *Tempest* to the big screen. **Summit Producer Sophie Cassidy**, for believing in *Tempest* from draft one. **Producer Sonny Mallhi** for his dedication to this story and continued encouragement, for me, as a writer. **Roy Lee**, for that amazing message he sent me, saying how much he enjoyed reading my book. I know *Tempest* the movie couldn't be in better hands.

Some of the authors who have influenced and inspired me before I began writing and early on in my journey: **Courtney Summers, J.K. Rowling, Stephen King, Judy Blume, Lois Lowry, Jay Asher, Ally Carter, Stephenie Meyer, Ann M. Martin.**

And last, but not least, thanks to anyone and everyone who picks up this book to read it for whatever reason – without people out there reading and buying books, my inspiration would be lost.

Coming s

VORTEX

JULIE CROSS

THERE WILL BE NO CALM
BEFORE THE STORM

The eye of the storm is a deadly place to be . . .

Jackson Meyer has completed his training to become an agent for Tempest, the shadowy division of the CIA that handles all time-travel-related threats. As a time traveller himself he's on his way to becoming the best of the best. However, everything changes when Holly – the girl he altered history to save – re-enters his life, and Jackson must make an impossible choice: erase the past or change the future?

Book 2 in the Tempest trilogy

JANA OLIVER

Riley Blackthorne.
Kicking hell's ass one demon at a time . . .

Riley has always wanted to be a demon trapper like her father, and she's already following in his footsteps as one of the best. But it's tough being the only girl in an all-guy world, especially when three of those guys start making her life more complicated:

Simon, the angelic apprentice who has heaven on his side; Beck, the tough trapper who thinks he's God's gift, and Ori, the strikingly sexy stranger who keeps turning up to save her life.

One thing's for sure – if she doesn't keep her wits about her there'll be hell to pay . . .

Look out for more titles in The Demon Trappers series!

STARCROSSED

JOSEPHINE ANGELINI

DESTINY BROUGHT THEM TOGETHER.
THE GODS WILL KEEP THEM APART.

WHEN shy, awkward Helen Hamilton meets Lucas Delos for the first time, she thinks two things: the first, that he is the most ridiculously beautiful boy she has seen in her life; the second, that she wants to kill him with her bare hands.

AN ancient curse means Lucas and Helen are destined to loathe one another. But sometimes love is stronger than hate, and not even the gods themselves can prevent what will happen next . . .